Threat

Level

RED

A Kristi Johnson Novel

L. Corbin Bey

Threat Level RED: A Kristi Johnson Novel

Second Edition

Copyright © 2012, 2018 by L.Corbin Bey. All rights reserved.

Published by Tempestuous Erotic Delight

Edited by Patience C. Mitchell

ISBN: 978-0-9991308-7-2 Paperback

To Tyz

Thank you darlin

For supporting me

If you love what you read

Tell somebody! Hit me up let me

know what you liked

L Corbin Bey

Foreword

Mr. Corbin Bey really shows his prowess as a brilliant light in the writing arena. I delighted in the fact that he takes his time and walks you through the lives of his characters. I was unknowledgeable of some aspects of how the world really works prior to reading this novel. I, now, find myself fascinated enough to stop and begin an elongated voyage into uncovering the mysteries of life entitled, 'I didn't know that".

From the opening to the middle and on towards a remarkable and intriguing crescendo, I found myself unable to put this captivating novel aside. I wanted more, and more was what I received. The mere fact is that the author took his time and researched the nuances of all of the details to make this story wonderful. One would want to know, "Is this stuff really real?" "Are there really places like that?" "Can this happen?" "Am I really free, or am I just playing the part of a freed person that is directed to re-audition on a daily basis for something that is actually a very bad movie?"

The world that we live in is a complicated place, and there are factions within and around us daily that enables this thing to function somewhat. This publication shares some very intimate and scary facts that says, "In an instant, what you have worked on to create and call "Your World" can be taken from you immediately". You can be placed in a compromising position that would rival no other. IMAGINE that!

Mr. Corbin Bey's characters are real; the issues are real and he writes this novel in a manner which subconsciously causes you to turn the next page…

So sit back and Buckle up, get ready for one helluva ride. Always remember that the next time you hear the words "Threat Level RED", in the next instant, you might be dead!

Chapter 1

The party was in full swing. The grounds of the magnificent old money mansion were lit up like early afternoon despite the 11:30pm hour. Sylvia glided across the impossibly high gloss marble floor to a short hallway just around the corner from the restroom suite. Little known to the rest of the partygoers, this blank wall she faced was not what it seemed to be. Removing her diamond encrusted brooch, she twisted the bezel to reveal a sophisticated marvel of electronic wizardry. Currently, the little doo-dad was pointing to a spot in the center of the wall, pressing a small recessed button caused a panel to slide open revealing a glowing keypad.

Punching in the expensively procured numeric string rewarded her with the side sliding of the door to the hidden elevator, slipping inside activated the sensitive electronics. Hidden very well inside the two hundred year old mansion, this modern addition was quite amazing. Not only did this "vator" go up and down, it also went forward, backwards and sideways, delivering one to any secret opening you wanted to exit from in the house including the opening inside the panic room. This was Sylvia's destination.

Once inside, she activated a timer to track how long she was absent from the party. She had left quite a number of horny drunken suitors in her wake, always perfect alibis. Noting her starting coordinates she punched in the panic room cell on the spreadsheet-like destination panel. Arriving less than twenty seconds later the door opened inside the secret living compartment. Walking through with the confidence borne of thirty separate VR trips through this same space, she went directly to the wall safe located behind the mid-sized refrigeration unit. Using the supplied back-door access code left by the designer for maintenance purposes, she opened the safe.

Barely visible in the darkened space, the beating hearts audible to all of her senses, they sat: The Rainbow Collection. The most perfect diamonds in the world comprising the color spectrum from brilliant flawless white to rose, red and black. Pulling off her silk evening gloves, she lifted her gown and pulled her thong to the side.

Pulling out the tampon-shaped storage box she unscrewed the cap and poured the Kings ransom worth of diamonds into the receptacle, reattached the tip with the braid and slid the tube back inside herself.

Rearranging her clothes and slipping on her glove, she replaced the refrigerator and retreated back to the vator. She checked her timer; two minutes had elapsed. Once again deferring to the Virtual Reality practice, she selected an exit point in another alcove just off the main ballroom dance floor. She had left a swarthy Kenyan gentleman waiting for her. He moved extremely fluidly on the dance floor when he moved in behind her with a sexy Jamaican styled slow wind. She was pleasantly surprised … too bad she was 'on her cycle'. She would have to find some other way to please him that would keep her on his mind. She exited to the dance floor and he was right where she had left him

"Kijana, there you are. I had thought that a splash of cool water would make me feel better, but I'm afraid it didn't work. I need some air and a little more privacy. Would you like to escort me home?"

The look in her eyes basically told him he could take her however he wanted. Directly, they were waiting for the valet, Kijana's silver Bentley came floating around the parking circle. The valet opened the door for Sylvia and accepted the tip from Kijana and they were off. Cracking the rear windows so that she could get some invigorating fresh air, he couldn't take his eyes off of her. He didn't know if it was exhaustion, the strong drinks or what, as she lay her head with its beautiful inky locks back onto the auto-comfort headrest. By the third traffic light she was breathing deeply and seemed to be asleep.

The night was actually young by standards of this west coast city, so he took it upon himself to drive up to a pinnacle area with a spectacular view of the city below. Once parked in a secluded area overlooking the twinkling lights, he watched her. Her beauty was almost unbelievable; her large breasts rhythmically rising and falling, the body- hugging top of her gown leaving nothing to the imagination. Kijana reached out to touch one and her nipple responded immediately. This caused a reciprocal stiffening of his. Not being a professional date rapist, he didn't know what to do with a drunken sleeping woman, so he touched her to see if she would awaken. Random touching caused several reactions: moaning, a slight shiver once and finally, after stroking her neck lightly she spread her legs still seemingly asleep.

He took this as a good sign and prospected beneath the

myriad layers of her gown until he felt the silky thigh high stockings. His hand continued to explore north until he felt bare flesh. He was so excited he was almost ready to come untouched. He counted to fifty, composed himself and continued to climb.

Upon reaching the lace covered apex of her spread thighs he detected the slight shudder that ran through her body. He stroked her there gently until her hips began to rotate sensuously. He pulled the thin panty crotch to the side and was confronted with the deal-breaker: the unmistakable feeling of the braided tail of a menstrual cycle tampon. Nasty freaky thoughts quickly crossed his mind but were just as quickly crossed out.

He started to remove his hand when she began to tremble and moan. Her orgasm caused her head to toss from side to side. As the sensation subsided she opened her eyes with the most sensual look upon her face and said, "Well, well, well, for a Kenyan, you sure have Roman hands! You don't have any idea how badly I needed that; but look at you, is there something I can do to show my gratitude?"

Without waiting for an answer she reached across and unzipped his tuxedo pants. His eyes glazed over and she took him to heaven with a first class oral ticket. Kijana dropped Sylvia off at her condo an hour later after she subliminally implanted the suggestion that they had been together the entire evening into his mind. She solidified the thought with another pornstar worthy blowjob while he was driving on the freeway. She vowed to call him the next day or so as he pulled off. She went around the back of the anonymous house and jumped into her low-key Lexus and drove home.

Chapter 2

Watching the numbers steadily click by at eye level Ronald had to wonder, how come doors on elevators were so short, even though there was plenty of headroom inside? Strange thoughts always drifted through his mind on elevator rides especially long ones. It probably stemmed from his seeing Damien: Omen II when he was much too young to be watching R-rated movies. The scene where Damien's enemies were sliced in half before being dropped to their death–by-elevator was a classic. To keep thoughts of that classic at bay, he thought of other things.

At 6'7", Ronald always noticed the small forest of shorter people he commonly rode with. It seemed like he was the tallest guy here at Tech Works Computer Systems Solutions. Every day was the same in that respect. He was a jazzy dresser, which gave people a valid excuse to look at him and an occasional opening to speak. Those that didn't speak, looked. When he noticed this he had to smirk just a little bit. Women of all races had an itch to know if the myth of a large penis were true. Just because a brother stood 6'7" and wore a size fifteen shoe, everyone thought that he had to be hung like a mule.

Myth or not it was true for him! The self- fulfilling prophecy of the thing was when they showed too much attention to it. It woke up to bask in the attention. To his amusement, the shocked looks on some of their faces, both male and female, were priceless. Moments like that created an instant "no fly" zone, probably afraid his zipper would explode and put everyone at risk. People were funny, especially the Corporate America types, afraid to express their sexuality or societal fears or questions out of concern that they would be branded "sexually harassing" or just harassed or the fact that they would be seen as inferior and overlooked for promotion because of bias or bigotry. That was the reason Ronald was an Independent Contractor. He never took a contract with a company for more than a year, and always with a break in between multiple contracts with the same company.

As their lead Systems Analyst, this gave him enough time away to let them see he was irreplaceable, but not enough time to let the replacement totally wreck his infrastructure. Every blue moon this strategy would work against him. The company would find a 'pool temp' that was worth his weight and always dreamed of being tethered to Corporate America.

This uncommon situation wasn't as bad as it seemed, his contract included a clause that paid him a healthy lump sum, approximately one year's salary in the event that his contract were to be replaced by a full-time employee position or an alternate contract situation. That was a pretty nifty clause he had come up with himself. He had a blackberry full of past and prospective clients; he had no worries. The car finally stopped at the 68th floor. He stooped his head and shoulders and stepped into the corridor, only thirty steps to his office and the beginning of his day.

His secretary had the three stacks of daily work requisitions at his work station, as requested, in the order of importance: Blazing, Flaming and Smoldering. The fact that his secretary is a bisexual woman was not lost on him. Her sense of humor was different, but he found her amusing and very efficient. It seemed having the best of both worlds worked very well for her; he just had to take her word for it. This morning his hottest requisition, the blazing assignment, would take him all the way up to the executive realm.

He had to tweak the executive micro-track Wi-Fi system. This secure wireless connection he had created for executive level users offered Wide Fidelity long range wireless connectivity with a micro beamed secure signal that only transmitted to the person authorized on that particular frequency. In essence, instead of the wireless connectivity being a cloud available wherever you worked, it was a beam that followed you - you were your own hotspot. Security was 100% unless a person jumped into your skin with you, the signal tracker was sub dermal. Ron arrived with his micro beam toolkit at the office of Chief Operating Officer Paul Truelea. Paul was touching all of his electronic devices and none of them were responding to him. He looked stressed.

"Morning' Paul", greeted Ron!

"Morning' Ron, wish I could say it was good but, I'm offline everywhere; it's a disaster!" Exclaimed Paul!

"Paul, this is your official calm-the-hell-down call. Whatever the problem is, it's fixable. Ok? From a reset to a full replacement, in thirty minutes max, you'll be back in the game. Alright?" assured Ron!

Relief flooded the COO's face like waters to a flood plain. This was how Ron could demand such exorbitant contracting fees; he was the man, undisputed. He took out his tool kit and scanned Paul's body. As he approached the implant, the scanner failed to register a signal activator pulse. However, he did detect the marginal power source.

"Paul, what did you do yesterday? Did anything out of the ordinary happen?" Inquired Ron. "I didn't do anything; just stayed at home with the wife and kids. I tinkered about in my … oh, well, I was in my workshop polishing a wood project my son had started and abandoned when the polisher started acting wonky. I went over and jiggled the cord and got a pretty massive tingling from head to toe. For a second I couldn't let go and then the plug slid out of the wall and it was over. I plugged into another socket and everything was ok. Damn, I had forgotten that quickly", retorted Paul!

"Well, there we have it Paul, you electrocuted yourself! It was mild, not as if you had stepped on a live wire in a thunderstorm. But to your implant, it may as well have been. The heat sensor power supply restarted itself, but all the programming has been wiped. Here, lift the back of your shirt", requested Ron.

Ron took the restore tool out of the toolkit. It looked more like a trigger activated syringe than any computer tool, but these were twenty second century technology tools being used in the twenty first century. The "port" for the implant was just above belt height and below the kidney line. It was a flesh colored overlay; beneath this was a very small aperture into which the syringe tip fitted. The system was populated by intelligent nanobots. The first action was to pull out the shorted out bots; he did this by turning the control stem to "remove"; a small meter on the side tracked the progress.

Next, he clicked the control stem to "apply image" from the internal memory. The device applied Paul's personal DNA password to the preset programming necessary to allow his personal beam to follow him and unlock all of his highly sensitive electronics.

Lastly, he clicked the control to "replace" and this repopulated the implant back to pre-electrocution status. After removing the restore tool and repacking it in the kit, he told Paul to redress and take a long gaze out the window at the mountains where the fog was just now burning off with the first rays of sunlight.

"Now take ten deep breaths, in through your nose, out through your mouth", Ron instructed. Ron liked to add a touch of meditation, eastern Zen, and mystery to his work. It relaxed his users and added another dimension to his legacy as one of a kind. The implant had been working from the time he had removed the tool, but extra was extra. Extra rewarded extra, and executives expected extra as a given.

As Ron was packing up to go back to data central, he told Paul he was back on line. Paul picked up his palmtop and stroked the fingerprint recognition and it sprang to life. You would have sworn someone had just given him a new lease on life. Ron went back to his floor. The system lord of the executive floor off to fight the smoldering flames.

Chapter 3

On the other side of the country, a tall very light skinned model quality woman strode confidently through a parking lot, leaving the motor running on her spaceship-looking 1973 Peugeot. The flowing, colorful wraparound dress she wore with the simple pillbox hat drew a lot of attention away from the plastic surgery mask onto which she'd expertly drawn the damaged face she used today.

The body, the walk, the hair uncomfortably pushed up into the hat and the bad plastic surgery look would make most people hypersensitive to her outward appearance. Questions too impolite for the public would make her job much easier. Entering the door, she asked the security guard the location of the information station where she could find withdrawal slips and supplies. His eyes noticed her disfigurement; she watched them slide south to inspect more pleasing areas of her anatomy just as she knew he would. He escorted her to the supply station. She was quickly taking mental note of everything and everyone in the bank: one at the drive through window, three tellers, four patrons and a manager.

"Ok", she thought, "Security first, and then the manager, all heroes die", she continued. Upon reaching their destination, she stumbled as if she had stubbed her toe. She reached inside the wrap of her dress and withdrew a .50 caliber Desert Eagle from her thigh holster. She stuck it forcibly into the guard's mouth simultaneously disarming him and pointing the .9mm Beretta at the manager. In her best little-girl-lost voice, she asked the manager if he could please help her by ensuring that no panic buttons were pushed which would result in nobody getting hurt. He was totally caught off guard by the casual tone of her voice. The guard's back to the tellers blocked the Desert Eagle from being seen. The hip level of the Beretta aimed at the manager left just enough menace to know this situation could get really bad, really fast. Just like that, she was in control.

The manager stumbled up from his desk trying to keep his composure once he realized that the robber had not yet alerted anyone else in the bank that they were being robbed. That was when he realized that this was to be his job.

With hands at their sides and Dulcet at their backs, the manager began to dictate her requests. "All cell phones on the floor and everybody gather in the middle of the floor on your knees in a semi-circle facing away from her", he yelled! They were then instructed to shuffle backwards on their knees until told to stop. Lifting her left leg up to toe the supply table with balletic ease, she revealed a plastic wrapped thigh with pre-cut lengths of duct tape affixed; her right thigh held extra, just in case.

She used the manager and the security guard to strip everyone naked then tape their hands behind their backs. She dumped purses and wallets into a convenient backpack worn by one of the patrons. She escorted the now naked manager around to empty all the teller stations and to open the safe to get to the packs of larger bills, after he deactivated the dye packs; of course. By now she had a full backpack and two very large Coach Bucket bags filled to the top with currency. She led the manager back to the group in the lobby to the showcase of her twisted sense of humor. She had arranged the duct taped group of patrons and employees into what is called a daisy chain. Basically a cluster arrangement placing one person's genitals within easy oral access to another person's face in a chain configuration until the last persons genitals are snugly placed against the mouth of the first person.

She took a sign out of the maintenance closet labeled "Closed for repairs", then taped the sign onto the front door and stepped out into the still early morning sunshine.

***

Sixteen minutes had elapsed since she left her car. She stepped into the Peugeot and drove sedately out of the parking lot. Two blocks down she turned into the downtown mall parking structure. Grabbing a ticket she drove up to the fourth level and double parked. She took off the pillbox hat from the back, and in the same process peeled off the stretched, shiny burned surgical mask exposing her perfect café au lait colored creamy smooth skin. After unpinning the spiral, she let loose her mid-back length, tomato red pony tail.

One tug of the concealed wraparound string and the dress came off leaving her clad in a short unitard workout outfit. She balled up the articles, squeezed both eyes and popped out the dark brown contacts revealing her emerald green ones. She switched her sneakers for pumps and added a Boston Celtics baseball cap with the ponytail threaded through the back. She was ready.

Dulcet hit the door open-auto start button for the Mercedes E Class and backed it out of the space replacing it with the Peugeot. Her carry bags stowed away in the trunk and the 'burn bag' with the 'tossables' went into the passenger seat. She drove down and around to the back of the mall by the loading dock; she tossed the bag into the Chemical Composting Compactor.

Every so often, according to its computerized schedule, the 3C would smash its contents, then, douse the compacted trash in decomposing chemicals, shove the result down into a steeping chamber where the gasses were collected and burned to help defray the cost of powering the mall. After all, one must do what one can to help the environment. She sped off sipping on a Fresca and sliding on her Dolce and Gabana shades and thought,

"Maybe I'll go to the nude beach and catch some rays.

***

Right around this time Thony (with an H) was deep into rehearsal. The show was due to open in thirteen days and the carpenters were running late. They had a two-story set that they were rehearsing on in their imagination, but the reality was they were in a church basement with lines and lines of masking tape representing walls and doors. The tape for the steps had a number that showed how many stairs were supposed to be there as they pretended to go up or down. The cast had been off book for the last three days, now everybody was antsy to get back to the theater to rehearse on the actual set they would be performing on.

The few props they had to practice with had been returned to the theater. Nobody spoke out loud about the carpenters or the safety and integrity of the structure they would trust their lives to for at least the next ten weeks. The first six weeks were already sold out! They could add just a tad bit more pressure into the mix, ya think?

But for now, rehearsal went on. His leading lady, Suzan was hitting her marks and performing her 2-dimensional blocking perfectly, even though this was their first show together, you couldn't tell. As far as musical theater went, this was Thony's (with an H) twenty second production. He had been singing and dancing since he was six years old. His adopted parents were patrons of the arts and took him to the theater at a very young age. He became enthralled and they enrolled him in classes; the talent soon showed.

From classics like "The Wizard of Oz" and "Lil Abner" onto off-off-off Broadway versions of the "Wiz" and "Cats" with stops here and there at Colored Museums, "All That Jazz" and other steamier Fosse-esque shows that combined light and shadow song and dance costume and nudity. He had done it all. Lately, he had cashed in on the fad of taking theatrical musicals to the Big Screen with substantial but non-speaking roles in "Chicago" and "Dreamgirls". In his circles he was starting to get noticed, which was a good thing. So when Suzan asked him if he did any dressing up when he was off, he stopped in his tracks. He totally broke character which was something he never did during rehearsal. "What do you mean dress up? Are you asking me

14

if I'm a drag queen", asked Thony?

"No, no noooo, Thony, I don't think anything like that", exclaimed Suzan! She rubbed the inside of his thigh, knowing that drove him crazy. "I know you're all man baby, I'm the first one that will parade a flag for your sexy mono-sexual ass. But I saw something the other day, only because I know every millimeter of your wonderful ass could I say this. But there was a guy and he looked disturbingly like you but at the same time not; he had on a long flowing gown", she said in her defense.

"Baby, did I tell you that you were making a whole lot of sense today? I didn't think so, because you're not", explained Thony! "Ok, if I notice or see him again I'll point him out to you, how's that", she said. "I think you are just falling so deeply in love with me that you are morphing my face onto every man you see, and probably some sexy-ass women too", concluded Thony.

They both broke out laughing at that. Totally disrupting rehearsal, the director thought the disturbance was brought on by the stress of being off the production schedule. So before they started a revolt, he gave them a fifteen minute break. At this rate they would have just five of the Actor's Equity contract recommended ten days of on-stage rehearsal before going into late night tech rehearsals. He hated to be the one to tell them, but as the quarterback of this theatrical team he was stuck between Unions. He had no choice.

He was glad he had Thony with an H. It was crazy that he had heard him say that enough that he thought it to himself now. But the guy had an infectious personality on and off stage. Little did he know that he was helping out immensely just by telling him things first. Because of this, by the time it was time to tell the full cast about whatever was coming down the pipe the sting was off, and hard decisions were made that much easier. Yeah, Equity Union Representative was in Thony's future if he so chose and Wilbert de 'Silver would cast the first vote. Will checked his watch and pressed "play" on the instrumental track, after every break he brought them back playing a random song from the show.

As they came back into the rehearsal space, musical theater immersion therapy he called it, it wasn't broke, so no need to fix it. On with the show!

Chapter 4

Sylvania Collins woke groggily at 4:00 am; she could feel a warm poking behind her and was wrapped in the temporary security of a burly arm. She felt so bad at times like these…these early… early weekday mornings when she had to remember the name of the man in bed with her; she was truly not a role model for the young girls under her stewardship. She knew how Charles Barkley felt a few years back. Despite the strange feelings, some pretty familiar good vibrations were starting to course throughout her body.

Still facing away from her mystery man, she began to twist on her sensitive nipples causing an instant party line to open up to her clit. Her hyper-efficient body started to respond. It picked up right where she left off when she fell asleep. The almost subliminal fluttering of the muscles of her sex spoke to his in a genital language only the two of them understood.

Her almost mystery man, though still fast asleep, began to stiffen, rising to do battle one more time like a good trooper. Feeling his soft flesh become steel, made her hotter and wetter. With no hands, just her sensual fluid hip ballet, she aimed him at the bull's eye, and as he grew and grew, he went deeper and satisfyingly deeper. Once he got to his full hardness, she was fully impaled...

Barry was his name, mmmmm ... Barry. She started to ride Barry's substantially awakened friend in an inverted doggy style, swinging her hips in arcs and circles, hitting every important spot inside herself. Gripping the bed sheets, she felt a major wake-up orgasm building. Just as it hit, she started to tremble, flex and squeeze. She felt Barry's strong hands grip her around her waist as he punched in for work. From that point on, her early morning solo became a pas deux das with thrust counter thrust and position changes like well-oiled bearings in a perfectly timed machine. As was her nature, by the culmination of their sex, she was on top, poised like a jungle cat holding his arms above his head; he loved the submissive position and assumed it gladly. In this position Sylvania rode across his body dragging her clit across his stomach, while alternately kissing him and sucking his nipples. The result was the tightest hottest ride imaginable.

She introduced him to internal geometry that he had never known until her. Then she would make him come, demanding every drop of his essence; the feeling made him want to braid his toes together. Afterward, they would kiss and cool off while she continued to have aftershock mini quakes. They arose from their love den, took a shower together, and ate a quick breakfast of juice, toast and half a Texas omelet apiece. Then left in their separate directions. Twenty minutes later, she arrived at Independence Elementary school.

Sylvania Collins was not the typical vision of a school marm. She tried to tone down her sexiness when she came to school, but she was cursed; even if she wore hip-hugger granny panties and a shapeless mumu dress she was sexy. Her large breasts and proportioned hips and butt were undeniable. She tried minimizer bras and butt reducer panty girdles. Nothing could conceal her God-given shape. All of the male teachers were distracted and most of the females thought she was doing something on purpose, but for her it was only about the kids.

She couldn't exactly do a poll to find out if she was dressing too sexy from the kid's perspective, so she just dressed in the middle of her road and hoped for the best. All of her students loved her and made great strides to please her. That meant that her classes had the highest grade point averages across the board in the entire school. This convinced the Principal that there must be a method to the madness after all, and gave Ms. Collins a lot of latitude because she got results. She just wished her religious trips to the gym would give *her* some results similar to Ms. Collins.

Today was a special day, Ms. Collins' fourth grade class was going on a field trip. All twenty of the parental permission slips had come in so nobody would be left out. They were going to the Tennis Open. Barry's company was one of the sponsors this year. Once Sylvania discovered that tid bit, magically a group pass for her, the kids and two parent chaperones appeared. She had a way of getting what she wanted from Barry. So, in just about two hours the busses would arrive and they would be off for their adventure. The Tennis Open wasn't part of the pro tour like the U.S. Open or the French Open; it was more of an exhibition of pro tennis athletes. She had a feeling the kids were going to love it.

The week before, they had done an entire segment on sports, team and individual. The last part of the series was about sports that could be both like tennis and golf. During that time she came across the passes. A quick permission request to the Principal and twenty parental forms later they were on their way. She thought, "Putt Putt" next! Today she was wearing a below the knee alpine white skirt with a sleeveless silk button down white shirt with a tennis motif. Around her shoulders was an off white pink and green cardigan sweater.

As usual whenever she went on field trips she wore her maternity bra; it had the fold out flaps so that a mother could whip out a nipple at a moment's notice to feed her baby. She had never had children, but she learned the hard way on her first field trip; her nipples got hard literally when the wind blew and they were quite the distraction. So, she used the breast feeding bra to insert pads that would distribute the pucker of her nipples, negating the distraction factor.

The truth was, she was excited to be going to the Open! She loved tennis and she loved her kids; she loved expanding their horizons and doing something she loved just made this the best day ever. The room buzzer on her desk glowed green telling her the bus was there. She got everybody up, did their preparatory stretch, then, went in desk order through the cloak room and got their jackets and lunches. Beverages would be provided by the arena. She lined everybody up in single file order and marched to the front door.

They all waved as they passed the Principals office; a couple of the boys saluted on their way to the big yellow bus. The students were instructed to check in front and behind to ensure that the same people were there all day until they got back. This was one of the security exercises they performed to ensure that no child was left behind – literally.

As they mounted the steps and took their seats they recited the standard, "Don't talk to strangers", and "Report everything weird"; there were bound to be new and strange things on any field trip, but kids knew what was weird. They were instructed to use a "Grapevine": one tell the next and the next until it got to the teacher or chaperone. That way everybody knew what was happening. If it were an emergency, "scream and point". That last tactic was the bane of the school bus drivers in the 21st century; "The scream and point exercise". On three, every child screamed at the top of their lungs "Stranger Danger!" and then pointed at the bus driver.

As soon as the scream died down the bus started and they were off. The tennis stadium was downtown by City College. The bus dropped the kids, teacher and chaperones at the front entrance. Ms. Collins went to the ticket window to claim the passes; they all got programs on their way inside. The souvenir programs listed all the people who would be playing today, the old timers: Andre Agassi, Jimmy Conners and Billie Jean King. The kids thought this was the funniest thing, it was like watching their grandparents playing tennis. To Sylvania, they were comical, but still in surprisingly good shape; their skill level was still high.

After they took a quick break the youngsters came out, the up and coming tennis pros of the future. These kids were close to her class's ages of nine and ten year olds, and they were doing an exceptional exhibition of skill for their years. This was the main focus of the field trip for her, to show the kids that they could be anything they wanted to be. If they could see something somebody else their age could do, they could do it too… if they wanted.

The next break was for lunch. Sylvania sent a text message to the bus driver to bring the cooler with the kids' lunches to the front gate. A chaperone mom met the driver and took the named bags to the prearranged table space that was provided for the group. The stadium package included juice drinks for the kids and an official hat and tee shirt. The latter two were the end of the day surprises. They would get a chance to get them both autographed before they went home.

After lunch was Prime Time! The Williams sisters, Martina Hingis, Pete Sampras, Maria Sharapova and Anna Kornakova, amongst others, came out and put on a world class exhibition of skill, strength and stamina. The kids applauded at the right times. It was so cute to watch their eyes and heads going from side to side in unison during the volleys – priceless.

The last match was with home grown talent, Dutchess Singletary. She was the unseeded local champion who was burning up the tour tournaments on her way to the big win. Dutchess was a sight to see! Tall, at least six feet, beautiful, light skinned, with a sensuously sexy, feline, body with similarly catlike reflexes. Most striking were her emerald green eyes and her flaming red hair.

Right about 1:30 the exhibition was over for the day, which was good; the kids had about as much as they could take for now. However, as they were single filing out of their club seats, they were stopped by a Tennis Open official and escorted into a room off the main tunnel, where the players emerged from their dressing rooms. This was the press room.

That fact was lost on the kids as they were led into the room with no knowledge of what was happening. But since the adults weren't worried, neither were they. They were instructed to stand in line with their backs to the tables. All boys and girls could be heard whispering behind them; they were then directed to turn around. When they saw their official tee-shirts and hats, they all screamed and clapped their hands. The officials thanked them for coming and asked if they had had a good time, they all yelled, "Yes!"

Then when asked if they had any questions they raised their hands politely and the officials told them to keep their hands raised. That's when all the pros they had seen playing on court came in and answered their questions. They spent time speaking to the kids and signed autographs on their hats and tee-shirts. Last but not least, they signed tee-shirts and hats for the adults. They spoke and signed in the same order that they had played, so Dutchess was last in line. Being the local sports celebrity, she spent the most time with the group. She thanked all the kids for coming and was pleased that they had a good time.

Before leaving she spoke to Ms. Collins. Surprisingly, she commented on her beauty. There was that short awkward moment when two obviously attractive women meet, but it was there and then gone. They had an instant rapport; Dutchess gave Ms. Collins one of her cards and told her that she wished she could have had a teacher like her in the 4th grade, there's no telling where she would be now.

Sylvania blushed and thanked her for her kindness; unexpectedly Dutchess gathered the kids in a huddle and whispered for a few seconds. They all turned around and on the count of three they screamed, "We love you Ms. Collins, thank you for a wonderful day!" They sounded like a choir of Angels; it was the sweetest sound she had ever heard. Dutchess winked at her and turned to leave. The kids and parents alike would talk about this field trip for weeks.

Chapter 5

Flashpoint:

Southern United States of America, summertime - record heat wave...

Landing at the International airport and preceding from first class to the Diplomatic area, two men stood out amongst the glamorous first class passengers to disembark. One beautiful man was about 6'7", comfortable with his size, he strode easily to the diplomatic area in his immaculately tailored suit. The other man was shorter but with a presence that belied his size just topping the six foot mark. This milk chocolate gentleman was also decked out in a perfectly tailored suit with blindingly shiny alligator shoes. His facial hair was groomed to perfection and it framed a face that some brave women would call beautiful! The pronounced scar on his left cheek somehow leant more to that estimation not less.

The outstanding article of clothing he wore was the traditional Gutrah Saudi Headdress with the heavy golden braids wrapped around the crown of his head. By Middle Eastern standards, this denoted a member of the Royal Family. But in this instance, he was representing the ministerial ranks in the country under Diplomatic passport for a two week junket. Other than these two men, the balance of the crowd was composed of drab typical looking travelers, nothing to catch one's eye. Neither men knew the other, but fate being the wheel that it is… they would meet again.

Both men climbed aboard the special internal train that whisked the VIPs to the diplomatic baggage area outside the perimeter of airport security. The diplomatic pouches and luggage was not inspected and the underground access was reserved for limos and diplomatic transport only. The tall man with the regal bearing took off his custom made Gargoyle sunglasses revealing his off-putting intense hazel eyes.

He offered his diplomatic passport to claim his pouches and, after stacking everything on the luggage cart, wheeled it out to the waiting limo. Robert was driven to his five-star hotel and shown to his suite. He was pre-registered, so, there was no stop at the front desk. Although they both arrived at the same time, his luggage was already inside his door when he arrived, earning the bellman a healthy tip.

He opened one bag and took out a digital text pager. The old fashioned technology still had some uses. The coded message of random digits was a jumbled contact number that he needed to call within fifteen minutes of checking into his room. He dialed this number through the hotel phone, knowing that the number would be disconnected immediately after his call. The phone rang twice; it was answered with "Yes, the clock is ticking,"

Then, disconnected. That was his confirmation that his assignment was still a go, and that no order had come down, cancelling any further action. Robert relaxed just for a minute, he knew he would be getting an encrypted email on his cell phone any time now, giving him coordinates and times for the "meeting". The euphemisms in his trade were almost humorous, almost.

Walking around the bed he looked at his bags, the tall diplomatic bag had a lock on it very few people had ever seen. The key looked like a small corkscrew, and the tip had a tiny sensor chip that was like no other. Twisting the key deep enough into the lock released the cylinder. He twisted the cylinder until the correct combination popped open the top of the bag. Inside were the tools of his trade.

At first look his trade looked to be photography or astronomy, the high tech lensed "cameras" that he pulled out would indeed accomplish these goals easily.

But the remaining hard ABS plastic cases got to the heart of his profession. The .50 caliber BMG sniper rifle with three five round magazines was accurate to 1700 meters, close enough to a mile for government work, especially if he actually worked for the government.

This was the reason his employer of the month insisted and arranged that he travel on diplomatic passport; diplomatic bags were never searched. This made procuring the correct tools for a job much more efficient than having them dropped at the hotel or going on a scavenger hunt to put them together, which he had also done. This option gave him ample time to physically reconnoiter the kill zone, to create a box from which the target could not escape. From one thousand meters in, no matter the weather, it was the equivalent of a slam dunk in the NBA by a seven footer.

Robert's phone chirped twice. That signal always sent shivers down his spine: assignment confirmed, target acquired, location set with backup location planned. In all of his years as a hitter, he had never had to avail himself of the use of the backup location, but it was procedure.

Slipping his tools back and locking his bag, he walked over to the wall socket where his phone was charging and opened the Ocean digital minicomputer phone. The mail was there. Completing the prescribed ritual of de-encryption took about one minute; the result was a map of a small block with a pocket park in front. The main feature of the park was a mini gazebo; this was ground zero. The target would be speaking from here at approximately 2:00pm tomorrow. Time check confirmed 10:30am local time. According to the attached text, the kill zone was ten miles south east of his current location. The map showed a basketball court within two blocks of the zone. Robert was going to work out. Memorizing his coordinates, he popped open a garment bag and removed a pair of knee scraper shorts, a light weight sweat suit, a pair of size fifteen Nike LeBron's and a headband. A pair of Oakley MP3 shades rounded out the ensemble.

From another bag he retrieved a flattened leather oval and an official Bob Mcadoo version, Spaulding basketball. A small zip bag held a fingertip inflator and a rechargeable mini pump. He licked the needle-like tip and poked it into the rubber filled hole. The inflator blew up the ball to its optimum

PSI and cut off. He dribbled the ball and got the perfect "ping" sound from the bounce back. He was ready.

He grabbed his keys which included one or two standard looking keys which were actually retractable razors and a bright yellow tourist picture viewer. The viewer appeared to be a cheap looking magnifier one could find at any tourist shop or amusement park in the world that magnifies an internally applied picture. But, of course, this was not the case. This viewer didn't hold a picture of loved ones, it was in reality a high-powered spotter scope with an internal range finder. Before, during, or after the game he would scope out the box from the ground. Fully prepared, he clipped on his "burnout" Boost mobile phone and left for the playground. The other man had collected his diplomatic bags and was also picked up by a blacked out limo. He was also whisked off to a hotel; this one a four star where he was given the red carpet treatment befitting an emissary of the Royal family.

***

Because this hotel lacked the fifth star normally attributed to lodgings for Royalty, they went the extra mile in terms of service hoping to attract more of the same caliber guests in the future. The main request was privacy; he was assured that once he had been given the list of amenities and services that he would be left alone until he requested to be bothered. He was prepaid for two weeks in the Presidential Penthouse. Once the preliminaries were out of the way, he tipped the representative $50.00 and locked his door. He took off his headdress, removed and hung up his suit. Using his keys, he opened the multiple locks on the diplomatic pouch. He removed the contents and set them out on the bed then bowed and said a prayer

"Allah Akbar...ALLAH AKBAR..."

Thomas Margolin AKA Abdullah Dubashi was on a mission for the faithful. The infidel, Mitchell Johansen, must die in as publicly a manner as possible, with much media coverage. Twenty seven hours from now, if Allah wills it, he will be roasting in infidel Hell all alone, suffering for eternity for his sins against the Holy Land.

He extracted two packs of lithium batteries and inserted them into their respective units. He took hold of the power pins and the associated trigger. Holding one piece in each hand, he pressed the trigger and felt the strong shock. It was powerful enough to make him jump with pain. He smiled, and this was good. He went through his other bag and removed an outfit befitting a low level drug dealer on any American street: Girbeau stonewashed oversized green jeans, with more than enough pocket room to conceal the eight bricks of C-4 plastic explosive, duct tape, and the power pins.

He put his map in his front pocket, put on his Timberland boots, pulled on a supersized hockey jersey, and cocked a fitted baseball cap to the side. All set, he crept out of the penthouse and down the service stairs two floors where he used the room service elevator to get to the basement level. Here he left out through the employee entrance and directly to a Ford Taurus. The keys had been left on the floor under the mat. He started the engine; it sounded strong. The gas tank was full, "Allah is good and most beneficent", he thought as he began following his directions. He drove towards the freeway.

On the way he looked through the other paperwork from his package. The design of the gazebo, the hollows beneath the columns were the best places to set the explosives. But for maximum yield he would combine the bricks and duct tape the package tightly around the power pin and place it dead center in the crawl space. This way all available dirt, rocks and wreckage would amplify the angle and provide extra shrapnel. Five minutes to target area he noted, as he pulled off the exit. Passing by a basketball court in full battle, he filed it away as a landmark to use when he came back tonight. The effective range of the trigger / pin system was just over one mile across open land, line of sight, but inside the city with all of its obstructions, it was just under four city blocks. Abdullah rode around the area from different directions looking at ground zero, then he parked.

Walking the two blocks to his destination, he observed everything. Finally arriving, he took a seat on a bench and lounged. He spent several minutes kicking at the fat, begging pigeons. They would all be fried tomorrow, he smiled broadly. It was Allah's will, so it would be done. An enemy of Islam and his infidel supporters would be eradicated tomorrow to the good of the world. "So be it", he thought looking at the area around the gazebo. He assessed how much collateral damage there would be. Surely this bench less than twenty yards away will be blown to atoms and the building at the gazebos rear will be severely damaged. Yes... This will be a message heard loud and clear.

Chapter 6

"Damn, why the hell is it that I can order forty cases of Fed Shock explosive tipped .40 caliber rounds and get them by first thing in the morning, but an order of pastel blue and pink post-it notes is not here two weeks later?"

The little things were starting to pile up on Special Agent Kristi Johnson. Her new command in Center Vale Maryland was barely six months old, and in those six months she had been turning in good work. Whatever it was, luck or her ability to hand pick talent, they had run down numbers six and eight on the top ten list in less than 180 days. That was simply not heard of, it was an agency record and it was done by a girl! In the parlance of the intelligence world, she was a Single Black Female, eight year vet of the FBI and the youngest SAC. Special Agent in Charge of her own subspecialty division. Her charges were tie-ins and interstate crimes. Jokingly, they called her shop the disorderlies because she had jurisdiction over non organized crimes, leads and links to major crimes not indictable under the RICO Act - basically freelance high profile criminals. Little was known of her work until results poured in. Hostage rescue, mob task forces, and Homeland Security interagency co-ops always got the headlines.

She was good with that, it made her feel like a non-military Delta Force unknown results producer. Besides, the less known she was, the less publicity, the less publicity, the less pressure, the less pressure, the fewer mistakes. That all worked its way down the funnel of more money in the budget which bought more and better technology and technicians to do the work. Things were working well. She had perused a new case overnight; a jewel theft of major proportions and a strange kinky bank robber. Hmmm, "Kinky bank robber she thought, she wondered what that was about, robberies of all types crossed her desk but this was the first with the official description "kinky."

She was no prude by any stretch of the word; she was a healthy, horny, sexually active Jet centerfold quality black woman. She could have been an Olympic medal winner for all the running around the campus she did, outpacing madly waving dicks on the yard of Howard University where she did her undergrad. But, she knew, the only time to get stopped was when **she** stopped, not when she **was** stopped. Football, basketball, baseball players, senators, want-to-be senators, they all chased her. She was a cross between Flo Jo, Halle Berry and Janet Jacme – or so they told her: Flo Jo for her runner's legs, Halle Berry for her curves and beautiful face, and Janet Jacme for the pornographic wet dreams she inspired.

Because no one on campus was known to have gotten the punnanni – this was subterfuge. She had a contract with the lovers she did see. If one word came out regarding anything about her sex life, they would be cut off from the most flexible, fantasy fulfilling, willing come-back pussy they were ever bound to get this side of heaven. To ensure nothing got out she would shave icons out of her pubic hair interesting enough to be irresistible not to talk about, if you were a contract breaker. Once, she shaved the McDonald's golden arches with the middle bar forming an arrow down to the best meal in town. If that didn't get around campus, nothing would. The cut off threat was solid, her security was intact.

She pulled the bank robbery file, the perpetrator was a woman or an incredible impersonator. She was tall, muscularly built, and disguised. She was solo, which was different. Usually, banks get hit by crews, not a singular person. She appeared out of nowhere and disappeared the same way. Witnesses reported a vintage car they couldn't identify. An older gentleman thought the description sounded like a Jaguar XKE 12 cylinder from the late 60's, but none had been sighted in the area.

They continued to look for the car locally, probably a dead end. Says she was totally prepared, down to pre-cut lengths of duct tape with extra just in case. Thoughtful, she used that on the manager. But that didn't spell "kinky" to her; the next page explained it all. The clothes that the victims had been wearing had been tossed into the safe and time locked. They were duct taped in a sexual daisy chain.

"Oh my God!"

They were left behind genital to mouth, Kristi had no choice but to cross her legs and put her hand to her mouth as she read. Apparently, from the officers that reviewed the tapes, it started with the men. Erections poking onto the lips and faces of the women caused a chain reaction which caused the women to get turned on. In the beginning they were all moaning and upset because they got robbed. Then the relief over not being hurt dissolved with the sights before their eyes. Incredibly, the women and men started one by one until they were all engaging with the sexual organ within their reach in oral sex!

It was unbelievable. Leave it to a woman to stage a robbery that turns into an oral orgy. Kristi had to refrain from rubbing her thighs together like a cricket making music. But, she was definitely turned on reading this criminal action report. This was a first, but it was also a harbinger of a very imaginative criminal mind at work. This one would be hard to crack at best. She would have to delve into criminal practices and behaviors from across multiple platforms to try to profile her. She hoped it was a she because if not, trying to track down a homosexual with this level of psychological know-how would be a nightmare.

Though the lack of male-to-male pairings pointed to a heterosexual woman, the female-female pairings seemed numerically coincidental. Kristi reluctantly put down the robbery report and referred back to her incoming crime log sheet: gang related kidnapping, fifteen cars stolen from a parking garage, which sounded like an inside job. She giggled, absolutely no pun intended. Triple murder suicide, which sounded like a completely closed circle, but murder suicide was the new fad now.

This was started by cowards too afraid to pay for their crimes, so they kill themselves instead. Two cops murdered in Georgia, Cobb County – she had heard of that place. Supposedly they dealt out harsh punishment for some of the pettiest things. Oh yeah, that was where they imprisoned that poor, young boy for consensual oral sex; ten years with no parole for getting some head. If she could remember correctly, it was a young black boy getting a blowjob from a classmate, a white girl. Both of them were underage, but he got ten years in prison, she got a reputation. Sad.

The report was about two hard core deputies that worked at the detention center. Apparently, they pissed off the wrong person – jeeze. They were shot, gutted, and left in their personal cars in the jail parking lot. The crime scene photos made her stomach clench. Deputies Reed and Paul both had long careers with that county. But between them, it says they had an entire book full of grievances against them, meaning it could have been anybody. Considering how many people get locked up and warehoused in this facility, that number was huge.

Kristi put that report away sighing. She was glad she was a Federal cop, especially SAC. She made the decision about what she participated in and delegated everything else. With this position and the uniqueness of her shop, she had the juice to pull resources from virtually anywhere to assist in her investigations. This cut down on local Agent depletion during a big case. She could fly into an out-of-state locale with three agents and be met by a task force at her disposal. It did cause some friction when some SAC's, male SAC's, realized how much bigger her balls were than theirs.

In those situations she did have a gift. Her looks and confidence gave her the ability to take command while still letting her male counterparts feel as if they hadn't lost control. It was sort of like faking an orgasm: it accomplished the goal of getting an ineffective man up off of you, and then at the same time, making him feel like he'd done something. She just had to make sure not to play that card unless it was absolutely necessary. She scrolled through the rest of the listings to see if there were any more standouts. Diamond theft, oh hell, this is one they're gonna try to keep below the radar: twenty two million dollars worth of naturally colored diamonds stolen under the noses of the owners during a high profile party at their house with a full complement of security. Whew!

The local office had requested still shots of all the guests and the invitation register and guest list. This was going to be a bear as well. Damn! How come the week had to start like this? The actual listing had about three hundred incidents that had occurred over the last forty eight hours. And they had been sent to her and out of them all, these few stood out as the most intriguing.

She would put out a support proposal to Georgia. Doubtful that these rednecks would accept help from a black girl. They would probably keep it in-house with their good-ol-boy GBI. The bank probe would get a pair of agents dedicated and two agents flown to the jewel heist location on the coast. Secure company emails had already been shot to local offices letting them know to expect the pairs. She would stay behind in the nerve center to monitor the teams; she'd know when to step in if necessary.

Chapter 7

Sylvia deplaned at DFW airport in Grapevine, Texas; she rolled her carryon bag to the limousine and stepped into the shuttle bus destined for the Crown Plaza Hotel in Las Colinas. She had a suite reserved for today and tomorrow. If all went well, she would be returning by a totally different route. The driver helped her with her bags and offered to take them up to her room for her. She flashed her thousand watt smile and declined his offer sending him on his way feeling good. No sooner than she had checked into her room, the phone rang.

The gentleman was very polite; he had a Middle Eastern accent, spoke slowly and pronounced each word deliberately. She was informed that a car had been dispatched for her and was waiting in the carport downstairs, a burgundy Mercedes 600SEL. whenever she was ready to join the men for their meeting the car would be waiting; it and the driver were at her disposal while she was in Dallas.

She thanked her caller and let him know that she should be ready in about thirty minutes. Hanging up she pulled the simple black shift over her head, clad only in French cut bikini panties and textured pasties to keep some kind of reign on her large sensitive nipples, she went to start up the shower.

Making sure all the available security devices were in place, she hung her portable screamer motion sensor around the doorknob and removed her panties. She reached into her "safe", removing the fake tampon and setting it on the sink. She stepped into the steamy shower and washed the air travel off her body and out of her beautiful black hair.

Stepping out to the fluffy beach sized towels, she dried off and donned a plush terry cloth robe that felt like a mink coat. She grabbed her safe and walked into the bedroom. She reached into her carry-on pocket and retrieved a 10' by 10' turquoise cloth square. Carefully placing it on her nightstand, she unscrewed the 'tail end' of the tampon and poured out the diamond collection.

The way they glittered and multiplied the small amount of available light, it made all the sense in the world why people called diamonds ice. Letting them spill through her fingers cemented the reason why they were a girl's best friend. She had usurped a couple of samples for her troubles, two nice two carat sized baubles. But the balance was here. What they didn't know wouldn't hurt them. The total weight of the collection was worth $22 million, but today she was in Dallas prepared to unload them for a cut rate price of $10 million. Most people don't know how many Middle Eastern men were in Texas in general, Houston and Dallas specifically, but the population was substantial and their oil money was long.

Twenty minutes later, dressed in a crème white Chanel two-piece business suit, three-inch closed toe Ferragamo pumps, matching silk pasties, and a double-breasted jacket, Sylvia wrapped her prize in the turquoise velvet. She deposited that bundle into a black velvet bag that went into her alligator and ostrich skin briefcase. She was on her way. With a severely pulled back hair style, and the four strand twisted pony tail at the back could put her in the spotlight on any catwalk in the world. She was ready.

***

As she stepped outside the front door of the lobby the Mercedes pulled to the curb and the rear door automatically opened. She climbed inside and they were off. Fifteen silent minutes later they arrived at the meeting site, a simple plain fronted building two doors down from a barber shop. The driver personally opened the rear door for her and subsequently the door to the building. The difference was ten times greater than night and day.

The entire entry was blood red and gold. The next set of mahogany double doors opened to an ultra-high end strip club filled with Middle Eastern men featuring Black, Puerto Rican, Asian and Brazilian women. They were served by uniformed bartenders and waiter staff. It was truly the most lavish club of any type she had ever stepped foot into, and that was saying something. Her hosts rose as one from the bar; she was expected. They escorted her to a VIP area just off the bar to a private access room off the VIP. There was a marble table set up with a halogen natural light and an 18" by 18" black velvet cloth. For just a second she allowed herself a small smirk for her choice of contrasting colors to offset the colored gems. Sylvia sat in the chair being offered to her. This was not the first time she had dealt with this particular client, just the largest transaction so far. Considering, there was no need for small talk.

Two briefcases were brought out and opened; her quick inspection and a glance at the integrated scales confirmed the weight. She opened her case, removed the black velvet bag and opened it to reveal the turquoise splash of color. She then laid the corners within the black corners and turned on the halogen sun. The marble table exploded with brilliance.

The collected buyers shaded their eyes except for Sylvia whose glasses automatically darkened to compensate for the rapid change in luminosity. The buyers were almost moved to clap, but held back keeping calm in the face of their contractor. The buyer clicked a switch on to halogen and the spectrum of light changed; the gems on the velvet square went from reflecting the light to actually projecting from inside the diamonds. The effect was impressive.

The inner luminosity lit up each still heart of each diamond, resulting in a soft but clear light emanating from each and every facet. This was a technique for finding flaws in gemstones, the uniform glow, no matter how the stones were moved around proved the point – flawless. The eeriest glow came from the black diamonds, light coming out of darkness. It was a sight Sylvia would never forget. With the authenticity confirmed, the quality demonstration over, the normal subdued lighting resumed and conversation was finally allowed.

"As always, we appreciate all your efforts and ask that you always continue to contact us first whenever you acquire new merchandise. You can rest assured that any leads we hear about will be passed on to you forthrightly, to our mutual benefit of course."

She inclined her head slightly, accenting her lithe neck, a very Eastern gesture indicating thanks and acquiescence.

"And I look forward to further business ventures with you and your partners in the future."

"Were the accommodations suitable?"

"Yes, thank you, the short time I've had to enjoy them has been more than satisfactory."

"And I presume your transportation was adequate?"

"Oh yes, more than adequate."

There was something about the power of a full sized Mercedes Sedan that made Sylvia wetter than Niagara Falls, but that was not something these Middle Eastern men needed to know.

"That's delightful...it's yours! As with your departure plans; arrangements have been made to fly your vehicle home with you, it's already registered in the name of your company and listed with Internal Revenue as a paid leased diplomatic transport in your company fleet." Sylvia was stunned, but only for a beat; her recovery was so smooth nobody saw the pause but her. "I appreciate the gift, I presume the cash will be distributed throughout the vehicle and arrangements have been made with cargo freight security?"

"Very astute, and yes as a matter of fact, your car will be awaiting you at baggage claim once you land."

"Thank you."

With that business concluded, the group adjourned to the VIP area of the club and shared a toast of Cristal champagne and snifters of Louis XV Remy Martin Cognac. The atmosphere was decidedly masculine, but the level of class made Sylvia comfortable. The incredible beauty of the dancers, the naked female body being one of the most beautiful sights on the planet, the procurers had chosen well. The fact was that Sylvia wasn't entirely cemented into her sexuality, for her, sex was about pleasure, whatever pleased her and made her feel good – was good.

Although the dancers were all exotic beauties, Sylvia knew she could strip down and easily compete with these professional nude women. But, giving credit where credit is due, the writhing, toned, oiled bodies were starting to have an effect on her. So, keeping her professional power projection, a millionaire amongst peers, plus knowing how women were treated in the society that these men hailed from, she reminded them that they were in the States.

Reaching into the humidor she extracted a Macanudo Cuban cigar, clipped the end and flamed the tip. Expertly wrapped her lips around the stalk wetting it, and puffed it to an impressive ash. She tapped it into the large bear claw shaped Tiffany crystal ashtray, crossed her legs and sat back to review the ladies. The assembled men had never seen anything of the sort in their lives. Coming from Muslim countries, women would never even have been admitted into a place such as this, an establishment just for men. But this black American woman was establishing herself as an equal.

At first, when they noticed how well she handled her liquor they were amused, and then the cigar shocked them. But after she got the two most beautiful women in the club, a Persian and a Puerto Rican; to give her a simultaneous lap dance that had all of their erections tenting their expensive slacks. They resigned themselves to the fact that this was a different country. If any more proof were needed, they just had to remember the $10 million they had just paid her, no matter the circumstances. Back home they would never have given a woman money like that!

Chapter 8

The smoldering and flame messages were nothing really, compared to the importance of the executive situation. These mortal user problems could have been handled from his command and control console right here in his office. But there were a couple reasons that precluded that. First was the fact that once he took over remote control of their computers, they lost all functionality, which only made them make more calls. Then when the systems starting working on their own, they would flip out and sometimes unplug them, totally defeating the purpose of the diagnostic.

Secondly he had established a policy of face time. Most people that saw him didn't know what to think, which was bad. Not knowing meant the UNKNOWN! The unknown meant fear. The last thing a 6'7" black man needed was an automatic fear response. So whenever he started a contract, his first days were spent meeting his users, fixing problems. He used his internal heat measurements to make sure the hottest topics got handled first knowing that even the smoldering coals could start fires.

He made sure all heat got handled the day of the report if possible. Those first days were interesting to say the least. His sudden appearance above the forest of cubicles drew attention from everybody. Women actually pushed their purses deeper under their desks.

However, once he walked into their cube and introduced himself, the deep baritone voice and radiantly beautiful hazel eyes made everything ok. He made sure all systems were in good working order and let them all know that he was available on speed dial or instant messenger.

The men were different, but not much. They all started the conversation with NBA references unconsciously showing their intimidation and insecurity. So he learned to sit down as soon as possible and to move about by scooting his chair from place to place. He constantly kept his anti-static band on his wrist. He would plug himself into a socket to ground himself before touching any systems because this form of locomotion built up a major charge of static electricity.

Sometimes, even now the women would talk with him as the obvious subject matter. Having been this size for years he was used to his body image and the way other people saw him. When the women would put in a work order regarding their ergonomic workstation chairs, they wanted him to come make adjustments they could've done themselves just because they wanted to feel him move them around in their chairs.

When they sabotaged their CPU, they wanted to see him on his knees underneath the desk doing his diagnosis of the processing unit and the physical connections. More than once he had looked up and behind himself to catch a user-woman stuck in fantasy, staring off into the distance while looking through him. He had even caught a couple of them diddling their nipples through their business blouses with definite color rising up to their necks and cheeks fantasizing about all this black man, doggy style, behind them using the equipment that came with those big ass size fifteen shoes to pummel them into submission, to use their corporate asses for his pleasure. Then he would announce that he was done, that everything was ship shape, mainly to give them a chance to compose themselves if that was necessary.

Sometimes they would still be tranced out, nipples poking out stiffly, and breathing hard. Others realized what they were doing and would turn their backs and busy themselves doing something else; the play off. Eventually, everyone got used to him and he only became an anomaly when visitors came by. After a few "house calls", a soft reboot, a driver version update, a loose network cable and, the most time consuming, a laptop system file re-image, his day was pretty much on auto pilot. Now he had a chance to think about what he would do after work.

***

Ron was a happy hour fiend; he knew the best happy hour spots in this and four surrounding districts. He knew who had the best food, drinks, bartenders, selection of females and entertainment for each day and each place. He had them stored inside a matrix in his mind.

Tonight, it would be either old school karaoke and open mike with pizza and pasta, or the jazz jam session with the seafood buffet. Hmmm, the choice was always who or what would he choose: the stomach, the big head, or the smaller big head. There was usually a tug of war between the first and the last. Tonight he thought it would be karaoke. The old school slow jam karaoke always drew a crowd of ladies that loved to be serenaded, usually single and if you could carry a tune. Nine times out of ten you could carry one of them home too! His baritone was perfect for singing Gerald Levert, Will Downing, Teddy Pendergrass - all those old school 'throw your panties on the stage' type singers. He had to admit that he was pretty good; his results spoke for themselves.

Ron checked in with Wendsday to see if anything else had popped up on to the radar.

"Naw boss man, it's cool runnins in dem reehdah screen rut naw", she said in a very bad Jamaican accent. Let her tell it, Community Theater was in her near future. She was going through an artsy chick phase; Ron was just glad she was out of her young rap boy stage.

"Sooo, awl ya gotta dew is stretch baack n relax gov'nor qui en time'll be on ya quickeren shit love. Just kick your ginormous dogs up on ya desk." Her British cockney was even worse. "Ok Wen, you keep up the practice, I won't fire you so don't quit, ok?"

They both laughed at that one and she went back to her desk. He followed her advice and kicked his enormous gigantic feet up onto his desktop and before he knew it, it was time to go. That was another of his personal dictates unless it was a real emergency. He would not leave early. It was much better for him to put out a fire late in the day than to have to be called in the middle of the night to deal with something that could have been done already. So, with nothing else popping up for today, he was on his way to 'Oke Dokeys'. The name sounded really wak; but just like smuckers, "with a name like Oke Dokeys, it's got to be good".

After re-inviting Wendsday to accompany him, she re-refused, she was on her chick-a-dee mission, exchanging platitudes:

"Be safe",

"Wear a rubber",

"Get home safe",

"See you in the morning".

***

They went their separate ways. Putting himself in big-dude-casual-stroll mode, Ron made his way through the grid of city streets, avenues, and boulevards until he arrived. There were a few others getting in early, vying for seats at tables with their co-workers or a coveted stool at the bar. The buffet was in full swing. However as Ron was approaching, fresh steaming hot pizza pies were being placed on the steam heating tables. He stepped through the line adding selections to his plate followed by a small bowl of pasta.

Carefully he made his way to the bar and snagged a seat close to the stage, giving him a perfect overview of the tables from front to back, as well as the entrance, exit, and ladies room paths. As an added bonus, his bar seat gave him great acoustics to hear the live band that was currently jamming and would later play for the contestants. The mood right now was smooth jazz. Later, slow jams would start non-stop, except for the band's breaks. Ron ordered a twenty two ounce draft beer satisfying the two-drink minimum in one shot, and sat back to watch the festivities.

He loved watching them come in; it was a real social science experiment. The ladies from work would come in together, scout a seat and designate a purse watcher. The balance of the group would go to the 'powder room', leaving the last one to go alone. Girlfriends, on the other hand would go in shifts, never leaving one alone. Coming in with a man was a ballet of another kind. Men with *their* women, would scout the seat that gave him the best view of the door just in case someone came in that he didn't want to see. Once they were seated, the woman would leave her purse prominently displayed, take out what she needs and she's off to the ladies room, leaving her universal calling card, which to all women meant "TAKEN".

Compare that with men that came in with a woman, co-worker, friend, and beard, whatever. They will choose a prominent table where they can see and be seen. He will order the first round of drinks, she'll go to the rest room with her purse leaving him to use the second waiting drink as a conversation piece until she returns. The game was funny, but it did have rules... and oh the players. That was one thing about being paid and single in the city. Whatever you wanted for the night was bound to come walking through the door: tall and thin, short and thick, and every combination in between.

Ron fancied himself a connoisseur of women. As such, had grown very picky about which kind of woman he would share himself with. There were some that would be instantly head-over-heels in love. Typically, they were not accustomed to a man, an actual man that knew how to treat them like a lady.

Then there were the ones that were looking for another 'baby daddy', one with some money this time. That's the reason they would spend all day at home sprucing up, getting a babysitter and borrowing clothes just to go to happy hour. They plan all of that just to pose as if they had gotten off work so that they could mingle with people with jobs. You had to be careful. Some were very enticing until you discovered that they took the bus to the club and had no way home.

Ron wasn't looking for any time bombs tonight. He wasn't pressed. If 'she' walked in, he would know it. The fact that his secretary could get quality women easier than he could, was a major kick in the ego. The slow jams were about to start. The band was tuning up and a tiny woman was approaching the stage. She was going to sing 'and I am telling you, I'm not going', the finale song from Dreamgirls. This ought to be interesting, he thought. After the first note, the first giant note out of this tiny woman, everybody knew that this was going to be a treat.

Chapter 9

Oh yes! The sun was so hot, it felt as if every inch of her body was being steamrolled by the intense heat. The rising temperature was cooking her, her muscles melting, her bones heating up and cooking her from the inside out. She could feel the fiery sensation all the way through her back to her middle. She turned over and applied Kiwi flavored SPF 300 suntan / block lotion all over her front side and pulled her tan thru UV mask over her eyes. No more than twenty minutes, her sensitive fair skin could not take too much more without burning. Damn those light-skin-ass genes! She wished she could have been born black as a cast iron skillet.

Very quickly those thoughts fled from her mind. The sun started to do its job. Her skin began to speckle with sweat as the organ heated up and her body's radiator started to work its cooling action. Her perky 36d breasts were broiling, warming up her whole body. The pinkish tan nipples were stiffening from the suns attention, the large sensitive nubs growing and sweating. The gentle breeze over the water evaporating off her nipples, exciting them all the more sending signals down to her sparsely haired sex.

Dulcet had been laying straight out with her arms to her sides, now she slightly spread and lifted her knees. She could feel the swollen lips of her sex separate stickily. This movement caused a hot shaft of sunlight to penetrate her, painting her rapidly stiffening clit with dappled sunlight.

The direct sunlight was on her now totally exposed clit, reminding her that she needed to apply some sun block to that sensitive area. Splashing lotion on her finger tips she reached between her raised thighs to gently dab the protective lotion on herself. The dabbing motion was irresistible, she started to lightly swirl her fingertips around and around on her slippery unprotected nubbin. Her lips grasping and releasing the dedicated shaft of sunlight that was now fucking her deeply. The heat was reaching the very depths of her.

Her hips started to move with the motions of her photonic lover. Dulcets orgasm attacked her, her stomach muscles cramping down on her ghost lovers long thick penetrator. The creamy liquid spurting like a small fountain recoating her fat swollen lips and sweat oily ass. She fell back breathing as if she had just run a marathon, smiling as though seeing a long lost lover. She lay there rubbing her overheated body from her boiling breasts and their stiff rubbery nipples down to her still throbbing cauldron of a twat, still tingling from orgasmic aftershocks. This was the best feeling on earth.

Dulcet had come to the conclusion over the years, ever since she had been molested by her foster brother in one of the government homes she had been assigned to until she ran away for good from that system. She always knew she was different sexually, not like the confused lesbians or the boy crazy whores. The actual categorization of Dulcet: she was a solo-sexual, she was addicted, worse than any alcoholic or crack head, to masturbation. No matter where, when, with what, she knew nobody could please her like she could please herself.

She had been exploring herself, every inch of herself since she discovered her clitoris. Intense yoga exercises gave her the flexibility of a contortionist. She could suck her own toes, and touch 100% of her body inside and out. She found not needing a partner came in handy, she never had to wait for anyone. If she wanted anticipation, she knew how to delay her gratification. Tantric studies gave her almost supernatural energy control.

Her tantric orgasms could last for ten to fifteen minutes at a time. No man, woman, animal or combination thereof could compete with that. After Dulcet had totally vacated the scene earlier, she took several different sets of ID and distributed cash throughout safe deposit boxes across the city. She put the rest of the cash and the other miscellaneous jewelry into a "You-store-it" facility space with a one ton safe bolted to the floor and locked inside. Once work was completed, she drove seventy-five miles towards the sun to her favorite nude beach. It was deserted at this time of the day so she was free to have her love affair with the sun. Being nude felt so right to her. Clothing always felt like a disguise, like the many costumes she wore to do her work, something to come out of once the job was through.

She stood on strong legs and made her way to the gently lapping surf and stroked her way out to the beckoning blue water. It lapped at her feet, then ankles, knees, thighs, and now it was just nipping at her cunt. A tingle buzzed through her, just knowing the incredible violence that this water was capable of. To have it lapping at her most sensitive parts like a small puppy with no teeth amazed her. She felt herself growing horny all over again. She started slapping her clit with handfuls of cool water. She felt so close to nature. It felt as if her clit was a large swollen tea bag and she was flavoring all this water with the essence of herself. With that thought, she started to come again. This time she dived into the surf, stroking smoothly, athletically cutting through the water still shaking through her orgasm; every kick stroke stimulating her and extending her pleasure.

She flip-turned and started stroking back towards shore. Getting to the sand she arrived on her knees riding out the last of her orgasm with the water splashing over her back dripping down her oily breasts. At this point she realized that she was starving. Dulcet walked back to collect her effects, towel, oils, blanket and confidently strolled to the car. Popping the trunk, she deposited her stuff then slid into the driver's seat and cranked up the big Benz. She slipped on some ballet styled slippers for diving and drove to the commercial district.

She dialed in using her satellite navigations Bluetooth cell phone. She ordered shrimp and crab in garlic butter, egg noodles, linguini with white sauce, two orders of bread sticks with melted cheese dip and a Sprite to go.

She drove around the city center window shopping, with the air vents sending in the city air with just a tang of the river water scenting through. Her timer told her it was time to pick up her meal. She arrived at the drive through pick up window, still gloriously naked behind her tinted glass. The man with her order slid open the window, the small display next to his head showed the price of the pickup. She rolled down the window just enough for him to see her eyes. She winked at him and he smiled. She rolled the window down a bit more, enough for him to see her beautiful face and hair framing those incredible green eyes.

Looking behind him she indicated a question he looked back over his shoulder. When he turned back around, the window was all the way down and his jaw dropped. Had the counter not been there, it would have gone all the way to the floor. Dulcet, beautiful, freshly tanned, buck-naked, held out a handful of cash. The poor cashier felt a trickle of liquid shoot down his leg. He grabbed and spilled the money all over the counter and he was speechless. She showed him everything she had. Pulling her leg up to the front edge of her seat, she dropped her knee towards the passenger seat. As open and exposed as she could possibly be, she calmly asked, "Is my stuff hot darling?" In response, she was almost sure he was going to pass out on the spot.

Finally, breaking his physical paralysis, he handed her the bags still in a daze. She accepted the bags and ran one perfectly manicured fingertip through her excited nether lips into her mouth. The other hand rolled up the tinted window and then she stepped on the gas and was gone. Dulcet saw the boy/man leaning out of the drive-through window, waving frantically trying in vain to get her attention. She laughed and shook her head. Sometimes she amazed herself with some of her antics, but that was what she called fun. Her tendency not to wear clothes was the reason for the limo dark tint on the car in the first place.

She kept some type of wrap–around something or another within reach just in case. She had a mental map of all the public and private places she could go nude, and when they were crowded or secluded. One thing Dulcet did not pay attention to was sports news, therefore, she had no idea that

Dutchess Singletary existed, but she was in the growing minority.

Dulcet motored home. She had condos in different gated communities in cities around the country; eight at last count. All were furnished nicely with giant flat-screen TVs mounted throughout with integrated audio built into the walls and floors.

All of the bills were arranged through corporate executive arrangement firms, so the fact that they were paid quarterly or bi-annually wasn't strange. Automated account debits kept all bills paid quarterly in advance. She drove up to the garage and was automatically recognized from the sensor in the Mercedes. The door opened and the floor came flush with the driveway. This little design modification was a security feature she had noticed in an architectural digest she had run across. When the sensor recognized the car, the door rolled up like an industrial freight door.

Once the car drove in and the door closed, the garage floor sank down four feet. As long as the garage floor was flush with the driveway, access to the house was impossible, as the baseboard for the house entrance was flush with the floor when it was down. As the garage floor locked into position she stepped out of the car, brought out the uneaten portion of her meal and walked into the sunken-den / entertainment room.

Dulcet went straight to her computer to check her recipe program. This specially designed software tracked numerous types of information: surveillance, random sweep numerical and alpha checks, over one hundred different types of input all coded named 'ingredients.' These ingredients were combined to mix up certain dishes. When a dish was ready a timer would ring and the optimum serve time was listed.

For instance, four days ago she was given a message that it would be time to eat this morning at 10:00 am. The recipe program gave her the probabilities. The program had been 99% on the money so she heeded its output. Today's meal, code named "breakfast," listed the probable number of employees as four; there were five. The probable number of customers as eight for that time of day; there were six. According to the schedule, the security guard would be armed and approximately forty eight years old, which fit.

So, using the breakfast breakdown she designed her disguise and wove her tactics around the generated data. She knew the control aspects of exposed sexuality, especially around strangers. This was why she used sexually adverse situations as major parts of her strategies. Amongst the hostage/victims, this ensured compliance and warped eyewitness statements, especially, when the last thing you saw was the winking asshole of the person in front of you in your face.

Currently the only output from the recipe was a cake still baking with an 80% probability of success due to be done four days from now. Everything else was still cooking. That was cool, she could use a couple days R&R; She deserved it after all. Walking upstairs she checked her mail. Receiving bills was comical, she opened a computer generated electric bill that said her current bill was due on the 29th. You owe - $90, 278.56. Please send your payment with mailing time in mind or pay online.

The package compartment of her mailing center had two packages. She scanned her index finger and the access door opened. She retrieved the two cylindrical boxes and closed the door. Plain, no outward markings, quite heavy. These were most likely from Dildo Depot. As a confirmed solo-sexual, she had a disgustingly complete collection of dildos, vibrators, butt plugs, beads, balls; she had sex toys from every corner of the globe. Some of them looked like torture devices but brought so much pleasure. They could make one wonder how they had ever had an orgasm before. And she was serious, not everything was a toy.

She had a machine room, it resembled an auto repair shop more than anything remotely sexual. She routinely spent blissful hours in the 'mach 'room. Dulcet was her own best friend in every way possible. So no matter how much time she spent by herself, she was never alone.

Chapter 10

After school Sylvania wrote up her journal report, along with the standard lesson plans and other requisite paperwork. She had designed a journal to keep track of the pleasures and trials of teaching. One day she may write her memoirs and she wanted to have material to draw from. Today's field trip would surely be one for the book.

This was the happiest and most fulfilled she had ever seen her kids. The entire experience was perfect. The preparation, teaching them how to keep score was priceless! She had to do some research to explain why the scoring was love, 15, 30, 40. There were several theories but the most accepted one held that the French wanted to score by 15s. However, the love came about from a French word that meant egg, like the common 'goose egg' term for zero. Being young, they took to the scoring naturally without question. Then, to be there seeing the scoreboard and knowing what score was coming next was such a joy.

They spoke to each other between sets just like any other

adult tennis fans. The gifts, and the meet and greet was so special. Though she had seen the things listed on the brochure that were included in the group rate special, seeing it on paper and being there to witness the kids reactions were two hundred miles apart. She looked at her autographed hat and tee-shirt. She intended to buy a special frame and display both items as momentos.

Meeting and then having a chance to speak with Dutchess Singletary was a rush for Sylvania. Even though others thought she was fashion model quality, the reality is that she's just a simple woman. She didn't have famous friends and she didn't go to high profile places. She was no fuddy duddy by a long shot. She loved her sex, nice sexy clothes, she enjoyed nice things like any woman. But she lived with a subdued style, dinner and a movie was an ok evening for her.

So an opportunity to meet someone that she had seen on TV or to go backstage at a concert she had just seen was a major treat for her. She had expected to have some minor players come and talk to the kids afterwards, but to have Venus, Serena and Dutchess come talk to the kids ... Uncharacteristically, she was having a hard time finding words to express her feelings. So she cut that entry short.

The next thing she needed to do was to put in a purchase request authorization for tennis racquets, balls and a portable / temporary net as soon as possible. She had no doubt that the kids would still be amped about tennis when they came back to school. With her journal update complete, she grabbed the phone to call Barry. She really wanted to repay him especially for everything. This perfect day would never have been possible without him.

Luckily for her he was a simple man as well, with big appetites but not complex ones. No swinging from the ceiling fan or anything like that. It seemed that everything she liked to do to him was everything he liked to have done to him. She was working on her dirty talk; she knew that turned him on a lot. She had once thought about tying him up, but that would mean that she would probably have to return the favor at some time. She wasn't so sure about that. She did want to broaden her horizons and if Barry was going to continue to be part of her life, she was willing. Her only caution was that she didn't want to slip up and have that part of her world encroach into this part of her world.

Most teachers of the young had to have two sides. The babies had to stay young no matter what because once your innocence was gone there was no turning back. So she cherished the innocence that was so scarce nowadays with the information overload that characterized society today. She was glad her kids didn't know everything, their questions were so refreshing so she ... Barry answered on the third ring sounding busier than ever.

"Hello, make this quick I'm juggling right now", he said.

"Oh, I see. I hope you're not juggling axes or swords, you already told me how I pull your attention", chided Sylvania. His tone changed drastically.

"Oh, hey baby, my bad. I didn't look. I just snatched up the phone, it's kinda crazy over here. How are you baby", retorted Barry?

"Baby, I don't think the thesaurus has enough words to express how I feel, but I know how to show you how I feel; my appreciation for the gift of this day knows no boundaries," explained Sylvania.

"Baby doll, I'm just happy my small token could brighten your day, but sadly, my day has a thick cloud cover."

"What do you mean", she asked?

"Well, through the miracle of technology you called my local number, but unfortunately, I'm about fourteen hundred miles away from that phone, that's why I'm juggling so many things right now. A major client's campaign just fell off the tracks. The guy that was at the head of the marketing push dropped dead last night! I didn't get a chance to call you because as soon as I pulled into the parking lot this morning there was a shuttle waiting to take a group of eight of us to the owner's private plane. Apparently my stock has risen without my knowledge.

I was put in charge of the group, and the group was tasked with taking over the client. This is my first time in the Learjet and if I pull this off at the last minute, I think I'll be fast tracking.

But I'm still staying put, don't let that idea get into your pretty little head. I should be back day after tomorrow, the latest. The launch is tomorrow night and this guy was sharp as hell and very detail-oriented. So all the technical aspects are moving along smoothly. However, the integration of my team into their project management took a little getting used to, but now we are running smoothly."

"But you're ok, right", inquired Sylvania?

"Oh yeah. The thing that keeps me going is the fact that I don't have to sleep without you. I'm not going to sleep until I get back to you", promised Barry.

"Don't count on much sleep when I see you mister. I owe you some gratitude, remember? And I intend to pay my debt," she replied. The sexy smile transmitted itself through the phone and Barry smiled with her. "Ok, then I'll get a nap on the plane."

They chuckled a short laugh full of meaning: disappointment, well wishes, hopes that, not that the assignment would fail, but rather that the success of the assignment didn't change things too much. They disconnected, he having said that he would call to let her know when he landed. Now she looked at the phone, her body had responded to Barry's smooth voice, her nipples had hardened almost painfully, but were still unseen beneath the thick collection of pads inserted beneath her maternity bra flaps.

The effect was just a fuller roundness without the obviously excited nipple giving away her lusty feelings. Now she had energy to burn off and no Barry to burn it off on. She could go dancing. It had been a while since she had gone anywhere by herself, so she set her mind to thinking of a place to go. As she left the building, she stopped by the principal's office to drop off her PRA form for the equipment and left using the rear door to the teacher's parking lot.

The custom painted Toyota Cressida was a thing of beauty to her with its off gold paint job and asymmetrical flashes of black. The same inky black as her hair, it gave the impression of a leopard running down the street with her driving as the queen cat. She drove away from the school zone doing the required 25 mph trying to think of where she wanted to go.

It was early, still time to make happy hour, which was when she remembered that she hadn't eaten today. Her excitement and the associated adrenaline rush had dampened down her appetite, now that she had thought about it she was ravenous. So now she was thinking about food as she leisurely drove into downtown proper, she stopped at a light and saw a sign over a club on the corner.

She had heard about Oke Dokeys but thought it was a kids place because of the name. Several of the substitute teachers had mentioned the place. It was a karaoke club with different themes on different nights, but they had happy hour every night. Sylvania turned right and then left into the parking lot. She put on her cardigan to keep from looking too much like a tennis groupie and walked around to the front entrance.

There was a small line as the doorman checked ID. She walked through the soundproof double doors and was washed by a sound wall punctuated by lights, smells and bodies – she liked it. As she walked in, she smelled first, and then saw the pizza buffet. All through college, pizza was the perfectly balanced meal; it even included veggies and was deliverable! She strolled over to the delicious sensory offering and put a couple pieces of veggie on her plate. Then the spinach Alfredo called her name, followed by the bar-be-cue chicken. She conservatively added one piece of each to her plate and looked around the club. Most of the tables were taken, the only seat she saw available was at the bar on the other side of the room. She was starving and didn't want to appear to be so.

She took a handful of napkins to hold beneath the plate and walked away from the food. As she approached a visual obstruction she turned her back and took two big bites from one of the slices, it was sooooo good. Holding her napkin to her mouth she turned to see if she had been noticed, so far so good. She walked to the next visual obstruction, a nice bushy plant and repeated step 1 twice more. Stepping around the plant she tossed her plastic plate in the trash and strolled to the buffet as if she had just now noticed that it was there. She chose the spinach Alfredo again and a slice of apple dessert pizza. The seat at the bar that she had seen was still available, now that her voracious appetite had been sated, she could do the dainty hor d'oeuvres nibble that was ladylike and sociable.

Excusing herself and leading with her plate, she made her way to the bar to claim the empty seat. Sylvania perched her beautiful ass on the plush swivel stool and swung around to face the bar, she ordered a rum punch thinking that would give her a nice sociable buzz that would be absorbed by the food in time for her to drive home. The band was rocking, playing a mid tempo jazz tune, she thought it might be Herbie Hancock, but it also may have been the Crusaders. She wasn't the best when it came to name that tune, but she knew what she liked.

***

The first round was good, although the initial tiny woman with the lion's roar of a voice was hard to match. Other folks from the first set had different styles, admittedly, nobody could match her for sheer power. But there were a couple of Anita Bakers and a Regina Bell that sounded as good as the originals. Ron was on his second twenty two ounce when something caught his eye... or rather somebody. He was watching the room and listening as the talent got better and better, and not just because of the beer. Ron's body worked well. He gave back as much beer as he bought, savoring the effect along the way. But he could've sworn he had just seen a flash of white atop a set of legs that could support a heavenly body, say Venus.

Ok, now that was the beer talking, truth be told, he did like everything about a woman! He couldn't see how a man could say he was just a breast man or only a pretty toe aficionado. How could you not enjoy the entire woman? Ron considered himself a "Woman Man"; head to toe and all the lovely juicy parts in between.

So, when he saw those legs moving through the crowd, his mind mapped out the proportionate parts to stack on top of them, creating his perfect fantasy woman. Then she disappeared, simply vanished, not lost in the crowd, just gone! Of course he blamed it on the beer, he then turned around to look at the older guy singing 'a house is not a home' by Luther Vandross. The old dude could really go; he had a couple people in the front row flicking lighters and waving them from side to side.

After he got his round of applause, a dark skinned brother with dreds walked up to the stage. There was no intro music without which you couldn't tell what the guy was going to sing, but he had his theatrics down. The lights onstage went dark and silence ruled for that second.

Then the strum of the guitar came; it was unmistakable, the idea that this Bob Marley looking dred was about to do this was amazing. On key and on time as the lights came up on his bowed head he began,

"I never meant to cause you any sorrow, I never meant to

cause you any pain, I only wanted one time see you laughing, only want to see you laughing in the purple rain."

The crowd went wild! As soon as he hit the first chorus, people were standing up rocking from side to side just like in the movie. Ron stood and clapped giving credit where credit was due. This guy had Prince or symbol or whatever he was called this week, down like a science. As he played air guitar to the 'oo oo, oo oo, oo oowooo's' at the end of the song, he got a standing ovation! It was going to be a hard night for the next up.

As Ron was trying to sit back down, he almost knocked over his chair, it was a totally surreal moment. The only comparison he could come up with was, the scene from weird science when the two little white boys created their perfect woman from magazine scraps and she actually appeared exploding from their closet. The woman Ron had created in his fantasy was nowhere near as incredible as the woman sliding onto the barstool two down from him. His timing was impeccable; he caught the minutest sliver of a glimpse of panty as she was spinning to face the bar. That one picosecond glimpse sent a chill down his spine and a rush of blood below his belt.

Beyond the glancing glimpse, the total package was so much more than he could have imagined. He had to catch himself when he noticed his tongue was starting to dry out, that was the only way he knew his mouth was hanging open. He played it off with a long pull from his beer; the cold shock brought him back to reality. He was much too smooth and suave to react like a juvenile virgin, but on some level he felt as if he had never seen a woman before, until that moment.

Fully readjusted except for his trouser snake (that guy

refused to behave). He turned to the bar and glanced at her through the back bar mirror. He had not been mistaken, the luxurious inky black hair, the curves showing through the cardigan, her eyes looked like pools of oil floating in space. Damn, it couldn't be the beer, all traces of a buzz were gone, but he was still waxing poetic inside his head, he knew what to do.

He placed a napkin atop his glass and motioned to the bartender. He whispered that whatever the lady two doors down was drinking, it was on him, with instructions to take her money, then give it right back. He then quickly maneuvered his way down to the songs table where they had a catalog of the bands' repertoire. He had to make this good. Ron had done a bit of singing over the years and had close friends that made a living from it. They told him that he officially didn't need a bag with which to carry a note. They knew how much he loved his job, so they told him not to quit. He chose 'come on and go with me' by Teddy Pendergrass, the one that starts out

"I don't feel like being lonely tonight I think I want, I want some company."

He got the song all set up with the band, he would be fourth after the next singer. He moseyed back to his seat at the bar, he snuck a look at the goddess nibbling on her delicious bar-b-que pizza. He knew because he had eaten damned near half of a fresh one. She was such a lady, just looking at her was hard because somewhere in his mind he knew he would have to look away.

He was on the wrong side to see her left hand so he would have to leave that to fate. Sitting back on his seat, he felt like he was sitting on an ant hill. He was jittery with butterflies in his stomach. To let his body tell it, he was about to open to a sold out show in Madison Square Garden, not sing in a local karaoke bar. He felt as if this one song was going to change his life. To try to control the nervousness, he mentally rehearsed, cleared his throat, and said the first note out loud clear as a bell. He was ready. He stood, willed his Johnson not to betray him and walked over to the vision. He stood next to her until she noticed him,

"Excuse me, could I ask you your name? My name is Ronald, and I seriously would not be able to live with myself if I didn't at least know your name." She hit him with a dazzling smile as she realized that this tall man she was looking up at was looking down at her with the most incredibly complex hazel eyes she had ever seen. She looked into them and was instantly lost. For fifteen seconds that felt like fifteen years, she couldn't move, talk or breathe, the breathing thing brought her back to reality.

She forcibly inhaled, the oxygen feeding her brain and unlocking her reflexes.

"Excuse me?"

"I said my name is Ron, and I would like to know your name."

"Oh, my name is, uh, Sylvania", she replied.

"Uh Sylvania huh, is that your name or your club name", inquired Ron?

"What does that mean", She asked very confused?

"I was just kidding actually, some people have another name that they use when they are out that's not the one their parents gave them. Which is usually because they don't want to be bothered", explained Ron.

"Oh, well no, that's not my club name, that's the name I've had all my life", she assured him. Now that the initial shock had worn off, she began adding to the conversation.

"Are those your eyes or contacts?" Ron winced at the turnabout, "Touché, and I apologize, I didn't mean anything by that."

Once again, she had that same confused look on her face.

"Excuse me, once again", she said. That look made him look deeper into this woman Sylvania. What he thought was a jab at him for doubting her was actually just a simple question. "They're mine, I've never seen color contacts that could actually reproduce natural color. They all stay the same, mine change from time to time so, I've been told", assured Ron.

"Well, I'm sure those people told you, and you're probably tired of hearing it but, I think they are beautiful", she replied appreciatively. "I don't know how any man could tire of hearing that from you", he retorted.

In the silence, they continued to look at each other and he broke it by forcing himself to look away first. Then he asked what she was drinking. She replied, "Rum Punch." He asked if that was what she really wanted. She hesitated and said,

"Yeah, I'm feeling kind of tropical right now."

Ron offered to buy her another but she indicated that she wasn't finished with the first one yet, so he offered to buy her next round. Sylvania looked at him whimsically surprised, "Is that you?" He nodded,

"So all that, and you can sing too?"

"All what?" he asked smiling. As he walked away, he winked and told her that he was going to dedicate this song to her. As he approached the stage, he felt as if he were about to do the State of The Union or sing the national anthem at the Super Bowl.

As soon as he touched the mike, the band started to play. As an unexpected bonus, the percussionist was a woman and she knew all the sexy adlibs on the song which made his rendition go over like gangbusters. All the while he kept his eyes on Sylvania. The close seat, the white skirt that incredible bouncing foot attached to that wonderful leg, made it easy to keep focus on the love song. When he sang "You look like you're just my type", he could see her put her hands in front of her face to hide the blush. Her reaction was so innocent it almost threw him off. She was so beautiful. After he finished to a very decent round of applause, he returned to his seat.

The bartender had refilled his beer and Sylvania had switched seats while he wasn't looking, and was now sitting right next to him.

"That was very impressive Ron, you're a good singer. Do you come here a lot?" she asked.

"No, every now and then, although I do a lot of different happy hours. After most of my days I need a little wind down. But don't get me wrong, I'm no alkie. I mainly go for the food." She looked slyly sideways at him while playing with her straw, an action so sexy, yet subtle. She probably had no idea what a reaction it would elicit. Instantly Ron was embarrassingly hard. Just like that, he could feel his boxer briefs tightening up all along his upper thigh.

"A little challenged in the kitchen", she asked?

Pretending much more confidence than he felt, he grinned a mischievous little boy grin from his childhood and said, "There are two rooms in my house that I have absolutely no problems in, and the kitchen is one of them". As expected her eyes grew wide and she stifled a laugh at the racy audacity of this man. Assuming that the other room was the bedroom by the way he put his smoldering eyes on her.

After the appropriate "comprehension time" he said,

"The other room was the bathroom. What were you thinking?"

By now, Sylvania had decided that she liked this guy. She didn't know what that meant. Was it the excitement of the day, followed by the abbreviated then abandoned anticipation of seeing Barry, just to discover that he would be gone for a while? Was this a mini-rebound situation? She thought not. However, had this evening happened like this with Barry sitting right next to her, she had a feeling she would still feel this way.

For the first time in a long time, she wanted this man in a purely lustful "What-does-your-I'm-coming-face-look-like" sort of way that she hadn't felt since college. Not that she was a slut or anything, she was mainly a one man woman. However, her one man was MIA, and a girl does have her needs.

"Ron, are you this flirty with all the hungry girls you meet at happy hour?" Sylvania asked. "Tell me the truth", she added. "No, actually I'm not. I usually mind my business and avoid eye contact as much as possible to keep people from asking about my eyes and trying to flirt with me", he said as a matter of fact.

He tried but could not suppress a huge grin that totally melted Sylvania, sending all her liquid contents to her panties. She was so glad that she remembered to put the pads into her bra, otherwise he would have been blinded by her 'lights' and he would have been able to truly read her like a newspaper front page! "Well, ok Ron I was just wondering. I don't want to get caught up in the net with the eyeball groupies, I was just asking", said Sylvania sarcastically.

Now she was feeling the tension, the sexual heat was building and she had to think of something quick or she was going to do something she might not regret.

"Well, when in Rome Ron, how do you get the band to play what you want to sing", she quickly added, changing the subject. He gave her the surprised look and then asked,

"What, you can blow?"

It took her just a second to reorganize her now awakened dirty little mind and realize that he meant sing. "I don't think I do too badly in the shower, the cats out back in the alley don't seem to mind", she replied coyly. Ron broke out laughing, her unintentional humor was right on time, and the tension was broken.

Once again, the nosey, ever vigilant bartender reared his head and silently slid up behind them and handed Sylvania the song book. He tapped it twice and as silently as he appeared, he was gone.

"Well damn, ask and you will receive huh? I've got to hang

out with you more often", she said. Sylvania rolled her eyes and picked up the book. Looking through the slow jam play lists, she noticed that this band could play just about anything. She flipped through page after page of songs that she loved from back in the day. Then, there it was, her absolutely favorite song. There was a murky haze surrounding its significance to her. Just seeing those five words sent tingles all the way down to her toes.

"That one Ron, I want to do that song, but you're going to have to help me", said Sylvania. "Damn, you don't pick the easy ones do you", stated Ron. "If it's not a little hard it's not worth it right?" She replied in a challenging manner.

Her hands flew to her mouth as if she could push the Freudian slip back in, but as an old New Englander once said, "Done bun can't be undone".

"Difficult, I mean difficult", she said through her fingers.

Ron was a little slow to catch it, but catch it he did and once again, burst out laughing,

"Ok, ok, I'll go talk to the band",

He said as he succumbed.

He quickly turned and walked away trying not to let her see the undeniable hard-on he was trying to meditate away. Talking to guys usually made it go down – he felt no sexy feelings for the same sex. It worked like a bucket of ice cold water, but he had to be careful he was working with hair trigger activation. Some days he wished he could just tie it into a knot and make it behave. But, of course, that would only make it worse. As he approached the songs table, he heard

"The lights are already off Teddy, whatchu want now?"

With a chuckle he said,

"I wanna flip the script, I need a duet and could you squeeze me in soon?"

Inquired Ron. He took the slip of paper and read it,

"If this world were mine by Luther Vandross and Cheryl Lynn. You pulling out the big guns, aintcha Ron?"

Yelled Songman.

"Naw, this one's ladies choice", replied Ron.

Songman's eyebrows shot up. "The newbie up to the bar? Sheeeit? I been dying to see that since I noticed her up there. You know she ain't never been here before? I know every skirt that shakes its way into this spot. You lucky you caught her quick because I'd'a been on her like white on rice." Songman assured!

"I hear ya talking old man", said Ron as he slipped him a $5, bill just because. "Damn, you feeling something, huh? Alright young dog, you'll be up in two", said Song man. "Cool. You know if I play my cards right you may not see me for a while", said Ron.

Ron strolled back to his seat, eyes locked on Sylvania the whole way. She in turn, was watching the way he moved. The common perception was that you could tell how a person was in bed by the way they danced. That was true, but also misunderstood. It's not just the dance, the dance needs music. Actually, it's the movement. The way a person moves tells you everything you need to know, if you know how to see it.

The walk, confident, long striding, just enough hip movement to know there's weight that's shifting. The torso, fluid, ready to move any which way on a dime. mmmmm. The way he maneuvers through the crowd, like a Lamborghini going through an obstacle course. The automobile touched nothing but making its way through efficiently, as if the motion expended no energy at all. It knowing the power to sprint to 100 mph lay just below the surface, twelve cylinders, and ready to ride. She knew that the reciprocal was true as well.

She had been told that when a woman walks, her hips speak every language. The attitude with which her shoes beat their tattoo, the rhythm, the beat that the sheer mass of the perfectly balanced ass, swaying, creating its own syncopation. The heavy breasts playing their own counterpoint and the up thrust chin, confident in the tune her orchestra was playing.

She snapped out of her research fantasy and Ron was standing directly in front of her sipping his beer. Subconsciously, but unavoidable as the tide, she looked from his size 15 shoes up those long legs. A subtle twitch hit her as she passed the distinctive print, up past the matching belt, button by button until she was sitting on the bar stool, head inclined all the way back looking into those magical eyes again.

"Hey", she said.

"Hey yourself. Everything is good, we are up after these folks singing right now. You ready?" Ron asked. She imagined it must be the alcohol. Yeah that's it. That's the only thing she could think of to give her this euphoric feeling!

"Yeah, I'm good, I mean I'm ready! She said assuredly.

"Damn Syl get it together, you keep sliding these unintentional comments out of your mouth. What's this guy going to think about you?" she thought to herself.

As she slid off her seat, both their eyes looked down; hers to judge the distance to the floor, his to the extra bit of thigh the leatherette chair helped to expose. Standing in her two inch heels they were aware of where they stood, so to speak. Her head came even with his solar plexus, she could look just above her eyeline and see his Adams apple. She couldn't ever remember having this particular vantage point with anyone before. She was at least eye-to-eye with most people she interacted with during the day. And, of course, although growing daily, she still had the advantage over the majority of the students at the school.

She determined through her slightly alcohol-filtered gaze that Ron was the tallest person she had ever met. She giggled a quick musical sound. She had just remembered a comedienne from the old Def Jam Comedy show. She had made a joke about climbing Michael Jordan and sitting on top of his head beating her chest. It was official, that fleeting image of Ron wearing her as a hat told her, her drinks were cut off.

"Do I have time to go to the ladies room?" she wondered aloud.

"Maybe just, there's one down the aisle by the stage that'll probably be the best one to use", directed Ron.

"Ok, be right back", she said as she grabbed her small purse and sashayed.

Ron was certain he had never used that description before, but it was the only one that fit. The old cartoon jungle beat, boom boonka-boom boonka-boom, infiltrated his body as he watched her deliberately stride away. The skirt material was trying in vain to keep up with the sway of her hips. It mimicked the counterpoint swing so familiar on the catwalks of Europe and New York. He realized at that moment that he had to be very careful; that water was deep, and if he wasn't careful he was going to fall in.

Chapter 11

Wilbert looked at his vibrating phone, usually he would not answer during rehearsal but this was the call he had been waiting for. He said, "Ok, ok hold what you got right there, everybody gather round." They had been back from their break for about forty minutes when he got his call. "Ok, update: rehearsal is going to end early today, something has come up", he continued. "So we're over, right in the middle of Act II?" inquired someone as an ensemble of about four or five people from the taped up stage. "That's right, rehearsal is over but you are not released. Take five, gather up all of your things and let's meet in the parking lot in your cars in ten minutes", instructed Wilbert.

The announcement generated quizzical looks and the associated murmuring buzz throughout the cast. "That's all", he continued. And Wilbert turned and strode off walking towards the rear of the practice facility where two Production Assistants were going over some paperwork. Thony and Suzan had shared a ride in, so they met at his car both sipping raspberry iced teas from the vending machine. By the time they'd arrived the rest of the cast was waiting. They all turned to them as if they knew something that nobody else did, they shrugged their shoulders indicating that they were in the dark as well.

From behind the church they all saw the PA's in the production van pulling out turning right and riding out. Just then Wilbert came out of the church basement door with a pronounced sour look on his face. He passed by everybody without a word and got into his car. Wilbert's window slid down and his arm made the follow-me gesture as he pulled off. As he hit the street he turned on his hazard lights. The lights ensured that all the people following each other knew who they were following. This wasn't so necessary in the city, but it became a stroke of genius once they got onto the freeway. They rode for about twenty minutes and got off at the exit. After three turns they pulled into the lot of a large venue and rode around to the back stage access area. Curiosity was building all along the route.

Wilbert parked in the Director Only spot next to the door and hopped out. Gone was the sourpuss face, replaced by the neutral look. He waited for the cast to assemble around him. Then without a word, he turned on his heels and walked away assuming they would follow, and they did. They entered through a side access entrance to the proscenium space. If they could have seen Wilbert's face in the dark, they would have recognized the ear-to-ear grin he kept for really, really good news. As the cast filed into the dark space they couldn't see anything before them as their pupils had not yet adjusted to the lack of light. "The last person in, close the door please", he said in that same affected monotone. As the door closed he yelled, "Lights!"

The stage lit up brilliantly – the set was finished and it was BEAUTIFUL! All the days of imagining reality through the taped out walls and doors were over. Now the next phase could begin. First things first, they took the tour from the lobby to the main audience space, from the balcony to the orchestra pit. That done, they went downstairs to see their newly assigned dressing rooms, the wardrobe room, and make-up and hair departments. Now, for the first time the cast could feel destiny calling.

The tour was not designed by accident, Wilbert wanted them to feel the force of the audience before they even had their asses in their seats, to know where exactly the back of the house was, to know who they were performing for. Most of all, the tour was designed to show them exactly what sold out, standing room only actually meant, since their first three weekends were already sold. This put even more weight to that statistic that the basement rehearsal hall could not even hint at.

The balance of the rehearsal time was taken by the technicians explaining emergency procedures, fire extinguisher locations, etc. The sound guy was demonstrating the Lavaliere styled wireless microphones and the sound equipment built into the set walls, floors and the overhanging booms. Wardrobe would be there the next day.

Their measurements had been taken by the designer weeks ago, and now all the costumes were completed and hanging in the appropriate rooms. Everyone would get a final fitting to ensure a perfect fit. Rehearsal time was over, but the cast wanted to do a quick run through of Act I. Wilbert convinced the necessary crew to stay a little while longer, and they readily agreed because they were just as anxious to get started and back on schedule as the rest of the cast.

Act I felt good everybody agreed, although it was similar to the giraffe walking on one day old legs; by the intermission they were in full swing in three dimensions. As the cast was officially filing out of the backstage door, they received maps to the venue from all points of the compass. Whichever direction they were coming from the venue was dead center.

***

Thony and Suzan were en route to her house in the Center City Lofts when they ran into horrible traffic. They hadn't been listening to the radio, they were actually running their lines, practicing on the way home. Seeing all those seats made the fact that this was a job and not just an adventure hit home for the entire cast. Every spare minute was spent in character.

But this was something else, all four lanes of the interstate were backed up, it was a parking lot and he needed gas. He turned on the local radio station. The news reported that there was a big rally going on smack dab in the middle of the city. Mitchell Johansen, a Swedish Pacifist Party activist was convening a rally for both sides of the Middle Eastern situation. Those who were for leaving the entire Arab world alone to their own devices, and those who felt that their record of human rights abuses called for permanent occupation. They wanted to ensure everybody's rights were adhered to, and that those that abused others paid the price in U.S dollars.

Thespians were apolitical; it was all about the art, whatever the part called for, that was who you became. The actors union gave certain latitude to changes or refusal of parts you auditioned for, but too many changes and people, casting people and directors started to know your name for all the wrong reasons.

So, he sparked up his GPS navigation box to find an alternate route around the snarl. A map popped up leading them by back streets to her condo complex. The neighborhood used to be commercial. Instead of tearing down the warehouses and office buildings, the city hired contractors to do the asbestos abatement and gutting. Then, the buildings were bidded out for architectural suggestions for mixed residential / commercial use. Loft construction went wild. Full floor-sized lofts were made out of the office buildings and multi-level custom homes were designed for the warehouses.

The entire body of the district changed while the face stayed mostly the same. Factory smoke was replaced by rooftop bar-be-ques. Loading docks and inventory spaces were transformed into quaint patio bars and five-star restaurants. Storefronts, restaurants, bars, coffee shops, and bookstores started to bloom. From above, it was a whole 'nother rodeo. Rooftop tennis courts, putting greens, and gardens flourished in the sunshine. Foot by foot they got off the freeway and used the surface streets to creep through the city. At least off the freeway the lights guaranteed they would move at some point. The closer they got to the loft, the more foot traffic they encountered. It turned out that the center point of the rally was a block and a half away from their destination in a pocket park that had been created on the previous land of an old dilapidated parking garage.

They pulled to a stop in front of her building, they had seen a couple walking their way fumbling for keys. Observation being the greater part of luck, the couple walked to the car they were directly behind, double parked. Once they pulled off, Thony scooted directly into the vacated spot. Suzan suggested he come up for a drink so that they could continue doing lines until traffic lightened up. He couldn't argue with logic like that, so they went up to her place. Hers was one of the converted old warehouses, so there were two floors. The furnishings were eclectic enough so that each different area could have been another country. She even had a small corner alcove with a distinctive colored remnant of carpet, a very plush shag with a pin spot dedicated as if it were illuminating a work of art. This was her spoken word corner.

The fan out from the corner could have fit a nice intimate audience. But because of the way the furniture was arranged, you didn't notice that unless you were standing on the carpet looking into the room. This was his first time actually being in her home, although he had dropped her off plenty of times. So he was given the ten cent tour, as she called it.

The place was pure Suzan. The smiling/frowning masks of the theatrical muse was integrated in several places. The layout was so unexpected he would not have been surprised to see an upside down staircase coming down from the ceiling. Each space had its own alcove corner, all were different and could be found in opposing corners of each successive room.

The playroom where the tour ended had a review corner. A slightly tinted plastic corner wall unit contained reviews of shows and pictures, signed Playbills of shows she had been a part of, and shows she had loved. The memento corner she called it, also had small hook holes for the insertion of armed shelves. Two arms were fitted into the wall. They both held awards for Best Actress and Best Supporting Actress, respectively, for work she had done at community theaters on her way to her current status.

During the tour, they had picked up snifters of Cognac and retired to the sofa in the playroom, with a large ¾ pie shaped cacao and crème round leather pit. They lounged and said their lines. They did dual speed practice. One time through, they would say the lines incredibly fast, sounding like chipmunks. The next scene, they would go slowly, like an old forty-five rpm single playing at thirty three rpm.

This technique ensured that you knew your lines and your timing. It's easy to know timing in real time, but if you know it going faster or slower, then you know you knew your stuff. The liquor was starting to hit them. After their second cocktail apiece and the Hawaiian joint Suzan produced from a secret box built into the sofa, Thony said, "Sofa designed by the CIA huh?" "You should see the manual, it's ten times thicker than the script! It takes a lot of technology to make a thing look low tech" she chided. They toasted, "to low tech" and sipped their drinks.

Suzan said, "I'm not feeling rehearsal clothes, now that I'm home do you mind if I change?"

"How could I mind, anything you want in your fine abode is simply my pleasure to behold", he replied. "You are so the actor. I'll be right back and you know where the refills are", she instructed. She log rolled twice on the couch until her feet hit the floor and she was off.

One disadvantage of loft construction was that whenever water was in use you could hear it everywhere because the pipes were basically all exposed. So, Thony heard the shower running, then shut off. About ten minutes later, Suzan came flowing into the room. That's the only way to describe what he saw. There was a billowing of midnight purple shimmering silk. Had it been plastic with a hood it would have been one of those rain ponchos. It had a sexy V cut neck line surrounded by tribal embroidery. It billowed and flowed in the wind of her motion as if it weighed less than air. She floated down to the pit, refreshed her drink, and announced that she was ready to rehearse.

Thony had caught sight of a leg, a wonderfully muscled calf leading to a streamlined knee and there, overflowing into the soft sexy thigh just before she plopped down onto the leather. He had unbuttoned three buttons of his Oxford shirt, kicked off his loafers, and melted into a nice mellow buzz from the Maui Wowie mixed with the Cognac effect. He was floating on auto-pilot as they started to run their lines leading up to their torrid love scene in the play. Because the set had not been ready, the four poster bed they were supposed to do the scene on was not available at the church rehearsal hall. It had been constructed on casters so that it could be rolled on and off stage. Plus, they didn't want to practice simulated sex in a church. So this was the scene they had spoken of but not blocked.

Theatrically, blocking is the act of walking through a scene using the dialog and the timing, the actor must have an entry place, action points throughout the scene and an exit place. Considering these elements, there must be motion to move along dialog. Even when there is no dialog there is blocking. The love scene had been blocked to keep the lovers faces to the audience at all times, while using the dialog, speaking into the microphones and most of all doing the same thing over and over the same way every performance. And of course, it had to be believable.

So, they were speaking their way through the dialog thinking about blocking when Suzan slid up next to him as though they were in the bed and she said,

"Pause, do you know what they decided our wardrobe was going to be for this scene?"

"I think my 'drobe is just a pair of boxers, probably with a speedo underneath, they mentioned a teddy or boy short ensemble for you I believe", replied Thony.

"Well since we're short on time, I think we should ask Will for some extra rehearsal time with the props to make sure the PA's have their timing down", she added.

"Yeah, that makes sense", he agreed.

"Ok, unpause", she directed.

The scene progressed. The emotions ranged from low sexy pillow talk to shouting, which had to be timed perfectly so that the sound man could adjust the volume to compensate for the change. They went over and over the cue words that would take them from one level to the next alternately whispering, then shouting, then whispering, then shouting. After the shouting match the whispering would return and they would have their make-up sex. While they were going over the volume cues, Suzan repositioned herself kneeling on her side rubbing his chest. She threw her hands up and practiced other natural reactions to the verbal cues until she found something that felt natural and believable. She asked him, "Are you wearing boxers?"

"Yeah, why", he asked? "Take off your pants, we need to be as close to wardrobe as possible. Until we know what I'm wearing for sure we'll just improvise, but we already know yours", she directed.

The weed and liquor, their practiced and natural familiarity with each other made the request a no-brainer. He just complied because he knew they would have to do it eventually. "Ok, give me some room", he replied. She slid up on her side and he slid off his slacks and dropped them to the floor.

Chapter 12

Robert was stiff and sore from all the games yesterday, he couldn't help it, he was competitive, and the team that he played with was remarkable. Blacktop champs, with him as the big man they ran the court. They played fifteen games straight and didn't lose one. Robert took some time to rest. They sent one of the loser teams to the store to buy them all cold drinks. In between games, Robert took his time looking around at his possible perches. He had established that nobody on the court spoke Portuguese. So he communicated badly that he was from Brazil, which also explained his unique hazel eyes. He was a foreigner, but fuck it, the dude could hoop, no language barrier there.

When he went off into his solitary tourist mode they left him alone. One thing Robert found interesting was the number of people he saw on rooftops as he scanned with his ocular. He had identified four possibles from the ground and now had to do some aerial recon. Leaving the court, he stopped by the public library, procured a temporary library card number in order to use the internet connected computer. He logged onto Google Earth and put in the coordinates for the pocket park. The wide view that had the park dead center was the default. He zoomed in four times until he had a clear view of the tops of the surrounding buildings. Two were automatically crossed out, they had public access recreation areas. One was too short with too many other buildings looking down on it, but the last one was perfect.

Double checking the elevation of the structure versus his ground level recon, he determined that he would need proper park side access to ensure 100% terminability. The problem was never the shot, the challenge was always the exit strategy. The perch he chose was tall, a requisite piece of business considering the number of buildings with rooftop activity nowadays. But that was going to add to the time to the street which in turn adds to the time out of the area.

He dressed casually in his specially fitted sweat suit with compartments to break down and hold the BMG and the five shot clip of .50 caliber ammo, he could still jog without bringing suspicion that he was a shooter.

The prick of a target decided that he wanted his rally to go through the night so he decided to move up the time of his appearance to 7:00pm. The time change had come to him via urgent priority text message while he was leaving the library. The result was that he now had to push back his plans. He had intended to spend the night in his perch, but night and day was out of the question. The Arab presence was overwhelming the area, the streets were mobbed for several blocks in each direction.

Robert reversed his suit to the yellow side and dressed, filling the compartments with the broken down parts of the sniper rifle. Feeling the expertly distributed weight as he stood, it didn't seem as if he had five high density milled, perfectly balanced components surrounding his body. In fact, the heaviest and bulkiest thing was the five shot magazine sitting in his jacket pocket. He approached his destination, and turned his brisk walk into a steady three minute jog. He dipped into the loading dock, silently checking out the scene. Nobody, no noise, apparently, everyone was outside on a simultaneous smoke break, gawking at the ocean of Arabs from every stripe on both sides of the issues. One thing he could say about this Swede, he knew how to draw a crowd. Creeping to the human sized freight elevator, he elbowed the button for the top and bottom floors, then took the ride up. He exited in an attic type space and saw just what he had thought he would see. By judging the shape and age of the building, the top most floors looked to be mostly deserted from his scope view yesterday.

His scope had been accurate, this floor was the second smallest compared with the two above him, those led to the roof itself. His view of the gazebo was of the rear left corner with a perfect view of the microphone stand and the two square feet surrounding it. He had plenty of room to get head and shoulders in his cross hairs. Using his spotter scope he judged the distance to target to be 765 meters. Robert realized that this would be like shooting a cow standing next to a barn.

The crowds were getting thicker, people breaking into factions, reading each other's signs to see which group to stand with for the media. Truly, that was all this really was, a media circus. Johansen's circus atmosphere followed him all around the world.

The media knew it, and he loved it, but apparently somebody

had no love for the loquaciously solicitous Swede. Otherwise, he wouldn't be perched right now as he was. So now the order was to wait. Wait for the target, wait for the optimum time, and then perform for the client. After the performance, exit the stage and the area as quickly and efficiently as possible, invisibly, preferably. Once en route to the major conveyance provider, check in, then disappear until the next call.

**

Suzan started the scene again, laying beside Thony. They shared pillow-talk until he told the lie. That was the cue, she spun up onto her knees, hands flailing the air screaming at him. He defended himself right back. Then, the realization came that it wasn't a lie, but a misunderstanding. At this point, she bent over, kissing him and apologizes. She asks for his forgiveness, he accepts. He doesn't like the way that feels.

They cut and start over from the top, this time around he makes it much harder for her to apologize. The change was noticeable, but her response was a little off. They both drained their snifters, and with a good idea of what the other was going to do, they started again from the top. As they got to the familiar place, Thony really became the man. His response to the lying accusation was so intense it shot a twinge through Suzan that she knew would reverberate through every woman in the audience. She felt herself get a little wet, her pheromones were percolating. Now she stepped up her game as well and she begged for his forgiveness. Once he acquiesced, she took the scene farther by throwing her left leg over his waist and looked down on him as she kissed him. Voicing love for his character's name and promising not to disbelieve him again.

***

Abdullah was in the crowd, right in the clear separated space between factions, while the Americanized media whores mingled around the gazebo jockeying for position so that their homemade placards could be seen on the televised newscast. Oh how surprised they will be when their love for the media spotlight sends them straight to hell live on their precious news. The infidel and all of his puppet media prostitutes will be handled at one time, praise be to Allah, Allah Akbar.

Abdullah walked all the way to the gazebo, he was within three feet of the first step, six feet from the center of the stage where the large chunk of C-4 high explosive currently resided. The remote controller was in his pocket, his hand caressing it with love, waiting, and waiting. Where was this devil of an infidel?

The time was just past 7pm. Just like the white infidel devils, late for his own appointment to hell. Just as Abdullah cursed Mitchell Johansen, the crowd began a low murmur. Large black SUV's began to appear. If one didn't know better, one would think the President of The United States of America was about to speak in the little gazebo. As the small group of blacked out vehicles started to arrive, Abdullah knew that he should leave, to get himself to safe ground. According to his sources he should be at least two blocks away, just about at the basketball court. He would need some time to get there. High explosives, unlike his precious Allah, are unloving and most unforgivable, but he needed to see him. He had an overriding need to look into the face of the devil before he sent him back to his everlasting home.

The vehicles crept along their approach, the security cordon around the gazebo grew tighter as the barricades grew farther away. From three feet to five feet, the security finally stopping the crowd twelve feet from the structure. No worries, the steel barricades would only create more killing force to send into the crowd. Suddenly, out from the crowd there he was. The infidel, Satan, himself getting out of a white limo as if he were a hero from some child's story riding in on a white horse. Ha! "Your horse and rocket will be of flame momentarily, yes, just as soon as I get clear", he thought to himself.

***

From Thony's mellowed and blissed out point of view, this blocking practice was going quite well. He was feeling his character. The outrage he felt at being wrongfully accused of being a liar, standing up for his points and having Suzan beg for his forgiveness, it all felt right. Suzan was a wonderful actress, they complimented each other seamlessly. The kiss was good, open face, lots of lips giving the audience a good visual; he could almost feel the stage crew manipulating the guy wires that would rotate the bed to keep the audience involved.

Suzan reared up onto her knees facing him, spinning them so that he was downstage and she was upstage facing the audience again. Now, she grabs his head and they do the passionate kiss; "Hmmmm wait, this is new", he thought. "The script stage directions call for her to hold my face from the side and kiss me. She just threw her leg across me and she's staring down into my eyes, hey this is good, nice improv. Now the kiss, yeah, her lips are so soft, they're juicy too, umm, the tongue is the perfect touch, adds to the realism. Her body feels so sexy atop mine he thinks, this fabric is so soft, so diaphanous" he continued. "Well now, we can't just lay here, this is where we need to work on some choreography", he thought. "Yeah move babe, I'll follow your lead", he said aloud. Thony was thinking, "Damn this feels good, imagine doing this in front of a sold out house, all eyes on us; a special spot light dedicated to the bed, Suzan on top of me, the crinkly soft hairs of her pussy tickling my shaft, her wet lips sliding up over my head, mmm she sure can kiss".

The passion light began to penetrate the liquor fog just as Thony slid wetly inside Suzan. Her heavy sigh into his mouth punctuated the penetration with actuality. Suzan pushed her steaming sex down onto Thony's rampant hard-on until she reached the root, once at her destination she grinded her clit onto his stalk releasing her first pent-up orgasm. Breaking the kiss to whimper her pleasure, she started to slowly ride, doing figure eight patterns, tracing the infinity sign with her educated hips.

As she rode, the large fabric tent rose and fell with her motion. He reached underneath to move it out of the way. Mission accomplished, he gripped both of her breasts and delighted in their mass as his thumbs played wicked circles on her stiff nipples. This onslaught to her sensitive breasts sent her into another convulsion of orgasms, her internal muscles rippling up and down his pistoning dick. The feeling was too good, he reached down and gripped both her perfect ass cheeks, cocked up his knees to get more leverage and proceeded to pound into her in earnest. Her body responded to his hands direction like a yo-yo master with his weighted toy, her hips seeking out maximum clitoral pleasure from Thony's steady long strokes.

He gathered her ass to him with one strong hand while the other traveled to her neck to add pressure to their deep soul-stirring French kiss and he came torrents inside of Suzan. Throb after throb he came and she milked him with her strong internal muscles turning her aftershocks into full blown quakes all over again. They lay within the purple cocoon upon the cacao and crème leather alternately throbbing and twitching…

***

Robert saw the approaching vehicles, he switched from his spotter scope to the ocular on his rifle. Painting the bull's-eye through the reticle of the scope onto the mike stand, he saw a man's face standing right at the bottom of the steps leading up to the front of the gazebo. He dialed in on the man's face, at first just checking optimal targeting range but then he saw something familiar, in his business there were no coincidences, ever. If he thought he knew that face, then it existed somewhere in his memory, but from where, from when?

The man looked around, he was kind of out of place, and even though he looked to be Arab he still looked out of place as if he didn't belong. He backed up so that security could expand the barricades. He walked straight back; backwards on the line of demarcation between both sides of the issues, not choosing one side or another in this totally polarized crowd. He did not take his eyes off the gazebo in front of him.

It bothered him that the man looked familiar, but his target was exiting the white limo now. He paused to look for the guy in the hockey jersey once more but he was gone.

The target was approaching ground zero now so all thoughts of the guy, Mr. Mysterious yabba dabba doo Arab were fading. One strange thing he had noticed was that the guy had a tent in his pants like he had a hard-on and his hand was rhythmically moving in his pocket like he was jacking off. Oh well, fuck 'em, if it came back, it came back, it all does eventually.

The target was climbing the stairs to the gazebo, now he was tapping the mike, checking for signal to the many well placed speakers. Robert put one shell in the chamber, locked and loaded. He was ready. He began to gently hum the tune –

"Got you in the box and now I'm, gooonna to kill you" to the melody of going to the chapel. He pre-tensioned the trigger to 2.5 pounds of pressure; trigger pull was 3.5.

***

Abdullah was now almost to the basketball court, he had passed mobs of people moving in the opposite direction, some giving him strange looks wondering why a good Muslim would be backing away from the rally. Now as he leaned against the fence, he looked back at the gazebo. The man whose eyes he had just looked into was climbing the stairs and advancing to the microphone, checking it. Abdullah wanted to make sure he had the right person, not just the introducer, then the infidel began to speak. He noticed a peculiar look cross his face and he stopped talking, whatever had distracted him, was not his concern, he depressed the detonator button he had been waiting three weeks to push and the whole world lit up.

***

As soon as the target began to speak, Robert applied the extra pressure to the trigger sending his projectile silently through space to the destined 3-dimensional point towards which it was directed. In less than one second it found its mark, the impact pushing the skull forward to bursting. However, before the cranium could explode showering the familiar red and grey matter across the podium, his eyepiece lit up with impossible luminosity. He knew that nothing he hit could have possibly done that, so what the hell just happened?

Per his training, he automatically closed his eyes and rolled to the left, which saved him from being pelted by several large chunks of shrapnel that seemed to be parts of the gazebo.

***

Thoroughly sated from the day's events and the culminating copulation; Thony and Suzan slept in the same position they had wound up in, she atop him, he still inside of her. When the blast rocked the gazebo they were awakened by the nocturnal animal instinct of mating Foxes. As the sonic wave of energy expanded throughout the neighborhood they rolled away from the window down into the thickly carpeted wedge of emptiness in the sofa. This third eye reaction saved them from the two panes of glass that were explosively blown into the room. That was the extent of the physical damage done to her place, but two blocks back down the street, the damage to the park and the career of Mitchell Johansen was complete.

Chapter 13

Dutchess awoke to the high pitched whine of the Bombardier Airliner whisking her across the country at six hundred miles an hour en route to her next tournament. The road was a lonely master, but she couldn't really complain. After all it was much better to be traveling, playing, and being paid for it than to be playing her heart out every weekend, only to have to clock in to a job Monday morning. This was definitely what she would rather be doing. Though she was only well known regionally, she was now beginning to be recognized in broader circles.

The USA Today had a big picture of her in the sports section a few weeks ago, that was big time, a national paper! She was on her way. Now she was being invited to tournaments instead of having to pay her own way. Hell, Venus and Serena knew her name, and that meant something. And, she was winning! She was undefeated in her last twelve outings. Admittedly, some were other unknowns, but she had just faced some stiff competition: seeded players, nobody in the top seventy five, but they were ranked in the world and Dutchess Singletary had mopped the court with them.

The tournament she was on her way to now was in Florida, and she would be playing on grass. She had her most wins on clay, but her grass game was steadily improving. The worst part about all this travel was the fact that she had to do it alone, that was what she missed the most about her days starting out, her friends. They could always be there because everything was local. But now with her flying all over the world playing and training, she'd lost touch with the people she most loved being around.

Even with the growing fan base, nobody cheered for her like her old friends. Dutchess was in the mid-state of celebrity sports, too known to be an unknown, but at the same time not known enough to rate an entourage. She fell under the category 'relatively unknown professional player'. She thought back to the other day at the Tennis Open. She had felt like an A-list player that day, the screams of the crowds and the autograph seekers. But the most memorable thing about the Open was the class of school kids and their teacher, Ms. Collins.

Dutchess was open with her sexuality. She was bi-sexual and anybody that needed to know, knew; but none of that was public knowledge, yet. She knew that added fame was reciprocally tied into decreased public privacy.

Sooner or later somebody would find out and then she would have to defend herself. She would, but she wasn't looking forward to it. Facing any kind of storm alone was never easy and she didn't have anybody right now, man or woman. But she kept drifting back to Ms. Collins. She never even found out her first name. She was behaving as if she were still in the fourth grade and had a crush, not asking, simply adjusting to 'Ms. Collins'. She found that she even liked saying it. But she was not the ordinary elementary school teacher, this woman had made quite the adult impression on Dutchess.

Her daydreaming took her back to Ms. Zydwiki, her fourth grade teacher. She was truly nothing to look at, not like Ms. Collins. She was from Eastern Europe, her accent made her beautiful to Dutchess. Dutchess's adopted parents were all American, apple pie and baseball. But they felt as if the adoption agency had misled them. They thought that they had brought into their home a Caucasian baby girl with green eyes and red hair, they had no idea that black baby girls came with those options.

Little black girls were supposed to have black hair, brown eyes and brown skin. She looked like she lived with a year round tan. But anyone who saw her naked would have no doubt as to her ethnicity. Her beige nipples and nether lips told any seasoned observer that she was not Caucasian, they would be pink, like uncooked meat. Her facial lips and cheek bones, not to mention the definition of her hips, ass and legs all pointed out the heritage she alluded to. No flat butt here. She wished every day that she knew who her birth parents were. One would suppose the mix to be a red-haired, white woman and a black man; she was the recipient of the recessive genes. The Lucille Ball red hair and jade green eyes, it was all a mystery to her.

That was one of the hidden motivators behind her determination to rise to fame. She wanted to locate her birth parents and call attention to the plight of foster and adopted kids.

She intended to be so famous that her parents would stand up and claim her. Even though it had been twenty one years, she still looked like she did as a baby, except for the obviously grown up parts. Did she have sisters, brothers, and pets? What would she do if she had a family that looked like her? But once again, her thoughts turned back to Ms. Collins.

They weren't that far apart in age, she couldn't be more than twenty five; Dutchess couldn't stop thinking of her as an authority figure. The attention the kids gave her made Dutchess want to be a young girl again, just so that she could look up to her.

This was nuts, she is a grown woman, professional athlete, solo, on her way to joining the best tennis players in the world on their level, and she was determined to succeed. And here she was with a puppy love crush on a fourth grade teacher. It could have been the fitted shirt with the tennis racquet on the breast or the way she looked at her like a bonafide star tennis player. She had really meant it when she said that she wished she had a fourth grade teacher just like her. What Ms. Collins didn't know was that she was talking about right now. The flight attendant stopped to ask Dutchess if everything was ok, she replied, "Yes, I'm just thinking about some things."

When she lifted her head to look the attendant in the eye, she got a reaction she didn't expect. "Hey! You're Dutchess Singletary! Could I get your autograph?" inquired the Attendant. She said this last in a whisper, realizing that she had lost her Professional Demeanor for a second there. "I'm so sorry, I don't usually do that, really, it's just that all this time I've been walking past you and you're just chillin with your hat pulled down, but once I saw your eyes, I knew. Nobody told me you would be on this flight. I hope I'm not bothering you", she continued. "No girl, you're fine, I'm just not used to being recognized", replied Dutchess. "Well, you better get used to it, you are on a roll", said the Attendant.

The flight attendant then proceeded to run down her stats, her last matches, everything. This woman knew her career as if she were her manager. She asked if there was anything in first class that she wanted, since it was too late in the flight to move her, they would be landing in fifteen minutes. Had she known she was aboard she would have upgraded her on the spot. Dutchess said that she was ok and didn't want to put her through any trouble. Come to find out, the flight attendant whose name was Sandy, was her first big fan that she hadn't grown up with. She gave her the 'wait a minute' finger and disappeared through the separator curtain. Just a few minutes later she returned with a covered tray laden with exotic fresh fruits so fresh she could smell them before the tray lid was removed.

Sandy told her they would be landing soon and she knew that she had to prepare for the tournament starting tomorrow so she didn't want to get her anything too heavy. She thought fruit would be good, just a token of appreciation from an adoring fan. Dutchess pulled out a piece of personal stationary and signed an autograph for Sandy and one for each of her two kids thanking her for all that she had done and them for watching. Sandy was in tears by the time the 'fasten seatbelt' sign came on. Dutchess buckled up and prepared to land. Her only thoughts: winning, one game at a time, one game at a time, win by two, win by two, game-set-match, game-set-match.

She repeated this mantra everyday of her tennis life the same way hockey players wore the same socks or baseball players used the same bat. It brought her luck and as long as she kept winning. She'd keep doing it. It had become like a Zen meditative chant. She would overview her play before she even entered the stadium. She watched film of her opponents' best, worst and all the matches in between before she left home. Then she'd use her notes on their high and low lights to study. Once she saw the name she had to play, their list of stats would pop into her mind.

For instance, a certain Czech 18 year old that she would have to play. She had good speed in one direction, ok backhand, weak bi-directional lateral motion, sluggish 3-d power coming in, and inadequate serve to the exact same area 90% of the time. Strategy: Ace whenever possible using the service stats, volley lead right, volley lead right, volley left, volley right, volley left, soft touch reverse spin right. If the second set of reverse volleys didn't knock her off her feet, the reverse directional close court shot should trip her up.

Her mind was full of these strategic tidbits. She was anxious to get to the stadium, suffer through the obligatory meet and greet and the welcome reception. Her biggest concern was who was before her, what was the makeup of the field she was up against. She knew as an unranked player that she wouldn't start out in center court playing top ranked opponents. But she did know she would be playing women and girls that were ranked in the world, as well as possibly some really good unranked players like herself. The plane was on approach, she was looking through the player packet provided by the tournament officials. Inside was everything she needed to know about the upcoming week of her life, from media day to the closing ceremonies.

She learned that every tournament was like a mini-Olympics with players from all over the globe, maybe not every country. But the list was impressive, protocol was the order of the day. She was to be assigned a protocol chaperone to assist her with the new world she was entering into. TV, ESPN, the Tennis channel, the interviews, the pitfalls of the limelight were many. She had thought that she would be sitting chilling in the hotel room.

The first person she'd have to find once she landed was her coach. They had reservations at the same hotel, and he was coaching a total of three people that were in the tournament this week. One of his players was ranked; the other girl like herself was not. This transition wasn't easy, she thought, "One minute big fish, small pond, the next day small fish in the ocean". This even applied to the amount of time she had with her coach, the ranked girl got more. That was the reason she did so much self-study and technique practice. If her coach was going to spend so much time with others, she needed to let him know what she could do without him; outshine his protégées as her stock rose, he would be forced to see where the addition of his years of experience could take her to the next level and beyond.

She would give him the chance to act accordingly or else thank him for everything he had done and get herself a coach that would spend all of his time dedicated to only her. Too bad Ms. Collins wasn't a coach. Ok, ok Dutchess, enough of the crush, focus now and maybe she'd look up Ms. Collins when she got back home, as long as that wasn't too soon. "Thanks for flying, have a nice day. Thanks for flying, have a good day, Thanks."

The typical de-planing freight train had begun. The Bombardier was not a large plane, which was both a blessing as well as a curse. The height of the curved bulkhead was not very loving to Dutchess' six foot frame, but there were not that many people to have to wait for. The aisle was narrow, but at least the line of people was moving along at a nice pace. She was still fingering her way the through her packet waiting for the rest of the people to disembark. As the line started to trickle, she stood and reached into her overhead bin for her rolling case.

She had a specially designed case in which she kept her computer, racquets, purse and a couple pieces of clothing, all the things she didn't trust to anyone else. This bag was always in her possession. She anticipated big things from this week. If she could prove that she was worthy to compete on this level it could really pay off.

After taking group pictures with Sandy and her other crew members and receiving a guarantee that Sandy would upgrade her to first class in the computer, personally, she walked to the gate. Dutchess was met by a uniformed driver loosely holding a sign that said 'Dutchess' with a small tiara atop her 'D'. Apparently the marketing blitz her manager had spoken about was underway. Her manager, Henry had come from the ranks of the music industry. When he was courting her he introduced himself as a 'cross-marketologist'. The majority of his clients were in the music/entertainment industry. But their money, the majority of it, came from other ventures, creating a brand and running with it. So they continued to see each other, each time he had something new to show her for approval or not.

Of the last ten things he had presented to her, the tiara over her 'D' was the best. It was classy, not too much, it played well as a one-word name logo plus it made for a distinctive autograph for merchandise. It was a start. He had said that he got the idea from a downtown building in one of the Carolinas. He redesigned the tiara, made it more regal and placed it over the first letter of her name, simple, yet elegant. So, seeing her logo for the first time in print on the sign was heartening. The driver was on the phone making sure that she was indeed on the flight; since most of the tournament players flew first class, they were amongst the first off their planes, not last. He worried that she may have missed the flight. He needn't have worried. She would have chased this plane down the tarmac and hung on if she would have had to.

He reassured his employer that their charge was indeed on the ground safely and they proceeded to baggage claim. Dutchess expected the normal executive car or a baby Lincoln limo or even a minivan wouldn't have been out of the ordinary, but when they stepped to a super stretch platinum Chrysler 300 limo with the Bentley grille she really felt as if she had arrived.

The ride to the hotel was too short; she almost wanted to tell Javier to take a couple spins around the city just to luxuriate in the extreme creature comforts of the 300. He explained that she was expected but added in that he would be her driver for her stay and would keep himself available. Spirits recharged, she stepped out as the doorman did his job, there was actually a red carpet covering the carport. She had only seen those on TV and felt they were cheesy.

But as she stepped onto that carpet, doorman trailing with her bags just out of sight of the photographers, then to see the welcome banners in all different languages, she was doing her best not to appear overwhelmed like an Iowa corn farmer's daughter on her first trip to the city, but it wasn't easy. She checked into her room and there was an envelope on her lamp table from her protocol chaperone informing her of the proper attire for the initial reception, interviews etc. She read the small packet and put it to the side. She called the front desk and asked to be connected to her coach's room. He picked up on the second ring; she said simply,

"Dutchess room 1535."

His reply was as expected, "Dutchess! Welcome to Florida, how was your trip?"

"The plane was ok, the car was better. Can you make some practice time for me?" The directness and no nonsense tone made him verbally stumble, "… uh, when were you thinking about?" "As soon as I find out whom I'll be playing first. If you are too busy just tell me and I'll have Henry arrange a coach, a local tennis pro or something. I'm really serious about this Lou. I intend to kick some ass this week, and I would love to have you in my corner. But if you are too busy, I still intend to kick some ass."

"Ok Dutchess. After we do the meet and greet reception, come talk to me, we'll put some time together." "Ok Lou. Thanks." "No problem. It's my job, right?" "That's right, and don't you forget it."

She chuckled to take out some of the venom, but she meant every word. She thought of the station in life to which she had arrived. She needed to make sure that she was treated better by all those around her, old and new. Lou replied, "I know you won't let me forget, I'll see you in a few Dutchess." He disconnected, she dialed the front desk. "Hi, this is 1535; could you tell me about what time the welcome reception will be over?" She heard computer keys tapping, "It's scheduled to be completed by 8:00pm." "Ok, great, I noticed in your amenities catalog that you have a rooftop tennis court?" "Yes" replied the receptionist.

"Is it reservable?" Inquired Dutchess. "Of course it is Miss Singletary, what time you would like?" she asked. "You do have lights, yes?" asked Dutchess

"But of course, we have several different lighting scenarios for you to choose from, switching between them is very simple, instructions are on the power panel", added the receptionist. "Thank you, I'd like to reserve the court from 8:30 to 10:30, is that doable?" asked Dutchess. "Very much so, we have another reservation for 11:00 so that fits perfectly", assured the receptionist. "Thank you dear, I'll be on time", she said. "Is there anything else you desire ma'am?" asked the receptionist. "No, I think that'll be it", said Dutchess.

Dutchess took off her travel clothes and jumped into the shower, steamed away the travel miles and readied her body to do battle of another kind. The reception was all that Dutchess had heard it would be. It included the giant ice sculpture in the shape of the tournament logo, the formally dressed press photographers, all of the gladiators she would do battle with and those she would love to just watch. Everybody was dressed to the nines, their powerful bodies moving, wild, animal like beneath the thin trappings of civilization.

Henry was there, he was like a butterfly, fluttering and landing all over the reception, the difference, this butterfly had a sidecar. She met reps from Reebok, Adidas, Nike, Met Rx, and Perrier – all the major brands she had ever heard of. Racquet manufacturers were all interested in her brand image. Henry had arranged for more meetings predicated on the results of her performance; the more she won the more meetings.

She asked Henry if he could find it in his heart to make this a bit more stressful. He actually laughed at that and gripped both her hands, looked into her eyes intensely until she looked back and said with all sincerity, "Welcome to the big time precious."

"You know Henry, I've been dreaming of hearing that, and now that the words are out of your mouth, I don't know what to do."

"Yes you do – play tennis."

"That simple huh?"

"Yeah, just like that."

He hugged her and told her to eat light. She mentioned her possible problem with Lou, he said he'd look into a personal trainer without so many other priorities. She thanked him and double checked to make sure she had her set of all the business cards of the people they had spoken to so far. As she looked up from her tiny jeweled clutch she saw Lou, he was by the bar with his young ranked player, Victoria something. His hand was really low on her back. They were drinking and carrying on in a particularly non-professional way. As a matter of fact, with a closer look she could see his hand moving, but that's not her back, that hand was definitely moving in slow circles over the cheeks of her ass!

Now it all made sense, why he didn't have time for her, why she had to fly all over the place alone and the reason he was almost never at her side court during a match. And to top it off; he was married with six kids! Dutchess couldn't stay any longer. She stopped at the beverage cart on the opposite side of the ballroom and ordered a Sprite. No sooner than the glass was in her hand a young Puerto Rican man was at her elbow. "You must be Dutchess. Your beauty far exceeds your description."

"Well thank you sir, but I'm at a disadvantage, you know me, but I haven't a clue."

He whipped out a card, "My name is Carlos De La Havana, and I work for Coke Brands. Like you, this is my first assignment in the big time. I have been following your career ever since I first saw that incredible red ponytail and those green eyes. Of course since I've been working for Coke, red and green came to have a special significance to me. Red is Coke; green is Sprite, that's my life now.

So, when I saw you, then noticed you drinking Sprite. I don't want to say that I saw dollar signs for you and me, although that was part of it, but more than that, I saw the possibility of my first 'x' in the win column." She took his card without looking at it and said, "Carlos, we may be able to talk, give me another card for my manager. I'll call you or I'll have him call and set up a meeting, ok? If you'll excuse me, I have to go put my tennis brain on."

She walked to the lobby to catch an elevator up to her room to change. On the way, she noticed a hotel employee with a cart filled with golden easels and placards with schedule and tournament information to be placed around the hotel and convention center.

When she asked if those were the schedules for the tournament starting tomorrow, he said, "Yeah, tickets are available at the..." Then, he looked up and saw Dutchess. He straightened upright. Apparently, there was one placard with pictures of some of the tournament participants. Looking past him she saw herself in action. Now, she knew why so many people had her image on their minds. That Henry, she was keeping him no matter what.

"Would you like one of these for yourself?"

"If that's ok, sure thank you."

"It's my pleasure Miss Singletary. Just go out there and slam some ass, pardon my French. But I like your vibe on the court and now I see it's not an act. Quiet as it's kept, we're all rooting for you. I'll be watching. Good luck." He gave her a tissue-wrapped placard. She got on the elevator and pressed fifteen. Once in her room, she tore the tissue off the full colored board and saw the brackets. The first round had her matched against Kikakio Konikami of Japan. Dutchess felt her scalp tingle; she had notes on the Japanese girl. Digging through her computer bag, she pulled out her extensive note file. She searched through it by country and pulled Japan and picked out Kikakio.

The card said her forearm was wicked, her short court game was kind of weak, and her backhand was unpredictable. She was known for high numbers of unforced errors. She had made a special note with an asterisk that said: temper. Thinking back to the tapes she had watched, the young Japanese girl got totally off her game once she got frustrated. The best way Dutchess knew to accomplish that was to chase her from side to side stroking the ball with a side spin while aiming at her body. Inhibiting her power would frustrate her in her own backcourt, then dropping the ball just over the net, infuriating her, causing her game to collapse.

Her confidence at an all-time high, she was determined not to be denied wins: one game at a time; one game at a time; win by two; win by two; game, set, match; game, set, match; She chanted as she got dressed. Her practice outfit, as well as her competition outfits, were name-brand less until she got a sponsor. Pro rules forbade her from wearing any logos. She grabbed her two racquets and some balls and set out for the court.

Chapter 14

Kristi was about to shut down her corner of the shop and hand over operations to her number two, Chad Morrow. He would oversee Ops and Intel until 7am, when she came back on board. Before she could get out the door, she heard a tone from her personal high security link, four double beeps.

"Oh, shit, that's major."

She took off her coat and sat back down at her computer. She logged on and went to the secure area of her system where she saw a large red blinking dot sitting directly over top of the city of St. Louis, Missouri. She clicked the red dot and a password input box came up. She entered the same password forward then backwards. The red dot disappeared, and was replaced by a real time overview of the central city. The screen showed what at first glance appeared to be a large crater. After zooming in, it looked even more like a crater with charred remains of wood and other debris.

The next zoom level confirmed her worst fear. Those charred pieces were not wood. They were the smoking remains of body parts. "Oh my God! What the hell is this?"

She double clicked the image and a strip appeared with picture frames chronologically arranged. The frame at 19:03:02 CST was a blindingly bright frame. She scrolled back to the 10:00:00 frame and her stomach turned over. This frame showed thousands of people approaching a central location. It looked like a round structure, maybe a gazebo in a tiny postage stamp-sized park. Two distinct groups of people were gathered, almost like revolutionary war soldiers.

Regretfully, and with a heavy heart, she zoomed in to the crowd to see if she could tell the makeup of the multitude. They were brown skinned. The facial features were similar, they looked like Arabs, definitely Middle Eastern. "Oh my God, look at all the children. They're right down by the gazebo surrounding the barricade gates." She saw a placard on the ground face up. It said, "Out of the Middle East forever, everybody". Digitally shifting to the other side of the skirmish line, she saw just as many kids with an equal mix of all ages. These signs, from what she could see said 'man rights 4 all, stay the cour'.

Suddenly, these two sides of the same issue seemed all too familiar. Panning over to the gazebo, she first saw what looked like a Presidential security detail. Still panning past the big black Suburban, she zoomed to the gazebo. The network news and the twenty 24 hour cable channels were all there. The lights made sure the object of the attention was visible from all angles: Mitchell Johansen, official spokesman for everybody and everything.

This month's two-tiered rant was to bring together all sides of the Middle Eastern debate. As usual, under the cloud and distraction of a major gathering to discuss issues, he had done this before, semi-successfully, but never with zealots vs. fanatics. Staying zoomed on Johansen, she tried to see what gesture he could have made. What the fuck had happened in three minutes that could …

She stopped cold at frame #19:02:59 CST.

Johansen's head from this angle seemed to change shape to an elongated, oblong stretching in the area of the upper left cranium. She used the arrow keys to go backwards and forwards between 19:02:59.5 and 19:03:00.0. The latter frame was blinding white. Even the onscreen image was bright enough that she had to shield her eyes. Staying on that frame she zoomed out – out-out-out-out. The view she now had was the nucleus of the gazebo as yellow/white as a small sun with heat flash pouring out from the gazebo in all directions. Zooming farther out showed the entire postage stamp park. Within four clicks, the park had disappeared. A large smoldering ring of destruction was all that was left. The crowds of people were gone. The periphery was scattered with the dead and wounded. It was by far the worst bombing she had ever seen and this was St. Louis, Missouri, USA! Without looking, she speed-dialed transportation.

"Transpo, Rich speaking."

"This is the SAC, I need Air. Helo to me ASAP; Lear to St. Louis, Mo. Helo waiting. Are you monitoring countrywide?"

"Checking countrywide, Missouri detail. Yes ma'am, there's a rash of activity: EMS/Fire Police, all first responders. The office in St. Louis is on Red alert, and something big is going on in Missouri."

"You bet your ass. I need to get there. What's the ETA for that chopper?"

"Checking ETA. I've got two. I can have a Huey to the Lear to you in five minutes to transport, or, in fifteen, a Blackhawk can take you through to destination."

"Get the Blackhawk ASAP."

"Yes ma'am. It's done, 15 minutes or less, rooftop heliport."

"Thanks Rich."

"Catch some bad guys. That'll be thanks enough for me."

"Rich, wait."

"Yes?"

"Keep the other scenario open as well, all three pieces. I'm going to round up an ops team for that five minute Huey to the Lear. Make sure they have chopper support at landing. They will be tactical, and count on six."

"Roger that SAC, anything else?"

"Wish me luck."

"As always."

She disconnected and rang the TAC room. These were the Hostage Rescue Team trainers, and the best of the best the FBI had to offer. They were all cross-trained in other disciplines: computers, forensics, crime scene analysis, etc. Weapons expertise was a given. They were scrambled for five minute readiness at the alternate ground level helipad. The mini brief given to their CIC would be bolstered in the air once they were on the Learjet. A preliminary game plan and the photos from the micro burst transmission she had received would also be made available. This was the worst. Kristi updated Chad on her new mission and informed him that breaks, leaves, and vacations were cancelled. He was to be on watch until she returned.

She invested all of her confidence in him and he knew she would be monitoring everything from her arsenal of electronics. Due to force of habit, he felt no animosity. Kristi contacted her personal team and advised them to be ready in ten minutes on the roof. They had to roll.

She went to her office closet and stripped off her business suit jacket and blouse. Took off her sexy front clasp Victoria's bra and replaced it with her Kevlar enhanced underwire tactical bra. She slipped on her Projectile Penetration Resistant vest, and strapped it tight. She wiggled out of her fitted skirt. She pulled on a pair of black SWAT tactical pants with steel flexi panels beside the zipper, thighs, and integrated into the flexible kneepads. She zipped up her Gore-Tex SWAT boots and pulled on her flak jacket. She was ready.

Her grip stayed packed. Leaving the closet, she popped two 400 Gigabyte USB keychain drives into the slots of her computer and hit 'synch'. All files on the daily office computer that were not already on the hardened Pelican Pack laptop were copied and ready to upload. Seven minutes later, she was on the elevator en route to the rooftop helipad. Her two men were already there, identically dressed with their grips as well. They looked like a well-armed Special Forces triad more than the administrators of this entire division. That was the nature of this job.

Nobody was immune to working in the field. All ops were field ops and you don't get the required respect to run field ops until you were proficient in the field, especially for a woman. But Kristi Johnson was not only proficient, she was one of the best the FBI had ever had. Her special responsibilities did not come lightly. Everything had been earned over and over. Her autonomy was such that she had her own mini FBI and authority to run multiple jurisdictional ops without needing any other approval. Oversight came after the fact. As she was leaving her office, she caught sight of the Huey H-60 taking off for the airport with the other team. They should get there within thirty minutes of their direct flight arrival.

She briefed her guys with the short version as she knew it. Phillip was scanning CNN and Headline News Network on his cell phone, trying to keep up with the constant spin factor that occurred when the truth had to be filtered through 24 hour news networks. Life dealing with facts must truly suck when you need new stories twenty four hours a day. It takes recycling news to a highly scientific new low. The actual truth takes a side-of-the-road seat to new news, even when there is no news. So when there is news, like your camera crew and equipment being blasted into vapor live on the air, there is nothing you can do but play footage from before the event. Until that is done, you send the payment that will connect your signal to the fastest local affiliate that can replace their dead team, to cover your dead team.

It looked like Headline News Networks check was good. They had a local affiliate, KABC, online with their weather/traffic helicopter in the air showing the crater. As they were huddled around the phone, they heard the seriously silent but unmistakable sound of the Blue Thunder Stealth Blackhawk just before it rose up the side of the building with its tilt rotor wash assisting in its perfect landing in the center of the 'x' on the helipad. They crouch-ran to the open doors and climbed in, connected their gear to the wall hooks and were airborne. They sped west at max speed within forty five seconds.

***

They hovered over the news copters, surveying the carnage. The crew in the Blackhawk waited for the return of the priority one message Kristi had sent to the Director of Homeland Security en route to St. Louis, recommending raising the Terror Alert Level to RED. This was unprecedented for a field level SAC to invoke this type of security blanket. The Red would be in effect temporarily until this situation was classified and the resulting threat assessed regarding the rest of the country. As she looked at the before and after photos of this area, she considered the horrific nature of the situation. The very fact that the entire area below them had been filled with people and in literally a fraction of a second this result had occurred. This was a devastating war zone nightmare; a scene straight out of Sarajevo or Iraq. But, this was Missouri!

The news choppers began to disperse and head back to their respective perches. Kristi had invoked the Level Red for just this reason. To rule the skies and the media without RED, say a code Orange, freedom of the press to interfere into a national security situation was still valid. Under Red, not so. Looking up, she saw the K-130 circling. The Blackhawk coordinated with the tanker and elevated high above the city to match speed with the giant flying gas can.

Its receptacle was awaiting the funnel shaped connection to come reeling out. There it was, complete with its guiding lights and rubber hose unspooling from the back once the propeller blades were clear of the assembly, the funnel attached to the receptacle. The red lights turned green and the fuel began to pump. The process took nine minutes at high speed pressure.

Once full, the green lights simultaneously clicked off and turned back to red and the funnel reeled back into the KC-130s aft end. The pilots exchanged good natured insults as they broke off. The Blackhawk de-elevated straight down, then adjusted the attitude to get a better look at the situation through cleared skies. The pilot scanned the area for an optimal spot to land away from the bodies. They chose the closest side street to the blast zone. The landing position was encrypted and bounced via satellite to the incoming chopper with a GPS lock for accuracy.

Once on the ground, the pilot discharged his passengers. He checked the video link from the nose of the chopper to the portable clamshell units each one of the trio held. Satisfied with the signal, he jumped off into the sky, just like its namesake, to hover and circle until it was needed on the ground. The entire area smelled of death. What couldn't be seen from the satellite above was the blood; the darkened, burned, sticky blood covered everything, as if a sticky red rain had come down only on this block. Kristi reached into her grip and pulled out a respirator mask dabbed with her favorite perfume. This was first level protection. Next came the gas, then the biohazard masks. She looked around and saw Phillip and James donning theirs as well. The first job was to speak to survivors to see what they remembered and ascertain where the rest of the people went.

The fire department was steadily pulsing water up into the air so that it could rain down to douse the small surrounding fires. The rim of the crater was littered with bodies on fire, smoldering and wet. They were obviously victims of the blast, blackened, charred and blown to bits. This was the reason the firemen rained the water down. The high pressure stream would break the remains of the bodies in pieces, as well as washing the wet, burnt, flesh and bones down into the crater. The size of which, from her vantage point, seemed easily thirty feet by about seven or eight feet deep. Neither Kristi nor her two backups had served in the military. So this level of carnage was incomparable to anything they had ever seen.

James tossed his cookies into a partially standing trash bin as they were approaching the death zone. In this area, the fires were out, everything was soggy and steaming.

They tried to keep their minds from shutting down by thinking analytically, trying to find some type of clue as to who would take risks this big. They looked for a calling card or something left behind to point to a reason. The enormity was such that between the three of them they could not fit a reason into their collective minds. Looking at the hundreds of mangled bodies and parts, charred and smoking, was too much. They retreated back towards the side street they had landed on.

They heard the Huey approaching. Phillip and James became impromptu landing beacons as the chopper swooped in and landed in the middle of the street. The six-man team filed out ready for whatever they had to do, but Kristi doubted that they were ready for what they had here. There were no bad guys, nobody to shoot, nobody alive. This day had already torn chunks from Kristi's heart. She knew in part that her job was chronicling man's inhumanity to man. But this sheer scale of carnage, the men, women, and children all these civilians, was an act of war.

Judging from the before picture, at the lowest of the low range, there were a thousand people in the park for the rally. The upper estimate, she didn't even want to think about. She detailed the new fresh team up the street in the opposite direction of the park to try to find survivors, witnesses, any living person that had seen anything prior to the time of the blast.

Any clue would be usable, a shout, cry or anything that may lead to an identity of the people responsible. The crew canvassed the block, noting the blown out windows along the way, storefronts and apartments alike. The shockwave must have reverberated back and forth like an echo through a box canyon destroying fragile glass all along its path. Kristi called the personal cellular phone of the DI, Director of Intelligence, FBI, he answered on the first ring. The amount of time before she spoke told the Director the depth of the situation. Kristi Johnson was, bar none, one of his most level headed SACs.

That was the reason she had been given the responsibilities that she had. When she called Homeland Security and demanded code RED, epicenter St. Louis, there was no doubt that it had to be a catastrophic situation. Looking at twenty seven seconds without a word, the Director started to think something had finally put Kristi beyond her limits.

The Director began to speak when she started. "The situation on the ground is much worse than the satellite could convey sir. I printed out stills from t-minus three seconds. The, the, uh hmmm, the estimated number of people from a preliminary estimation before getting an expert count looks to be upwards of 700 people. Local fire crews are onsite putting out the last of the fires. I've got a team with me as well as my personal detail. Once the fires are out, I intend to take over the forensics and control the media. Any suggestions sir?"

"Not really Kristi. You seem to have made some headway. National Guard troops are being deployed countrywide to all of the targets on the Homeland Security 50 state threat grid. Between you and me, I authorized 24 hours at code RED with a subsequent drop to Orange, unless we get more action. Kristi, are you ok? Will you be able to handle this operation, it seems pretty rough." "No and yes, sir. I'm not ok right now truthfully, because I've only heard about scenes like this from war zones, and the reports pale in comparison to the reality. But, I will handle this situation. I refuse to cave and destroy your faith in me sir: Whatever, whenever, wherever, sir."

That was one of his sayings. She remembered everything when it came to this job, he was proud of her, but he was worried. "I'm going to send the component investigative parts of the St. Louis office to perform the large scale forensics. I want you and your team overseeing operations locally. We clear?" "We are clear sir. Is there an ETA on the support troops and could you include a satellite imagery specialist?"

"Regarding ETA, they have been on alert ever since you have been on the ground. The alert status has wreaked havoc with traffic. The air traffic control system is trying to land every plane over the U.S. and re-route anything on its way here. So look to the ground.

You should have backup within thirty minutes, full accompaniment. Lastly, yes you will have experts in every category you will need, photo recon included. We are also trying to chase down all available morgue units to start DNA matching ASAP. This is gonna be a long process, but we have authority to max resources, that comes from the top."

"Roger that sir, I'll pull my team in and advise. Will you be tracking?"

"I'll touch if I need to. I have to go up to the round place and check in."

"Copy. Thanks sir."

"No need, you earn yours. Out.

***

They disconnected. Kristi felt much better considering the Directors confidence in her meant everything to her. She knew that she had the latitude to make the decisions that had to be made. Grounding every machine in the air, over the entire country, turning back any plane or ship in the world that was on its way to the U.S. was a major decision. Major-major. Before 9/11/2001, it would have been a Presidential decision. That alone spoke multitudes of volumes about what the Director thought about her.

***

Several years before, the law enforcement apparatus in the

U.S. looked into the future of engagements and realized that traditional methods of handling urban issues were beginning to fail to keep up with the new society: firepower, disrespect for the law, etc. An analyst at the FBI Quantico, Virginia Training Facility, which consulted with Special Forces teams came up with a worst case scenario, Urban Conflict Scenario Simulation. This involved training for elite troops within local law enforcement that, in the event of localized uprisings, could quell the situation through magic: appear and disappear. The simulation, using Top Secret technologies used the hiding in plain sight principle to develop a totally innovative method of domestic urban warfare.

Radio spikes were punched through the asphalt in a constructed test city. These spikes picked up signals from the then Top Secret classified Global Positioning Satellite system, establishing a link to the Palm Pilot personal digital assistants with maps of the city used for underground navigation using the existing and out-of-service sewers, maintenance tunnels and other unseen accesses.

The assault squads could pop into an area loaded for bear, with secure communications, monitoring the outgoing situation. At the optimum time, they would rise up through the manholes and crush any uprising. Then they would disappear as if they had never been. The scenario totally disabled the effectiveness of lookouts or police scanners and created heretofore unknown capabilities for undercover operatives to keep their cover intact while doing their jobs.

So, when the Director advised her to "look to the ground", that meant for her not to be surprised when, out of thin air, a platoon of backup arrived sometime within the next 27 minutes. Kristi fingered the talk button and whispered into her throat mike,

"To me, ASAP."

Her wireless headset chirped,

"Copy, 1 through 6."

Her team was coming in.

Chapter 15

Ron had just finished his beer and was waiting for Sylvania to come from the bathroom. Thoughts of her walking away had him slightly in a daze. He looked up and he was in the dark, half way to the stage, the MC called out.

"Ron it's that time again. Where are you and your partner?"

Totally forgetting that protocol called for the band to start playing as soon as the microphone was touched, Ron reached out and grabbed mic one from the MC. At once the thrumming bass boomed from the subwoofers...Duhoom, Dum Duhoom. Duhoom, Dum Duhoom. Automatically, Ron kicked the baritone into gear.

"If this world were mine..."

His delivery was so smooth, he had women in the front row swooning. He had gotten so into the soulful groove of Luther Vandross, he had closed his eyes and was fast approaching the Cheryl Lynne part. He opened his eyes in time to see

Songman giving mic two to Sylvania. She strode up to the stage exactly on time with the band. She sang,

"If this world were mine, I would make you a king, with wealth untold, you could have anything…"

She walked that walk up to him standing center stage, the act seemed rehearsed. The moves were so flawless. The harmony was so tight. She wound up in front of him facing the audience. The swell of her ass just grazing his hair trigger and it was on, the beast was let loose. He started to grow hard. The lights on them both making the growing bulge impossible to miss. She felt it before she had totally finished her pass in front of him. Now they were dueling, doing the back and forth overlapping.

"When I'm in your arms…"

"When you squeeze me yeah, the way that you doooo…"

"The way that you, love me boooyyy. Oooo, the way that you woolohhhoohhahoow."

Several times during the song Sylvania couldn't help looking down at Ron's distress and smiling. It was really unfair because her nipples were so painfully hard, they felt a foot long.

When she did her cross in front of him, it was almost as if he kicked her a little bit right in the crack of her ass. Then she looked back and smiled while still hitting her notes. Ron was truly the man to be able to keep his composure and sing the song perfectly with such an obvious lack of blood to his brain. She was proud of her own multitasking ability because that thing felt huge. Thinking about that and the song made it hard for her to move, but she knew she couldn't just stand there. Finally, they came to

"If you bee lieeeve".

They stood looking into each other's eyes facing each other, Ron's arm enfolding her into him. His throbbing erection pulsing against her with the final heavy sigh at the end of the song. He pulled her tighter and kissed her. The crowd went wild. It was the highest number recorded on the decibel meter used for judging the contests. It maxed out and looked as if it were stuck there.

The audience was on their feet. The band was clapping. Even SongMan was clapping and wiping his eyes. Ron and Sylvania, the immediate spell half broken, made a small bow and waived as they held hands and half ran off the stage. The MC came on stage and asked for another round of applause for Luther and Cheryl, they got it.

Working their way through the crowd, they found two small splits of champagne where their drinks had been. Even though Sylvania had told herself no more drinks, this was celebratory champagne, complements of the management. On her first time at the club, she couldn't refuse. Besides, there was no way she wasn't going to have this man named Ronald tonight. A little bit more liquid courage may be just what she needed to ensure that outcome. They toasted one another's skills, then just one another. Before they could finish all of the champagne, they were on their way out of Okey Dokey's. He was walking her to her car.

"Oh Ron, I'm so glad I met you."

"I'm not really sure I did."

She looked behind her, back at him.

"What do you mean by that?"

"It feels too much like a dream. I'm not even sure that I'm not dreaming right now. I know I can't ever come back here without you, if this is not a dream."

They both laughed a nervous laugh at that.

"Well, what would it take to prove to you that I'm real?"

"Wooh, that's not easy. I have some pretty vivid dreams. Sometimes it's hard to distinguish dreaming from reality."

Sylvania, acting very serendipitously, reached out and pinched his nipple. Tweaking it caused his hand to go up to protect his sensitive flesh, his eyes bucked open, mouth forming an 'O'. Then, knowing the alcohol was coursing through his veins, he got a mischievous grin on his face and pinched her nipple back. His grip on her nipple was so good it had to have been hard already.

Her response was similar but she reached crisscross and held both her breasts unconsciously caressing them with her hands. That impromptu pinch had caused moisture to flood her sex. Her lips had swollen so much from her prolonged excitement, the added tightness of her panties was all that kept it from running down her thighs.

"Where's your car Ron?"

"It's at work, about five blocks that way."

"Come on, get in."

She popped the doors with her key fob, and jumped into her car. Ron was pushing the passenger seat back farther than she knew it would go. They made it around to Ron's job in about three minutes.

"O.k. Ron, I know I may be doing things all wrong, but it's out of my hands now, are you married?"

"No."

"Do you have a woman living at your house with you?"

"No."

"Are you gay?"

"No."

"What was the status of your last AIDS test?"

"Negative and yours?"

"The same, do you live far?"

"No, as a matter of fact I live here in the city, right on the outskirts of the CBD."

"Good. Get your car, I'll follow you."

Ron got out of Sylvania's car and hauled much ass to retrieve his. He squealed his tires six times speeding through the parking structure. He didn't want to wake up if this was a dream. If he wound up screwing a pillow, then this dream would be an Academy Award winner, but not to worry she was still there. He beeped his horn and pulled out, she followed. She couldn't imagine what fate made this possible, what kind of planetary alignment was responsible. She thanked those lucky stars for every second of the last few hours.

They pulled into the parking structure for the high rise. He spoke to the on duty supervisor, instructing him to give the car behind him a visitor's tag and to keep the date open, just write his unit number on it. They parked flanking the elevator and almost raced to the button, he got there first and pressed up.

The doors slid open to the empty car. They stepped inside and he pressed thirty seven. The small jerk threw them together, they flowed easily. He scrunched himself down into the corner, she walked between his open legs and gripped both sides of his head and kissed him hard. Her tongue thrusting into his mouth lustily; she was hot as a firecracker. Then she switched up and tenderly kissed his lips without tongue. This change was much more sexual then the frantic kissing. Ron was thrown for a loop. The doors slid open on thirty seven they tried to calmly walk up the hallway holding hands. Ron stopped at 3710, popped the lock and ushered Sylvania in.

The whole space was dark, impossibly dark, when he closed the door. The blackness was complete. He held her in this pitch black darkness and gave her a full-bodied hug, crushing his erection against her. She could not see her nose on her face, but she could feel the hairs on his chest. He reached out like a blind man and started undoing the buttons on her blouse, reading her body in Braille like a blind man. He actually had his eyes closed.

With the last button undone, he used the palms of his hands to rub circles around on the front of her bra but could not feel her nipples hardening. He now used his fingertips to explore the face of her bra. His fingers found what felt like a pocket; he pulled and it came away. Sylvania gave an intake of breath. He could tell that her teeth were clenched. Behind the opening, he felt fabric, upon touching it, it fell away.

Now he felt the long rubbery stiff nipple he was looking for. Ron bent forward and took the long stiff nipple in his mouth and sucked gently. Using his tongue to rasp around it in circles, his lips milked it. While his mouth was busy, his hand freed the other nipple and he pinched it gently. As he switched to sucking on the other nipple, he reached around behind her and unhooked the bra. He slid her shirt and sweater off and down her arms, he then slid the straps down off her shoulder and off her arms as well releasing his prize just long enough for the bra to fall away.

Sylvania was close to an orgasm from Ron's nipple play. She was wondering why she couldn't see anything still. Her pupils should have dilated by now, but she didn't care. The blackness added another dimension. Ron was sucking her turgid nipples and licking her bare breasts so well she had to do something for him.

She reached ahead feeling for his belt. She quickly loosened it and began to unbutton and unzip his slacks. Once open they slid down, she heard them puddle at his ankles. The noise she heard next was comical in the dark. Along with his mouth pulling off her breast to keep his balance, he grunted as he tried to unburden himself of his shoes to remove the pants, made her giggle. She reached out and caressed Ron's massive dick. The giggle turned to a moan, once again she felt wetness gush, wetting the crotch of her panties totally.

Ron was finally free of his pants and shoes, Sylvania was nude from the waist up and dripping wet. Ron said, "Lights, 5 percent." And a glow so soft you could barely say it was there illuminated the room, her pupils had indeed dilated from being in the absolute blackness…and now she could see. Ron led her to a satin wrapped king sized futon, and with a deft flick of the wrist, transformed it into a bed.

He lay her down on her back and pushed her away. She went sliding over the silky material looking between her knees at Ron. He was now crawling between her legs with his head down lightly nipping at the insides of her thighs. She had only been done orally once before, because the person doing it didn't know what he was doing. It wasn't pleasant, but this was a whole 'nother rodeo. His lips felt so sexy moving up to her inner thighs. Then he was gone. She looked and pulled her skirt up over her knees to pool around her waist. That was the cue he was waiting for. He moved in and captured her whole panty crotch and sucked it into his mouth. She squealed,

"Yes, do it."

"Do what?"

"Do IT!"

"What's it?"

"Lick it."

He licked her panties one time

"Like that?"

"Yes, no, more."

He licked her twice,

"Like that?"

"Why are you teasing me?"

"I want you to tell me what to do so I make sure I please

you."

"Ok, lick me down there."

"No baby that's not how you ask me to do that."

"What do you want me to say?"

"Tell me to eat your pussy."

"Oh damn, um, eat my... ppp, eat my pussy mother fucker, eat it good too."

"See how easy that was? Now look what you get."

Ron used his tongue and teeth to pull her panties away from her engorged lips and began to eat her in earnest. Within two minutes he felt her hard clit scraping across his tongue and she was squirting juice into his mouth and babbling in an ancient orgasm language.

While she was on her orgasmic roller coaster, the buttery soft fabric rubbing him almost made him come while rolling around keeping up with her. But he managed to slide his boxer briefs down and off and to reach the end table to grab a Magnum condom and open it when he came up for air. He had switched tactics and was sticking his long tongue up into Sylvania as deeply as he could, trying to get her to say the word, but all she could do was moan and come again.

Finally, he sat up and removed her stretched out soaked panties and unzipped and removed her skirt. At last both naked, he ran his hands up and down her body. Scooting between her legs he bent over and held her breasts together sucking both fully awake nipples. The head of his covered dick was bouncing on her clit, he asked,

"What do you want me to do now babe?"

"I want that in me."

"What's that called?"

"A Penis?"

"No, for the purpose of this exercise, it's my dick and this,"

He tickled her pouting lips with the big head,

"This is your pussy, say those things."

"Your dick, my Pussy."

"Good girl, you are getting the hang of this huh?"

"Ok, I know what you want me to say you nasty man. Ron, put your dick in my pussy. Don't tease me anymore, I want you to fuck me Ron."

This was what he wanted to hear. He just didn't know the words would be filled with such passionate emotion. He notched the very tip into her wettest point and started to rock in and out just a bit, slowly wetting the rubber with her juice. The wetter it got, the more it slid into her until half of Ron's nine inches was rocking smoothly in and out of her. She had two orgasms while he was getting that much in. She said she wanted to get on top. Ron readily complied.

Once on top, she was a different person. She pulled him out until only his head was still inside her, internal lips nipping at him. Then, she wiggled and slammed down, taking all but the last inch. She rose up again, this time getting it all and burst into another orgasm, this one thunderous.

She rode through her heavy quakes with long, tall bounces,

taking all of Ron as deeply as she could. She felt him start to lose his rhythm, the first showing of his control slipping. So, she pinched and sucked his nipples while using her perfect ass to rebound off him and back down. Suddenly, Ron swooped up her legs in the crooks of his arms and spun her to her back with her thighs against her shoulders and her channel aimed straight up in the air.

Ron rocked her world. He was fucking her now, just what she had asked for. She could feel his well acclimated dick coming all the way out before slamming back in to the hilt. Her orgasm count was forgotten long ago. But this time, she felt an orgasm coming from her entire body. This was new. Ron was kissing her through every thrust. Then, he reached beneath her, gripped her ass and squeezed, sending every bit of himself into her and he came.

He came forever. The throbbing of his thick muscle inside her, the growing balloon of hot boiling semen filling the rubber, and her locked, but fluttering, muscles made this the best orgasm either one ever had –bar none.

Ron was so excited, he could not go soft. Slowly, he let her legs come down. But instead of adhering to gravity, she locked them around his waist and just rocked him. Eventually, they fell asleep. This had been the best day either one of them had had in a very long time. Or, this was just the beginning.

Right about 4:45am, Ron's alarm went off. He awoke quickly and said,

"Stop, its Saturday."

The alarm silenced. Ron was amazingly still atop Sylvania; still semi hard and deep inside her. When he stirred, he felt the vacuum seal of her lips causing him to regain his former rigidness. He gripped himself by the base and slowly slid through Sylvanias liquid heat. Sliding out from her depths felt like he was being bitten by a mouth with no teeth as her strong muscles snapped shut. He slid off the rubber and reached for a fresh one. Using his long fingers, he painted her internal juices along the new rubber. The sight of her laying there in his bed, so beautiful, unimaginably beautiful, yet here she was, he felt as if he had bedded Ms. Universe. But, somehow, not just bedded, it felt as if they had made a real connection.

He wasn't sure what type of connection, but he could feel something more than sexual. Just watching her sleep told him that. Gripping his rampant stiffness he stroked his latex-clad head against her clit, the two slippery surfaces sliding like ice. Her body responded with a jerk. He pulled one leg over the other and urged her onto her stomach; she moved automatically. For the first time he beheld her ass, it was a work of art. An entire museum could have been dedicated to it.

He flattened his large hands and placed one on each cheek and held them there, feeling the strength, the heat flowing from inside. Using the base of his palms and thumbs, he separated her ass cheeks right at the crease with her thighs and there, just below her winking hole, were her plump lips parting for his exclusive view. Straddling her thighs with her butt spread just so, he aimed and penetrated. Slowly, he allowed her to remember him.

But this time, the penetration was from a totally different angle. He somehow went deeper than before. When he hit bottom it really felt like bottom, like some mystical place inside of her that he had just discovered. Whatever this place was it brought her out of her deep orgasm-assisted sleep into a moaning, orgasmic wakefulness. But, this one seemed to start around her toes and shook up her thighs, through her butt, which responded in ripples, then through to her torso and shoulders until her entire body was shaking. Ron kept himself buried inside her until her tremors subsided. Then he kissed the back of her neck and said," Good morning sunshine,"

Then he pulled out incrementally as he kissed down. Then, he went back in as he kissed his way back up. Not wanting to be passive anymore, no longer totally in awe of this beautiful black giant, she pushed back. Raising up on to her knees, she wanted it doggy-style. She wanted him to do like he did earlier. Then, she remembered her sex talk lessons, 'ask for what you want.'

"Ron"

She said wiggling her hips loving his size in this new position

"Yeah babe?"

"I love the way your big dick feels in my little pussy, but I want you to do something for me, will you do it?"

"Anything for you, Sylvania."

Her dirty talk had made him twitch deep inside of her. Hearing him speak her name caused her to clamp down in reflex, especially considering her request.

"I want you to hold onto my hips and fuck me; fuck my pussy until it fits your dick like it's yours. Please fuck me, Ron."

Ron almost lost his mind. He gripped his hands almost fully around her slim waist, slid them back and held her natural

142

hip points and began. Watching her head snap, gave him a fear of whiplash. But this was what she wanted. It's what she would get. He reached underneath and held her clit tight to his shaft as it rocketed in and out, the other hand weighing a breast while squeezing the long nipple.

At one point he totally took his hands off of her and let her throw back onto him. She was fucking like a porn star, hair thrashing, and inky black against the other blackness. Ron scooted back to the edge of the futon walking her back with him. He thought of something he had seen and always wanted to do. Once at the edge of the bed, he stepped down the side closest to a wall.

Standing now behind her he leaned over her back and stroked into her deeply. Then he gripped her by the undersides of her knees, gripped and lifted. She moaned,

"Oh shit Ron, what the hell are you doing?"

Ron stood up with her impaled on him, her arms went behind her head to hold onto Ron's neck as she defied gravity. Ron used the wall for stability and they started to move. Ron sucking on her neck while she brought her arms down trusting so that she wouldn't fall off Ron's cock. She was even thinking dirty now. She gripped a nipple and stroked her clit and his dick as one, she felt so wide open and free, her orgasms shook her and she felt weightless in his strong arms.

Once again she felt him falter and grow harder. Sensing that this was a cue that he was ready to come, she told him to sit on the side of the bed. He did. She rode him facing away from him. Just when he was gripping her to pull her down and come deep inside her, she jumped off of him and turned around.

His face was pure agony until, without breaking eye contact, she pulled the slippery rubber off of him. She stroked his raw, naked, head against her clit and jacked him, using the copious juices from her own source. It didn't take much. With both hands gripping and stroking, Ron broke eye contact and his head fell back, mouth open. She now watched the tip of Ron's dick as it puckered and spit a column of white creamy semen straight up.

Four or five spurts, she kept jacking until the spurts stopped. Then, she squeezed the last out of his tube, holding the still stiff, but, shrinking love machine. She rubbed it side to side, across her clit. Scooping up some of Ron's semen from his lap, she applied some to her nipple and sucked it off. She must have liked it because she did it three more times. While still holding him she said,

"Good morning dew."

He smiled a huge toothy grin.

"Sylvania, why are you in my life? Are you just here for a day? Tell me now so I can kill myself."

"Actually Ron, I don't know. I have a, well, I guess nowadays, I should call him a 'friend',"

Accented by air quotes.

"But at the same time, I'm feeling something here, and it's something I like, even though I just met you."

"I thought that was just me."

"No, I think it's a 'we' thing. I don't know what it is, but I don't want to leave you Ronald. I feel safe with you, even in this sensory deprivation chamber you call your home."

"Oh shit, sorry – 'windows 50 per cent.'"

The day outside instantly became blue, every color blue she had ever seen, it was the pre-pre morning, post night sky.

"Fold this up Ron."

He folded the futon with the same ease with which he'd folded it down earlier, disregarding the pool of semen on his lap. She straddled him and sat with his half-stiff dick between her legs like an airplane control stick and cuddled up beneath his chin. She relaxed in his arms and watched the sunrise. As the giant star arose to prominence she started:

"I'm a fourth grade teacher, Ron. I'm basically single, and live alone, unless I want company"

Chapter 16

Dulcet was relaxing in her wave massager. This was one of the larger machines in the mach room. It was aqua blue and very expensive. It worked by suspending a sleep-styled mat surface above super salinated blue water, while the subject stayed dry. The water was forced through jets under super high pressure that created a strong wave motion when matrixed through the multiple channels.

The result was a concentrated wave action that rippled through the mat providing several types of massages from head to toe. Of course, Dulcet had modified the machine to fit her needs. She had installed a small Symbian device that was sensitive to wave motion. Its randomness sensors decided what response Dulcet would get, for how long, and in what combination. With the modification, instead of lying flat on the floating mat surface, one would climb in laying either on back or stomach; the sensors could tell. After the lid was closed, the wave motion would begin.

The Symbian was placed so that as you straddled it, you could crush your thighs against it and even wrap your legs around it and kick it to you with your heels. The device had peripherals, two dildos, and a sucking set of lips with a warm realistic probing tongue. The entire unit vibrated and matched body heat. The randomness ensured you would not know which or in what combination you would be assailed with. That was most of the fun.

She had set her massage for an hour. She was dozing while the dildo was slow-stroking her ass, the lips were clamped to her pussy with the tongue plunging in and out between the lips. In the distance, she heard a tone. Rising from her orgasmic therapeutic massage, she popped the hatch, deactivating everything. The tone was louder now, it was an incoming text message.

The irony of having her sexual massage interrupted by a business message was not lost on her. Padding in nothing but silk slippers, she sat down at one of the networked computers in the condo. The message said:

For long off-the-hook relaxing island destinations

Attach, above information: bring cash, play the pick 6, support the schools. RASSVAPP

"Hmmm, interesting."

Of course it was coded. One of her miscellaneous criminalistics investors had some Intel on a job, a quick turn-around at that. The code broke down like this: the first letters of 'for long off-the-hook relaxing Island destinations attach', spelled out Florida; 'above information, bring cash play the pick 6, support the schools. 'Bring cash' was self-explanatory. Pick 6 was the number of digits. And the 'm' in imformation was a mis-spell that was off by 1. The RASSVAPP was a jumble of rsvp and asap. The result was an ASAP job in Florida. Price of the Intel was $100,000, respond to get the balance of the details. Recipe said nothing she had going would be ready for at least four days. This should be an in-and- out. She text messaged back to the unknown sender.

"Stressed out, need vacay, en route?"

'deet deet'

The double tone told her the message was received and was being read. She knew the person would have to ID themselves in order to get her to the next phase. But she was indeed en route. She grabbed a light soft-sided bag and plopped some flimsy things into it. After all, it's Florida, right?

Dulcet strolled to her vanity and looked into a peephole. A bright green light scanned across, up and down her eye. The retinal scanner activated the servo motors built into the wall- mounted vanity to reveal her closet sized safe. She went in and rifled through her various ID packages. She decided she would be Chilean for this trip. She grabbed the Chilean passport, green card, a stack of cash, and a couple pieces of jewelry, including a nice chunky wedding trio, and left the safe.

Using the name on the passport, she contacted the private jet partial ownership number and checked to see if anybody was going to Florida. There were two businessmen leaving at 8pm on their way to Orlando. That would do. She got herself on the flight using the cut out, Cayman Island corporation user ID and pass code. She left her return city open just in case Orlando wasn't her destination.

After all, she still didn't have the ID confirmation nor the details. So, she had a little time on her hands. She tightened up her manicure and pedicure to ensure she matched all the outfits that were tossed in the bag. Her tan was intact from earlier, so she could fit in as a Floridian if she had to, depending on the job. She'd need to pack a mini gig bag with tools of the trade, the typical generic stuff. Duct tape was the best ranked criminal tool available on the market. Guns were for intimidation; duct tape was for everything else. Most people didn't know that kidnapping was the #1 use for duct tape world-wide, good old American exploitation.

Nylon Rope, a good short-handled razor for cutting rope, gloves, CN spray, just in case she had to put a small group to sleep for a while, and gloves: calfskin fitted, surgical and Playtex. The last stop was the arsenal on the way out. She looped a Sarong around her neck and slung her bag over her shoulder. Slip-sliding her silk slippers over the thick pile carpet caused static to build up inside her body. It would be released on either metal or human contact. Dulcet went into the dining room and leaned her nipple into the handle of the china cabinet and ZAP! She could see the spark jump from her nipple to the metal handle. The feeling was indescribable but always reminded her of home. Sliding the china cabinet to the right revealed a short hallway. Stepping in, afforded views of glass cases filled with weapons.

Everything was represented from Japanese throwing stars and darts to original traditional ninja katana to HK 91 and

MP5 full automatic machine guns and a back pack mounted .50 caliber Gatling mini gun. She chose a short barreled Sig Saur automatic pistol to bolster her pack, there were no security screeners on the private jet tarmac.

Although air security was tight, because of the high profile people that flew this way, to board, you drove directly to the plane on the tarmac and boarded, just like that. It was surely worth the $50,000 yearly membership. Twenty four hour access to aircraft was important in her line of work. Her last act at the house was to call for a limo. She speed-dialed the car company that the homeowners association kept on retainer and ordered a 7:00pm pickup. .

She gathered up everything and filled a roller bag with compartments for her weapons and a couple of toys. Packed, she lounged on her oversized lazy girl recliner, turned on the massive wall mounted flat screen and hit the random channel button. The forty eight paned picture-in-picture screens popped up, randomly shuffling them brought one up on the central main screen.

Headline news was showing a war zone somewhere that looked hellish. It seemed like a missile or something crashed and made a big ass crater with what looked like body parts burned up and scattered all over. She didn't know what the hell was wrong with those damn Palestinians or whomever these nutcases were this week, and then she noticed the slowly blinking live in the upper corner and KRDK St. Louis Missouri,

"Oh shit, that's here? St. Louis?"

Just as the realization was dawning she heard the front bell.

Slipping on a pair of four inch pumps she went to answer the door. Distractedly opening it and handing out her bag totally out of character, not to mention her sarong was still casually hanging around her neck and she was naked except for her pumps. Her driver, ever the professional, took the bag and made sure she wasn't looking before he took an eyeful for later. Dulcet went back and turned off the TV and set the random schedule security system. She wrapped her sarong around her back, adjusted the straps to cover her swaying breasts and tied the intricate knot that would turn the whole thing back into a long piece of cloth.

Walking out to the Lincoln Town car. She sat, the driver looked, smiled his approval and closed the door. As he entered his cockpit, she told him the private airport she would be going to and when she needed to be there. She rolled up the privacy window and they were off. During the entire ride to the airport, Dulcet wondered what this job was and how it had come to a head so quickly.

Her thoughts were interrupted by the slight humming from her roller bag. Opening the zipper compartment containing electronics, the Asian IPhone was twittering and buzzing with a Chinese rhythm. This version of the popular apple device was sold only in Asia; the tenth generation wireless multi-function device was much faster and more feature-laden than the American version using 7.56.

The Asians also had programmers that created applications to customize the 9g device beyond the wildest imaginings of the creators. Dulcet's IPhone had scrambling software far simpler, but much more effective than the MIT programmers at the NSA in Ft. Meade could develop. Therefore, the fact that this phone was ringing at all meant half of the ID was confirmed. She answered,

"Arigato mamacita Bella"

Japan, Spain and Italy that confirmed Giancarlo's identity.

"Ciao Bella."

"ETA 8:30 your time, where do you want me?"

"Where are you coming in?"

"Rat town exclusive"

"Copy, I'll be there."

The phone disconnected and the screen went black. They pulled to the airport right on time. The two businessmen she was hitching along with were boarding as she pulled up. Her swinging Polynesian wrap dress made the obviously married men stare with lust. But one look at the monster cluster of diamonds on her left ring finger, let them know she was way out of their league. They made pleasant introductions and offered to take her bag inside. She refused their offer and the men settled into their seats.

Dulcet, after deliberately waiting for them to sit, stood to fit her bag overhead into the bin.

She purposely gripped a bit of fabric, reached up, with her sarong riding higher and higher until the rounded naked cheeks of her ass and the fiery red tuft of hair peeking from in between made a peek-a-boo appearance.

She knew they would be looking, hoping to catch a glimpse of panty beneath the short, but not too short dress. But, they dared not hope to spy the dewy lips of her fat sex close enough to touch. She heard the sharp intake of breath from one of them. She turned back around and watched them both busy themselves doing nothing. She let her dress drop into place and took her seat. Both men reminded themselves not to be gentlemen once they landed.

She was happy with herself, her nipples were stiff but hidden in the folds of her sarong halter-styled straps. She knew all the attention was on her; that's how she liked it.

Any cover story she had in place would take precedence over any old lying eyewitness testimonies. Who would you believe, me or your lying eyes? It's truly amazing how that worked in the world of the rich and privileged. Of course, after being caught, there wasn't much that could be done. The magic worked by keeping things from getting that far. She knew that she had made their day, but that was a by-product of making her day.

The plane took off slightly early, since all passengers were on board, there was no reason to wait. Before they knew it, they were cruising at 35,000 feet doing mach 1.5. The smooth sailing Gulfstream G650 made the speed feel like they were standing still. Fifty-seven minutes later, they were in Orlando airspace. The fasten seatbelt light came on prematurely. The pilot came through the speakers,

"Due to suspected terrorist activity in St. Louis, the Homeland Security threat level has been raised to Red. We, as well as all commercial non-military flights, are being grounded. Orlando will be our last stop until further notice. Hope you had a good flight. Pray for America: the latest casualty numbers are hovering between 900 to 1000 people dead … God help us all."

Unconsciously, all on board crossed themselves, though

none were Catholic, nor did they wear any type of religious jewelry. There was something about being this far from the ground and still having to land.

But land they did. Five minutes later they were taxiing to the Private Jet hanger. Even with the horrific news, the two men remained seated to catch another look beneath the rich woman's dress. Hoping to store every detail for later recollection. As she made her way to the bottom of the jets stairway, Dulcet was met by her driver. Using the name on her Chilean passport, he also informed her that the code RED had caused troubles across the country, but the problems should not affect her assignment.

Halfway to Coco beach, she got the details: five World Series of Poker players were on board a personal yacht, three women and two men. They all had their winner's bracelets and a pot of,

"It's said to be $3 million in cash on the boat right now. Security is in on it, they expect to be roughed up; the $100k is to ensure your entry and exit from the boat. The cut up goes, based on the $3 million – 1:2, the 1 comes to us to pay off all involved, the two is for you for doing the work and leaving a calling card. Lastly, after you leave the boat, set it free. Unlatch the mooring lines and your job is done."

"Ok, are we on our way there now?"

"Yes, the game is in progress now, it's due to go for two or three days."

"Ok, I need to change, what should I expect from security?"

"Their biggest security is the fact that nobody knows that they are there. That was the $100,000 detail.

Dulcet reached into her gig bag and took out a wrap for her hair. It was like a stocking cap, but it had the consistency of mousy brown hair. Next, she changed the look of her eyes to brown as well; now the features of the Chilean she was supposed to be, were coming out. She pulled out a G-string pair of slingshot panties. They were basically a cup for her lips and the hair on her mons. Other than that, it was just a thin string. She fitted this on to conceal the red pubic hair and to ensure that none was left behind for CSI technicians.

Her last piece was a pair of rubber dive shorts. They looked like boy short panties made of rubber, in case she had to get into the nasty U.S. Ocean water. It's so polluted she didn't want to risk anything going up into her.

All the way to the marina she was formulating her plan. Of course, she preferred to work according to the dictates of the recipe program, especially since she worked alone. But this did seem to be a walk in the park. The code Red thing was buzzing around in the back of her mind. Like most Americans, she had no idea what it comprised of, considering they had never seen one since the system had come into effect, The highest they had ever seen was ORANGE.

This was unprecedented, but right now she had other things on her mind, like two million dollars to put into a safe deposit box tomorrow. The marina was in view, from their vantage point on a hilltop overlooking the yacht slips. She was given a pair of Starlight Photonic Light Enhancing Binoculars. They used all available light to paint objects and create the eerie green or red effect they called night vision, not to be confused with thermal vision which picked up heat signatures and outlined them against their relative backgrounds. These binoculars did both.

Her contact counted the number of yachts, starting from the right to the target, there was really no need even though it was dark and all but two of the yachts had the lights totally off. The darkened boat with the armed guards (three visible) was a dead giveaway. Unless one were appropriately equipped, they were all but invisible. She defined her entry procedures. Giancarlo gave her a clicker, a low tech device that would make the clicking noise of a bottle nosed dolphin to alert the security point man that things were in play.

He would then make the appropriate moves to ensure her passage inside. Dulcet removed the Sig Saur and slid it into the holster attached to the inside of her dive shorts. Her last piece of gear was the sleeveless black rubber zip-up hooded top. The top was so tight her breasts bulged from the top of the zipper. So attired, she would look like disjointed arms and legs walking in the night.

She carried the few tools she would need in her backpack. Its capacity tripled in size using tabs and zippers. Right now, all it contained was rope, tape, respirator, gas and a razor. She was pulling on the gloves now. Giancarlo explained which car to look for during her escape and wished her luck. She left. She made her way down to the marina. She was counting the boats she had seen from the hill. At two boats to target, she hit the clicker. She continued on and proceeded down the slipway to the boarding area. She was met by one of the men in black,

"Chile?"

"Si."

"Vamos."

He led her to a hatch opening, she could hear activity.

"Su habla ingles?"

"Si, yes I do."

"Ok, watch that light under the door. The generator has been acting up for the last hour or so. You see the lights go out, open the door and slip inside. The table is directly in front of you, ten feet; the money is to the left of the table. There are chips on the table; they are personal ones, they don't count. Of course, the bracelets are on all of their wrists. Give me three minutes."

"Ok."

He left off into the stygian darkness. Two and a half minutes later, the sliver of light at the bottom of the hatch went out. It was time. She slipped silently through the door pulling out the Sig Saur. Darkness always causes voices and sounds to carry. The perception is that things done in the light are louder. Subconsciously, causes people to speak softly in the dark, to whisper. The whisper allows you to think you can hear in the dark, which is why blind people have such an advantage born of their disability. They are never in the dark because of the absence of the light. The blind talk loud when the lights go out. But, all the conversation in this stateroom was whispered.

"Damn that generator."

"Don't you cheat woman, I know how you take advantage any way you can."

"Shut the hell up, I don't even know where the dealer is, I could mess around and blow you by accident."

"Forget him, blow me and I'll fold!"

"You guys are disgusting, and you're a slut. I guess they were right: you can't predict who your friends will be. Hey, why don't you ever say anything?"

Dulcet counted the different voices and took in the context. There were supposed to be two men and three women players, but now according to the talkative woman it seems the dealer is a man as well, hmmm. She did a quick recalculation, three: two female-advantage would make the men act sensible, whereas the opposite would make the men want to protect the women causing everybody to get hurt.

An even three: three changed the dynamic as well as her final scenario geometry. There was still hope though, surprise was on her side. With this thought, the lights came on.

"Hallelujah! Thank you Lord, lets pla…"

"I hate to be contrite, but, put your hands where I can see them or I'll kill you all – NOW!"

Automatically all six people raised their hands.

"You, dealer, come here, the rest of you stand up and turn around!"

The dealer walked over to Dulcet, she cracked him across the side of his head with the Sig. He saw stars, then, she stuck the gun against the base of his skull. Told him to strip, toss his clothes into a pile in front of him. To the others, she gave the same command a minute later.

"Toss those pretty bracelets onto the card table if you don't mind, or, even if you do, I don't care."

The now naked players tossed their WSoP bracelets onto the table under protest. Several grumbled their disapproval. Dulcet sensed a change in the energy of the room. The competitive nature of the gambling women was throwing off the balance of power, so, Dulcet changed the game. Reaching into her bag she palmed the respirator mask onto her face and twisted the nozzle feeding her fresh Oxygen. Then, she dropped the CN gas canister while pushing the dealer to the floor by the back of the neck. The gas worked amazingly fast in the closed-in room; the would-be protesters crumbled to the floor. The dealer being closest to the canister was out first, she retrieved the gas and closed the pressure release to shut off the flow and returned it to its place inside her bag. Out came the duct tape.

The first woman was arranged on her knees, face down taped to a straight-backed chair, arms, head and shoulders stretched through the back arms taped to the legs. The first man was placed behind her with his flaccid penis nestled against the woman's sex. They were taped together at the knees with his wrists around her torso below her hanging tits. Already his body was realizing what was going on. Even though he was unconscious, he began to stiffen. She aimed him up into her and went about taping the next woman behind him. Slumping her knocked-out body over his back. She taped her arms to his thighs and positioned the next man behind her. The last woman seemed to be the one that would have caused the uprising, the talkative one.

After she was positioned and taped by arms to the man in front of her as well as a strip attaching her neck and long blond hair to his back, the dealer was placed behind her. His large member hanging half hard. Still wearing her gloves, she spat on a finger and poked it into her loose unconscious ass and positioned the dealer's penis inside.

She jacked fresh blood into his member until it stiffened and slid deeper into her. They were taped at the thighs and knees with his hands around her torso. Her tableaux was complete. She went to the table and slid the pile of bracelets into the bag. They would be dismantled of diamonds. Then, the platinum and gold melted down and separated. The cash was in a display case, nice and classy, a glass case with a pearl handle, and bundles of $100,000 in $100 dollar bills. She extended the backpack to its maximum capacity and dumped the cash into the bag still looking at the chips. She noted that they were real Las Vegas chips. She scooped them into the bag as well. It seemed that there were as many chips as there was money, made sense.

The backpack was heavy now, she was ready to go. Then, she noticed that she had overlooked the pile of clothes and jewelry. The Rolexes, rings and two necklaces would fetch a nice return. The wallets and loose cash brought a few thousand loose extra dollars. All the cards and information she'd find something to do with later. The black clad security types were nowhere to be seen. As instructed, the last thing she did was to unhook the mooring lines fore and aft. The rippling waves gently floated the boat away.

She knew that anybody boarding the vessel anytime soon would also get the gift of the gas. She was only now taking off her mask and stowing it away in her pack. The car was straight ahead. She hit the dolphin clicker and the door popped open.

She crouched by the door, Sig in hand waiting:

"RASSVAPP"

She got in and pulled the door to her with her foot.

"Chile, all is well?"

"The boat is free floating, all the people are unconscious... conveniently forgot about the dealer huh G?"

"Unfortunate oversight by the mercenaries hired for security. No worries, they only got half their promised amount, the rest comes after you got out safely. Unless they forfeit the other half of the money, they won't live past tomorrow."

Dulcet was squirming out of her back pack. She reached in and counted out ten of the triple banded bundles of cash.

"Where do you want these?"

He passed back a drawstring bag.

"Fill this."

She dropped in the bundles and cinched the bag. As she passed it back up front she asked about the code RED. He told her that National Guard troops were being scrambled, air traffic was grounded countrywide.

"I'm sorry, but you can't go home as we promised, it looks like instead of an in and out, it's gonna be an in and stay."

Not likely Dulcet thought.

"I need a car, clean, untraceable."

"Can do, we are on the way to where you can have your pick."

She was back down to just her slingshot. She replaced her mission gear back into her pack. But, she kept the Sig Saur locked and loaded in her hand; you never knew when the smell of some more money would make an individual lose his sense of reason. She also knew that she was partially to blame; she knew that men didn't think well when their dicks were hard, but she wasn't going to go to a gas station to change.

She wound up in a halter top and a long, tennis skirt just above the knee, and a pair of white mules. Their destination took thirty minutes. Finally she looked through the window as they cruised past a selection of cars. She saw a 1979 S-450 convertible, older, low tech, just the way she liked it.

"Stop, the Mercedes, no extra electronics right?"

"Nope. All the cars here are swept twice daily and this lot is secure."

Dulcet rooted around in her backpack and came out with a sheaf of bills.

"Here Giancarlo, it's about $10,000, for the car, and call it a tip for getting me out of there."

"It's no problem Chile, it's always good doing business with a professional."

"I agree."

She stepped out of the car with her backpack and roller bag and transferred them both to the bench like backseat of the Benz. The keys were in the ignition, it started like a sleeping beast. She goosed the gas and slowly rode back to the road that brought her here. She had seen a freeway sign for I-95 South, she would go to her condo in Miami. It seemed like a thousand years ago she had heard some wise person say – 'If you invest wise, it'll end up saving lives'. She heard that voice every time she made a score. The condos she owned were at all the points of the compass.

Now it was time to work on her international permanent digs this time around. She could get to one of her properties within eight hours of a job, pre-planning. In another life, she had been privy to a principle called P7 – precise prior planning promotes, a predictably pleasing payoff. Using these bits of wisdom had kept her prosperous and safe through some harrowing situations, not to mention the disdain she felt for hotels and their-nosy ass staff members and their snitch bonuses.

Dulcet pulled into the Miami city limits in her three hour old Mercedes to the most unexpected sight: tanks on the sides of the roads and armed uniformed old men. The weekend warriors not prepared enough for international deployment. So, this was Threat Level RED, a mini unorganized martial law.

She reached into the bag with her Florida clothes and pulled out a long silk scarf which she looped around her head and tied around her neck, adding a pair of CoCo Channel Mickey Mouse frames, she rode right past the checkpoint. She continued to look back to see if anyone bothered to chase, nobody. It seemed there was no need since A1A south only went to Miami and the Keys, apparently they were only interested in people going north.

Once in the city proper, she drove fifteen more minutes to her house. She motored sedately through the upscale gated community to her property, and drove straight through to the backyard. The grass sloped imperceptibly and curved below the deck.

She pulled in and parked the Benz, got out and worked the combination on the access door. It took two trips to the car to get both bags into the crawl space under the pantry. Closing off the outside world at last, she swung the lever to move the spice closet open on its smoothly moving hinges and walked into the kitchen. Dulcet had created the master plans for her vaults and safes. She used separate contractors to do the work in each of the different locations, so that the décor fit the residence, but the functionality was the same across the board.

She made her way to the master bedroom where she used the retinal scan to access the area. She walked into the vault pulling out the stacks of $100 bills as she went, 20 bundles of $100,000. She broke each bundle and inserted $100,000 stacks into the specially designed cash carousel feature of the safe. To the layman, it was reminiscent of a giant pez dispenser, spring loaded and designed with two parallel tiers. It could hold up to $100,000,000 easily; it was almost half full.

The bracelets she took out and piled onto her jewelry lab table. This was a small lap desk that resembled a pool table without pockets or corners. The first bracelet would be the tester, she primed her heat source and applied it to the metal band to determine its properties and to test the settings of the stones. Right around 1600° the first diamond slid out of its protective setting. She kept the element attached and switched to a jewel puller and proceeded to divest the rest of the gems from the settings.

All together she had nine bracelets to disassemble. Those egotistical bastards had to wear all that they had to prove to one another who was the best. Dulcet knew that it was her! She worked on five more bracelets. She was impressed by the mini mountain of high quality diamonds before her as well as the slightly misshapen pile of gold and platinum next to it. Those would be melted and separated later. She put the other four into the drawer on the desk. Once she was finished, she knew a fence in Dallas that dealt in diamonds that would happily take them off her hands. But that would have to wait until after this National Guard thing was over.

Chapter 17

Peeking up from the wedge space in the pit, Thony and Suzan heard the pandemonium and knew that at the same time their personal lives had gotten closer. The world, as they knew it, had changed too, in some fundamental way. He pulled Suzan's purple wrapping off of her completely and started checking for injuries, they found none. She checked him as well with the same results. Naked, they found shoes and checked the rest of the condo for damage, all the other windows were intact.

They went back into the playroom trailing the vacuum cleaner; they crunched the glass with their shoes so that the appliance could pick up the smaller pieces more effectively. Thony looked out of the broken window. Down about two blocks, was a helicopter in the middle of the street.

"What the hell... Suzan, turn on the TV."

She didn't hear him over the noise of the vacuum, or, she was concentrating too hard on the task at hand to allow herself to be distracted by whatever reality Thony was looking at. He turned and looked at her naked body, the body he had only seen with his hands. He involuntarily started to harden as he watched her move. He moved away from the window, rampant erection bouncing in front of him and approached her. He grabbed the hand holding the upright handle to slow her down. He could feel the frantic fear just below the surface of her skin. He hit the power off button, the machines roar wound down to a whisper.

In the silence he heard her whimper. He turned her around by her shoulders, looking into her eyes. He had to readjust himself up against his stomach in order to pull her in for a hug. She hugged him back fiercely still whimpering,

"What's happening? Oh my God, I just wanted to love you Thony, why, what, I'm so scared."

She put her head on his shoulder and started to cry in earnest. He stood there, hard and soft at the same time, he stroked her hair and the back of her head until the crying subsided. They walked out of the playroom hand in hand looking like a grown up Jack and Jill. Off came the glass encrusted shoes and they made their way to her bathroom where he wet a cloth, wiped her face and applied a cool compress to forehead and neck. He asked where her bedroom was located, she pointed upstairs. Thony noticed a well hidden set of spiral stairs in mirrored alcoves at either end of the hallway.

Thony followed her, the diameter of the spiral was such that her ass was an inch below his face all the way up. This set of stairs entered the 2nd story within sight of the Jacuzzi tub.

The bed was in the middle of the long rectangular room with the other spiral at the far end. The front edge of the room was a balcony overlooking the entranceway. Offsetting the midway point, was a traditional stairway with a three tiered switch back that angled off towards the playroom and the dining room.

Suzan's bed was huge. It was an island unto itself. He led her back towards the pillow topped beast, it was definitely custom designed. The octagon shaped eight poster bed had gauzy material falling from all sides like civilized Spanish moss. They walked to the bed, he backed her up and sat her down, he looked into her eyes and they were red and brimming to overflow with unfallen tears. She grabbed him, her lip quivering.

"I'm scared Thony, and I don't know why. Make love to me; make me know I'm safe."

Thony laid her back. As her body slowly fell away, her legs parted and raised, opening herself to him totally. Half hard, he lay between them wrapping his arms beneath her shoulders, kissing her tenderly.

Her desperate passion was transmitting itself to him. He naturally flowed into her, her pouting lips welcoming him inside, tight and wet. By the time he was fully inside, he was painfully but pleasurably hard again. He experimented with his depth, grinding into her deeply. She was rocking her hips in circles working her clit against him, her strong muscles massaging his shaft all along her walls. Whenever he pushed deep she would moan into his mouth.

After her first orgasm from the deep marinating penetration, he began to slowly thrust, full long strokes, then slow half strokes, until he was just using the tip, driving her crazy. Finally, with one strong deep push, he came again, hard. Her entire body was shaking and tears were streaming down her face.

"Do you feel safe baby?"

"Oh yeah, yes. I know nothing can touch me when you are inside me, uh yes, give me more. Faster... I want you to come again."

He started to speed up his long strokes, her legs were flailing, going from spread out to both sides to gripping him hard on his flanks like a horse at gallop. Her tightness added to the hot, constant orgasm that was making him crazy. He pulled on her shoulders rolling her up to him kissing her deeper. His gentle pace was increasing, working up a froth between them.

He sighed into her mouth as his balls contracted and sent their load down into her depths, only to reappear smeared along his length trickling down her rounded cheeks and rewetting her swollen lips. He broke the kiss and looked into her eyes. She looked much better. She exhaled a huge breath in a sigh. She let him know that that was just what she needed.

"Ok, now, whatever it is, I'm confident that I can face it, with you by my side."

"You sure?"

He was panting, out of breath. She, on the other hand, was as content as a spoiled housecat. Her orgasmic aftershocks communicating to him internally, keeping him hard.

"Reach up to the headboard, wave your hand across the

top."

This caused a panel to light up, she stretched and pushed the screen and TV/cable buttons. Through the scrim of fabric he watched a large screen come down from the ceiling, an image slowly coming up on it.

The view was a war zone image of carnage and destruction. Something about the scene was familiar, disturbingly familiar. Then he recognized what it was, the fire trucks and EMS vehicles. The image was so huge, it was like sitting at a drive in movie. The letters were clearly visible STLFD. Those were St. Louis Fire trucks!

That explosion was here, the blast they heard was right down the street, maybe two blocks away. The broken window was their only physical damage. The announcer was saying that "this was the worst terrorist action on U.S. soil since the World Trade Center. It looked to have been aimed at one man, but hundreds of people on both sides of the rally's issues had died in the explosion. Authorities are still waiting for someone to take responsibility. So far, nothing. No one has come forward. The country is at Threat Level RED for the first time since the color coded system has been in use. Countrywide, the National Guard is patrolling the streets. Until something concrete is known, checkpoints will be set up randomly.

The Homeland Security Director, in a statement, said"

"We don't know if this is an isolated incident or a prelude to something else. So, we are going to err on the side of caution until further notice. The emergency broadcast system is in effect; if you hear the tone, know that it is not a test."

"Thank you Director. That was the Director of Homeland Security. We are currently awaiting more information. Air Force One and Two are currently scrambled with the Presidential and Vice-Presidential families aboard.

The city of St. Louis is 'under curfew until further notice; no one is allowed on the streets after dark, those caught out could be 'dealt with harshly'. That is the official word from FEMA, the Federal Emergency Management Agency, according to the USA PATRIOT ACT*. After a confirmed terrorist act and the threat level goes to RED, the Government is suspended and FEMA takes over. The failsafe is a SEVEN-day clock starting from the time the code RED is declared. If a stand down to ORANGE or below is declared, the government regains control."

Suzan turned off the TV. They sat in the dark, not saying a word.

"So what do we do now?"

"I'm not sure Suze. We're actors, not soldiers. I'm not sure if I told you, but we're within sight of the blast zone. From the playroom window, I saw a helicopter in the middle of the street. I saw soldiers, at least they didn't appear to be in space suits, so it looks like there's no radiation. It wasn't a nuke. But it was right here, way too close for comfort."

"It's so strange, I knew something terrible had happened. I don't even know how we wound up on the floor. But I just felt something telling me to "Get down, bad's coming.""

He looked understanding at her. They rolled over, separated, and wound up laying next to each other wordlessly. They looked at one another in the half light. The echoes of emergency lights from two blocks away were faintly bouncing off the walls, and the wails of slow sirens joining the fray.

Chapter 18

Two blocks down and one over, within sight of the crater and the basketball court, Kristi sat in the MCU, (the Mobile Command Unit) provided by the local field office of the FBI. The MCU held everything you would expect from a local office building: break area with coffee and food, restrooms, work areas, and meeting rooms. The MCU was actually two units, both the size of double-wide house trailers.

The combined unit was self-contained in the event of a biological, chemical, or nuclear incident; it could provide a sterile and safe environment for up to two weeks. Multivariable motors powered up battery farms that ran generators that kept electricity and life support systems working. These were all part of the security systems as well as the air purification, water reclamation. And filtration systems were linked into the internal computer and communications systems.

Kristi sat at one of the computer systems now with John Eagle, the FBIs most experienced satellite imagery specialists. John was a Blackfoot Indian, and he'd first joined the Bureau as a profiler. Years later he had been working a case that had everyone stumped. The satellite imagery held the key.

When John stepped in, he explained to the experts that the art of tracking prey, works from ground level, often getting down to the ground and finding tracks or broken twigs, the same can be said of tracking from the sky. Later, with further research, this activity he had known from childhood on the reservation was discovered to be an offshoot of the Chaos Theory**.

After breaking that case, he was seconded to Satellite Imagery Analysis Division, but still primarily a profiler. John could see a photo taken from space and see things with his naked eye that most couldn't see with advanced equipment. Add the two skills together and he could find a baby with a specific birthmark in a crowd. She had witnessed this herself. John Eagle was who she was thinking of when she had made the request of the director.

They were sitting at an ultra-high resolution monitoring system, she had inserted her jump drive into the USB slot. They were going over shots from before the blast from the two stills she had shown him. He confirmed that this was a double: an assassination and a terrorist bombing at virtually the exact same moment. John Eagle agreed that the bulging of Mitchell Johansen's cranium was caused by a projectile entering his head from the top rear of the frame.

The next partial second of a frame would have shown the entire frontal lobe of his skull punching out explosively, except for the fact that the frame in question was the blinding sunburst of the bomb, becoming, fulfilling its purpose. A bomb's only purpose is to blow up. There is absolutely no other reason for it to exist. This one determined the destiny of hundreds, if not more, inside that micro second it took to become its intended purpose.

Next, John Eagle wanted to look at the actual footage that the stills had been taken from. It came up after her password routine. For material of this nature, the passwords were imbedded into the data, not the system or the software. This allowed for one grace re-try, then, the data permanently erases itself. As she was scrolling to the time designation on the pictures John Eagle wanted to see, he stopped her. He wanted to see the footage in its entirety, because something he had noticed during her scrolling had troubled him.

The MCU had gathered skads of data during its short time onsite. They now had the final seconds of the cable video footage as well as an audio feed from the collection of vaporized correspondents.

Now, with the earlier microburst from Kristi and their real time-sat feed available to do the live overlays, John Eagle was compiling a primary scenario. John Eagle took the previous pictures of the gazebo. He used the structure and the natural landmarks, like streets, to determine the direction the bulge pushed out from to ascertain a projectile path. John Eagle looked at the possible sites from the location he had calculated. Laying this computer data aside, he went to the other half of the dilemma.

"According to the second by second, the explosion came from the gazebo. No matter how high you zoom out, the gazebo is the epicenter. Now, the rally was advertised to start exactly on time, 7:00 pm sharp. But the explosion frame, which is ½ second after the apparent shot from the back, happens at 7:03 p m.

That points to a remote device, ok? See what I see? First, we are being led to believe that, according to context, Arabs, of two different minds, the perpetrator is either an Arab pissed off with Johansen, or, that a hate group aimed at Arabs in general. The placement of ordinance this powerful is significant. The place with the most impact would be closest to the most impactful target. That, we can agree, is the gazebo which points to Johansen.

"If the crowd had been the target, the explosive would have best been placed facing the perimeter around the gazebo in order to get the maximum number of people. The fact that the bomb didn't go off at exactly 7:00pm, tells me that it wasn't on a timer. Somebody waited to be sure it was Johansen and not somebody else standing at the microphone before blowing the charge. With that being said, going back to the shooter, why did he pull his trigger at the same moment?

He had the advantage of being able to watch him approach from wherever he came from to get to the gazebo."

"That would be here."

Kristi pointed to the group of black security SUVs surrounding the white limo in the before shot.

"Ok, so how come he didn't shoot him out here in the open?

He must have had a clear shot all along this path, unless shooting him at the microphone was in his contract. Ok". Now Kristi, this has been a glimpse into the mind of the Great John Eagle," he said theatrically. "Now, I'm going to show you how this works."

As he had been talking and free-flowing information, he had also been taking notes and sketching diagrams.

"These questions and observations must be done, listed and thought out before pictures and the aftermath in order to go backwards in time and know what to look for, ok? You with me?"

"Of course I'm with you John Eagle. It would take a much bigger crowbar than you could wield to pry me apart from you right now buddy."

With her tendency to downplay her attractiveness, Kristi had no idea how attractive and desirable she looked at her base. In her special ops gear with the fitted PRRV breast protection, her sheer will and tenacity gave her a glow, and the underlying determination just took it over the top.

"Ok, let's set the zoom here, center of the gazebo in the center of the screen, altitude at about 30 feet, we get a good perimeter. Now, set the video two steps backwards at - 0:00.05 increments. Watch to see what, according to our notes, stands out. We have to almost assume that the bomb was pre-set, because something with this kind of yield could not have been invisible. It looks like it could have been a cruise missile warhead. But, I digress. Ok, here's Johansen, 19:01.00 stepping into the gazebo."

The frames crept backwards with partial seconds in between. The crowd was moving out away from the speaker as the frames kept going backwards and the anomaly showed itself. Grounded placards were picked up, but there was one small dot that seemed to be going towards the gazebo. Facing it, walking forward, meant that this person, in real time was walking backwards in a straight line from the gazebo while everybody else was walking towards it. "And there we have it, an anomaly, something that doesn't fit. This is how you determine 'persons of interest'."

John Eagle did some tapping on the keyboard then grabbed the mouse. He click-zoomed in on the anomaly and click-dragged a box around him. After the box was set, slight shading came over the person; right clicking on the shaded area opened a menu, he chose 'track'. This command put a blinking arrow on the shaded area. He then zoomed out until the entire park was the center of the screen. The people on the ground looked more like a solid mass than individual bodies from this height, but the blinking arrow still indicated the position of the shaded one. Kristi had to interrupt,

"John, I'm not sure where this is going, but I want to thank you right now. Anyplace this goes from here I have to credit you for taking me. If at any time I thought I wanted to toss my computer out of the window and go back to the way things used to be done, as they used to tell us at Quantico. You have truly reaffirmed my belief in technology integration with the right people. I want you on my team John Eagle. But, we'll talk about that later; let's finish."

It took John a second to get back to speed. The things she said with the intensity that she said them caused sweat to break out on his scalp, upper lip and underarms. But, he was a professional, so, he retained his composure. He set the step timer to 0:00.35 to step forward this time. The arrow was steadily moving backwards away from the gazebo. Then, the arrow began to move erratically; he paused the frame.

The change happened at exactly 19:02.50.0, using the arrow key, he tapped until he was at 19:02.58.0 and zoomed into the arrow. He got to a height of ten feet and saw the man. From this height, you could see facial hair, but not enough detail to determine if it was real. Zooming further down to six feet they were looking at the top of his head slightly magnified. They could see a device in his hand. It was red and held as if it had a trigger, but it didn't resemble any weapon either of them had ever seen. The man was still looking in the direction of the gazebo. John Eagle clicked one more frame and the device was being aimed at the gazebo and the man was shouting something.

The next click brought the blinding light in from the right side of the screen. Zooming back out, showed the arrow being blown to the left and coming to a stop. John Eagle scrolled along the path and zoomed back into where the arrow had stopped. The image was as surreal as any they had ever seen: the man was on his back slammed tight up against the fence surrounding the basketball court, laughing, actually laughing with the device still in his hand. John Eagle zoomed in maximum until the face filled half the screen.

He saved this face to the hard drive and Kristi's USB drive, then printed several copies. Kristi pulled one of the high resolution printouts. It was almost like magic that this clear picture was taken from 24,000 miles away in space. The detail was so crisp that you could see the frightening dichotomy between the laughing mouth and the deep dark black penetrating eyes. A shiver passed through her. This man looked like he was capable of anything and the worst part of all, despite all the destruction around him, it appeared that he was still alive.

**

Thony vowed that anything she needed him to do he would to ensure that she didn't go through the fit and near catatonia he had witnessed earlier. Not to say that he wasn't scared shitless as well, he just knew that this was no time to show it. He had to maintain the strong man, "Me-Tarzan-you-Jane" effect in order to get through this. Suzan stared into Thony's deep black eyes looking for promises only to see barely checked-fear, but checked, nonetheless. Something about looking into his eyes always made her feel better, she couldn't say what it was specifically. Maybe the blackness, so indicative of deep mystery, more than likely it was the fact that when she looked at them, she could see the reflection of herself.

Whatever it was, she was glad he was here, that he hadn't just dropped her off and left. She was especially glad that she had crossed the line. Finally making love to him was everything she had thought it would be. The panic attack, hadn't happened since she was a very young girl, but he had the magic to make that go away too. Maybe he was the one, she sure hoped so.

Chapter 19

Sylvia was blithely riding in first class on her way to the East coast. She hadn't wanted to supply the Arabs with too much information, so, she changed her destination spontaneously just before she was due to go to the airport. The car had already been packed and her things retrieved from her suite. The change in destination didn't seem to cause any concern, everything about the transaction had gone smoothly, until…

"This is the Captain speaking, I'm sorry to have to be the one to inform you, but this flight will be abbreviated due to a hydraulic problem. The airframes failure to maintain altitude has nothing to do with our ability to land, but in consideration for the safety of everyone, we will be landing in Atlanta, Georgia, for repairs. Ramp agents will inform you and direct you to alternate modes to reach your destinations. We thank you for flying with us we appreciate you".

The captain signed off and the Fasten Seatbelt sign popped on. Food was still being served in first class. The attendants sped up the service just enough to have all of the carts stowed away before the plane went into landing operations in fifteen minutes, one hour early. This turn of events didn't change Sylvia's plans much, in fact, it was even better. Now that they didn't know where she would be landing, the first thing she needed to do was to make a call.

Complimentary Cellular phones were available to the first class passengers; they worked off the satellite transceiver in the nose of the plane directly to the satellites. Sylvia detached the phone from the armrest and dialed a 404 number in Atlanta.

"Hello, is this $ensation? Hey girl, what's crack-a-lackin? This is Fantasia."

The woman on the other end squealed with delight.

"Hey girl, where are you?"

"I'm about to land in the Atl in a few minutes. I'm..."

"You in the air?"

"Uh, yeah, why'd you say that?"

"You and the President must be the only ones, girl. Somebody did some 911 shit in St. Louis; they got the whole country on RED alert lock down.

All the planes in the country and the ones trying to get here are grounded, land where you can right now type shit."

"Damn, they told us it was a problem with the plane."

"Yeah, there's a problem alright; that bitch gotta land, now. At least you gonna land in the A instead of Mississippi or Alabama or some other place in the sticks."

"Yeah, look girl, I may need to see your brother about a car once I get there. You feel me?"

"Yep, I gotchu girl. I'll call him soon as we hang up, you coming by huh?"

"Yeah, I'll be through; I know you cooked,"

"You know this - - maaayunn!"

They both laughed at that; Atlanta, Georgia, was known for two things: strip clubs and soul food. Those things were common knowledge. But, it also had an undercover claim to fame, the large gay community and the down low sex society: live sex clubs, S&M shops, dungeons and massage parlors. The sex industry was flourishing, on a yearly basis. Not many corporations could count the same amount of income as the combined sex trades.

Sylvia's girlfriend, $ensation, was a long time stripper. She had 'danced' in most of the clubs in Atlanta. She routinely traveled to where the action was: bike week in Florida and Carolina, the Adult film awards in Las Vegas, spring break in Cancun and Cabo san Lucas, Mexico, Mardi Gras in New Orleans and Carabana in Montreal. She got around, and she had fans. One of her online groups had over 850,000 members. Whenever she traveled, there were people that knew her as well as others that she knew.

She had been out of the clubs for a few years now. She had a small posse of girls she took to different locations to turn out private parties, Atlanta style. They were known as $ensation's Pusse Posse; they were known for their girl-on-girl shows and live sex with audience members. After all, what good is a private party if you don't do something nobody is supposed to know about? She ran an equal opportunity shop, she had male and female clientele. She would bring males and females to the female events; but only women to the male ones, although for the right price, something could always be arranged. This was the main reason Sylvia knew $ensation, her discretion.

She had done private parties for the Mayor, Congressmen and CEOs and no one was the wiser. She would take her girls to an appointed meeting place where they would be met by blacked out limos that would whisk them to the private location. Up front money was always in the limo so everything else was a go. $ensation's brother was a retired drug dealer on the west side of the city, now, he dealt with other things.

He had a legitimate auto detailing shop that did aftermarket vehicular modifications and accessories. He could install 10,000 watts of stereo power, low profile ground effects or seamless stash spots that vacuumed away vapors and bypassed them through the exhaust manifold to kill illegal package scents. He was a self-taught electronics wizard; Sylvia knew that if anybody could find a tracking device hidden inside the Mercedes, it would be him.

"Ok 'Sashe, I'll be at Hartsfield in five minutes, give me about thirty and I should be to you. You still in CP right?"

"Yeah girl, this is family land. I'll be here forever, literally. We got the whole family planted here so after a while you'll be viewing me instead of seeing me, right out back."

"Whatever, crazy ass."

"I'll call Beeny now. If he's not here by the time you get here, I'll know what you need to do."

"That'll work shorty."

"Syl, you try so hard; be safe, ttfn."

"TaTaForNow?"

Sylvia didn't know where $ensation had picked up that little saying, but she had held onto it as if she had written it herself. The landing at Atlanta's Hartsfield-Jackson airport was uneventful. Sylvia climbed aboard the internal rail train and rode around to the baggage claim area.

She gave her claim ticket stub to the baggage supervisor and he reacted with an intensely strange look. It's not every day that a ticket like this one came across his desk; he was used to finding lost suit bags or computer bags, but a car? He would have to make a call.

He contacted his manager, the baggage manager for the entire south terminal. He was informed of the appropriate procedure and told not to let the passenger know that he was such a damned rookie; be professional. The supervisor called his assistant to oversee the baggage claim area and escorted Sylvia through a doorway hidden inside the baggage carousel.

They walked through a complex set of machinery used to ferry luggage from berths where the airplanes arrived, to the myriad different areas in the airport where the bags were destined to be picked up from. This led them to another door; the other side held a sparkling glass hallway with a moving sidewalk that activated once they stepped on. She had never known this sort of thing existed.

As they moved towards a drop off, the sidewalk transformed into an escalator. They went down two stories, at the bottom it went back to the sidewalk mode for about 100 yards. She hadn't moved a foot yet. The sidewalk ended with a loop at the end of the hallway, this was where they stepped off. The tall glass wall looked out on a large covered parking facility that seemed to hold only foreign luxury cars. The supervisor, trying in vain to hide his excitement at being here, probably for the first time, picked up the red phone and spoke the numbers from her claim ticket.

Two minutes later, the Mercedes arrived on the back of a specially made flatbed vehicle. The back activated and slid to the ground. The driver handed Sylvia the key fob, she approached the Benz and the driver's door opened. As she sat in the seat, it started up and a heads up display asked her if she would like to set her preferences. She held a conversation with the car for the next fifteen minutes, setting foot pedal height, steering wheel distance, lumbar support and at least a dozen other details.

With that session complete, she drove off. The lot had direct access to Interstate 75/85 North and South as well as I-285 East and West. She got on I-85 Southbound and rolled to $ensation's house in College Park. She pulled up to the compound. That was the only way to describe the property. After coming through the trees, the first thing she saw was the central house. A six bedroom, eclectic, beautiful place that had been renovated and expanded over the years as the family grew.

There were two huge buildings behind the house. One wide and flat, the other tall and long with two huge doors. The first one was for cars; it was like a dealership. Inside sat everything from sports cars to Hummers. The big buildings were covered garages and repair facilities for the tour busses.

When $ensation took the Pusse Posse on the road, she really hit the road! The Provost Superliner Tour Coaches were tricked out with big screen TVs, stripper poles, and plush with deep toned carpet and sofas. The busses were an incredible investment. They were literally strip clubs on wheels, of course. They were private clubs, very exclusive.

This mode of travel was mainly unknown, except to a very small circle that cost quite a lot of money to enter. Her business was growing with the help of her brother Beeny. They were working another angle. A fifty-three foot trailer was being customized as a two story split level club and casino with dancers, gambling, and a VIP area. The blueprints were the bomb and the weight calculated out to be no problem for U.S. roads. Just hook it up to the multiphase generators and off you go.

They had access to a Volvo and Two International tractors, the best on the road. Each trailer would be customized differently so that the patrons had a choice of floor plans and amenities. And of course, mile high air was in the planning stages. Sexual pleasure was very good to $ensation. Without having a single share of stock, she was a very major corporation. Sylvia rolled past the main campus and motored behind the garages and up a hill gaining access to $ensation's private residence. She was waiting on the front porch.

The circular driveway was a nice new touch. Sylvia stepped out of the Benz and approached her girlfriend. They embraced fiercely, it had been a long time. They walked inside and Sylvia had a seat. The private side of $ensation was the polar opposite of her work life: classy, wholesome southern living, from the slowly stirring ceiling fans to the wrap around porch outside, and the constant pot on the stove inside. Speaking of the pot, $ensation brought in a TV tray with collard greens, fried chicken, macaroni and cheese, pinto beans, corn bread, banana pudding and a giant glass of iced sweet tea.

"I told you I got chu girl, your ass looks like it's fadin away; other than that, you're lookin good Syl."

"Well shit, everybody can't work the badoonka doonk in their line of work, you know? Besides I don't get many complaints about this ass."

"Girl, you know you can roll on a pole tour with me and mine anytime."

"I might just do that girl, but, I'll need a new name though. You know Fantasia is permanently retired, American Idol blew that for me."

"Shhhiiit sexy woman, I can always call your good pussy ass Sunshine."

"Girl you are still crazy."

"Maybe so, but I'm not lying."

Sylvia knew it too, they had stripped together back when $ensation was first starting out. The private parties were the perfect cover for casing a beautiful house as well as getting secrets out of the men. After one of Sylvia's lap dances and a happy ending, there was no limit to what they would brag about to the dumb little stripper. They would want to make themselves look bigger than they really were, especially in houses they didn't own. Next thing they knew, they've been robbed. Those old days were fun, she had to admit. But now, she was in a whole 'nother league; after all she had $10 million outside in her new Mercedes.

"Hey girl, where's Beeny? I need him to scan my new car for any and all tracking devices, I have a feeling the folks I got it from didn't really want to give it to me."

"Well that shouldn't be hard. Beeny! Guess who's here?"

Beeny came out of the kitchen sucking on a pork chop bone and stopped in his tracks.

"Fantasia? Is that you?"

"Beeny, I'll be her for you baby boy."

She opened her arms for a hug and offered her cheek for a kiss.

"I'll grip that body proper like after you get your eat on. You look like you been missin a few meals. Now what's this about your car?"

"I need you to sweep the shit out of it. You're the only person I trust with my V12 anyway. I think I may have some high tech tracking shit that I'd like to be on its way south of the border while I'm moving north. You feel me?"

Beeny's eyes hadn't stopped scanning Sylvia the entire time he had been in the room."

"I want to …"

"Been, get your head out of her ass now, she needs your help. Knock the dust off your old ass mack game later after you do what needs to be done. These motherfuckers might be tracking her here. You think bout that?"

"Alright, shit, let me get the key; I'll be back 'taisia."

Sylvia smiled, hearing her old stripper name made her think

about doing something a little off the chain. She didn't need to be thinking like this, but she did have some time on her hands, and money in her pockets; she needed to get rid of that too.

Now that she was on land, she had entirely too many metal strips surrounding her to allow it to be found before she knew where it was or how to access it. Sylvia was so happy to see her girl. It was a good reunion. Plus, she was getting things done to her new car that could not have been done by anybody else, nobody.

She knew full well that wherever that money was, Beeny was going to find it and he wouldn't touch a dime. But, he would make diagrams leading to all the locations and detail their accesses. Any devices he found would continue to work, just like she asked. They just wouldn't work tracking her.

After Sylvia finished eating, she wanted nothing more than to go to sleep but she knew that wasn't how this thing worked. The secret to working soul food was to keep moving after you eat: walk, dance, run, fuck; something. Soul food only sits on you if you sit on it. It's the best food in the world in terms of nutrition; you just have to know how to work it, like everything else. She got up, stretched, and walked outside to check on Beeny's progress.

***

So far he had found a total of three devices, including the lojack GPS tracker. All of them were sitting on a work tray attached to a battery by alligator clips so that they continued to transmit, but they were sending constantly conflicting signals. The front of the car was going north at 80 mph, the rear quarter was going east, and the passenger seat was headed west. His equipment told him that there was another one. He was checking for compartments.

He had enough experience with all modes of transportation to know with certainty, no matter what type of vehicle, the exact amount of spare space that was usable for stashing and approximately how much of what would fit. It was a science to him. He was systematically working his way through the Mercedes, when Sylvia walked up and ran one manicured fingernail from his kneecap right up to his crotch. By the time the finger made its way to the apex of his baggy sweatpants, space was at a premium.

"Fantasia, why did you ever leave me girl? I wanted to make an honest woman out of you."

He said this while continuing to do what he was doing, not allowing the straining erection to distract him, much.

"I didn't want to waste your time Been', trying to fit my round ass into a square hole."

She was running her finger up and down his rigid shaft now.

"I knew what you wanted. I also knew I could never give it to you the way you wanted it. And you bein my boy, you know I couldn't do anything half assed, right?"

Now his attention was distracted. She could see his toes flexing. She scratched the head with two fingernails, and then as abruptly as she started, she stopped. For the first time he popped his head up off the floorboards.

"Hey, what the fuck boo? You know you the only one for me, you do shit to me nobody else even got license to try."

"Boy quit tryin to sweet talk me outta my panties, you know what to do. Find the shit you're tryin to find so I can have my way with you before you chicken out."

"Chicken… hold up, I got it narrowed down to"

He ducked his head back down behind the seats and wiggled a couple of times, feet twisting subconsciously balancing the handiwork. He reached back to the floor behind him and grabbed a tool by touch,

"Got dam girl, what in da fuck you been up to?"

She knew he had found the money. She had figured the best place to put a tracker would be inside the money bundles. She had actually expected that more than the trackers on the car. Now she had to wonder if the money was all in this one spot or distributed throughout the car.

"Girl, I thought I had seen some shit until I found this fiber wire under the seat. It was running right beside the wire bundle to the biometric power unit used to remember the seat preferences. This space is limited but useable. These corners are perfect for straight packages, the seat cushion cut outs look right for…"

He pulled out a $20,000 stack of $100 bills,

"Then I saw that this was where the wire was going to. It's attached to the band, a 'micro-mitter', very strong, it uses the cars security system for power. It sends randomly timed signals to a satellite that then bounces around and triangulates your location. This one is the most high tech of them all, but I'm pretty sure it's the last."

"How much money is in there?"

"It's hard to tell, you want me to pull it all out?"

"Later, right now I'm gonna pull out what I want."

Sylvia scooted into the back seat of her big bodied sedan, pushing Beeny further inside in the process causing his sweat pants to catch on the seat and drag down his butt. This gave her access to the bulging twitching object of her desire.

Sylvia and Beeny had been lovers off and on under his sisters nose years ago; as peculiar as it sounded, $ensation frowned on lovemaking between her people, employees, and family alike. Even though sex was her business. Fucking, on the other hand, was another Olympic event altogether. The reason being, fucking was sport. It was exercise. It was what her business was based upon: the stimulation, the fantasy accompanying it, the tease, and the promise. By contrast, lovemaking was emotional, non-pragmatic, and unpredictable.

Instead of arousing the fantasy, it became the distraction. That was bad for business. It's one thing knowing your fuck buddy was up on a pole spinning around naked and getting dollars stuffed into her panties; it was an entirely different proposition knowing that same woman was the one that you loved. The same thing worked, or didn't in reverse. To see what you consider your man, hoisting some bachelorette up in the air, spinning her around, and then sucking juice from her panties.

Meanwhile, a mob of her friends, fat, out of shape, the sexy ones, attack him in the name of money. All, of which, can be a perfect recipe for a psycho stalker. Compared to him just being your boy, then, you applaud and respect his hustle. Within that environment, they became secret lovers only on occasion. That kept it special between them. But, of course, after Fantasia left the erotica business, $ensation discovered the truth. Her brother was in love with Fantasia. He didn't even know Sylvia. But still, the damage was done. She could only be so upset with her friend, she had always been special. She not your ordinary sex worker. She did what she did for $ensation, her friend, as well as the marks she would set up to rob.

The brand new suspension in the Mercedes was no match for the long separated lovers. Sylvia held onto the doors armrest as she rode Beeny, bucking and thrashing through her orgasms. Their sex was synchronized as if the last time had been yesterday, not years ago. They sidled up in the roomy backseat and kissed deeply, re-waking the pathways they had trail- blazed years and years ago. They reconfigured until she was laid back against the seat with her legs up on Beeny's shoulders; he leaned in and sucked her nipples while steadily stroking her deeply in the small space. Once again, Beeny and Fantasia were flying below the Radar.

Sylvia had one last teeth chattering orgasm and Beeny followed directly, breathing harshly. With her legs still locked in position, Sylvia ran her fingers through his soft curly hair.

"I really needed that Beeny. I'm so glad my plane got grounded."

"Where were you going?"

"I've got some things I need to do out east. But now, I'm glad I didn't get there. With all this hardware, I wouldn't have gotten there alone." Beeny thought about that.

"So, if it wouldn't have been for the grounding you wouldn't have come around, huh?"

"It was time for me to be here B, everything happens in its time. You and $en' are never far from my mind, I think about y'all all the time, especially when I'm on one of the coasts trying to get some soul food. West coast is all Mexican; the East is all Asians. Those fat church ladies with the melted Hershey bar complexions can only be found down south. The only spot with a number one stunner burning in the kitchen is right here."

She grabbed Beeny by his prominent ears and kissed him hard on the lips, and then said,

"Now, let's liberate this money!"

It turned out the money was dispersed between seven really good stash spots. Only the one under the driver's seat was fitted with a tracking device. Still, they stripped all the bands off the cash and rewrapped it. When they were done, they had four cubes of bundles. Each cube had $2.5 million; 125 bundles of $20,000 each. Beeny shook his head and wondered what the hell the former love of his life was up to now. He gave her four Army styled duffle bags, one for each cube, then two gigantic fashion model duffle's of $ensation's ,that each held two of the smaller bags.

He lugged the two giant zip up bags to the trunk of the Benz. The redistribution did nothing to alter the stance of the majestic, now untraceable steed. He also handed her two medium sized titanium briefcases to use while transporting the money. He may not have seen her in a while, but some things never change.

It was common knowledge within the family circle that Sylvia didn't use banks in the conventional sense, she only used their safe deposit boxes, private and no questions; if you have the key, you get access. Her newest venture was to start a bank in the Cayman Islands. It was progressing nicely. She would be her only customer until she got more corporate monies flowing her way. Once her relationship with Banque Suisse in Zurich Switzerland was solidified, she could retire and work for fun with a legitimate background.

Now that she was taken care of in every way and packed, ready to get on the road she didn't really want to just up and leave Atlanta. She and Beeny walked back to $ensation's house. $en' was in the kitchen putting food away.

"So did ju get everything done you needed?"

"Yep, Beeny took out five trackers, got my oil changed and a lube and filter job."

"You know that boys been sprung ever since you retired Fantasia; when you left, his ass was puppy dogged out. But I wasn't about to call you and I wouldn't give him your emergency number. I knew you'd be back in time."

"I'm glad I came back when I did. Big baller, everything I see is new, even this crib. The big house and all that land is all that I remember, but look at chu now. Picture me rollin."

She sang a snippet of the Tupac song.

"I decided not to leave tonight since the army took over the country. Maybe this wouldn't be the best time to take a road trip. What's poppin tonight in the big bad city?"

"Shit, for you, any and everything you want. What chu wanna do?"

"I wanna go dancing."

"There it is, we go dancing."

Chapter 20

Abdullah was in his suite facing the east, Mecca. Praising Allah for bringing him safely and undetected through his mission to send the infidel back to the wretched hell where he belonged. The collateral damage of non-believers in attendance deserved the fiery end they got. He still had, after all, these hours, the burned in after image of the blasts sun in his eyes. When they closed, it was there. Everything was in slow motion. One second, the infidel was standing there with the look of surprise on his face, the next second, there was the great ball of fire.

It had been as if the sun had hovered inside the park, for that one instant and he had the privilege of seeing it. Then, the blast wave lifted him bodily and threw him into the fence surrounding the basketball court. The explosive was as powerful as the seller advertised. Praise be to Allah. Had it been any more powerful, he would have melted right through the fence.

As it was, he was probably dealing with a mild, at best

concussion. But, he was full of joy to be alive when so many were not. Abdullah finished his prayers and adjourned to the living suite; he turned on the huge flat screen TV to watch the coverage of the mission. He debated whether or not to claim any credit. However, he knew well, that the root of the word "terrorism" was terror, terror was 25% untold and 75% unknown. He turned to the news network and marveled at the giant image of the talking heads consulting 'experts' looking for people to blame.

He knew they would have their spies overseas and around the world torturing freedom fighters, especially in the Middle East. May Allah provide strength and comfort to them. Abdullah decided that he would not put a name to this bombing, he would leave it nameless. If after a time one of his brother cells wanted to claim the victory he would let them.

But until then, let them wonder. Let them quake in terror trying to predict when the next bomb would go off and where. This was one time Abdullah enjoyed television. The people would be in such a rush to keep something new coming from their stations that they would allow just about anybody to get a chair and microphone to spout whatever they thought had not been said yet.

The most entertaining thing is, the longer you watched the more desperate they became to get new information. This was when the secrets came out. After repeating and rehashing the same thing over and over someone, without permission or authority, would come on and say things just to establish that he or she knew things. Once these things were out it was impossible to take them back. The example of that very principle was named Julie Silverstein. Julie was a Zionist woman with lots of letters behind her name and probably a $20,000 check in her pocket to send to Israel to fund killing more Palestinians.

She produced a top twenty graphic of the best targets for terror in the United States of America. This was priceless. Abdullah grabbed a pad and pen from the sofa end table and jotted down the entire list. There were actually a great deal more destination targets than he had gathered from the Rand McNally travelogue: monuments, landmarks, as well as generic target descriptions like shopping malls, refineries, water treatment plants, and reservoirs.

Abdullah considered his remaining Diplomatic pouches. He had come well prepared: a small case containing vials of military grade Anthrax, six in all, and a secured aerosol can of Sarin gas, the deadly poison his brother freedom fighters had used in the subways of Japan. In addition to the poison, he still had ¾ pound of the C-4 and four hand grenades.

All in all, he had plenty enough to wreak havoc before he lost his life in the service of Allah. He admired his suicide prone brothers and sisters. But, he found that his destiny was many fold. Once he had completed all that he was destined for, then, he would gladly receive his reward of riches and virgins. Now Abdullah needed to exercise his cover. He dressed in his Diplomatic Saudi garb and rang the driver's cell phone. The 'driver' and the 'security men' were members of a radical cell of Islam that operated far off the radar like he did. They performed mostly support missions, like the one that had dispatched the diplomats in the name of procuring the motor pool. The men brashly came through the lobby, mini Mac10 machine guns barely visible, menace implied.

The knock came roughly fifteen minutes after the call. Abdullah strode down and through the lobby as befitted his station as Saudi Diplomatic Emissary. As a Saudi National and a Diplomat, the National Guard could do nothing to stop his men from carrying weapons, nor could they detain them. They toured the city admiring the massive Arch. How Abdullah wished he could bring down this impressive monument, but alas, he would need much more ordinance than he had.

As they passed by the river he spied an entrance to the casino area of the entertainment side of the River walk. Amazingly as it seemed, with the country at RED alert, with armed soldiers patrolling the streets, these Americans refused to stay indoors, at home with their families. This was one of the major signs that the Great and once Powerful America was on its last leg. The family structure had crumbled. Single parent homes were populated by adults that had to prostitute themselves just to be able to keep the bills paid, followed by further prostitution of themselves, or, even their children to put food on the table.

These infidels would destroy themselves in short order. Abdullah's mission was to light the fire of their destruction, to help the inevitable along. He watched the riverboats motoring along the Mississippi river filled to bursting with drunken tourists, still drinking and wasting the money they did no work to earn.

After a hard day of destroying lives worldwide with their computers and selling their scantily clad children in the sex industry, they came here to the river to gamble away their mortgage payments because they are addicts. They are addicted to the 'American Way'. Oh how he wished he could set the entire wastrel country on fire. But, he would do his part, piece by piece, as long as he could.

Abdullah directed the driver to escort him into the casino. As soon as he stepped foot onto the plush welcoming carpet, he was met by the manager, who had been alerted by his security of the presence of the Diplomatic vehicle. He gave the foreign dignitary the grand tour of the land-based as well as the riverboat facilities. The body guard acted as an interpreter, even though Abdullah understood the English better than the rapid fire Arabic the guard spoke.

The facility tour included everything, including the environmental systems. Questioning, using the possibility of opening a casino of his own, Abdullah asked about the desert heat effect on the specialized equipment, special sand blocking filtration filters they may need to block infection in the air considering the density of people, especially referring to the slot machines and the closeness of the chairs at the card tables. All along he took mental notes. At the end of the tour, the manager was assured that he personally would receive further communication regarding any plans or thoughts of franchising before he left the country.

The official word had come back from his reconnaissance and his superiors gave him a direction. This act was repeated in the food district, a sprawling gastronomical portion of the River walk complex. With the indoor/outdoor ambiance of the place, the airborne chemical would probably not be the best method. The heavy, water-laden river air would negate a vapor cloud, keeping it from working to its maximum effectiveness, as it would in a dryer air environment. The more humid air would be better to transport the Anthrax spores.

Abdullah made notes on all of these observations, once he got back into the limo. Now, it was time to go back to the hotel and lay his plans. Today was a good day. The reinforcement of the fact that even under a RED alert, the greedy infidels paid no mind to operational security. The stupid deserve to die. Abdullah got back to his suite and immediately knelt on his prayer rug and prayed to Allah to keep him smart for the remainder of his short walk on this Earth. All praises due.

**

Robert stepped from the bus at the end of the line. He was at the Northside Depot; he had waited moments before he had repacked his jogging suit and turned it onto its reversible colored side. He took the exit steps two at a time, jumping down half flights in some instances until he got to the third floor. There, he stepped into the hallway and onto the passenger elevator. The crowded elevator was full of workers from the building, some still dressed in athletic gear as the buildings gym was on the sixth floor. The conversation was abuzz with, "What the hell happened?"

"I was in the bathroom and felt the shock, I thought it was a quake."

"I was online instant messaging a client when the damned windows blew in."

"I don't know about you hero types. I hate to admit it, but I peed my pants."

"I thought something smelled like babies."

That brought a black humor chuckle that Robert joined in on, fitting into the nervous group fear of the unknown that Robert was only half pretending to be a part of. After all, he knew what these people didn't know. The bomb had been an assassination. What the assassin didn't know was that the target was dead when the bomb went off. The problem with that was, his employers also didn't know the target was dead before the bomb went off. Which was going to cause a problem with his getting paid.

Another thing the sheep in the elevator didn't know was that he was 99% certain that he knew the face of the bomber. The guy that was walking backwards from the gazebo, the guy in the oversized hockey jersey, the face and the clothes didn't look congruent, they didn't match. Add that to the hard-on, that looked like a tactical boner of a pro. As strange as that sounds, the professional knows there is a very thin line between sexual excitement and the appetizer for a kill.

When one gets the big game in the crosshairs, that superior feeling unknown to the prey that they are about to go from reigning their kingdom to laying across the front of your Jeep, and there is nothing they can do about it. That is the same feeling a lover gets with a desirable sleeping woman, laying on the bed wet and spread out before you, knowing that nothing can stop you from jumping her bones and having your pleasure. That was what Robert saw in the single-minded look in the man's eyes. The purpose, the 'I know something none of you know' look. That look plus the obvious erection appends the statement with 'you are all about to die'.

That face was one Robert would not soon forget, those obsidian eyes, and the scar on his cheek. But going a bit deeper, he didn't look traditionally Arabic. Although there could have been some mixing in the nationalities, but, to

Robert, the man seemed to be as black or African American as he was. The beard and the expression glued to his face was what marked him with zealotry. He had to remind himself that all fanatic Muslims were not Arabs.

The U.S.A. had its own proprietary sect of bow tie wearing, bean pie selling, and "Final Call" newspaper hawking Muslim followers of Louis Farrakhan. Based out of Chicago, Illinois, they were a far cry from the suicide bombing Sunnis and Shiites of Iraq and Iran. But ideology is for the individual. Over the years a number of privileged Americans have found their way to Palestinian or Libyan terror camps to learn their A, B, C s of bomb making and terror cell creation and development.

With the advent of the internet, recruitment, retention and refresher training has become even more prevalent. So, this man has features to be able to blend in. But, as a man trained to find one face at a time, Robert was not worried that he wouldn't find him. It was just a matter of staying vigilant. Robert stood at the taxi stand flagging down one to take him to his hotel. He had purposely gone seven miles away to keep the trace of his path as circuitous as possible leading back to his starting point.

Once there he went directly to his suite, he was not expecting any messages at the front desk, he knew where they would be. Inside its compartment in his Diplomatic bag, the message was waiting: what the hell happened? He responded using the secure text mode:

'Grandma Food poisoned before wolf could feed. Wolf not long for this world24'.

'Grandma' was the target, the wolf in this instance was a

lobo, phonetic code for a bogey, and U.S military slang an unknown or an enemy that has been inserted into a theater of battle already in play. The ending notation requesting 24 hours to look into the source of the crossed wires and try to salvage the balance of the money he was owed. Stepping over to the pouch he retrieved his handheld computer and logged onto the WI-FI connection. Using a programmer's backdoor entry, he performed a secure search on the situation in St. Louis.

The Web was awash with suppositions, theories, scenarios, body counts, multiples and multiples of the amount of misinformation available on television. He tried, in vain, to strain through the mountains of input attempting to glean one piece of truth, one shred that rang true. Over and above everything else was that face, those black, black eyes, with their singleness of purpose. How could he have missed that look? He knew how. It was the same look he had in his own hazel eyes. It didn't matter that his eyes were beautiful and those others were flat and dead. What mattered was the content, the single minded purpose. That's what made him look away from the man, the target, the job at hand.

Then the blinding light came back to him and he knew this man was still alive and he had to find him. He had to destroy that face if it was the last thing he ever did!

Chapter 21

The court was pitch black. There were glow-in-the-dark dashes that led to an illuminated light panel. On the face of the panel were diagrams detailing different configurations of light schemes. She chose daylight, center court. The roof lit up like it was noon. She could now see the 'Robo-Serve' automatic serve machine.

She stepped to the control panel and selected random, skill level mid and speed NCAA, using the best of the machines programming for college level just to warm up. The machine spit out serves at 55, 60 miles per hour. Dutchess easily returned them. After about fifteen minutes, she was warmed up and she readjusted the profile to professional women. The serve speed went up to 90 mph, and the randomness included spin serves and much more variety. With a bit more effort, she returned all of these serves as well, though it upped her physical output, she was feeling it now.

Her legs were feeling warm and her shoulders loose. Her backhand was awesome, the racquet felt as if it weighed nothing. She had only heard rumors of this machine before tonight, but she would surely be writing a thank-you letter to the manufacturer in the near future. She paused for a bit to sip some water and upgraded the profile to pro men's. This was far beyond what she would be expecting to face, but the challenge was why she practiced. If you practice against far more advanced opponents, that made the real opposition much easier to face and overcome.

These serves were coming at 120 and 130 mph. Dutchess was having a difficult time returning them all; out of 20 serves, she only missed three. By switching back to pro women, she was killing the best 110 mph serves, sending them right where she wanted them to go. She felt good. It was 9:20. She stopped for more water and started to work on her serve. She slammed balls at a maximum of 115 mph, a personal best for her.

Right around 9:30, Lou showed his face on the court. He was drunk; Dutchess ignored him for a full ten minutes hitting ball after ball, with precision working away in her mind against Kikakio Komikami. All of her tapes were playing in her head: she was hitting the balls directly into her body, frustrating her backhand and handicapping her forehand, causing her to stop short just to get the leverage for a return, then finessing the drop shot. This was the way she intended to finish her: one game at a time, one game at a time; win by two, win by two; game set match, game set match. Twenty-four points over two matches and she was in the second round.

Dutchess was amped; she was so full of energy right now. She felt that she could power all the lights on the roof off her body heat alone! She went to collect her balls, tossing them into her ball sack and walked directly up to Lou. She had him by at least four inches. She looked down at him; she could tell the future right now. Lou would not last, not with her, not with tennis.

She started to walk away shaking her head when he reached out to her. He missed. But she felt the attempt and turned on him.

"What Lou? Your little girlfriend gone beddy bye, so, now you want to come play with me? Huh? Look at you Lou. I had major hopes of you taking me all the way: number one seed, Wimbledon. But all you wanted was some in-shape young pussy. You're pathetic Lou, and you're drunk. I'm really not that mad at you. I'm pissed off at myself though, because I was looking at my success as the result of sporadic, but excellent coaching. All along it was my own discipline and practice, my research and note taking, me watching films till the wee hours, talking to other players, and, most of all, me playing tennis."

Henry's words came rushing back to her: 'all you have to do is play tennis'. That, she felt she could do, it didn't have anything to do with anybody else. A good coach would help her by watching her and providing observational feedback; a bad coach would do nothing she couldn't do by herself. She hated to fire Lou before Henry had gotten a chance to get another coach. But right now, just looking at Lou was making her stomach ache. She started to say something clever that would penetrate the fog of his inebriation when the elevator 'ding dinged' and the doors opened.

A tall man, at least 6'7" exited carrying a bag of racquets and balls looking at the court expectantly, not noticing the daggers shooting from Dutchess' eyes at Lou, nor his reactionary drunken confusion.

"Hello, is the court free right now?"

The clipped cadence of his European accent was enough to make her forget the clever hurtful thing she was going to say to Lou. She glanced at her watch and saw that it was 9:45.

"Are you the 11:00?"

"Yes, I was hoping the previous person would already be gone, I've heard a lot about this system and was looking forward to putting it through its paces."

"Well, I still have fifteen minutes before my time runs out and the 10:00 spot was vacant..." She looked him over, sizing him up as an opponent, at 6'7," he was a full 15 inches taller than her upcoming opponent, plus he was a man. Working with a robot programmed to serve like a man was one thing. To have a real one at her disposal was something else.

"Would you like to play?"

"I don't want to interrupt whatever you were talking about."

"Believe me, the conversation wasn't worth the breath."

She looked at Lou with disgust and walked away towards the court and the tall man.

"My name is Dutchess."

"I'm Franz, I'm in town from Sweden to provide support and overall services for a contingent here for the tournament. I'm basically a glorified translator for a group of 19 year olds."

"Well it's a pleasure to meet you Franz. Can you play or is this just a volley practice?"

"I've played a couple games in my time."

"Ok, you serve."

She knew it wasn't entirely fair since she was warmed up and he was not, but, she knew he had the power advantage and she had to neutralize advantages however she could. Franz served, the clock said it was 132mph. She thought he was either being modest or downright lying about his past experience. Whichever it was, she didn't intend to allow him another Ace like that – and she didn't.

Dutchess held her own and won the first match 6 – 4. Franz was slightly winded but still ready. He was a great player and a fierce competitor. Every point she won, she earned it. There were no freebees. By 10:30, Dutchess was ready to turn it in. She felt ready for anything, especially this little girl from Japan. She thanked Franz and explained that she was in the first round tomorrow and needed to get some shut eye. He understood and wished her luck. Before she left, he went over to his bag and took out a card. He wrote his room number and cell phone number on the back. She stuck it in her bag and left.

Once in her room she began to undress. She pulled out Franz' card; this time, she read it: Franz Grúber, Master Trainer, Swedish World Games Champion 2001, 2002, 2003. She was stunned beyond belief. She stared at the card for minutes before she could move freely. She had just beaten a three time world champion who was trying to beat her! She had to throw herself onto the bed and pull the pillow over her head just so that her skull didn't blow itself apart. She lay there like that thinking about every move that he had made until she dozed off to sleep.

Dutchess awoke in the same position, any bedmate would have been pleased: her head under the pillow, naked but for a pair of very small, very sexy panties, her substantial ass waving in the air. She awoke by falling over onto her side. It was early, rolling over onto her back and kicking her legs up to the sky, she greeted the day. Last nights practice session was still fresh in her mind as she reached over to scan the itinerary for today.

The media breakfast, followed by personal time for private practice, then the first round. She smiled knowing that the first round included her. She walked to the shower, bypassing the placard with her image looking back, and touching the edge lovingly, she went to wash. She spent a long luxuriating time cycling through warm-cold-warm water. This was one thing she loved about hotels, no matter how long you stayed in, you never ran out of hot water.

She toweled off and dried her long red tresses. She looked at her body in the foggy mirror, not the typical anorexic all muscle women's tennis body. Dutchess had curves. She had butt; butt that came with the Asiatic genes. Her breasts were a mouth-watering 36c with invitingly sensitive nipples. Unlike the typical redhead, she didn't have a milky complexion with the fan-out freckles all over her breasts; she was smooth, unblemished with the hint of color that let others of her race know that she was a sistah.

Her features alone should have been sufficient, even in this era of Caucasians with bodies approaching the dimensions of black sistas. Dutchess could have been dipped in chocolate and rivaled any black booty flick porn star. But for tennis, the sexy body sometimes got in the way. Too much ass could cause knee and ankle problems. Ask Serena, too much uncontrollable breast action could get in the way of your efficient backhand.

Dutchess went to her bag and unpacked her minimizer sports bra; this apparatus distributed her breasts. Instead of giving her the alluring mid chest cleavage, it took the mass and basically squashed them flatter. She used the traditional tight-banded areas of the bras architecture to push the breast flesh flat. It was much more comfortable than wearing a bra two sizes too small to keep from swinging and swaying so much. In addition, it kept the blood and air flowing, keeping you cool.

Aesthetically, it made her look like a boy with a well-developed set of pectoral muscles. Her ass and long hair ensured there was no confusion. But that was the extent of the gender identity inventory. Her musculature was professional class and she was as flexible as a gymnast, and had been all her life. She dressed in a sheer boy-short panty that matched the sports bra. She insisted on feeling sexy beneath her clothes, no matter what. She had on a light blue logo-less outfit with her signature "D", with the tiara on top. She may not be authorized to advertise a sponsor, but nobody could stop her from advertising herself. Adhering to these rules, she had even gone as far as removing the swooshes from her shoes. She grabbed her bag and strode to the elevator to start this momentous day.

And momentous it had been. After several demur interviews at the breakfast with the media, she downplayed her abilities to tell the future. She wished her opponent from Japan, whom she had never met, all the luck in the world. This was her first time playing a ranked player, but, she thought it should be a pretty even match. Dutchess wiped the floor with Kikakia Komikami, 6-1, 6-0. After the match, she was still in a state of confusion. Her body was telling her mind that there was still tennis to play, even as her mind was marking her name in the bracket on the poster in her room. Once again, the media pounced on the light skinned, green eyed girl with the long red ponytail. This time she let her manager lead, she offered sound bites and went to her room to change.

After writing in her name, she did a little victory dance, adding a small twist and shout. She was interrupted by a knock at the door. She answered; it was Henry. He hugged her again with congratulations. He informed her that his Blackberry was filling and his room voicemail was full of people trying to get a meeting with them. All the usual suspects, plus some he hadn't seen coming, loved the logo. Henry told her that now he wanted to keep her out of the spotlight, stashed away for a while. Since everybody wanted to know her she would become kind of scarce.

The lack of public exposure would actually make her stock rise; absence truly does make the heart grow fonder. The fonder the heart, the more it was worth to court. Dutchess gave Henry his copy of Carlo's card from Coke Brands from the night before, and told him about their conversation.

He thought the red and green pick up line was very unique, and that if his style went beyond the first impression, he might be a good addition to Team Dutchess. She was a tennis player; Henry wanted to promote her like a NASCAR rap star. He had big plans for her and all she had to do was to continue to play spectacular tennis. Henry left her to her thoughts and went in search of the new monetary gains. She told him about Franz and sent a text message to his blackberry since she only had one card. She had decided that she would make last nights practice a ritual for this tournament. She called down to the concierge desk and asked if she could reserve the 8:30 to 10:00 slot on the rooftop court for the rest of the tournament. The concierge said,

"I've been expecting your call ever since I discovered your name on the log from last night. I figured after your performance today that you may have been calling.

Dutchess was amazed, until she remembered the bellman that said that the employees at the hotel were rooting for her discreetly. The rules stated that no employee could be outwardly partisan to any person staying in the hotel or involved in the tournament.

"That would be wonderful, and please inform anyone that's rooting for me that I said thank you."

"You keep on winning; that's all the thanks we need Miss Singletary."

She hung up and wiped a slowly tracking tear from her face. Right now, she still missed her friends back home; but knowing that there was a growing base of fans here, confirmed to her that along with her old friends, there were others that had her back. Additionally, they supported, hell, maybe even liked her. She looked at her picture on the bracketed placard, then, to the mirror and had a Sally Field Oscar moment:

"They like me, they really like me."

Then, she fell back on her bed and turned on the TV to the tournament. She thought of nothing but what name was going to go into the second round bracket along with hers. As excited as she was, with all the adrenaline pumping through her blood, Dutchess dozed off. She awoke to the ringing of the phone and knocking on the door. Totally disoriented, she checked out her environment. She was lying across the bed in her panties, her winning outfit draped was across the chair next to the bed; she had already decided to wear it every day.

The TV was still on and the phone was still ringing. She said

"Hold on a second,"

For the sake of the knocker.

"Hello?"

For the caller.

"Dutchess, what are you doing?"

It was Henry,

"I'm waking up Henry, is that ok?"

"No it's not acceptable. Look at the TV."

She turned and looked, the tournament was over for today.

"Oh damn. I missed it?"

"It's ok, I'm sure the excitement got the best of you; but let's not slip up like that anymore, ok?"

"Ok. Any luck with the coach search?"

"Lou is not too happy; he actually heard through the grapevine that he was on the outs"

"He heard no such thing, unless you have officially changed your name to grapevine. Henry? Henry are you there?"

"Ok, ok, maybe a cocktail napkin may have been left with the trash at the bar with a reminder to replace him. But what are the odds that he is going to read the trash?" "Henry, you are dastardly. One more minute, Henry, somebody is at my door. What else do I need to know?"

"Ok, the short version: Lou is pissed knowing that you want to drop him. His seeded player lost today and his two unseeded prospects are all that he has left. You are going to be playing Tashia Wawbinka from Switzerland. She is seeded number 34 in the world, and I'm free for dinner a 6:00 pm."

"Ok, good, let me compose myself and I'll comment on those things at dinner in that order. Now, let me go answer my door."

"Right, call me before 6:00."

"You got it, bye."

She wrapped a fluffy robe around her and went to the door.

"Coming, coming, sorry for the wait."

She felt bad about making the person wait, security was the farthest thing from her mind. She opened the door without looking out, the chain was still on the door. In the sliver of hallway light, she saw Franz.

"Oh, what a surprise, hold on."

She closed the door and disengaged the chain, then, reopened it fully, admitting the tall Swede.

"Dutchess, I wanted to congratulate you in person on an outstanding victory. I have trained people that have been dismantled by the person you beat so effortlessly today."

"Thank you Franz, I appreciate someone of your caliber working with me last night. I apologize for not recognizing you, I don't know how I could have missed that."

"Your focus on your pending match was complete, I could have been a famous American cinema star and I doubt that you would have noticed."

That brought a chuckle from Duchess along with a question,

"So how did your people do today?"

"Of my five coaches, four of their charges went through. One will, unfortunately, be watching from the stands."

"Well, more through than not is good, right?"

"True."

There was an awkward silence while Franz was trying to formulate his next words. His English was very good, but sometimes the mental translations took a second.

"I have come by to ask you two questions if you don't mind."

"Ok, shoot... I mean go ahead."

She had to remember this guy was a Swede, he probably thought she was a white woman.

"Alright, first question is, are you busy for dinner later? I would like to dine with you, if possible."

"Ok, negative for that one; I have a dinner appointment with my manager at 6:00. Ok, and the second question?"

"I would like to request a rematch on the roof tonight, if that is at all within your scheduled free time."

"Now that I could arrange. I have a reservation for the court for the same time tonight. If you could show up at the same time, your rematch will be waiting. Don't be soft on me."

"I will not be soft, Miss Singletary; need some recompense."

The double entendre hung in the air as Franz realized what he had just said. It dawned on him that Dutchess was standing in front of him with her breasts nakedly swaying beneath her robe; an impressive amount of cleavage showing from his vantage point up there. He felt a twinge in his crotch that could not have been missed as it was right in Dutchess' sight line.

As for her, she watched the slightly lusty sheen come over his eyes and realized how sexy this tall man was. Now that she realized that she could have him, that he was a mortal and not just a collection of statistics, he shrunk a little bit. Now he was his actual 6'7", his credentials had made him seem ten feet tall until just now, this was better.

"Yes, same time, same place, once again, I want to thank you for coming by. But, if you'll excuse me, I have to study for tomorrow and prepare for tonight."

He grabbed her hand and kissed her knuckle. The unexpected action causing her robe to part just a bit allowing a sliver of skin to peek through from her cleavage down to the open space between her feet. As he was straightening up and releasing her hand, the shadow of red beneath the minimal slice visible of the crotch of her transparent boy shorts, was enough to make him gasp. She casually clutched her robe back together and opened the door to let him out, not even acknowledging the slight faux pas.

***

Dinner with Henry was a mini/marketing sales meeting. Dutchess had a high protein salad and a Coke; for some reason she wanted to get used to drinking Coke products. Henry gave overviews of the short meetings he had had since last seeing her. He planned on playing hard to get, possibly working towards a sponsor for the finals match. Dutchess informed him that whatever was to happen, if and when she beat this Swiss woman, she would continue to wear the same outfit for the remainder of the tournament.

He understood the sports religion, superstition, or whatever you wanted to call it. As long as the client was happy and winning, he would continue to be ecstatically working.

After dinner, while half listening to Henry rattle on about business, the other half of Dutchess was steadily solidifying her battle plan for Tania Wawbinka into a strategy. She was going to be a lot more of a challenge than Komikami. Her ranking was higher and her fundamentals were stronger. She noticed from her notes that she had more patience than the Japanese girl, but she could be beaten. Dutchess went through her weaknesses, mental, physical, and her strategic history. If she could use the best of her strategies from Komikami with the power she used against Franz. (Of which she would try again tonight, just to make sure it wasn't a fluke), then, she thought she could see a clear victory.

On the court she went through the same workout she had the night before, finishing each of the time segments by feel. Her internal clock telling her when enough was enough, and, right on time, there was Franz. While preparing for the late night practice session with Dutchess, Franz was excited like he hadn't been in a long time. Back home in Sweden he was seen as a tennis God.

Then, this young strangely beautiful American woman whooped him like an amateur last night. It was so refreshing not being shown any respect or courtesy because of who he was. However, he memorized from earlier, the incredible sexual energy that had been in her room, the bare sliver of skin, and the hinted glimpse of red pubic hair.

Once again, he was hard as a rock thinking about the young tennis player. It had indeed been quite a while since he had taken on a lover. Ever since he had taken over the Swedish National team and developed his own personal coaching staff, the opportunity had not presented itself. While in the shower, he considered masturbating to take the edge off of the physical stress he felt regarding the upcoming rematch.

But, he wanted that edge; that bit of extra energy would be what he needed to make him victorious. Besides, he thought, "It was much better to water the grass than to water the water". As he was exiting the elevator, he saw her, warmed up and ready, a healthy glow of sweat covering her, waiting.

The match was intense. She was bringing out new weapons that he hadn't seen the previous night; the difference was night and day. She was slicing like a pool shark, using extreme English to make target balls do what seemed impossible. Her body would say one thing, the ball would come from the expected direction then bounce off in a totally different direction.

His ego was deflating, but his pride and admiration was

steadily growing point by point. He got a couple high speed aces past her, but her serve was steadying out at around 112 mph with gusts up to 118. With this level of skill, this woman was going to have a long career in this sport if she stayed healthy. She wound up beating him again 6-4.

She toweled off and sipped some water, eying Franz, going over his moves to determine if he had played his best or if he was pulling his punches. Seeing him still breathing slightly hard she realized that he had actually put up a fight. Maybe not 100%, but he had put up a fight, and again, she had won.

"Thank you for another opportunity to play with the best Franz."

"Oh no, no, no thank you Dutchess for the opportunity to play the best. You've beaten me fair and square as you Americans say, and I am duly impressed.

I can only assume that the older gentleman I saw outside the court yelling and screaming at the end of the day was the same inebriated one I saw last night, your ex-coach?"

"You assume correctly."

"Could I also assume that the skills that you used to trounce me were instilled by him?"

"Then you would be wrong; the one thing he did do was to repeatedly tell me that I could do anything, even though I think he stole that from a pep talk from a movie.

Franz shook his head,

"You do have my card with my private cell number. You know what I do; if at any time you feel in need of a coach as time goes by, I implore you, call me. I will keep space and time available for you."

A slight flush began at his neck and ran straight to his ears.

"You have managed to do something that I was not counting on when I arrived here; you've made me a fan. Get me a Dutchess Singletary flag and I'll wave it proudly."

"Thank you Franz."

Suddenly flummoxed from the simple raw kindness, Dutchess said,

"I'll keep that in mind."

With that they went their separate ways. Dutchess kept her thoughts split between Franz Grúber and Tania Wawbinka. She slept deeply. She would go on to win her 2nd, 3rd and 4th round matchups; the placard in her room had only one empty slot left: her opponent for the tournament finals, the opposing space held the name Dutchess Singletary.

Chapter 21

At last, finished telling her story, Sylvania listened patiently to Ron's tale. It turned out both of them had been raised similarly; starting out in an orphanage for Ron and straight to adoption for her. They both floated between private and public schools and finally on to college: education for her, computer science for him.

The careers they had chosen had paralleled their upbringings. His instability as a baby was manifested in his refusal to be an employee. He insisted on being a contractor and making his own rules, moving from contract to contract and back again. This was his way of establishing his own extended family. Every time he would go back to a site, it was like a pleasant family reunion of sorts. Reunions from his childhood never had good memories for him, just more strangers that didn't look like him, staring, knowing that he didn't belong.

Sylvania had similar circumstances that led her to teach children. She had a special attachment to childhood. The essential joy that children can feel in a healthy learning environment was a daily epiphany. The light bulb in the eyes of the young kids made her days so fulfilling. Sylvania loved kids, even though she didn't have any. It wasn't because she didn't want any, it was because she refused to bring any babies into the world without knowing that they would have the best possible environment to come into.

Not materially, though she was comfortable, she wanted her man to be her husband, unlike her own past situation. She wanted her child to come into a world where their mother and father looked like them and acted like them. No more alien relationships, not family. So, she felt shocked by the echo of her feelings coming from Ron. Considering the context, she had just wanted a happy ending to a good night. But now, the very real possibility existed that she had met her soul mate for life.

Decisions were made. They felt that they needed to be together, their meeting each other felt pre-ordained and meant to be. Had they not met the way they had in Oke' Dokeys, they both knew, unequivocally, that they would have met somewhere else.

Ron could still not believe how incredible this woman was; she was the angel from his dreams that he had subconsciously compared every woman he had ever been with to. That was the reason everything seemed so seamless now; she had always been in his mind, now she was in his arms. They arose and went to shower. They used the warm water to reinvigorate themselves. Then, he pumped up the Jacuzzi tub and added a cupful of baby oil to the aromatherapy body wash.

He lifted Sylvania and delicately deposited her in the

bubbling tub, then went to make breakfast. Ron whipped up an incredible garden vegetable omelet, which he set atop specially made thick, wide, French bread with four melted cheeses on top. This, he took to the Jacuzzi room where Sylvania was lounging. Her hair cascaded like crude oil rippling over the side of the tub.

Ron attached the tray to the attachment holder on the side of the tub and caressed her hair reverently. Instinctively, he separated it into three large sections and began to braid.

He got to the tip and split the loosely connected base and threaded the tip through until she had a neat box crown resting atop her head. She was so easily beautiful; he read appreciation and surprise in her expression, as if a 6'7" grown, straight man was not supposed to know how to braid hair and create a wonderful Jacuzzi-proof hairdo.

Ron slid into the tub next to Sylvania as she was leaning over to sample the gourmet breakfast that Ron prepared so quickly. It was delicious. She was loving the food so much that she had scooched herself further to the left so as not to drop anything into the water. Her action exposed both soapy globes of her juicy peach to Ron. She was so engrossed with eating that she hadn't even considered her positioning. Ron having cooked the meal was totally distracted. The light sparkling off her soapy body, her plump, hair-covered lips with just the hint of pink clit peeking out at the water line was driving him crazy. Ron's periscope was up to full mast looking for a target.

"How is everything babe?"

Sylvania replied,

"Cd quality singer, Casanova quality lover, and gourmet

chef, I think I found a home. Ron, do you mind if I stay?"

"I don't mind at all, as a matter of fact I was just about to ask you to."

"Really?"

That question stopped her fork in midair; she turned her head to look over her shoulder. At that moment, she realized that she was bent over the tub doggy-style, throwing down on this wonderful meal. Wiggling her ass with joy, her eyes followed the slippery line of her backside, until she spied Ron's ample periscope poking above the water line. She put down her fork and waved her target around in view of his rangefinder. Taking the hint, Ron rose up and moved in behind her, just far enough so that he could see his target in range.

It was wavering above the bubbling foamy water. Sylvania was still looking back over her shoulder watching the torpedo aimed at her bull's eye. These war-games were getting serious. She hadn't seen such a large bullet before, and this one was pulsing at her. She felt a shiver and began to quake in the pit of her stomach, her appetite for food had been sated, and now, her other hunger had returned.

The plump lips of her dewy sex opened slightly as she flexed her hips; the tiny bubbles from the jets causing her clit to expand. She turned back around and dropped her head to her crossed arms. Ron took this as a signal and proceeded forward on his maiden voyage. His first time uncovered inside the beckoning coral pink vessel of his fantasy. Then he stopped.

He reached behind the tub into a small fishbowl, he pulled out an extra-large Duret 'barely there' condom. He ripped it open quickly with his teeth, pulled it out, and proceeded to roll it onto his tip. As he was rolling it down he was also sliding himself into her, in short in-and-out increments. By the time it was fully rolled on, he was fully embedded inside of her. He used the side of the tub for leverage and stability and the round cheeks of her ass for bounce-back.

Ron went to work making his point while she answered in counter point, both trying not to splash all of the water onto the floor. So, they took their time, including the water as a third lover, exploring different angles and motions. She loved this position. He reached so deeply inside of her and the tub's juxtaposition, cool on the outside while the inside was boiling hot felt like a combination made in heavens own workshop. She felt herself building to a massive orgasm. She had been avoiding the little ones using her muscle control, but now that spring had wound itself so tightly, when it let loose …

Ron slid out of her and positioned her in her original position in the corner seat of the Jacuzzi. She lay back and put her feet on his shoulders. The powerful jets were hitting her from every angle. It felt much better than it had before now that her body was a ball of sexual excitement. He re-sunk his missile into her smoldering cauldron. She was clutching and could feel him flexing. With less than ten slow, deep thrusts, the tightened band released.

Her propeller went spinning, her tremors clutching at her from so deep inside, her muscular reactions were so strong they threatened to pull the snug rubber off of Ron. That was his last thought before he came, totally filling the rubber. She was clutching him rhythmically, up and back down her walls, just to be washed away by the jets.

Not knowing that he had slipped on the rubber, Sylvania thought about Ron's semen inside of her. He saw the concern on her face and reached down to pull out of her. As he did, he removed the rubber and cleaned himself off at the same time making sure to fully empty his chamber. He showed her the filled used rubber and watched the relief flood her face.

She mouthed the words 'Thank You' to him. At the same time, Ron took aim and slid back deep inside her, flesh to flesh. One full stroke to her core, and there he stayed buried to the hilt.

The surprise and the feeling was too much for her and she began to come again, just as hard as the last time, eyes wide, mouth open staring into his eyes. Her strong contractions and boiling hot wetness on his raw sensitive flesh was so intense he had to close his eyes with the pleasure. He pulled out just in time and came again, all over her wet soapy breasts. An unbelieving look came over him as he watched her massage the baby oil, soap and semen into her skin. He looked down, still holding himself, and kissed her full on the lips.

"You know, I think I'm in like with you, lady."

By now she was gaining control over her speech as her system slowly cycled down. "I'm pretty sure I … uh mmmm, like you too mister, damn! You do know how to do things to me, don't you??"

"You give me inspiration. What can I say?"

They reconfigured themselves into the opposite corner of the tub where the underwater landscape was more conducive to a couple chilling. They stayed in for about another fifteen minutes to allow the hot water to cook their muscles a bit more. Then, they stepped out to dry off. He wrapped her in a huge fluffy towel so big it could have been used as a toga. She wrapped it twice around herself and picked up the finished breakfast tray. Ron threw a towel carelessly around himself and they adjourned from the bathroom.

The sectional sofa in the entertainment room had recliners on both ends. Included, was a service station between them with a mini refrigerator, air suction ashtrays, and heat/cool cup holders. They lay back and Ron hit the remote power button. The cable news network Headline news report was on. The strange thing about that was the fact that the TV was set on a local channel. They both reclined back and let their fingers play a goofy game of footsies.

Ron turned up the volume; it turned out the cable news network had taken over the local affiliate station. They had just switched from the main story to the wide world of sports. In sports news, the tennis tournament is still underway in Miami, Florida. In the men's arena, the results are pretty predictable. Federer and Blake are still ranked numbers one and two, respectively. They will be the most likely matchup for the Men's finals as their brackets continue getting closer and closer.

'The big surprise is on the Women's side. In singles competition, a first timer to the tournament chase. There's no way that her anonymity will last any longer. Dutchess Singletary is cutting the grass with opponents as if that was her job here, one that she is eminently qualified for.'

"Hey! I know her."

"You know who? The anchor or the player?"

Sylvania slapped Ron's hand,

"Dutchess, she was at the Tennis Open downtown, I took my 4th graders on a field trip and afterwards, she came to the meet and greet. She was the most wonderful person; we exchanged numbers and everything. I'm so glad she's doing well."

"Shit, it doesn't just look like she's doing well; she came from a who-the-hell-is-she status, to looking as if she could take the whole thing."

The sportscaster continued,

"In the first two rounds, Dutchess defeated Kikakio Komikami of Japan in straight sets 6-1, 6-0, to move into the second round where she faced 34th seeded Tania Wawbinka of Switzerland. This match was more difficult, but the outcome was the same with a 6-4, 2-6, 6-2 win. She has moved into the third round, a solid favorite to be in the finals. For her first time in the lime light, Dutchess Singletary is the one to watch."

"So, that's your new home girl huh? Maybe you can get us some good seats for Wimbledon."

Ron said in his best 'I'm a groupie' voice.

"No, really, I'm kidding, I don't have any spare time to go to sports outings. The best I get is happy hour. But, if you're convincible, I'd like to spend those hours being happy with you. What cha think?"

He winked at her so slyly that she smiled and melted at the same time.

"I think something can be arranged, Mr. Smoothie..."

Then the real news came on,

"The top story from overnight, St. Louis, Missouri. The death toll from the terrorist action last night has topped 1300 in its current estimate. The bombing of Mitchell Johansen's rally stands as the largest loss of life on U.S. soil not involving a building. The country is still at threat level RED. Roberta Johnson from our Washington Bureau is at the Homeland Security briefing, Roberta."

"Thanks Doug. I'm here at Homeland Security Headquarters in D.C. The briefing from the Director is pretty much a rehash of what we have been hearing since last night. No person or group has stepped up to claim responsibility for the bombing. The fact that the bomb killed Arabs and supporters on both sides of the Middle Eastern discussion as well as Mr. Johansen being the obvious target, tends to narrow down the list of persons of interest. However, that brings no surcease to the families of the estimated 1300 families that want to see someone brought to justice. Roberta Johnson, live at Homeland Security in D.C., Action 12 news, back to you Doug."

"Thanks Roberta. She will be onsite in D.C. to keep us abreast of any new developments from Homeland Security throughout this time of crisis. The President has been unavailable for comment, still onboard Air Force One due to the Code RED. Stay tuned to Action 12 as more information comes in regarding any new suspects, threat level color changes or National Guard deployments.

The following national numbers will connect inquiring loved ones to database operators standing by to identify locations of traveling relatives stranded by the mass groundings of all the airlines, an action unprecedented since 9/11/2001. TSA has kept meticulous records of all passengers on the ground, as the grounded flyers were made to go back through the security checkpoints once the code RED was declared. Cable News will return after these words from your local affiliate."

'Have you ever felt, well, not so fresh? Well, today we...'

Ron clicked off the TV, the room was filled with stunned silence. Without noticing, Sylvania had magically appeared in his lap, curled up inside his arms. Nothing sexual now, purely the need for security, knowledge that nothing would or could hurt her.

"1300 people..."

She said,

"St. Louis, shit that's too close."

Ron was wondering if this was an isolated nutcase or if this was the first shot in a war on U.S. soil. He held Sylvania in his arms until her fear shakes abated. He understood her anguish. She was a teacher; the mass deaths of hundreds upon hundreds of men women and children. Not to mention the unprecedented aftermath, which was going to reach into her classroom. How do you discuss senseless death with children? How do you not?

Soon, he sensed that she had made a decision. Either a way to handle the situation or a decision not to decide right now. Whichever one she had made, she was now laying in the recliner cuddled up to Ron, content.

The British woman's voice caught her off guard; Ron was startled from her reaction, but not from the voice. It was his work alarm. When he was in the streets he had an armada of electronic gadgets between his body and his vehicle. At home, the gadgets all rested in their various cradles: the Uninterruptible Power Source controlled nest of chargers. At home, he would more likely than not be naked or sleeping. Instead of having fire house alarms going off to indicate trouble, he had programmed different personalities to warn him of incoming message traffic.

The British woman was the voice of the current client contract. Her message regarding warm weather on the 15th floor indicated a warm alert in the server department, something that needed very quick attention, but wasn't maximum priority. He explained this to Sylvania, the fact that he had to go into the office to troubleshoot a system problem. She understood, besides, she needed to go home and check on her house as well.

"I've got a few things I need to unknot and take care of, will you be long?"

"No, I shouldn't be, maybe an hour, two max."

"Ok ... well, do you want to see me later?"

"Do birds, pigs and airplanes fly?"

"Two out of three, sounds good to me. By the way, here, it just occurred to me that you don't have my number. I'll be home, call me when you finish what you have to do and I'll see you then."

She stood and held out her arms to help him up, as simple as it was, it was the sweetest gesture he had seen in a long time. Probably something that had she had picked up from the kids, he thought. They hugged, both still bare chested and in towels. Their unquenchable thirst for each other simmered just below the surface. They walked through the house at 50% daylight, gathering clothes from last night, like Easter eggs. The majority of the wayward items were at the front door, right where they had been discarded.

Ron saw the small scattering of pads on the floor, then he noticed the maternity bra. He picked them up in one hand, her skirt, blouse and cardigan in the other. Looking at the first hand he looked a question at her.

She volunteered to physically answer, deftly slipping on the bra with the flaps open, she tweaked her nipples to awaken them to full hardness and carefully slipped on her blouse. Without even buttoning it, Ron could see how prominent her nipples were. They stuck out so thick and rigid. The sight was so sexy to him that another tent shaped erection was in the process of forming beneath his towel. She then closed one nipple access panel on the bra, the effect was nearly identical.

Finally, she inserted the pads into the other nipple access and closed it before buttoning up her blouse. Now he knew the reason for the pads. One breast looked as if you could literally suck it through the blouse, while the other looked as round and smooth as a bullet.

"Nuff said."

Ron told her as he was moving in to plant a dry, lip bite on her still protruding nipple. They kissed. He slid on his pants commando. She shimmied her skirt up over her hips. Her panties, that had made their way into the pile from the futon, were in no condition to be worn right now. So, she balled them up and shoved them into Ron's back pocket.

"Here nasty man, damn, I feel so… naughty. No panties on under my school clothes? What are you doing to me?"

"Let me think about that and we'll discuss it later, how about that?"

"You can count on that conversation mister."

She playfully raised up on her tip toes and gave him a quick kiss, then they made their way to the elevator and her car. Ten minutes later he was on his way to work.

Driving home felt so foreign after her extended one night experience with Ron. Her thoughts were clouded. Ron, she had never met anybody like him. His height, those eyes, and the way he made love; no, the way he fucked. As hard as Barry had tried to get her to talk dirty to him, Ron had made it want to come out of her so easy.

She couldn't believe she had said the things she had, nor the fact that she had liked doing it so much. But now, she was back in her car, her reality. She looked over to the passenger seat and noticed how far back it was, and felt tingles just remembering his being so close. She couldn't help but smile, feeling her swollen, pantiless sex warming the seat, and thinking about where her panties were right now. This was followed quickly by another feeling, guilt. Barry.

He wasn't really her man, he was more like an extended date. She had been with other people since she had started seeing Barry. It's just that this felt so different, like something totally new. Ron made Sylvania not want to be with Barry anymore; that had not happened before. For the first time, it felt like the date was finally over. It was time to go home and consider the next date; but she couldn't see that far. When she thought about being with Ron, she couldn't see anything past that.

She needed to call Barry; her cell phone was on the floor, still connected to the car charger. She waited until she stopped at a light and picked it up. There were four messages, all from Bman1, the name Barry had programmed into her phone. The first text message said: [stuk, all planes grounded, almost have campaign complete, waiting 4 actors 4 comercl cb if any change.] The next message read: [missu lk crazy! Still stuk, planes still grounded, all rentals gone.☐.] The third message was a repeat of the second, the last one had a different tone: [R U O K? no answer 3x, tried 2call no signal. Try u @ home – B.]

She hoped he had a signal, she didn't trust what she may say to a machine. Even though email and text messages were the en vogue methods of breakups nowadays, she was too old fashioned for that.

She rang Barry's number, he answered before the second ring. Old Barry, how was she going to tell him it was over? She didn't want to hurt his feelings, nor did she want to draw it out and hurt herself. She wanted him to know that it wasn't ok to come back. The major problem was that he had done nothing wrong, nothing to deserve this, it was simply his misfortune to have had to work one day too many.

"Hey B,"

"Hey Van, you finally got my messages.

"Yeah… I got them Barry."

"What's wrong Van? I hear wrong all over your voice."

"I … it's this whole terrorist thing that has me down, driving through National Guard checkpoints in Atlanta. It's got me reevaluating some things. Barry, I need some time to myself."

Silence.

"Damn babe, what did I do?"

"No Barry, you didn't do anything babe. It's all me, fickle, menstrual old me, putting my life under a microscope lit by floodlights. I give you permission to go to sleep without me. Handle your business; this is no time to go rushing around the country, and these Guardsmen don't seem to be having too good a time. Remember Kent State? Those were stressed-out National Guardsmen that killed all those kids? So, take your time, do it right. Call me; let me know you made it home safely. Then, I'll call you when I've straightened things out, ok?"

"As you wish, Van. Are you sure it wasn't anything I did?"

"Absolutely."

"Ok, try to feel better, ok?"

"Goodbye Barry."

She hung up gently, even though that didn't matter on a cell phone; a click was a click.

***

The "warm" really should have been a "cool"; but just as well, it needed to be done. One of the secondary web servers needed to be rebooted. The actual servers that facilitated the internet interface were proxy servers that lived in the DMZ. As a matter of routine, he rebooted and defragmented the hard drive anyway. It wasn't exactly a waste of time, and, as he expected, he was done in a little less than an hour.

With time on his hands before he had to see Sylvania, he swung by the upscale Lenox Mall. He was feeling an impulse buy. Stepping into this mall was like walking into an exclusive club; valet parking on every side, Hummers, Ferraris and Bentleys held their place at the front entrance to the material palace. Ron never had been a big shopper. However, when it came to material purchases, he knew what he wanted, found it, bought it and left.

This purchase was simple – a pair of 1.5 carat Diamond earrings with surgical platinum posts, classy, undeniable. Next he went to the Cacao Loco and got a Grande Café Cacao. The earrings had been placed in separate tiny airtight Ziploc bags filled with purified water, Ron dropped the little baggies into the drink and watched them sink to the bottom. Then, he strolled the mall on his way back to the car.

***

She dropped off two briefcases full of cash into a safe deposit box at Wachovia Bank's self-serve access, a 24 hour direct access Concierge service that gave special customers access to their Safe Deposit boxes without having to go through the bank. She did, however, step into the bank where she made a $300.00 deposit into a savings account and added $1,000.00 to a checking account. Mission accomplished, she wanted to go and pick up an IPhone from the Apple Store. She knew that there was one across the street inside the Lenox Mall. It seemed like such a waste even starting up the big V12 Mercedes engine for the trip across the street. She valet parked and went in search of her electronic gadget.

She rode the Tiffany crystal elevator to the second floor and exited a few yards from the store. She was impossible to miss, even in this cumulous cloud of beauty and excess: the four inch heels and mid-thigh, dark purple, body hugging dress left nothing to the imagination. Just knowing how hot she looked caused her prominent nipples to lead the way. Her eyes were hidden behind a large framed pair of black and gold Gucci shades.

Twice Sylvia and Ron crossed over and under one another until finally, Ron was walking up from behind the down elevator as Sylvia came strutting off the moving stairway. The tiny Apple IPhone bag was swinging from the crook of her left arm. Her G-string created the illusion of nudity beneath the dress, and her naturally swaying breasts, which all moved to the rhythm of her own jazz quartet.

Ron couldn't believe his eyes. He knew that body, that hair, his manhood knew too. It reared its stiffening head to say hello as well to the vessel he had been nestled in all night. Ron walked a bit faster, catching up to her profile. Her obviously braless breasts made his mouth water, he felt that he had to take a sip of his drink just to keep from drooling.

As he walked up beside her and her big stiff nipples met his gaze, something clicked in his mind. He turned his head away from her and called her name; no response. He did it again, same thing. She wore no earpiece, no headset so he knew she could hear him, but what he'd said didn't seem familiar to her, her name! Sylvia stepped off the escalator, pleased with her new purchase and amused by the new erections she was leaving in her wake.

***

She was ready to go. Most likely, she would get a room at the X Hotel, then, check in with $ensation, to see what was going on tonight. She still had four more stops to make and the bulk of the cash would be evenly distributed across Atlanta.

Well, well, she thought to herself, what we have here, a giant boy scout with a mission-ready package. He was closing in on her like a heat-seeking missile out from nowhere. Hmmmm, he's tall. She decided to test his commitment. If he passed the test, she would step up her game while she waited for the car. He was calling out to somebody. "Oh well, he must have seen somebody he knew, and they had to be something to have tendered a better offer, oh well".

As the distance between them grew, she put a little more bounce in her walk. She knew he was watching. Ron pulled his cell phone out, he knew it was crazy; he'd had many, many women in his womanizing career. He could remember just about all of them by face, body, or name. But Sylvania was not only the freshest in his mind; she was the game changer. So, he knew even after this short time, that he knew her!

As far as he was concerned, he could recognize her in his

sleep, literally. But now, she's not ten feet away and didn't respond to her own name? He dialed her number, she picked up the phone on the first ring,

"I'm expecting a call, is this who I think it is?"

"Sylvania?"

"Of course, who else were you expecting to answer my number?"

Relief filled his voice but his body was overcome by tension, the woman in the purple dress was not on the phone.

Chapter 23

<u>*St. Louis*</u>

There was nothing normal about this scenario. Now that they had distilled an image of a high priority Person of Interest, she released John Eagle to return to the task he was originally assigned, body count estimation. He had rounded the ground zero and park proper numbers to 1,300. He was now trying to factor shrapnel and other collateral damage. It would take some time and footwork to uncover the number of fatalities from imploding glass, and even more research to ascertain the number of wounded.

These vital statistics were important, but the only thing Kristi could see was the face of the POI. Where was he and where did he come from? Using all the satellite recon they had available, she had determined that he entered the park from the same block that he had fled to. Other than that, he was a ghost. But Kristi was a '70's baby. She grew up watching Scooby Doo and his weed-smoking buddy, Shaggy, and the gang solve mysteries where the ghost always was a mask with a real head beneath. If you had the tenacity to keep going and a little bit of luck, you could solve every case in thirty minutes. The similarities ended years ago, but she still knew that criminalistic ghosts always had a face beneath the mask.

Using the vast computer resources of the MCU, they recreated an almost 3-d image of the POI's face and distributed it electronically to the task force. The numbers had grown geometrically since she had landed here. The actual numbers of feet on the ground was way past her count. The number of field command contacts had grown to fifty, so the octopus had grown prodigious. They all had the picture and were using every modicum of authority granted them by the code RED status. Even though nationally, normal life was being encouraged; National Guard helicopter fly-bys and an increasing number of road blocks did not describe the picture. Americans had not had a normal day in the USA. Beirut maybe, but not here,

A priority tweet came through the MCU communications center. An image was being transmitted, it was marginally grainy, but the resolution was good enough for Kristi to see those black penetrating eyes. The milk chocolate complexion, the nose, was the face they were looking for; she was sure. Kristi printed the screen shot and compared the photos – identical. She didn't want to trust her excitement or her vision, she called for John Eagle. He used his expert vision; he immediately determined that the faces were identical, even though the scar disturbed him just a bit.

"Where'd this come from?"

"Recon team36 looking at the resource allocation grid that puts us right … here".

The grid magnified with her touch, the area was commercial, and it was an art's district. Punching up this grid coordinate brought online all the active cameras in the area including the three man recon team. They saw the large theater complex, zooming in showed a shelf of photos; one of which was the POI with no name caption below.

"Hold position, team leader en-route to sector 36 command, come in."

A moment of silence was followed by

"Go for sec three six command".

"Three six, this is team leader, I've got your current location, under 100 meters from your recon point, verify."

"Copy that loc team leader, we're standing by."

"Link to grid 654 / 520 confirm when synched."

Seconds …

"Synched."

"Copy, ok my birds hot, eta 5 minutes, I need three six above and around when I land."

"Copy that team leader, above and around."

"Team leader out."

Kristi took the two pictures and stepped out to the ready and waiting Blackhawk, the three members of her personal ops team: Phillip, James, and Marcello. She left the five man balance to keep security tight at the MCU. Phillip had her grip in hand. As soon as her ass hit the seat, the Blackhawk's rotors cycled up, angled forward, and shot up and away.

The grid coordinates were already programmed into the hop computer. The FLIR (forward looking infrared radar) unit in the nose had a camera view that was currently checking the horizon for obstructions. They increased altitude to 10,000 feet and maxed air speed, three minutes to target.

Dennis 'Dragon' Kuntz was commander of Section 36 Reconnaissance Operations Team. He was one of 50 teams spread out over the grid searching for the POI, to bolster the on the ground reports to the home office team. Each section was comprised of a full complement tactical operations team. Currently, they were spread out beneath the city and surrounding environs using the tunnels and sewers to get around. Motorized sleds with hydraulic come-alongs were used to transport equipment quickly and efficiently.

Dragon's team was surrounding the theater complex. A four-man contingent was sent out to locate any direct entrances to the basement areas of the building itself. The balance of the team went to coordinated access points to have theater perimeter cohesiveness, in other words, to surround the place.

Reading one minute to engagement.

He gave the countdown to his sub-commanders, every access point was manned by the 'above team'. These teams ensured everyone 'below' got above ground as quickly as possible and into formation, in this case, alternating left and right until the perimeter team met another perimeter team member visually, practice time for perimeter formation: 26 seconds. At: 30 seconds to 'T,' all teams moved out.

***

The stage crew was putting the next coat of shellac on the floor mikes and the other mikes that were hidden in the scenery. The sound vents were covered over with tape and the entire painted unit blended perfectly into fore and background, adhering to their respective areas. The fabric-covered ones were sewn into the upholstery and bedding. In the sound booth, the technician was checking the input levels. Even with the tape in place, the sensitive mikes could pick up the smallest noises.

He was checking for 'house' noise; creaks, transformers, plumbing and refrigerators, anything that would interfere with the fidelity of the show once in progress. In less than a weeks' time they would have preview audiences, time really flew when one was behind schedule.

Wilbert had been doing cut-out rehearsals with portions of the full cast, scene mates. Cue critical people were doing run throughs with the newest cast member, the set. Everyone had to be familiar with their movements around the set and the passes of other members of the cast and crew that would be constantly moving, as the show's life matured.

During these rehearsals, they would pretend the other cast members were there. As the groups cycled through, they would factor in the previous cycle moves; in that way, they that rehearsed overlapped would be practiced before full cast rehearsals. The cast was on a five minute water break; all breaks were held on stage in silence because of the ongoing microphone work.

The technician heard a fluttering noise in his headphones,

he had heard something like it before, but couldn't recall exactly what it was. Then, he heard another fainter sound. It seemed to be a metal scraping, the flutter grew in intensity. He happened to look up into the blacked-out house in confusion.

The next thing he knew, all of the doors in the venue opened at once. The blinding light was quickly blotted out by the dark hulking forms. Panic came over him like a switch. Only now did thoughts of the code RED trickle into his mind, but, something told him that these were not National Guard troops. The fog machines were empty and would not be filled until dress rehearsal, so the air in the theater was clear which made the rhythmically roaming red dots from the laser sights stand out even more. At that point, he lost it altogether. He pushed the stool back and tried to crawl underneath his sound console, no such luck.

Before the rolling stool could come to a halt, he had a Heckler & Kotch Mp5 submachine gun pointed at his head. Behind him which, a face straight out of an Xbox 3000 war game, was glaring at him, the technician passed out.

As soon as Kristi's Blackhawk touched down she was on the ground, with tactical machine gun with the integrated rocket launcher in hand. She wore a Kevlar facemask with the Auto Responsive Filtering System, checking for over 700 detectable breathable toxins including teargas and the full spectrum of pepper sprays.

From outside and above, the exercise was impressive. The perimeter, once established, grew continuously tighter until the building was fully surrounded. Coms had already confirmed that the inside team was working their way upstairs, dividing backstage, orchestra pit and side wings, they would all be covered as they were advancing.

The outer perimeter split, half going in for the raid. The balance at one time taking one step to the left going into perimeter protect mode, guns drawn, pointed outward ready to kill anything that moved. The inside team took over. Within four minutes of the Blackhawks landing, every person inside the theater was sitting on the stage at gunpoint. Kristi identified Wilbert as the likely place to start.

He was taken away to be interrogated. Once he was segregated from the rest, the lobby headshot of Thony and the computer massaged picture of Abdullah were shown to Wilbert. They demanded to know his whereabouts. Everything he could think to say came spilling out of him at helium speed. Cell phones were called, addresses were translated into GPS coordinates. Within minutes, the Tac-laptop showed Thony's house, exterior, as well as the thermal view if the interior confirming the lack of occupancy. Now, the screws tightened. The real interrogation began.

"I swear that this is the address and contact information I have had for five years. If there is any other, I don't know about it."

"When was the last time you saw him?"

***

Robert lay perched between the chimneys on the roof, his sweat suit was turned to the matte black non-reflective side, and the same material covered his rifle and scope. From this perch, he could see ground zero and blocks in either direction. Helicopter traffic was sporadic but consistent. The code RED had lasted longer than he had expected. He had been doing recon of the area from different perches with the onsite headquarters always in view.

He was very careful not to use any type of electronic communication, the interceptor E4 AWACS planes were circling constantly, and no doubt, monitoring any and all electronic signal traffic between towers and satellites. This mission he was on now was entirely reconnaissance, looking for that face. Nothing close had come within his crosshairs, but like himself, he believed in returning to the scene of the crime.

Traffic had been light, very light, vehicular as well as foot. The National Guard's presence everywhere had a lot to do with that, specifically, the black ops types coming and going in this particular area proved to be a major deterrent. He had seen the woman jump into the Blackhawk and roar off about 30 minutes ago. In her absence, some really dark-looking types surrounded the headquarter's vehicle. Robert used his spotter scope to scan up and down the block scanning for live bodies. A small group of kids, all holding hands, were walking towards an apartment building carrying grocery bags. He kept his eye on the street checking everybody for its corresponding face,

"Thony, I want to get out of here, can we go somewhere? The curfew won't fall for a few hours and when it does I'd like to not be here, there's a smell, it..."

"You don't have to say anything else babe, you want to leave, we leave. I will never doubt one of your feelings again. Come on, let me dress you."

This got a wry smile from Suzan.

"So what, you bucking for a wardrobe job now? Tired of working the stage?"

"Let's just say I'm cross training."

"As long as you don't plan on cross dressing ..."

They both had a laugh at that. Thony knew that he would make an ugly woman, adding fuel to his fire. Suzan was thinking that he might be pretty cute adding to hers.

Thony went through Suzan's closet and picked out a dress. He had noticed that when he touched it, it had made her smile, which let him know that it had happy memories attached. He pulled it out and lay it across the bed. It turned out to be a simple wrap-around dress, knee length, kind of swingy with pleats. It was a very simple geometric pattern of ice, royal and sky blues, short sleeved, with a simple cut.

 He went to the other side of the walk-in and chose a pair of two inch high, grayish blue tinted, closed toe pumps. He looked at her for approval; she smiled in acquiescence, agreeing with his choices. Not done yet, he went into her armoire and pulled open her lingerie drawer. He chose a pale lavender teddy with spaghetti straps.

He approached her with the teddy balled up in his hand, bouncing the sheer fabric to see if it would float away on its own. As he stepped to her he offered his hand, lifting her to her feet; he indicated for her to lift her arms above her head.

He unballed the teddy and fitted her hands through the straps. She was standing before him, arms raised, breasts stretched with her nipples looking up at him. He let the teddy slide down her arms; it bunched up temporarily around the swell of her breasts, as he lightly touched her arms back down to her sides, the obstruction cleared.

The excitement of dressing her had caused his manhood to do battle with gravity. The proximity causing him to rise between her legs, her hairs tickling his tip. He pulled the teddy the rest of the way down, forcing himself back and moving to her side. Kneeling, he reached through her legs to grasp the rear half of the crotch closure. As he pulled it through his palm formed a perfect cup for her puffy lips. He leaned in and placed a loving kiss on her clit before attaching the front snap, half completing the absorbent cotton crotch.

He stood and looked over his very own cocoa brown Barbie dol. He walked around to see the rear view; the teddy's panty portion framed her delicious ass so perfectly. There is nothing more beautiful than a black woman's ass in the perfect pair of panties. She stood still as he approached her from the back, still rampant as ever, he slid smoothly into the welcoming gap between her legs. He kissed her on the neck and she moaned, at the same time, she tightened her grip on him.

The volcanic heat on the top of his shaft drove him crazy as he tried to withdraw. She felt his breathing on the back of her neck begin to catch, so she loosened up her grip under protest and allowed him to pull out. He held her arms out so that he could slide the dress on as if it were a coat. Then he walked around front and pulled the tie string around the loop then wrapped the dress and tied the intricate bow at her hip. She stepped into the shoes and was complete, almost.

He took both hands and extended his fingers and fluffed her hair on both sides one good time, laying her beautiful brown locks on her shoulders, perfect. Suzan loved the way Thony had dressed her; she was still trying to figure out how he had known that this was her favorite dress, and that the shoes she had never worn were bought to go with it.

She was outdone; her emotions were everywhere. But right now, and at this very moment, she felt as special as she had ever felt. Standing there, fully dressed, emotionally seduced by her still naked lover man that she had physically seduced, she was impressed. She had never thought having a man put your clothes on could be so sexually stimulating.

Thony was standing in front of her, basking in his creation. He was so hard he was bobbing up and down with each heartbeat; that was because of her, she thought. She took a step closer to him, gripping him with her right hand, stroking his face with her left. She kissed him tenderly. She rotated the burning tip in her palm and dropped her left hand to pick up her hem. She descended to her knees until she was face to head with Thony's hardness. Slowly and sensuously, she licked the palm that was rotating his tip, gripping it and sliding her fist around applying lips and tongue while spinning her gripping hand around the shaft.

She licked and sucked the head only, looking up into his eyes. The tendons on his neck stood out tensely, his head was thrown back in ecstasy as she started to jack him firmly. She toke more and more of him into her mouth, corkscrewing her slick hand, adding another dimension to the mix. She felt him start to move with her giving her some counterforce. She heard a crackling sound and realized he had tightened his fists until his knuckles popped. She felt the throb at the base of his shaft; her mouth filled with his steaming creamy essence. She kept stroking him until he was done. She continued to kiss and lick her lover's magic stick, feeling him shudder with each sensitive post orgasmic touch. She looked up and saw him looking at her with love and appreciation. Now, they felt inseparable.

They walked back to the playroom and retrieved Thony's shoes. He redressed in his grey slacks and periwinkle shirt, a strangely matching color combination. They prepared to leave the house. No matter how much Suzan felt like taking back off the outfit that Thony had dressed her in, she still had the feeling that they needed to leave. They affixed cardboard and duct tape to the windows, then, went back downstairs and out to the street to Thony's perfect parking space.

There! Robert saw a couple coming out of a warehouse loft complex. The man looked somehow different than he had on the day of the bombing. The fanaticism was gone from his face, but the eyes were the same black. He was with a woman, a beautiful black woman, they were dressed in semi matching outfits. Fuck it, so he had a girlfriend. They were going to a car parked right outside the building, about 1.5 blocks down from him on the right. No problem for a shot, but still, he had that nagging feeling in the back of his mind.

He traded the spotter scope for the ocular on his rifle as he sighted in on him, the car pulled off. Robert was about to pack up and take off, it was too late to follow them. He had seen and memorized the license plate for future reference, even though the car was most likely stolen. The presence of the woman disturbed him. She wasn't with him when he blew the park; a mad bomber with a girlfriend? It wasn't unheard of, but it didn't seem to fit the Middle Eastern terrorist profile. Why wouldn't she have been with him during his historic bombing but she's with him now? In the seconds it took Robert to ponder this question, he got an answer to something he never thought to ask.

***

"Son of a BITCH! Are you telling me that this woman he left with lives at the same place we just left!? Contact the MCU, roll section 1, NOW! I'm on my way."

Kristi was fuming, she turned on the captive audience on the stage.

"Not a word, any of you, it would be considered a National Security Felony; you remember Guantanamo after all? That will be like a study hall, we clear?"

"Yes, we are clear ma'am."

Kristi signaled to Dragon.

"Drago, the bastard's in my back yard, I want you back below ASAP until I see where we are, you copy?"

"I copy team leader, abracadabra, we're out, team 36 back to 2 ... ride out."

"Sky, this is team leader."

"Team leader, sky is hovering over your 20."

"Come down."

"10-4"

Kristi strode outside, her personal detail surrounding her. The Blackhawk came down directly in front of Kristi, nobody made a sound, they all knew she was pissed, the pilots only words were:

"ETA 4 minutes."

***

Robert was dismantling his rifle when he heard an unmistakable sound... the "whoomp", "whoomp" of a silenced helicopter. It was so familiar because the same sound just left here some 35 minutes ago, the Blackhawk. Before he could search the sky for its direction, motion on the street caught his eye. He looked up and down the empty street, looked back to the command vehicle, then looked back again and he saw at least 30 black clad commandos, they literally came from nowhere. Robert was amazed. He said,

"What the fuck?"

He grabbed his spotter scope in time to see the last of the black clad figures coming from the manhole and replacing the cover. That was something new, soldiers from the sewers? Once above ground, they were rushing towards the same building the face and the woman had come out from. At that time, the helicopter question was answered as well. It zoomed into view and landed right in the middle of the street.

A woman in body armor, with tits, if you can believe that, hopped out of the chopper. Three men in front and one at the rear; a team obviously trained to protect her, proceeded into the building. Kristi headed up the insertion team. The order was stealth; sneak up on the target, watch out for booby traps. They used fiber optic periscopes to look under the doors to make sure there were no obvious traps set on the knob or hinges before they opened the lock. They spread like fog throughout the loft. As each and every room and hallway was entered, they checked in with

"Clear"

Until the section 1 commander announced

"All clear."

Kristi was livid; she had found and lost the POI within the same hour! They found signs of recent habitation, as well as signs that they should be coming back. Curfew goes into effect in three hours. After six, anyone caught out without reasonable cause could be shot. She would interface her men with the National Guard; each of their teams was about to grow by one.

Chapter 24

Dulcet stepped out of the shower and dried off with a giant sized fluffy beach towel that could have covered a twin-sized bed. She walked through her Florida house. She always felt liberated and open here compared to the house in the mountains where she felt isolated, but on top of the world. It was probably the slitted ocean view.

Her house had the effective exterior façade of an empty vacation home, with the hurricane shutters and storm doors permanently affixed. That way, Dulcet never had to worry about being bothered. She designated a time share company to open, air out, and clean the house under the auspices that another contract was in effect with the actual rental work during the season. Those people didn't exist. She padded through her bedroom, arrived at a chest of drawers and picked up a small, pale, pink contraption. It was called the Trojan.

She had ordered it from a Scandinavian internet company. Basically, it was a sheer pair of bikini panties with a six-inch dildo integrated into the crotch, the base of which was a clit tickler. Once on, they looked like an ordinary pair of panties, only the wearer knew the truth. A series of charms on the waistband controlled the power and intensity. She slid on her Trojan panties, the name coming from the horse that snuck in through the gates and took down Troy. She scooted her anti-static office chair over to the business center of her room and logged onto her system. Because her life was so spread out, she kept a secure server hidden in the mountain retreat that could connect and remotely operate all the other systems she had in the other residences.

She logged on and checked Recipe. The program put her through the usual password protocols, plus four extra steps, because it recognized the remote access. Recipe had updated the ingredients of the currently cooking meals to factor in the code RED, which pushed everything into different directions because of the current National Guard presence.

One meal stood out. It was scheduled to be ready in five days because of the number of Guard troops that had been sent off to various wars all at once all over the world. This meal was cooking in Atlanta; "hmmmn, soul food, nothing like it", she thought. She put an alarm on the soul food meal and signed off. If any changes occurred she would get a message on her phone. Otherwise, a secure menu would come through the computerized phone with all information needed to formulate the perfect insertion and extraction.

She felt good about the general shape of her world, she hit the diamond button on the Trojan and started the vibrations, perceptible but not mind-blowing. She walked over to the treadmill that stood by the boarded up window; the monitor integrated into the machine was connected to the ocean side security cameras. This meant that she could walk and be by the ocean at the same time without leaving the house. Walking while wearing the Trojan took a bit of practice, no vanilla stroll would work. The sexier, hip-swaying walk allowed for proper steps while the hip swivel kept up a nice agitation motion, sort of like a washing machine motion.

She started out at a leisurely pace just to warm up, then, after about 20 minutes she notched everything up. She pressed the shamrock button that caused the Trojan to wiggle back and forth. This added a very pleasant addition to the vibrating sensation on her G spot, eliciting a gut wrenching series of orgasms. She held onto the stabilizer bar as she speed-walked along the beach.

She was freely sweating now, her breasts swinging from side to side, body glowing, and her hair a forest fire raging around her shoulders. She hit the star shaped charm and started her run; this selection added thrusting to the already mind blowing internal acrobatics assaulting her. Dulcet almost stumbled from the additional sensation, but she was a sex trooper. She regained her balance and continued with the pre-programmed running sequence.

Once the full hour and a half program had run its course, the inclined machine lowered and the fast pace slowed down to allow her on fire muscles to cool off. Internally, the 4-way motion was still attacking her. She finally pulled herself away from the machine and fell shakily into the office chair. She tossed her legs outward over the arms of the chair, reclined and rode the wave. With the physical exhaustion, mixed with the sexual oversaturation, and the last of her strength, she clicked the diamond button turning the Trojans power off. She physically winded down through the quakes of her third plateau orgasmic journey. She dozed.

When she awoke, she was still reclined in the chair. The Trojan panties were sopping with her internal cream. The muscles in her thighs and butt were still throbbing from the orgasms and the run. She smiled and stretched like a cat. She brought her legs together and pointed them straight up into the air, then slowly pulled the panties over the swell of her ass. The sticky mess in her crotch allowing the dildo to slide easily out of her with a sticky pop as it exited her muscular depths.

The contraption felt much heavier sliding the rest of the way off her feet than it had when she had put it on. She spun around in her chair and it occurred to her that she was famished. She left the office. On her way to the kitchen, she stopped by the master bath, ran a sink full of warm water, and dropped the Trojan in to soak. After a quick ride on the imported French made bidet, she made her way to the pantry to break out the supplies.

The fresh utensils were still packed in their original containers; she prepared them for their inaugural use. She attacked the pantry, setting out jars of fruits and vegetables, Japanese noodles, a bottle of olive oil and the surgical steel wok. She placed the fire ring on the stove and applied heat to the steel. It was amazing how the new storage technologies could keep food so fresh. The snow peas in their pods came out as if they had just been picked. The kitchen filled with the fresh garden smell of the fresh produce.

The wok had reached its optimum cooking temperature. She added a teaspoon of oil and tossed in all of her ingredients. She worked the mixture expertly with the two scoops.

Next, the chicken and shrimp combination that had been

stored in its soy sauce and saki marinade went into the wok. The smells emanating from the kitchen could have come directly from Osaka. She let the juicy pieces of meat heat up inside the hot vegetables, the marinate mixing with the natural juices resulting in nothing less than perfection.

Within ten minutes, Dulcet had what she needed to replace the vitamins and minerals she had lost working out. She carried the tray into the den. She decided that she would drive to Atlanta tomorrow in order to be in place before Recipe's meal was ready. But for now, the steaming hot bowl in her lap was calling her; chop sticks were a must. She cozied up into her greedily grasping satin-lined lambskin sofa and hit the TV remote.

Dulcet wasn't a big TV watcher. The fake crime shows were boring and ridiculous, just the premise. They would take solved crimes and create an hour long drama showing the incredible prowess and resilience of the star, no matter how bumbling or inept they were. They could solve the most complex cases in an hour or less.

On the flip side, there were the true crime detective shows. Most of these lasted thirty minutes. These shows would run just enough of a criminal's profile information mixed in with the prescribed amount of Crime Scene Investigative technology, photos, and video of forensic labs to convince the average dumb criminal that they too can now pull off the perfect crime.

Unbeknownst to the viewing public, the producers leave out enough information to catch you if you try what you saw step by step; that way they know what your source was once you get caught. The idea that a Television show is going to actually walk you through instructions for the perfect crime is about as feasible as a cellular phone company that advertises in the inner city for all inclusive, unlimited cell phone service with an affordable monthly payment. This info is being constantly monitored by police, FBI, ATF and anybody else that wants to listen in on low budget criminals incriminating themselves. Actual thinking was fast becoming a lost art in the world today; that's why she depended on Recipe.

The worst brain lull was still the news. Despite the fact that she was used to making news and not watching it, she had to tune in. The whole terror alert thing was cramping her style, throwing off the timing of meals coming out of Recipe. So, she felt the need to see what the hell it was all about.

The first report out of St. Louis was a scene of an actual crater with the edges fuzzed out to avoid showing still visible body parts. A spokesman from Homeland Security was doing a press conference at the site in conjunction with the FEMA [Federal Emergency Management Agency] media representative. "The current official count was 1427 people, men, women and children killed at the park site with other collaterally injured people still being sought and listed as unaccounted for. This is a major strike back by the terrorists in the war on terror. The National Guard presence has greatly increased the confidence we have in our ability to keep our cities free from any further provocation.

So, at this time, we ask for your ongoing patience and cooperation regarding the roadblock checkpoints, re-routed freeways and the curfews. They are for your protection. Thank you". "There you have it ladies and gentlemen, over 1400 dead at ground zero in St. Louis. The threat level remains at RED until further notice. We have integrated the Alert Trac system here at the network. While watching any network show, the outline of your screen will indicate the threat level color. Mainly, it will be used to inform the public when the level drops down from RED to ORANGE or below. In lighter news, the Tennis Tournament is going into the finals today with Rodger Federer defending his title against the top ranked Russian, Sergy Nikozolv. But, the real excitement is shaping up in the women's ranks".

Dulcet got up to take her bowl into the kitchen to rinse it out as the sportscaster started to rave about somebody named Dutchess Singletary.

"First planets, now Royalty, what's next? Lexus? Mercedes?"

To Dulcet, sports were also a waste of time. Being a solo-sexual person, she had no need for teams unless they were victims. She strolled back to the sofa and caught the tail end of the tennis story. She saw just a glimpse of a red pony tail that looked the same color as hers. Her pulse quickened as her physical eye caught sight of what her mental vision was too slow to pick up, something wasn't quite right.

Chapter 25

The pomp, the circumstance, the ceremony, the crowd, the Finals, had been the most exciting ride of Dutchess' life. She ran through the rounds, beating the players ranked internationally on a world class stage. She couldn't believe it on one hand; on the other, she had worked hard every night on the rooftop of the hotel doing her specialized workout. In this short time she could feel herself getting stronger, more agile. The biggest change from last night's workout and the others was Franz. He was not allowed to work out with her because the end of the fourth round found the empty bracket filled by Anastasia Bjorkman, of Sweden, one of Franz's countrymen.

Thus, one part of her workout, that she had come to enjoy, the actual one on one human competition, compared to the machine play and solo mental preparation, was taken away. She missed it. But, she still felt prepared and strong. There was a twinge of excitement, not necessarily fear, but the competitive thrill of having a real opponent.

Not that the last ones were not pros, they were ranked in the world. Their skills had surpassed many others before she had come along. But this Swede had beaten as many people in this tournament as she had in the past tournament. She was a force to be reckoned with, not to be taken lightly. Dutchess worked harder by herself than she had with Franz. She remembered every defense he had used against her, knowing that if he was a National sports treasure in his country, his under-coaches idolized him for his accomplishments. Therefore, they would teach his theories and defenses as though they were Holy writ.

Then, she projected Bjorkman onto the other side of the court. She worked her slices, increased the power of her backhand, and worked some special tricks that she had held back from Franz. She had only divulged what she was working on at the time; professionally, he was still the enemy. He had no idea how balanced her strength was. She favored her left side when she played him. That was why she only played him after her own private skills practice and warm up sessions. Her transport arrived with Henry already waiting, a package in his hand.

"Dutchess you are looking as radiant as I have ever seen."

"Thanks Henry, is there a reason for this command appearance?"

"I wanted to remind you about the available photo ops following the Finals."

"I'll be sure to keep those things on my mind Henry. Boy, you sure know how to ..."

"No, no, no, you'll do nothing of the sort! I said, I'm here to remind you, you only do one thing Dutchess. Our thing, that is: they both said,

"Play tennis."

"That's right, play tennis; I got the rest handled."

Henry kissed her on the cheek and wished her luck.

"After all the hoopla, we have some things to discuss, ok?"

"You bet."

They pulled to the players drop off entrance. The red carpet was out, and the photographers were swarming. Henry led the way, reminding Dutchess to remain upright, bag casually slung over her shoulder, and not to rush. Let them take their pictures; her outfit was perfect, the same one that she had worn the entire tournament. It had become a story of its own. The 'Good Luck Gear', as it had been dubbed, was collected, hand-washed nightly in distilled water, dried, and returned to her room along with her half grapefruit breakfast and cherry filled Godiva chocolate. This turned out to be free publicity that Henry couldn't have paid for; it was great.

Adhering to Henry's rules, she kept her six-foot frame upright, bag casually resting over her shoulder. There was nothing she could do about her vivacious walk. As she shook and swayed, the crowd before her parted obediently. There was another thing that Henry had told her to do, it seemed silly and unnecessary when he had said it in the car, but now …

She stopped and looked quickly back over her shoulder as if someone that she recognized had called her name. The cameras were right on cue as they snapped. She looked questioningly, they snapped; she smiled, they snapped. Continuing the genuine full-faced smile, she waved. They continued to snap as her forward progress resumed. Henry was a genius!

That impromptu photo shoot was perfect; she felt it. The crowd outside the stadium was packed. It wasn't until she had gotten most of the way in that she realized that there was not one seat empty. There was standing room only, a term that just that moment had meaning to her mind, all sold out, and no more seats. Everybody was here to see me. Just the idea sent a sexual thrill through Dutchess' body. She could tell that she had gotten a bit wet from all the concentrated attention. She waved, the crowd screamed, she could get used to this. She felt like a rock star.

This was the way Venus and Serena were used to being greeted, she paid attention to every nuance. Bjorkman came to her seat on the opposite side of the judge line to her own screams and applause. Dutchess took a small sip of water and pulled out her racquets while awaiting the line judges' invitation to the court. As the unseeded player, she was invited last. That was ok; she didn't intend on being unseeded for long.

As she was stepping onto the court, she repeated her mantra: one game at a time, one game at a time; win by two, win by two; game set match, game set match. The Swede had won the toss and decided to serve. The first serve of the Championship was an ace, 110 mph, not bad for a girl, Dutchess thought. But, it wasn't the ace that was the problem, it was the smile. The Swede gave Dutchess a totally condescending smirk that conveyed all of her European confidence that she was entitled to and was going to defeat her. Mistake, which put Dutchess in the zone.

The next serve came; her method of practicing with faster

and faster serves caused the incoming ball to seem as if it were moving in slow motion. The look that came over Dutchess' face was captured and displayed in the next week's Sports Illustrated. She smashed the serve back, directly into her body.

Bjorkman was so unaccustomed to having her power serve returned, that she paused. Her reaction causing the serve to go to Dutchess. She played fabulously. The first set catching Bjorkman off guard, not having much to study from outside of tournament replays, the result 6-2, Dutchess. After the first game, Bjorkman recovered. From then on, it was furious competition. When the dust settled, it was 6-2, 6-7, 7-5 (10-8) with Dutchess winning the tiebreak. She had done it; she'd won her first major tournament. She fell down on her knees, hands thrust up into the sky and let loose a thunderous cry of joy.

The photographers had a ball chronicling her excitement: the tears, the laughter, added to the pictures from before the match. She had an impressive portfolio from her first major tournament. After the ceremony, where she was awarded the Tournament Cup, she thanked everyone on the tournament committee, her friends, old and new. She warned the world that she was now here. As a result of her win, Dutchess was now seeded; she was ranked 48th in the world. She had never been so happy. She spent more time crying tears of joy than she ever thought possible. Henry had been in the stands rooting her on, he was impressed. Usually, he would be behind the scenes making things happen, but this was the finals. For one of the first times, he used the tickets that came with his position as manager. After watching her performance, he looked at her with a new-found respect. She was remarkable, and he knew that he would now work much harder for her. Not that he was slacking now, but he felt as if he were.

As he passed the box office on his way to see Dutchess in the locker room, he was informed that there was a delivery for him. He retrieved it and continued on to see his star. The crowd of well-wishers and fans was much thicker than it had been on the way in; Henry had to grab a pair of security guards to escort him through the throng to get to his charge. She beamed upon seeing Henry, holding up the cup. He saw the little girl come out on her face. Henry stayed by her side through the interviews and autographs. At the first sign of fatigue, he shut it down. Surrounded by security, they made their way to the transport loading area to wait for their limo.

Before Dutchess could step to the limo, Henry whispered something to their lead security guard then disappeared. Puzzled by his strange behavior, Dutchess tried to run after him, but, thought better of it and stayed put with the security detail. Damn, she was big time, she rated security now. Just then, she saw the Chrysler 300 limo coming her way. But there was something different about it, on the panel separating the front and back doors was a sign. It looked to be painted onto the car in gold. It was her logo, the tiara D, and the D was sparkling like it was made of diamonds; it was so beautiful. This day kept getting better and better.

They piled into the Diamond D 300 and took off to the hotel with well-wishing fans clapping on both sides of the road. Henry pulled out the package he had been holding earlier,

"I didn't want to distract you earlier, but this package came this morning."

The package contained pictures of models; models all made

up to look like her with similar body types. They had on outfits similar to what she wore now, and others on both spectrums, super sexy to ultra conservative.

"Where did these come from?"

"One of the meetings I had over the last few days, along with shoes, equipment, vitamins and vehicles; a small French company was interested in creating a fashion line for you, on court and off. I thought that it would be a good tie-in to have a European company for one of your first endorsements. You know since they still do the whole royalty thing, it would be a natural."

The arrival at the hotel was one more part of her new life. Stepping out, she noticed that the brackets had been replaced with a huge board hanging in the atrium. On it was her, holding up the same trophy that was in her hands right now. The caption read 'Congratulations, we knew you could do it!'

Once again she began to cry, the employees made a dual line for her to walk through leading to the elevator. She and Henry went up to the room; the staff had set out Godiva chocolates all over like a golden Easter egg hunt revealed. She threw herself backwards onto the bed and gazed at the ceiling while eating a chocolate and exhaling very loudly.

"It's really real, huh Henry?"

"Yep, you did your thing miss lady, now it's time for me to do mine."

"And what are you going to do Henry?"

"Dutchess, I'm going to make you rich."

"Do I want to be rich Henry?"

The question caught him slightly off guard, but not totally. To know Dutchess Singletary was to expect something different.

"Well, I'd say yes. Simply because it makes it easier to play more tennis, which will raise you through the ranks faster than not playing; yeah, I'd say being rich is the best road to number one."

"Oh, well if you put it that way, go ahead Henry, make me rich."

Henry pulled out the catalog of people he had spoken to and the different deals they had on the table depending on which round she had gone home in.

"Remember, they had heard about you, but they didn't know that you had what it took to go all the way like we did."

"You thought I was gonna win Henry?"

She sat up on her elbow to look him in the eye.

"Of course I did, I'd never deflate the winning energy of my client. You wanna run for President of the USA? I'm behind you 100%, as a matter of fact, after today's performance, I think you could win."

"Get out of here Henry!"

"Seriously Dutchess, there's no doubt that I think you can win any contest you enter. Let's get something straight here lovie. I like you a lot, as a matter of fact I love you Dutchess Singletary. As a matter of fact you're not just my friend D, you are my job. I have to do for you so that I can eat, and in order for my 15% to be fillet mignon and not Taco bell, I have to work hard for you. So, you get rich, I get to eat consistently." He looked at her seriously, she looked back the same way. Then, cracked a smile and threw a chocolate at his head which he caught with ease.

"I'll always feed you Henry, I can't afford to have to put a kite string around your foot to keep you from floating away."

"That's comforting D, oh, and by the way I had a talk with…"

The knock on the door distracted his thought.

"You expecting somebody?"

She shrugged her shoulders,

"Maybe it's my first groupie."

"I'm looking into body guards as soon as possible."

Henry said as he walked to the door and looked out the peephole.

"Well, speak of the devil, almost."

Dutchess sat up on the edge of the bed to see who Henry was opening the door to. It was Franz.

"Dutchess, I'm at a loss for words, I'm sure it won't last long, but a loss nonetheless. I'm saddened by my country's loss, by my team's loss, by my player's loss. But, at the same time, I'm elated by your victory. I am so very proud to know you and am intrigued by the offer made by your manager."

At that she looked a question at Henry,

"We were just getting to that right before you knocked Franz, come on in, sit down. As I was starting to say before,

Dutchess, I had a talk with Franz, as you asked me to, regarding his possible availability for private coaching. He said, well hell. You tell her, Franz."

"The fact that I'm here Dutchess should be indicative of the fact that I've thought about you, your incredible skills and your drive to win. Admittedly, I've had some reservations, simply because whatever you have been doing on your own is working. After the first time you beat me, I knew there was success in whatever your coach was using to condition and prepare you for your matches.

Then, I discovered that your coach never really worked with you, that you were basically self-motivated, followed by the sex scandal involving Lou and his young players. That is when the origin of your rage-directed determination came clear. That's when I made my decision, as I mentioned to Henry, that I will keep room in my schedule for you, outside of my country; you will be my priority.

I want to spend some initial time preparing a conditioning program, looking into your diet, etc., to keep you healthy and strong. These are the two things, without which, you cannot be a champion."

"Dutchess, I don't want you thinking about replacing me too. I also worked on the other lead you gave me. Carlos, the guy from Coca Cola brands, I've got a meeting set with him about an hour and a half from now. You guys talk, I'll set the specifics and call you with the exact when and where."

"Ok Henry, I'll talk to you soon."

"Good talking with you Henry, we will surely be speaking again very soon."

Henry left. Dutchess and Franz were standing in the short hallway by the door. She was looking up at Franz.

"Sorry I beat up on your countrywoman."

"You are the better player, you deserved the win."

"So you're not mad?"

"I told you, I'm a fan of yours; your game is pretty good too."

This comment made Dutchess blush. The heat rising to her cheeks also sent a chill running down her body. The chill stiffened her nipples against the restrictive sports bra, creating small hard bumps nowhere near representation of her true excitement level. Automatically, she crossed her arms and cupped her breasts. Franz watched her response to the compliment, paying attention to the range of emotions flashing across her eyes.

He touched her elbow intending to lead her to a seat, he felt her shiver and her eyes closed. Instead of being led away to a chair, she turned into him embracing. She laid her head on his chest, wrapping her arms around his waist and squeezing tight. He embraced her right back. Visions of the last time they stood in this hallway filling his thoughts: the slight split of the robe, and the tiny glimpse of the fiery red bush. His erection instantly sprung up against her, running down and straining against his left pant leg.

She felt the throbbing fleshy response to her hug against her lower belly and smiled a nervous smile into his chest. It had been more than eight months since she had been with a man. Her last lover, Camille, had left her for another woman. Her excuse, too much time on tennis courts playing with balls and not with her.

She was nervous. Would this tall, strong, Scandinavian man, her new coach, be any better than Lou if she went to bed with him? Just as this thought crossed her mind, Franz tipped her chin up to him and he kissed her. Gently, yet, firmly on the lips, then his tongue invaded her lips and eased its way into her mouth. He wrapped his arms around her tightly she jumped up onto him, and coiled her legs around his waist.

He turned and effortlessly walked them over to the bed. Still kissing, unwilling to break the embrace, he sat with her in his arms on his lap. He urged her shirt apart from her shorts, breaking the kiss just long enough to pull it over her head, revealing the sports bra with the hard little nipple prints.

He rubbed his hands all over the encumbrance trying to find a pathway inside. Then, he found the key. The curious hook and eye mechanism was simple enough. After some digital exploration, the last hook came loose. The 32b breasts that he was expecting to see bloomed to their rightful 36c. His intake of breath and the look in his eyes telegraphed his pleasant surprise. Allowing her time to take off her bra, gave him the opportunity to remove his Polo shirt exposing a lightly haired muscular chest. She massaged his chest, then, pressed her hard nipples against him, teasing them through the hair, then going in for another kiss.

They ran their excited hands up and down each other's bodies, feeding the sense of urgency to both to be totally nude. She unlocked her legs from around his waist and pushed him down. He used the position to kiss each one of her nipples in turn, flicking the sensitive tips rapidly. She rolled off him while loosening his belt; then, she unbuttoned his pants.

She lay back with an efficient shove, and rid herself of panties and shorts in one motion. They dangled from the ankle of one foot, forgotten as she turned her attention back to him. He had lifted his butt to slide the pants and boxers down. While he was kicking off his shoes to make room to discard the pants, he heard her gasp. She was looking at the thickest penis she had ever seen. It was sculpted for work, big work. He had length, but the width was outstanding. He caught her eye with an expression that said his exception had been a deal breaker before. She responded by reaching out and encompassing it in both hands, like her tennis racquet and smiling.

"I like a challenge."

Is all that she said? His apprehensive look disappeared and he grabbed her. They rolled over twice, until she was back on top. She looked down at him and asked if he had any condoms.

"Well, no, I didn't have any idea we would be getting up to anything like this."

Her expression faltered, but only momentarily.

"Ok, I know."

She began to kiss her way down his face, throat, chest, and belly. He reached over to palm her beautiful breasts, tweaking her long nipples. She continued to kiss down his body; he was waiting for her kiss to stop at his sex, when it bypassed it completely. He opened his eyes to the sight of her smooth body passing over him like a slow moving freight train. He stretched his neck to kiss each passing piece of real estate. He felt her squirm as he tongued her belly button. Then, the little turf of   fiery red pubic hair was right on his nose.

Not as thick as he'd thought it was, her parted lips with the swollen clit poking through, was clearly visible from his vantage point. He wanted to lick and suck the prize so much. But, she had by passed, so would he. They were laying on their sides in a stretched out '69'.

"Well, since we don't have any rubbers, I guess we'll have to try something else, what do you think?"

"In matters of tennis, I coach, in matters of Dutchess, you coach."

"Good answer."

With that said, she filled one hand with his balls, and with the other, wrapped as much as it could around his shaft. She kissed his thigh and started to juggle and stroke, varying her pressure with both randomly. Franz in turn began to lick up and down her inner thighs. He reached over her hip and brought one hand through from the back, using two fingers like a peace sign he held and spread her lips. The other hand he brought from the front stroking between her lips; his wet journey ending by circling round and round on her hard slippery clit.

Mirroring Dutchess, his hands began to move in unison, his fingers becoming so slippery they began to slide in and out of her muscular depths. His middle finger was joined by two more. Her tightness felt as if it would break them off, the pleasure she gave in return made his eyes cross. As she stroked him, their movements mimicked the coordination of hard lovemaking. His fingers felt so big, she really wondered how she was going to fit his thick-ass prick inside her. But, she would find a way.

His fingers were feeling so good stroking into her as his thumb caressed her clit, "Oh shit, what was he doing", she thought? She started to jerk him faster while blowing moist hot air onto his leaking tip. It wouldn't be long now; but damn, she was about to come hard too. She couldn't remember her last male/female mutual masturbation induced orgasm, nor did she believe it had been this good. Franz started pulsing in her hand. She could feel the base start to jump, that was when he slid a slippery thumb up her ass. He still had three fingers inside her; that set her off. Her entire body cramped; Franz's fingers were unable to move, despite the hot juice that flooded his palm and down his wrist. His thumb was locked in her ass. She spun his tip around in her wet fist so smoothly, then, before he could acknowledge it, he was coming.

She continued to jack him; her strong grip caused his semen to shoot like a porno star. She aimed the come all over her breasts, the last spurt hitting her on the bottom lip, as her head thrashed back and forth from the force of her own orgasm. She licked it off, force of habit. Now, she was dying to take the drooling head into her mouth and suck it clean. But instead, she continued to squeeze the rest out and rub the tip across her hard nipples, relieving him of all that he had.

He was experiencing the same hunger to put his tongue somewhere, anywhere to taste this delicious woman. After all, it was right there, but he followed the rules set by Dutchess. He looked down and saw the wonderful sight of his come all over her beautiful tits, and his dick belched another shot of come. That had never happened before.

He stuck his fingers into his mouth and sucked her come off of them, luxuriating in the muskiness of her. This was some woman. That had been, by far, the best non-penetrating sex he had ever experienced, and to think safe sex in Sweden consisted of conversation. They lay there in the special afterglow of shared masturbatory orgasms, nowhere near the guilt of all out sex nor the worries associated. It could have been the 1970's for the way they felt. They raised up from bed with his hands, and wrists and arms a sticky mess; her chin, breasts and stomach the same.

They got up and walked together to the bathroom locking the privacy chain along the way. They turned on the shower and spent the next twenty minutes washing and sliding against each other's soap slippery bodies.

Franz was slipping and dipping dangerously close to sliding inside Dutchess. She was pushing and rotating her hips, so wet and horny she almost wanted it. The teasing dance lasted until he actually notched the bullet shaped head inside her lips. They froze in place; one move by either one of them, and there would be no turning back. Franz firmly gripped Dutchess' wet-ass cheeks, moved his strong hands around to clutch her slim waist at the very top of her hips, and pulled back from her.

He was so glad that he had when he did. Standing there, remembering the intense feeling, his dick began to bob, then he shot another load all over her soapy ass. The shower washed it away. They rinsed the rest of the way off, stepped out, and towel dried each other.

They sat, Dutchess in a robe, Franz fully dressed, and discussed what had just happened and what had almost happened. They decided on a perfect balance of mentor, coach and secret lover. If it became known, that was ok too. They were both grown and single and no one was getting hurt; they would keep it under wraps as long as they could. She kissed him goodbye, promising to see him later since the planes were all still grounded and everyone's stay was extended.

Franz left to get some rest and buy some condoms. Dutchess looked for the perfect thing to wear to her meeting with Henry and Carlos' boss. She removed a suit bag from her luggage, which contained her winner suit. She had tried it on the day she had packed. Looking at herself in the full length mirror, she knew that she looked as if she had just won the world.

So, she had packed that outfit and accessories separately, and vowed only to open and wear it if she won. Now, the outfit was on time. She opened the zip bag and removed her robe; naked, she reached into the bag and removed a sheer silk thong with a French band that made it invisible. She stepped into the thong, it was so light, and it was as if it wasn't there. To match the thong, she had an au naturale bra of the same material. She connected the front clasps and pulled on the simple black dress, classic.

The LBD fit her perfectly. It hugged every curve that she had like a coat of paint; the dress came to ¾ thigh high, just above her knee. The diamond tiara stud earrings and pearl necklace were the extent of the jewelry. Finally, the three-inch black pumps made the outfit complete. She was in the mirror arranging her hair when the phone rang. It was Henry.

"Hey, Dutchess, you ready?"

"I was just doing my hair."

"Good. I know you're looking perfect. Coca Cola is doing it really big for the tournament winner. They are courting you babe, unlike any boyfriend you've ever had. We are going to experience the best of the best tonight honey; don't trip."

"Ok, I'm not tripping".

"We're going to a private revolving restaurant overlooking Miami Beach. I've never been there myself, so it'll be a first for both of us. I'll be downstairs in about fifteen minutes; look for your Tiara D. The car is white and they said it's an upgrade."

Chapter 26

Atlanta

"Baby, where are you right now?"

"Exactly?"

"Yeah, exactly."

"I'm in my bedroom changing clothes. Now, I'm walking into the closet. Why am I giving you this play by play Ron?"

"Because I could swear, on two stacks of Bibles, that you are right this moment, twenty feet in front of me wearing a dark purple dress."

"That's crazy Ron, how could you think that?"

"Babe, I walked up to this woman. You know I know what you look like from the front and the back, right?"

"Well you should, I'd suspect."

"Right. I saw you, see you, I'm trippin. I called your name out loudly, and the woman that looks like you didn't respond at all. Maybe I am trippin."

"You got to be babe, after me, they broke the mold."

"Yeah, you're right."

"Ron, you don't sound too good, you wanna come over here?"

"Is there a park near your house?"

"Yeah, there's a big park right down the road."

"Ok, cool, I'll come get you and we'll go to the park."

"Ok, I'll text you the directions to my house."

"Bet, I'll be to you in about thirty minutes."

They hung up. It was common knowledge that if you were on the freeway in Atlanta without traffic, you could get from any A to B destination in about thirty minutes. Ron was going to test the theory today. The Sylvania looking woman was still walking up ahead. She was pushing through the revolving door approaching the valet.

He picked up his pace a bit to try to catch what kind of car she was picking up. He came through the door in time to see her pull up the dress farther almost until her ass was visible, then slide into the cockpit of a maroon big body Mercedes. It was at least a 600 series and brand new. He was sure that wasn't the car Sylvania drove to teach fourth graders everyday...

Sylvania stood in her full length mirror inspecting herself. She wanted to see what Ron saw when he looked at her. He had sounded so weird on the phone, describing some other woman as if he were looking at her. She turned around and looked back over her shoulder at the curve of her back where it flowed into her ass. The way her cheeks stood firm and proud all the way down to the concave indentations that formed her slight gap, making room for her fat poonani to nestle and live.

She gazed at the naturally progressive flow of her thighs into her calves. She was sure there couldn't be anyone else that looked like her that much, could there? But the man that saw this woman had not two hours earlier left her body. Nobody should have known her by sight better than him. She started to wonder, as women do, if she was actually as unique as she had always suspected she was. If the man that just finished making love to her all over his house, all night long, couldn't recognize her compared to some miscellaneous woman walking. Where was he anyway?

She couldn't remember the background noises she had heard, but there were some. He was probably inside and people were walking, but that could have been anyplace from an office building to a train station to the Underground. She would have to wait until he got here and find out. She pulled out a summery outfit to wear to the park. It was a long wrap-around, dark, lime green and white skirt, matched with a short sleeved translucent wrap blouse of summer weight poplin. She wore a pair of hemp fiber sandals, and an ivory and onyx choker.

Twenty seven minutes later Ron pulled up to her front door. As he was approaching, she pulled open the door before he had the chance to knock and swished past him heading towards his car with her purse slung over her shoulder. She got to the car, stopped and turned around waiting for him.

"Is that what you saw Ron? Did she look like me like that?"

Ron slowly walked to the car, he approached with his arms open, and she stood defiantly, testing his will and memory. He took one more step and she closed the distance and wrapped her arms around him, he felt the need to be holding her when he told her;

"Yes, that is what I saw, but she had on a short purple dress, pumps and she was driving a 600 SEL Mercedes from this year."

"You can look me in my face and tell me that?"

"Baby, I deal in details for a living, when I saw her my body told me it was you, I actually thought you had come back out and followed me, as strange as that sounds. That's why I called you, baby you have to know what it took for me to make that call. I needed to see if she would answer the phone, it was that serious, and it was uncanny."

Sylvania looked into his eyes as he explained, she was feeling this man, and she saw the distress in his face as he told her what had happened. She decided to chalk it up to mistaken identity and reclaim her day with her man.

"It's ok baby, whoever she was, she wasn't me, had she been, she would have done this."

She reached up and pulled Ron's head down to her level and gave him a deep passionate kiss. He wrapped his arms tighter around her, his quick onset-stress melted away. He ran his hands along her back, cocked his head, not breaking the kiss. She smiled. They broke the kiss, she smiled again up at him, and winked. This time, he kissed her.

She gripped his ass, pulling her all into the kiss, as his hands slid their way down to caress, what he thought would be, her silky panties. He felt none. Sylvania was naked as the day she was born beneath the pretty summer outfit. As they finally pulled apart, Ron looked at her with an amazed expression on his face, he asked,

"What about the special bra? No panties?"

"You bring something out of me. When I left my panties at your house and drove home, that was the first time I can remember ever being fully dressed without any underwear on."

She rose up onto her tippy toes and whispered into his ear,

"While I was just sitting there, feeling my pussy rubbing on the seat, I was driving in broad daylight."

She stepped back,

"It made me feel so nasty and free at the same time. I have you to thank for that. Then when you wanted to go to the park, I figured, hell, what better place to feel free? Just in case I lost my nerve, I put a pair of emergency panties in my purse."

"No need to worry about your nerves babe, I wanted to go to the park to chill and stroll around and lay back with my baby."

"And who the hell is your baby, mister?"

"That'd be you m'lady."

She smiled hugely as she took the proffered door and sat on the sun-warmed leather seat. Ron walked around to the driver's side, got in, and drove off towards the park. They left the car by the nature trail and walked for a while, hand in hand, until they wound up at a grassy glen atop a tree-lined hill. They held hands and continued to stroll looking at the grass and blue sky. Ron sipped on his coffee drink and offered some to Sylvania. She sipped the strong chocolate drink; he told her to go on and finish it. She enjoyed the taste; so, she shrugged and sipped the rest through the straw. When it was all gone she shook the cup. It sounded as if there were ice cubes inside, even though the drink wasn't cold.

"What the hell?"

"What babe?"

"It sounds like there's something in this cup."

"What do you mean? There shouldn't be, you finished it didn't you?"

"Yeah, well listen.

She shook the cup and indeed it did sound as though there was something rattling about inside the black coffee cup.

"Take the cap off, let's see what it is."

She ripped the lid off expecting to see some foreign object left from the coffee shop. What she saw was two shiny objects in tiny plastic bags.

Had she been more street savvy, she would have recognized the tiny zip lock bags that crack cocaine is sold in on the streets of the inner city. But, these baggies didn't hold any type of controlled substance. Inside each one was a titanium posted 1.5 carat diamond stud earring. They were brilliant cut and of magnificent quality. She stopped in her tracks, staring into her palm, her mouth slowly dropped open. Disbelief washed over her face; finally, she looked over at Ron.

He was looking up at the sky, around into the trees, anyplace but at Sylvania. She stared at him forcing him to look at her. His smile, ear to ear, and radiant, could not be contained. As soon as she saw it, she jumped up into his arms and wrapped her legs around him. She squeezed him so tightly she shook. She put her lips to his ear and said,

"This is the nicest surprise I've ever gotten. I can't believe how much you've impacted my life."

Her tears were flowing freely now, her body still shaking against him.

"I thought about what you said, how you were in "like" with me; that was so cute. But, damn, I called my friend on my way home. I broke up with him, Ron. I've made some room in my life for you, in case you want to sing a few more duets or something."

She realized she was moving, Ron had palmed the round cheeks of her ass and had started walking with her held up on him. Her legs were wrapped around his waist and her head rested on his shoulder as if she were eight years old and he was her daddy. He walked to the top of the small hill and set her down on the grass. It was a sun dappled spot with little beams of sunshine radiating through the leafy shade. They lay back. Ron pried open her still clenched fist and removed the two small bags. He opened one and shook out the glittering wet gemstone into his palm. He twinkled it in front of her eyes to emphasize the reason for the name, brilliant cut. Then, he gently held her earlobe and inserted the titanium post into her empty hole and screwed the custom security backing into place.

He sat back and admired the look, which was as classic as Dorothy Dandridge or Lena Horne. She turned her head to allow him to put on the other earring. Now, when he looked at her, she looked exquisitely finished to perfection.

They chilled there on their secluded hill, watching the clouds float by, enjoying each other's company. They spoke of their favorite pets (dogs), fears (drowning and fires), and all the small things that lead to big comfort. Then, their talk turned to fantasies. Ron, being the man that he was, said that his fantasy was to meet a woman as perfect as Sylvania. Now that he had, he was in need of an entire new set of fantasies. She, on the other hand, had fantasies all the way back to her childhood that she had never fulfilled. The ability to talk dirty, and be as confident as she was now during sex, was a fantasy that she never knew she had.

She thought it was something her last lover wanted. But once Ron persuaded her into it, she realized the amount of freedom and increased pleasure that came from being able to say what you want and get it instantly. There was no feeling like it: no shocked looks, and no comments about her language. This new confidence was driving other fantasies to the surface, such as, sitting here on the cool grass, naked, with her wrap-a-round beneath her.

"Ron?"

"Yeah baby."

"Would you think I was strange if I told you that I wanted to take my clothes off and lounge with you in the sunshine naked?"

"Would I think, well, no, not particularly. Why, is that what you're feeling?"

"Yeah, will you pull my strings?"

Ron's excitement was surprisingly organic; no rampant horniness came over him at the thought. He just reached over and pulled the tie at her hip, then tugged at the cord near her waist. At first, both pieces hung there, deciding to deal with or defy gravity; of course, gravity won. The slow sliding of the skirt material whispered across her thigh towards him. The weight of her breasts caused the blouse material to part gently.

Now, they were framed as a vest, and her thighs were displayed as if on exhibit in a museum. She layed her skirt out to the sides like a blanket and shrugged the blouse off her shoulders. She was magnificent. Her beautiful brown skin with the jet black hair cascading down, made her look like a goddess. The pose that she assumed was reminiscent of the pinup poster of Pam Grier from the '70's, except for the brilliant blast of light and color every time the sun hit her earlobes.

She had her eyes closed feeling the sun on her face. He sat back and watched her marveling in the fact that she was his, if he wanted. He could do whatever he wanted: lick a nipple, open her legs, and turn her into a quivering mass of pleasure. Or, even, pull her up, put her legs over his shoulders, and find her wet and ready to receive him. But to sit here and watch her was so much more sensuous than any action could be. The teacher, Miss Collins, was teaching him lessons in sensuality.

She opened her eyes and his erection bolted. It was like

being in a voyeur, caught looking even though you've been invited. Her beautiful eyes looked lovingly at him, as if all the things that had passed through his mind had gone through hers too.

Ron looked around and saw people far off in the distance. He chose not to tell her, for now, she was so peaceful. He leaned over and kissed her. As they slowly kissed, he reached up and fondled a breast; he stopped when the kiss did.

"Congratulations babe."

"For what Ron?"

"For crossing another threshold, this doesn't seem like the action of a woman with a pair of emergency panties in her purse."

He smiled at her, she beamed back.

"Let's go dancing Ron, no singing, no stage, just some out of the spotlight dancing."

"Ok, we can do that."

Ron stood up and offered his hand to help her stand, all he could do was shake his head. Her total nudity, outside, exposed to the elements, was turning her on so much. The warm air was making her nipples quiver, they were so stiff. As he knelt to retrieve her skirt and blouse, he could see the telltale traces of liquid creeping down her thigh from her apex. He handed her the two pieces of clothing and ran a finger up her inner thigh capturing the liquid, then, sucking the finger, "mmm, rose petals."

Shocked by his action, her mouth flew open and she

reached out to him for support as a strong quake rolled visibly through her body. Sylvania reached into her purse and pulled out the white silk bikini panties and slid them up her thighs before redressing.

"You are dangerous you freaky man."

"You just don't know my love, it's all for you."

Chapter 27

Sylvia checked into a suite at the X hotel. The first thing she did was to log onto the internet and activate her phone. Once activated, she called $ensation.

"Hey girl, what's up?"

"Shootin my reg-la girl, makin plans for tonight."

"That's what I was calling about. Where's the place to be?"

"Well, that depends. I got a couple things going tonight. We got a combo gig out southwest. Some young rapper type is having an album release after party at his producer's house. I got about fifteen girls going there, but that's not until late tonight."

"You say it's at the producer's house?"

"Yeah, one of those big pocket mansions behind the golden gates."

"Pocket mansions?"

"Yeah girl, you know how real mansions have 115 rooms, sit on twelve acres, got a helipad and a landing strip?"

"Yeah, big boy, old school money."

"Well this is new money. Think brand new subdivision, right, nice-sized houses, maybe $150,000 to $350,000, nice acre lots with a decent 1, 2 or 3 bedroom house, ok?"

"Right, you see them all the time right off the freeway, little look alike cracker boxes lined up in a row."

"Riiiight, well these fresh, new money types are building into the same concept, except, the houses start at a million, and the acres are maybe an acre and a half or two. They are long and impressive, but you have neighbors like, right there. Mansions are not supposed to have neighbors right across the driveway; that's why they call them pockets. Plus they build a bunch of cul-de-sacs to give the perception of privacy."

"So the money is there, but not the land."

"Exactly, that's why we'll be there late tonight for the thunderstorm."

Sylvia remembered 'the rain'. When a crowd favorite, as most of $ensations girls were, her included, would get on stage, get naked, and do a signature move. The money would be tossed up in the air above the girls, and come raining down, normally, singles, fives, and the occasional ten dollar bills. The thunderstorm was the same; but the denominations were larger and the frequency higher. Thunderstorms were the forecast for tonight.

"Well, you already know I'm trying to be there. You never know, Fantasia may be reborn if the vibe is right. Either way, there should be some things to look at and through."

"Cool, you know I always have room in the posse for alumni. It keeps these hoes on their toes."

"So what's poppin before the late night tip?"

"Well, you said you wanted to go dancing right?"

"Riiiight."

"So I guess we gotta go cut a rug. There's quite a few Jermain Stewart clubs around."

"And just what the hell is a Jermain Stewart club?"

"Damn, I forgot you crib out in the boonies somewhere, talking to wolves all the time. You remember the tall skinny guy that used to be in the group Shalimar with Howard Hewett and Jodie Watley, remember? Well, after he left the group, he was a one-hit wonder with a song called 'We don't have to take our clothes off to have a good time."

"Oh yeah, I remember that song, 'We can dance and party all night and drink some cherry wine', that's him right?"

"Yeah, that's why we, in the industry, call them Jermain Stewarts."

"Got it. So where are these clubs?"

"There are a couple new spots and some happy hour spots, im thinkin we hit one of the old school places where the locals go."

"Let's do that, go native, get our Atl on."

"Ok, let's kick it about 9, get a few hours in before the

bizzness."

"Ok, so about 8:30; where do you want me to meet you?"

"Meet me downtown at the Martin Luther King exit off 75 south."

"Ok, MLK, south 75, 8:30, got it, I'll see you then."

"Alright Syl, you got a garter, just in case?"

"You know I don't need one, but if you got one, I'll use it."

Laughing, they hung up. Sylvia thought about her Fantasia gear: about thirty yards of one inch gold lame' ribbon, crisscrossed from her neck around and stuck to her nipples, then, riding a wonderful path between her legs, forming an imaginary panty on the bottom. She must remember to stop by the fabric store. Sylvia had retired Fantasia when she left Atlanta the first time. Her subsequent line of work was too-high stake; low profile for her was the way to be identifiable by things she couldn't change.

She unpacked to let her outfits breathe. She took off her purple mall walker dress, stood in black thigh high stockings, and a small black silk thong. Her quest was for dancing party clothes. She laid out a swingy skirt of fuscia and black, with a pretty pattern inside the pleats that you could only see when it swings.

She had a fierce pair of four-inch fuscia and black pumps that she had bought specifically for this skirt; a black tank cut leotard top, and the ¼ length matching shoulder jacket killed it. She packed her clutch bag with a micro G-string, nipple-stick clothing adhesive, a small roll of cash, a mini-mag halogen flashlight, and her Mercedes key fob. It was ghetto, but expected.

Half dressed, she sat down to figure out what to do with her hair. She brushed it back until it looked like a uniform wavy puddle of oil. She wrapped a fuscia scrunchie around the base, giving her a long pony tail which she split down the middle, and secured with two black rubber bands. She draped her twin ponies over her collarbones; she liked what she saw. She then opened her hard case and chose a pair of slim, rectangular, glasses from Japanese designer Miki Moto. They had the subtlest hint of black pearl dusted onto the arms, and they brought out the Japanese features from anyone that wore them.

The overall effect was exotic: a beautiful, black-anese woman, fresh meat. If she said nothing, she could be whatever percentage she desired. Her Japanese was limited but passable enough, unless a real native speaker was in the house. She wasn't worried about that this evening. She would be the shining star in a local yokel dance club.

Later on, she would be the hard-to-get prize for the master of the house; or, whom ever knew the secrets; or, had the combinations to get to the things that would impress her out of her panties. He would be the master of the house to her. She made her way to the lobby. First, she stopped by the concierges' desk to retrieve her goggle maps driving directions to get to MLK to meet $ensation.

Despite all the years she had lived here, there were still places that tripped her up. Atlanta was a difficult city to navigate, mainly, because every time the wind blew, they changed the name of two streets, not to even mention the 96 streets with some variation of the name Peachtree. Sylvia got on the road, the freeway was surprisingly clear for this time of the evening. After riding twenty two minutes, she arrived at the MLK exit. She pulled over to the left and put on her hazard lights. She pulled down her lighted vanity mirror, and applied a coat of lip gloss, enough to make them unavoidable, not enough to look like a neon invitation.

She flipped up the visor and checked the rearview. There was $ensation pulling up behind her in a pearl white BMW M3. As soon as the exit traffic stopped, she scooted around Sylvia's big bodied Benz, the little roadster turning from white to blue to dark green as she passed. Sylvia tapped the gas, the big V12 easily keeping pace with the Beemer. They rode the freeway for another twenty minutes and exited in a suburb of Atlanta, Decatur. There was a dance club right off the exit. The parking lot had a nice crowd, not too many, not too sparse.

***

The National Guard checkpoint had been the most invasive yet. There had been reports of 'Guard troops overstepping their bounds in major ways over the last twenty four hours of the code RED. Some of the troops were taking the curfew too literally: shooting at cars and pedestrians out walking their dogs after hours. The news was filled with the abuses coming from states all over the country.

The troops, not used to guarding fellow Americans, were having flashbacks to the training given to them for dealing with foreigners and hostiles. Americans were not used to having their freedoms curtailed. Atlantans, with proper papers, were allowed to participate in commerce after curfew. There was no out-and-about idling allowed. As long as you were spending money in the metro Atlanta area, the council allowed exceptions.

These came with a price though. During an emergency session, the council had approved an extra post-curfew tax. You could still make money, but it was going to cost. Thus, boosting the city's coffers appreciatively, because they were the only municipality for miles that had passed such a resolution.

Once allowed into Chits parking lot, everything else was a go. The ladies got in for half price and the band was in full swing. They stepped to the bar and got drinks. By the time they had taken their first sips, the bartender got their attention and placed two new drinks in front of them and pointed to two guys at the other side of the bar.

They were decent enough at first glance, but the full gold grills they sported told Sylvia that they were looking for somebody else. But $ensation gave them both enough smile power to feel like they had done something right. Sylvia gave $ensation the side eye, letting her know that the gold mouth twins were not her cup of tea, and started towards the dance floor.

The club was set up with two distinct sides with the circular bar in the middle. The stage side had comfortable chairs and tables for dining with in-wall booths in the back; the opposite side was the large dance floor with the DJ overlooking the far end. At the top of the stairs was a promontory that stuck out giving a view of the dance floor immediately below and directly into the eyes of the DJ.

Sylvia stood there now overlooking the talent, checking out the new grooves in the 'A'. Quite a few of the Down South Georgia boys looked like they could hang with Sylvia. She polished off her Cognac feeling the heat worming its way down to heat up her stomach.

Setting down the snifter, she quickly turned her back to take a pick of the people she caught staring at her ass while she was overlooking the floor. At first glance she caught five guys and two women red handed.

Almost choosing a woman just because, she chose a light skinned guy with a nice build standing by the bar. He was obviously taken in by the old Al B. Sure light skinned pretty boy mystique, he obviously didn't know they hadn't been in style since the mid 90's. But, she chose him anyway, and they danced. With her four inch heels, she was his height, if not a little bit taller. He was an adequate dancer. As the next song came on, it occurred to her why he still had any self-esteem at all. He started to lick his tongue out like a snake or an iguana. So, he was short, with bad rhythm, couldn't fuck, but he could eat some pussy. That was why he could come to the club with a bit of confidence. He probably knew how every woman in the club tasted, and, looking at these broads, maybe some of the men too.

She cut him short with no explanation, walked up the stairs, leaving him to look at her silky stockings. At the top of the steps she saw a dark skinned tall brother. She wasted no time. She grabbed his hand and led him past Mr. light skinned. She felt much better about her new selection. This man reminded her of the guy earlier with the adorably glowing hazel eyes that was shadowing her at the mall. Something about him had made her horny, made her put extra wiggle into everything she had. Then, whoever he was calling out to, took his attention away from her. What would she do if she ran into him again? She turned her back to her new partner and gave him a standing table dance that would have made $ensation proud.

Chapter 28

<u>St. Louis</u>

Abdullah crept along the pier towards the casino boats. His resources were excellent, wearing an exact replica of the maintenance uniform of the casino fleet HVAC contractor. He walked with the slump in his shoulders as if he had been carrying this vacuum cleaner his entire life. If you looked quickly you could almost see the dent in his shoulder from the constant duty. Allah was most beneficent and merciful that he never really had to do this work. There was something in him that allowed him to believably assume any identity he needed to perform Allah's work. The slight limp detail drew focus to instill sympathy for a relatively young man injured in his chosen line of work. He approached the employee entrance.

His ID had been rushed, but it was good. The plastic pocket on his uniform made it so he didn't have to extract it to show it, which was good because the back was blank. Walking onto the boat gave him chills. Allah, keep me calm and I will be on my way long before the infidels have a chance to know it's me, unless it is your will. He wore a Glock .40 caliber semiautomatic in case something major happened. He would take as many as possible, then himself. The infidels will never interrogate or torture him. Never.

"Morning,"

Abdullah, temporarily "Billy", spoke to the security guard and the few employees standing around the coffee machine.

"Goddamn terrorist got me doing rounds sucking out filters all, damn it, over town. These last three gonna kill me. I saved the worst for last, but dese two boats, I hate fucking boats. Boats got my fucking leg gimpy at 30 years old. Can't chase my kids around cuz'a fucking boats. But hell, what can ya do? Gotta work."

He threw his hands up in despair. Everybody in hearing range felt this man's frustration, and admired his determination for not giving up. After all, they were whole and only had to deal with customers. This, obviously, injured handicapped, young man has to go up into areas of the ship were the dust bunnies are flesh eating wolves. They tried to commiserate with him, but none truly could. So, they watched him hobble away into the bowels of the ships ventilation system. Once beyond the door, the pretense was suspended. He donned a ventilation mask and went about the real job of cleaning out the ventilation system. He wanted to make sure the system was clean so nothing stopped the anthrax from making its way through the boat.

After vacuuming out the approach-way, and the induction side of the filter, everything was squeaky clean. He used his knife to cut down the filter to 1/16 thickness, then he replaced the screen into the track and locked it. Next, he retrieved a device about the size of a pack of long cigarettes. There was a small window screen on the top face of the device.

Near the center was a small aperture smaller than the diameter of a dime. On the back was a screen with a powerful fan mechanism. Small grappling type hooks attached the device to the portion of the filter screen. Abdullah reached inside his uniform for a small plasticized porcelain pill box with four compartments. Each contained a two inch long cylinder of white powdery substance with threads on the bottom edge. Abdullah pulled out one and screwed it into the hole in the front of the device; the screen lit up showing all zeroes. A winding knob was located on top of the device, which counted up the numbers from right to left. When the numbers got to 11.00.00 Abdullah pushed in the top of the winding device. The farthest right set of numbers started to rewind themselves in count-down fashion.

The first one was done. Allah a Akbar! Now, he had two more to do, one more boat and the main casino on shore. After thirty minutes per cleanout/install, it should be complete by 9:30; he'd be on the road by 10:00. The first one should go off at 5:30pm, St. Louis time. By that time, he'd be about twenty minutes from mid-town Atlanta.

The home of the terror mongers prime targets is the (CDC) Centers for Disease Control and Prevention. It is a treasure trove of the most deadly and contagious diseases, weapons, and compounds on the planet, all confined to one city, one place.

After all of the anthrax bombs had been placed and timers activated, Abdullah made his way back to the hotel to officially check out. The fanfare was needless, the Saudi Emissary was a very rude man. With a swirl of his robes and a bag full of cash, he was gone; the armored limo was not in place any more. The hotel was back to its normal routine, no more royal babysitter.

The diplomatic plates allowed Abdullah to travel the freeways. During the Threat Level RED condition, the freeways had reverted to total military and government control. Some people think that the small blue sign with the ring of white stars that proclaims the freeways the Eisenhower Interstate System only meant that he was president when they were instituted. Not so, the stars indicate that the true ownership and stewardship of the interstate system is military. During times of emergency, the interstate system allows the military to get in, out, and around the country on the ground the same way that air traffic is suspended to allow military use of the skies and airports.

Once the driver flashed the diplomatic passports with nationalities from a friendly country, their diplomatic vehicle was allowed onto the south bound interstate without further delay. Since National Guard was in control, highway patrol units were no longer an issue. The driver cranked the speed up to 99mph and used the fast lane to stay clear of military vehicles.

***

Riding out sedately with no particular place to go, they passed by the Anheuser Busch plant. They saw the giant Clydesdales in their pens trotting around and the misty

Mississippi river. They drove out of the downtown area sticking to the back streets. They noticed the cars that were out on the major thoroughfares; they were packed. The military had taken over the freeways and the checkpoints were a major source of congestion. Thony and Suzan wanted to get away from the madness. But once they got out of the house and the city, they made a little better time on a two lane back road that went for some ways.

They rode by farms with cows and horses that could give a damn about the color of the threat level. The radio waves were awash with expert commentary about the reason for the alert, theories about why the park was blown up, any and everything. On the non-news stations, they took the road that as many people as there were, was how many opinions there were. They shut down the record spins and opened the lines to callers. Every caller had something different to say. They clicked off the radio and listened to a jazz CD. By this time, Suzan had turned her back to Thony and lay with the back of her head resting on his lap and her knees lying atop one another on the passenger seat.

Thony's natural arm rest was just below her breasts, feeling every breath she took and occasionally grazing one of her nipples as the teddy tried valiantly to fight gravity, but ultimately lost. The bumps in the road were fun. The more they drove the more she fidgeted around until she found the position that felt right. She laid on her side with Thony's erection riding the crease between her neck and left ear. She went to sleep. The back roads of America were sometimes poorly maintained, and often badly marked. They were usually blocked by obstructions; flocks of sheep, families of deer or the occasional fallen tree across the original routes. Some of those little alleys in the city can connect and keep running until you wind up in another county or even another state.

About an hour passed. The small road had gone over an elbow of the Mississippi that actually looked like a small lake, so, he nor Suzan paid it any mind. Now, with Suzan sleeping soundly, he was casually rubbing his non-driving hand up and down her smooth body. The knowledge that he had dressed her and knew everything she had on was very exciting. This new love affair was a good fit. They shared careers, which always made time together better and it gave access to a built in fan, critic and confidant. It wasn't until he crossed over the next bridge that he realized just how far his jazz induced, sensuously distracted joyride had taken him. Lightly slapping Suzan on her ass to wake her, Thony said,

"Suz, Suz, honey wake up."

"Hhun? He slapped her a little harder.

"Hey, hey... Do that again."

She still hadn't lifted her head but he could feel by the rising of her cheeks in his lap that she was smiling. So he smacked her once more kind of hard; she yelped at that one and involuntarily yawned. Coming off the yawn she turned and put her teeth around Thony's shaft and gently bit down width wise. He swerved the car a little and she sat up looking out the windshield. Seeing nothing in back or front, she looked at his pants and saw the throbbing mouth shaped wet spot and let out a giggle and said,

"That's what you get, that last one stung."

"You asked me to do it."

"You knew what I meant, you sadist."

"Call me Marquis."

They both got a laugh from the S&M reference.

"But seriously babe, how do you feel about a Marriott Marquis?"

"Marriot? Out here in the boonies?"

"Well, that's why I woke you. We're not exactly in the sticks anymore."

She looked out at the passing scenery.

"It doesn't look like St. Louis. Where are we?"

"According to the last sign, we're about seven miles from Springfield."

"Missouri?"

"Nope. Illinois."

"ILLINOIS! I thought we were just taking a leisurely tour through the country."

"Well, we're still in the U.S. and you did say you didn't want to be back there when the curfew hit. We obviously won't be back there in an hour."

"Okay. Then, this outfit, you so expertly dressed me in, was obviously chosen for adventure. So, let's see what we can see in Springfield. Isn't that where the Simpson's live?"

"Duh, you are one crazy woman when freshly awakened."

"I blame you because you drive me insane."

And she inclined her head, stuck out her tongue and rolled her eyes around. Not as quickly as in St. Louis, but eventually, they ran into the surface street congestion and saw the National Guard posts at every freeway exit and some of the major intersections.

Once they got into the city proper, they looked into getting a room at one of the major chains. Then, making Thony look like the psychic he claimed to be, the Marriott Marquis was the hotel that finally had a vacancy. All the suites were taken already. So, they got a regular Room on the 27th floor, and were assured if a suite became available they would get a call and the offer of an upgrade on the house.

Room 2720 was a nice room not to be a suite; simply a single room with a bathroom, TV, and coffee pot, the expected 3-4 star amenities, and a big California king sized bed. Nothing like the custom bed at Suzan's, but it had a fluffy comforter and a firm mattress. They both fell back on it and bounced as if they were mattress shopping. She rolled on top of him grabbed his face and kissed him desperately and said,

"Thank you for taking me away Thony, mentally, emotionally and physically, internally and geographically."

A little sly smirky smile crept onto her face with this last. She wiggled her hot crotch on his and announced,

"I'm hungry my King, would you feed me?"

"Which mouth needs feeding my Queen."

She pointed to her face,

"This first,"

Then she picked up the front of her dress,

"This next."

"I do believe that can be arranged, but first I'll have to tame this tiger,"

He pulsed beneath her and she rolled off of him.

"Ok. Take your time,"

And she skipped into the bathroom.

By the time she reemerged he was only plagued by a chubby, though it had a hair trigger, it was under control. He had already called down and made reservations with the concierge.   Their table would be waiting in the restaurant when they got there.   They walked hand in hand to the elevator that rode down the outside of the hotel. The lights went out so that they could see the city through the tinted glass of the elevator. Landing in the lobby they stepped into the Italian-themed restaurant.

Thony was recognized by the concierge in that spooky way that concierges worldwide have of knowing every face they check-in. They know what their preferences are, among many other things, magically, even if they haven't seen you for a while. Now, in the days of computers and personal electronics, it was understandable, but still kind of spooky. They were seated in the rear in a booth. They sat across from each other so that they could look into each other's eyes. The melted candle in the Chianti bottle was a nice touch, along with the red and white checkered tablecloths.

She ordered Penne' pasta Primavera and king crab parmesan salad. He got the fourteen layer lasagna with two loaves of hot-from-the-oven Italian mini breads with garlic butter. Somehow, the fact that they didn't have a suite available for them had found its way to the restaurant, along with a slowly breathing bottle of house red at their table, complementarily.

They sipped wine and talked in hushed tones as though they were lovers in a play. The fact that they were lovers in life made all the difference in this chemistry. The ambiance in the restaurant and the lack of windows created the illusion that it was night time all the time. The food came and it didn't matter what time it was. It was delicious...

Chapter 29

The MCU was clicking overtime, the team leader was pissed off, and nobody could rest nor could they relax until something came from under a rock. The original crew from Maryland was overseeing the insertion of task force members into all of the National Guard posts all over the state. Every check point got a task force member effectively quadrupling the size of the task force. Pictures of the POI were circulated. None of the check points had confirmed the POI as having come through their sectors, none of the task force units had come across anything either.

Kristi was furious to have missed him by so short amount of time; they could still smell their scents in the woman's apartment. Kristi could tell there had been recent sex and the shower was still wet. They couldn't have missed them by more than twenty minutes. Now, she didn't know where they could be. It had been over two hours. Just then a series of beepers and bleeps indicated some activity coming through.

"John Eagle, what's that? Is it a lead on this son-of-a-bitch?"

"Don't think so SAC, it looks like an internal feed from CNN."

Indeed it was from Atlanta, home of Ted Turner's Cable News Network. A senior story editor was sweating noticeably on the live video feed.

"Is this Kristi Johnson of the FBI?"

"This is Special Agent Johnson, how can I help you?"

"I just contacted Homeland Security and they gave me the frequency to contact you. They said that you are the point person for this terrorist action. Is that you?"

This was news to Kristi. Now, the game was forming; all the big agencies were distancing themselves. Everybody was pointing to her, so that if this train came off the tracks everybody can say the black woman was in charge. She called the Threat Level RED, she fucked up. Fire her, crucify her and everything will be ok. Oh, and by the way, don't make that mistake again. She was probably on her period.

"How can I help you", she asked with icicles dripping from her voice?

"We just received a strange message via our website. It should be there on the Data channel now. We did not have a clue what it was or what it meant until a production assistant recognized something as a reference to St. Louis. That's when I started making calls."

"Ok. I'm bringing up the Data channel now. What is this I'm seeing?"

"Well, I've got to admit Special Agent Johnson, when we saw it we had the same reaction. You know as a 24 hour news outlet we get things every day, all day and night. The thing that stuck out the most about this was that it wasn't claiming responsibility for the bombing."

"Ok Mr.?"

"Wolfstein, Simon Wolfstein"

"Mr. Wolfstein, I'm going to bring my cryptologist up to speed on this. Give my assistant all the data in case I need to re-contact you. I'll have a pair of Agents there within the half hour."

She made a gesture to one of her men to make that happen. If she remembered correctly, the Federal building in Atlanta was within sight of CNN.

"They will have computer and Network credentials. Give them access to any and all locations related to this message; your system administrator should be a good place for them to start. We'll be in touch Mr. Wolfstein"

The agents from the Atlanta office would undoubtedly be descending on CNN, now, as a matter of fact. They should have been getting to Wolfstein as he was hanging up the phone, it just depended on what floor they were on. The message was cryptic but somewhat familiar.

[U suk amerikkkan pricks appropriate tools right into oblivion twice asshole cunt twats why you breathing so hard old miss? Keep lookin over the rainbow while your arch falls grip it on time? Don't bet on it Ha Ha Ha Ha!]

Everybody in the MCU was silent. The mental frequency was so high, the lower brain functions barely responded; blinks were suspended, mouths hung open, some forgot to breathe. But all were focused on the strange puzzle on the big screen in front of them. Popping out of the trance, John Eagle did a select-all to copy the text of the message. He had no doubt it was a message or a very clever decoy. The astute production assistant had noticed the reference to the arch singular, unlike a certain burger restaurant that used arches plural.

The St. Louis most famous land mark was its giant arch near the Mississippi river. He copied the text and pasted it into a program called Crypto Sleuth. This was a Government sanctioned software written by cyber criminals serving life in one of several Federal facilities. This program took the proffered input and ran it through all of the current cryptographic protocols to attempt coherent output. It was primitive, but it came up with good results more often than not.

He programmed in the criteria to match it against bombing, St. Louis Missouri dates, times, etc., and set it to work. In the meantime, Kristi was working through the problem the old fashioned way. Her first and most distressing question was,

"How come this message went to CNN in Atlanta with a reference to St. Louis? Any ideas?"

"It's anonymous, it came through the website."

"24 hour news, they knew somebody would get it."

"Maybe they were tired of keeping it to themselves?"

"Ok. So those are reasonable, but terrorists are not by definition reasonable people. Let's reach a bit farther afield people, think like the enemy not like your families, damn it."

"SAC,"

It was John Eagle.

"I got the first layer run through, it looks interesting."

Kristi walked back to the isolation room John Eagle worked in when he had something hot running. The print out showed:

[Breathing, miss, over, looking time bet ha ha ha ha tools. Oblivion arch]

"These keywords came out of the first layer search of the message. Next, I punch these words into the knowledge base for the artificial intelligence program which holds salient facts about every state in the country, as well as most cities in the world. Knowledge will extrapolate the words out, using fuzzy logic to make any connections that are St. Louis-centric."

The results came fast:

[Arch=St. Louis arch tourists archway to the southwest;

Tools = work, construction, maintenance, repair, language,

Looking = seeing, seeking finding, hidden;

Over = about, ahead, higher,

Bet = gamble, chance, wager casino,

Time = limit, current, target, origin, eta, delay;

Breathing = respiration ventilation, HVAC, fresh air, stale air;

Miss= single lady, elderly lady, Mississippi river, Mississippi state university extension;

Ha ha ha ha = laughter, laugh 4 times, 4 times laughing;

Oblivion = dead no more alive]

While the knowledge base was crunching along, John was staring at the problem in a zone.

"This guy is no dummy SAC; you see these first thirteen words? Do you recognize what they spell out?

[u Suck amerikkkan pricks appropriate tools right into oblivion twice asshole cunt twats]

"You recognize that SAC?"

"Something's knocking on the door. The words are throwing me off."

"It's acronyms, the first letters spell out usa patriot act."

USA patriot act then, the duh response,

She smacked the heel of her palm against her forehead.

"Shit, how could I forget that?"

Most people that had heard of the act never knew the patriot act was signed into existence by George W. Bush. Lil Bush, as he was called in the media, to separate him from his dad, signed the act into being immediately after 9/11/2001. New

York City came crashing down, this was one of the most controversial terrorist plots against the U.S. ever seen.

The statute basically created a host of new laws the U.S. could use, and watered down a lot of the freedoms that we have always taken for granted. But terrorists saw it as blankets of protection to hide behind when their nefarious plans started to fall apart. The Patriot Act allowed Government agencies to actually act. What most didn't know was that it was an acronym that stood for:

Uniting and Strengthening America Providing Appropriate Tools Required to Intercept and Obstruct Terrorism Act.

This message sender knew enough to bastardized the act and send it back into their faces. She was mentally adjusting her profile of this POI, upping the intelligence quotient of what they were working with. From the beginning she knew he was not the typical zealot. They would have taken themselves out with the first blast. This guy was still alive for a reason. And that couldn't be any good.

She remembered the smiling deathly grin on the satellite image after he'd survived the bomb blast. She revisited the thought that he was feeling more confident, invincible even. Enough so, that he would keep going until he died or was killed, Allah's will. Well, be damned that, her will was going to rule this one. She stepped back to the front of the MSU. The analysts were throwing out combinations from the knowledge base format. One of the junior analysts shouted out a string that stopped everybody cold. It sounded too terrible to be off by much:

[St. Louis tourists construction hidden above casino target

ventilation Mississippi River 4times dead]

Chapter 30

After the meal, they lounged, drank strong coffee, and settled their food. Suzan was feeling good; better than she had since this entire terrorist thing had happened. For the first time in quite a while she felt like she could relax. Slumping slightly and kicking off her shoe, she surprised Thony with a light creeping sensation on his inner thigh. She was creeping her foot up his leg to probe at his manhood.

The tablecloth was covering the end cap of the table; she was safe to explore. She kept a totally disinterested air about herself, casually sipping coffee as she explored all over the crotch of his slacks. He tried to keep his cool but couldn't help looking down seeing her talented right foot creeping along his rapidly stiffening erection.

She was amazing, her foot felt so educated, it could have been a hand. It stroked along the length of him causing him to open his left leg a bit to allow her more access. Not very practiced, but willing to try, he used the base of the booth bench to pry off his right shoe and judging by the angle that her foot was attacking from he picked up his own coffee cup to disguise his grin and ran his stocking foot directly up the inside of her thigh. He stroked his big toe in circles lightly until he got to the puffy damp place where they connected.

This sudden quid pro quo caused her to abruptly rattle her cup on her saucer. Her grin spread, trying to keep from making noises while she felt his foot exploring under her dress. He started to stroke his pointed big toe up and down over her puffy mound. On one particular down-up stroke, his toe got caught on an obstruction. They both held each other's eye. Then, he applied upward pressure and heard, as well as felt, the snaps give. His next down stroke was met, not by the puffy mound, but, by the wet separation of her lightly furred anatomy.

Her eyes closed and her mouth opened as that same toe came back up through her hot moistness to get lodged beneath her clit. She gripped the side of the table. He wiggled his toe, her foot gripped him and started to shake. She called for the check.

The waiter arrived with the leather billfold and lots of idle chit chat, they signed the bill charging it to the room. Suzan had retracted her leg but held his hostage. Her eyes locked on him while he dealt with the waiter. His eyes locked on the waiter to keep him from looking at Suzan as she rhythmically moved against his toe. She seemed intent on making herself come despite the presence of the waiter standing right there. It was crazy, but it seemed like she was almost there.

The waiter was busily earning his tip. He asked if they had enjoyed the wine and if they would like a bottle sent up to their room. Thony said that would be nice and managed to reach around his rock hardness to extract a $10 bill. Right then, there was a thump-rattle sound, the crystal salt and pepper shakers had knocked together as Suzan's orgasm hit. She was holding a napkin against her face as though wiping her mouth. Her closed eyes caused the waiter to inquire if she was ok.

She waved him off indicating that she was fine. On the contrary, her innards were spasming all over Thony's two biggest toes; he could feel wetness between them when he wiggled them. She let out a little squeal and let his foot loose. Smiling the smile of a deranged woman and breathing unevenly, she announced she was ready to go. Replacing their shoes, he informed her that in order to leave now she would have to walk close in front of him.

Walking in tandem this way, they shuffled to the scenic elevator; luckily they were alone, he punched twenty seven and Suzan attacked.

Popping open his pants, she dropped them enough to free his rampant manhood. One hand pulled her dress up in back, the other guiding him into her soaking wet sex. He grabbed hold of the guard rail and slid deep into her while they both looked out the tinted glass window of the elevator. He used the rail for leverage and stroked her deep and strong.

He had been so turned on from the advanced game of footsies, plus the fact that his two toes were still moist and sticky. This short elevator ride was ample time for him to work up an impressive orgasm that triggered her second. Now they were both throbbing and shaking, with him leaning his weight on her back as the bell rang for their floor.

They waited for the door to open to see if anyone would get

on. They saw the other bank of interior elevators close as their door was opening. They shuffled backwards out of the elevator into the deserted hallway still connected, still horny. Suzan, seeing nobody in the hall way, bent over and spread her legs. Thony still hard and embedded inside her gripped her hips, bent his knees and jack hammered her for about thirty seconds nonstop. Her legs buckled from her orgasm and he wound up picking her up and carrying her to the room where he lay her still-coming body on the bed. He undressed, then undressed her. They made love slowly, reliving their trip so far.

***

With the receipt of the CNN message, Kristi's crew at the MCU had automatically and seamlessly split into two; one still tracking the POI the other comprised of cryptanalyst types working to break down the message.

Considering the first set of questions she had posed regarding reasons for CNN to be the recipient, instead of a local station, they decided to widen their search methodologies to country wide. As implausible as is seemed, in the hours since he had slipped through their fingers, he could be almost anywhere.

So, the pictures the task force and National Guard had, began to circulate all over the country. First, to the National Guard check points, where they were located at every freeway exit in the country. Next, the patrols were up linked. Their laptops were equipped with facial recognition cameras and fully enabled military communications.

They checked neighborhoods for curfew violators. According to protocols, any accusations of looting, or other unseemly behavior, had to be captured digitally before a shooting could be authorized on the back end. As long as you had video you were covered.

Next in priority were lodging places; these places of refuge were the best haven for curfew violators: the motels, hotels and taverns. During times of stress, people needed food, liquor, companionship and a place to lay their head. Unless you were with certain Government sections, these basic human needs became catch all targets. As the radius widened out from ground zero, echoes started to ring back, negative, negative. But the search, as newly calibrated, was still young.

The reception clerk at the Westin Hotel in Springfield, Illinois pinged into the local National Guard frequency in regards to the urgent POI identification alert.

"Hello? Yes this is Theodore Bains, I work at the Westin in Springfield. Well, we seemed to have a man fitting the description that tried to get a room about four hours ago but we have no vacancies. So we sent him on his way."

"Was he alone?"

"Yes, he was alone, casually dressed. That's all I could tell you. We only keep our paying customers in mind sir."

"Thank you for your prompt response Mr. Bains, we will be in touch if we need further information."

The guard post hung up. The next call went to the National Guard Missouri Post, directed to the task force liaison, from there to the MCU to Kristi Johnson, SAC team leader. Once

Kristi got a whiff, she was determined that he would not get away again. She tasked the portion of the MCU not working the crypto problem to work every hotel and motel.

He had started at the Westin, so, he wasn't going to downgrade to a motel unless he had to. Starting in Springfield, they were to check the entire state. She put out a return to base order for her task force members and ordered sector forces #2 above ground to get ready to fly. She would split her force and leave half there and take half to Illinois once she had a confirmation with one hour or less surety.

***

The young crypto analyst was diligently writing down his take on the knowledge base output. He contacted tourist attractions, starting at the Arch Park and then the casinos. The casinos reported brisk business on both boats and the riverside casinos. The midnight curfew extension was welcomed, but it was a thorn in the side of the 24 hour gambling industry. When asked if anything out of the ordinary had occurred within the last 24 hours he was transferred to security operations.

"Yeah, security's tight here sir. We have extra men on the boats, and in the riverside, extra patrols on the River walk. They are all cooperating with the Guards patrols."

`"And nothing out of the ordinary?"

"Nope, looking at the dayshift log here, naw nothing. We did have an HVAC guy come do maintenance on the…let's see, vacuumed the filters out; been working all over town, young guy with a limp."

The analyst lost his breath. He wanted to say ten things at once but nothing came out. Finally, he composed enough air to ask the head of security to hold on. He grabbed his knowledge base break down and read it again:

[St. Louis tourist construction hidden above casino target ventilation Mississippi river 4 times dead]

Then looking back to the knowledge base output, he found that if he replaced construction with maintenance, and replaced ventilation with HVAC. He instantly got chills and an uncontrollable shaking in his hand. As an analyst, he didn't come in contact with the sharp end of the stick very often. He had to control himself. Touching his send button on his communicator he started off, ok.

"This is crypto,"

That was as far as he got, protocol went out of the window,

"I need somebody in here ASAP! I think I got something!"

At least he had the wherewithal to release the end button. The airline pilot voice of his tactical superior came back with.

"As you were technician, ETA 90 seconds."

The voice calmed him immediately, knowing he was beyond his depth but hearing a life line on the way changed everything,

"Copy that."

Taking his caller off hold, he requested and received the number to the HVAC Company. Keeping the security man on hold, he opened another line and called the maintenance company's security. He was sweating profusely. The dispatcher came on line. He explained his need to know the information, using FBI and Homeland Security credentials as his superior strode authoritatively into the tech area. The dispatcher informed the analyst that no maintenance rounds had been scheduled for the casinos or the boats for today...

Chapter 31

Luxuriating in the afterglow of good food, good sex, then slow love, Thony and Suzan lay satisfied. He was above her, massaging her back, and whispering sweet nothings. Suzan expressed the desire to stay here, to run as far away from ground zero as possible and stay in each other's arms forever. Maybe they could get some cameras and do an internet reality show, charge a subscription fee and live off the proceeds. He let her babble on, knowing full well that they would have to get back to St. Louis. They had a show to do that started out sold out. There was no way to back out of that without already having another line of work in mind.

Thony got down to her calves and feet and urged her to turn over. From foot level his view up was that of a topographical map; starting with the toes of the foot hills and rising up the plains of the shinbones. One could imagine four wheeling over the kneecaps onto the coco dunes of the muscled thighs.

At the crest of the dunes was the black forest, dark brown vegetation covered the violent volcanic magma spewing fissure in the landscape. A fall into the crevasse could mean weeks of pleasure attempting to regain the top. Above this, on the horizon, the twin dark chocolate tipped mountain range, he began his trek.

***

The call finally reached the Marriott Marquis. The registration clerk looked through the copies of the licenses for the guests and didn't notice anything out of the ordinary until he looked in the special registration area. This area was for VIPs, and other guests that were to receive special consideration of one type or another.

The guest in room 2720 was on the list to comp an upgrade to a suite if one was available. They had received two bottles of house wine. Apparently, the concierge had recognized either him or his companion as some type of actor from some recent film. But actor or not, special consideration or not, he held in his hand a priority dispatch from Homeland Security and we were at a RED Threat Level. These things must be adhered to the letter. He made the call.

Kristi's Blackhawk was cycling up; she had the sector 2 team as well as her crew. Altogether, four helos were preparing to assault downtown Springfield. They were waiting for the precise coordinates to the POI now, officially known as code name "Rabbit." Kristi's communicator bleeped, that was the wrong tone, and she answered warily.

"Team leader, go"

"Team leader, this is crypto lead. We have an acknowledged

threat as a result of some balls-up research. Pardon me team leader, the casino district has been identified. An anomaly has been detected."

"Explain the anomaly,"

She was feeling ripped in two, already trying to be three steps ahead of two situations. She had a second com device in her other hand sending a priority one text to Chad Morrow back in Baltimore.

"Repeat that crypto".

"Repeat, Riverboat casinos as well as the landside casino were subject to an HVAC maintenance check this morning.

The HVAC Company said they dispatched no such individual. Need immediate go approval. Both boats are on the water, the casino is experiencing, quote 'brisk business', please advise ASAP! Over"

"Copy crypto leader; team leader is en route to engagement #1. Stand by, Calvary is coming."

"Copy team leader, crypto leader standing by."

"Team leader,"

The Blackhawk pilot over her head set,

"We have coordinates data's streaming as we speak."

Then her com buzzed again,

"Shit! Proceed to target, Phillip, get the data as it comes in, analyze and advise.

"Hello this is team leader."

"Kristi, this is Chad, what's the deal, what do you need from me here?"

"I need a core HAZMAT team ASAP; get me specialists: bio toxins, airborne. Put'em on F16's. I need them in St. Louis, on the River walk at the casino in twenty minutes. Repeat two zero minutes."

She could hear typing in the background as Phillip was grabbing pages from the pilot.

"Done. Andrews is scrambling too. We got medivac choppers 60 seconds from lift off from Bethesda naval, all HAZMAT pros; one Harrier en route to CDC Atlanta; and two biohazard airborne Specs standing by. Your ETA of twenty minutes has been passed on."

"Copy Chad, keep an open channel to MCU. I'm going tactical, keep me posted."

"Copy that Kristi, I mean team leader. Vaya con Dios."

Disconnected from Chad, she grabbed the pages from Phillip. There were layouts of the Marriott Marquis, Springfield, with a hot infrared signal on the window of room 2720.

Chapter 32

Florida

Upgrade was an understatement, as Dutchess came gliding down the escalator from the mezzanine level of the hotel. The official photographers went crazy once they realized who they were seeing. The tall beautiful woman bore a resemblance to the Dutchess from the Tennis court, but, the ever present baseball cap and ponytail were missing.

In their place, was luxuriously wavy, red hair cascading down the back and laying on the collar bones. The magical green eyes were happy and mischievous as she did simple poses for the shutterbugs. She was handed a sharpie permanent marker at the bottom of the escalator. She signed a few autographs on her way to the carport.

As the doors swished open, she saw the unbelievable 1956 convertible Bentley limousine with the flying B lady leading on the radiator. The car was like something out of a dream, and on the side of the limo, was her diamond D tiara. Henry was sitting in the plush confines of the one cushioned back seat, smiling like a good ole boy with the key to the Jack Daniels warehouse.

The uniformed driver, complete with hat and gloves, opened the door, offered her a fur lap blanket and closed the door for her. The camera men rushed to snap pictures as she rode off for her date with destiny.

The main drag in Miami Beach is Route A1A, otherwise known as Collins Avenue. All of the famous names were here. The flagship Fountain Bleu hotel was a major fixture; the opposite side of the street was a waterway with slips on both sides near for access to the hotels. The other side was for personal access to the houses attached. The tallest building on Collins Avenue had no name; it was a silver cylinder with black windows.

The bottom ten floors were upscale, the upper floors were shopping establishments; the term ' mall' failed to come close. It was more like a multi-floored emporium of material excesses.

Above these floors were various levels of residential options from single floor, ranch style living to three-level opulent sky high mansions. This was, secretly, the most exclusive address in Miami. In fact, the address didn't even exist. The Bentley cruised up the avenue, looking strangely appropriate, rolling by the art deco buildings despite the modern vehicles around it. The Bentley was like a time machine, changing the date with every mile.

The turn off Collins on the un-named street was abrupt. The sun was blocked by the towering edifice. They drove up to a tall silver rollup door, the driver looked into a camera and was facially recognized. The door rolled up and they were admitted by a green light.

Once inside, the light turned red and the room they had driven into started to ascend. The elevator stopped at the 78th floor; the driver and his charges were expected. The back wall opened to a parking facility that looked much more like a living room than any structure Dutchess had ever seen. Looking at Henry, she saw it was mutual.

The driver opened the door helping Dutchess out first, then Henry. He led them to a golden elevator that had one button and a camera. As the doors whispered closed, the light on the camera blinked on; then, the button on the panel lit up and the camera light blinked off. No sooner than the light blinked on it went off that the doors slid open into the most lavish restaurant they had ever seen.

There, waiting for them was Carlos, looking surprisingly comfortable in this surrounding. This was his stage. He shook hands with Henry, then Dutchess, bowing and adding a kiss to her hand that made her blush. Henry's courting comment came back to her full force.

"On behalf of the Coca Cola family, I would like to congratulate you on your impressive win at the tournament today. As I had mentioned to you earlier this week, I have had my eye on you for a while. Not only because of your unique red hair and green eyes, but your beauty and down to earth realism. All of these things, in addition to your natural warrior's spirit, make you a winner and that is what we look for. Duchess, before I go any farther, I need to make a confession. I'm afraid I told a bit of a fib when I first met you."

Duchess was instantly on the defense; her posture changed subtly in response to her mental posture.

"Oh no, it's nothing bad or anything, it's just that I'm not on my first assignment. I was unnerved by your beauty in person, and when I saw you drinking Sprite, I saw my chance to speak to you. After having noticed you with your agent, I didn't want to approach you about any type of business without Henry around. I'm actually President of Coca Cola brands, Duchess; I apologize for the small mistruth."

"Well, I guess I can forgive you. It wasn't the best way to meet me. I do prefer the truth. It makes things easier as time goes by knowing that everything starts off on the up-and–up."

Chastened, Carlos bowed his head and extended his hand.

"Ok. Deal, no more deceptions, up-and-up from here on out."

"Deal, so what is this Carlos?"

"This, my dear, is the top of the world. Let me show you."

There were champagne fountains, an ice sculpture of the championship trophy, and a manned buffet with uniformed servers at every station. The restaurant was closed to the public; it was a private restaurant. There were twenty tables total, including the four incredibly plush booths, built into the steadily revolving architecture.

The round room had two rings and a center piece. The center was where the cooking areas and the bars were located. The outside ring was the dining area; this was where the tables were with plush rolling chairs at every place setting.

The booths were at every compass point with four tables in between. The waitresses could find their way to you anytime, whether they waited for you to come around or if they had to come to you. The service was very personal.

Once they'd gotten appetizers from the buffet, they stepped onto the slowly revolving outer ring adjourned to a booth. Carlos pointed to the inner wall. The wall was a tinted window that looked out right on the Atlantic Ocean; you could see the Keys from here looking like small stepping stone rocks. The yachts were beautiful against the blue water. Carlos pulled a slim keyboard from beneath the table and pushed a power button.

"Dutchess, we have some of the best computer and production professionals in the industry. Like I told you, we have been looking at you for a while; especially, on top of all else, you are a home girl. Atlanta loves you Dutchess, totally. For this presentation, we had our graphic artists and computer image specialists cobble together a vision along the lines of what we were thinking about for you."

The keyboard clicked, buttons were punched, and the tinted window became a presentation screen. On the screen, a bright red splash slowly revolved and zoomed out to show the top of Duchess' head; the red was the ponytail. It showed her playing on a bright white background. The ball was a sprite can and the music was hip. It looked like some kind of video game, Dutchess Singletary, Tomb Raider. Several different commercial presentations came and went. Dutchess didn't really like any of them, until she saw the last one.

It showed kids unsuccessfully playing on a tennis court. One of the kids was wishing that he could really play, when suddenly, a shimmering image of a fairy godmother with Dutchess' face (obviously pasted onto someone else's body) came down from the clouds. With a point of her racquet, a move she had used on the Japanese girl in the first round, she granted the kids wishes and they started to volley. At the end, they showed the kids surrounding a large trophy: a Sprite can with a tiara on top.

She clapped her hands for that one, bringing smiles all around. Carlos had begun to worry when none of the other samples had made her happy. But now, she sees what she likes; and he likes what he sees. Dutchess will be a major coup; he was prepared to give her $60 million over five years to sign exclusively in the beverage category. He was sure that she would have suitors coming out of the woodwork, especially if she goes for his max. It was time to see what her agent was worth.

"So Henry, I'm thinking a ten year contract for $4 million."

Dutchess heard the numbers and started calculating, but Henry reached under the table and stilled her shaking leg. With the other hand he grabbed a shrimp, dipped it in cocktail sauce, looked Carlos directly into his eyes and said,

"Come on Carlos, we're all bigger than that. Judging by the amount of time you put into this production package, and how far back some of that video capture went, you've been thinking about this for a long time. Well, so have I. I've been in negotiations with a lot of people this past week. Considering where Coke Brands sits on the 500, and the numbers some of the much smaller guys were talking, ten years out, no way. Max, four years, and, I want $100 million."

Carlos' eyes grew, he looked, not at Henry but, at Dutchess. Her eyes held fear; it was obvious that she had never heard numbers like these bounced around, especially in reference to herself.

"No can do Henry; how about eight years, $80 million?"

Henry was still holding Dutchess' leg, but now, to still himself, not her. She was almost catatonic.

"This is some really tasty cocktail sauce they serve here Carlos, I taste a hint of chutney, nice."

"Only the best Henry, Dutchess. How is your food? If anything is not to your liking, I can have any appetizer you desire whipped up right away."

"I'm ok Carlos, the orange roughy nuggets are delicious, and I just need some more sauces."

A server appeared instantly, pushing a recessed button on her headset,

"Sauces, get the saucier to create something special for Dutchess, plus bring out an array of the usual."

The server released the button relaying the request directly to the speaker in the kitchen. By the time she got there, the request should be ready. As expected, she returned directly with an artist's palette of colors; each one was a different sauce for Dutchess to try. Each of the fourteen small ramekins were good for about four dips each, the center section held fresh hot nuggets.

"Mmmm, that looks tasty Dutchess, now Carlos."

Right back into the game,

"That won't work, it's still too long."

"Ok Henry, you want four years, I want money. Ok, final offer."

"Excuse me,"

The server reappeared.

"Are the entrees ready?"

She inclined her head.

"Three minutes, sir."

"Thank you, we should be ready, just bring everything."

"As you wish."

"Thank you, the food here is so delicious, I don't want to let the presentation of it suffer. Now where was I...oh yeah, my final offer, five years."

Henry's face frowned.

"Sixty million dollars with a renegotiable extension. What do you say?"

Henry went from gripping Dutchess' leg to patting it like a docile puppy. She smiled, and he smiled.

"Carlos, I'd say we have a tentative agreement. Of course, we're going to need some time with the actual paperwork as well as a digit representing the signing bonus."

"The bonus can be negotiated with desert, extras always mix well with sweets I think. Dutchess, welcome to the family."

Dutchess had actually been holding her breath. She exhaled, and the tears came streaming down as the breath escaped her.

"Thank you Carlos. Henry, you're the greatest."

Henry patted her hand to show her it was never a problem working for her. At the same time, emotionally, he downplayed the $240,000, bonus he'd just negotiated himself for the next five years.

"Well, now that the big business is done, let's eat."

They stepped out of the booth and walked to the next table back. This table was laid out with the full complement of gold cutlery.

It seemed like there were diamonds integrated into the handle grips. They had emerged just in time for the meals Carlos had ordered to be set at the table. For their pleasure, there was Sprite and Coke in crystal decanters. This turned out to be a special formula; liquor, not at all like what you could buy, but familiar all the same.

"Membership really does have its privileges."

The lavish meal had at least four courses: the fish that stood out better than the rock lobster was the sautéed fillet of Dover Sole, then the standing rack of lamb. Dutchess had never seen so much food. Many of the things they served were so totally foreign she couldn't pronounce them. But she tried a bit of everything and commented to Henry and Carlos about her new palate discoveries.

The desert cart was almost as tall as her; with heels. They adjourned to another rotating resting place as they ate sinfully. Rich chocolate cake presented a flambé with cherries soaked in the same aged cognac as their snifters. Everything was wonderful.

Her day could not possibly compare to anything she had known in her life. She had finally arrived in the neighborhood she had always dreamed of being in. Now, she had to find her way to the top of the highest hill, the number one seed.

The conversation was light. The various landmarks of Miami and the Atlantic views were posted on the far walls by the windows to let you know which direction you were currently facing. In addition to what was there of interest, it was strange knowing that you had to face north to see South Beach. Then, like before, out of nowhere the game was back on.

"So Henry, what do you think would be fair?"

Not one to be caught off guard Henry slid easily back into the negotiations,

"Ten percent is always respectable, Carlos. I could see that, covering some of the personal things she would need to begin to be a face for your brands. But, it has to be acknowledged that all conflicts be resolved for her play. Is that agreed?"

"Definitely, the highest priority is that Dutchess play. We would never try to usurp her playing time under any circumstances. As a matter of fact, anything we can do to help, transportation or facility-wise, we would be glad to provide as a sponsor.

Of course as long as we can place products and add to our visibility as well as hers, we are there. As far as the ten percent, that's doable. Is there anything else?"

Henry cursed into his cognac and thought,

"That was too easy!"

He surely could have gone for more but the negotiation was closed. That's what he got for negotiating up-front money on a full stomach. The game was always played better on an empty stomach. After all, the hungry always pulled down the biggest prize.

"I think we're good Carlos. Dutchess, how do you feel?"

"Well, besides stuffed like a Christmas goose, I'm still waiting for the reality of this whole thing to settle in. Would it be polite if I asked you to ask me later?"

"I'll take that as an A-OK Dutchess. First negotiations have a way of being overwhelming. That's one of the reasons I wanted you to be here. I could have done this with Henry, and then consulted with you via conference call. But, I'm truly a fan Dutchess. I wanted your first taste of the corporate world of player negotiations to be a pleasant and educational one.

They are not often this way, the meetings Henry will be attending on your behalf in the coming weeks and months probably won't be nearly as civilized, and it's a shame, but it's true. I do hope you enjoyed yourself and learned a bit of the business?"

"Yes, and I do truly thank you, Carlos for everything. I did learn several very important things. The most important I think is how to insist on being treated. You did a very good job for the 'new guy' Carlos."

He actually shrunk a bit at the reference to his deception, but it kept at the front of his mind to always keep it real with Dutchess Singletary. He would never forget.

With the final part of the negotiations over with, there was one last thing to be done. They were now coming back around to the Atlantic view. Carlos made a quick phone call and pointed out towards the ocean. Within minutes the sky lit up with an awe inspiring display of fireworks, keeping to the green and red motif with healthy shots of blue and white. It was a 4th of July worthy show specifically for her that ended with a Coca Cola bottle and the word 'Welcome'.

She had lost track of how many times, but once again tears sprang forth from her eyes. The two men stood by and clapped for her success. She watched the last clouds wisp away from the display and got herself together.

They finally parted ways. Going down the short elevator, she hugged Henry, so thankful to have him as her manager. He in turn, accepted her thanks and thanked her for taking him away from all those gang-banging rapper types that only cared about making videos, getting high and avoiding the police. She laughed and hugged him again.

The elevator had been open for a minute or two. They stepped into the auto living room and the driver of the white Bentley was nowhere to be seen. Approaching the elevator was a stretched Lamborghini Ferrari Murcia ago. The sports car, usually only a two-seater, was the length of a Cadillac. To ensure her confidence, the driver that walked around to open the vertical Lamborghini styled door was taller than Dutchess. As before, Henry got in first and Dutchess last.

The driver, once again, supplied Dutchess with a white ermine lap throw; this time, for discretion rather than wind chill. He closed the spaceship-like red door and started the car. The engine sounded like a caged beast. He smoothly moved around the carpeted space until he was facing the door to the elevator. After being facially recognized the door opened, they slid inside and the bottom dropped out. It was amazing how fast they went down, considering they now knew how high up they were to start.

As they touched down, feather lightly, both doors opened and they drove out to the shadow of the building. Turning right, took them back to a slowly darkening sky on Collins Avenue. The following left turn allowed the driver to accelerate to the speed of traffic. Dutchess looked at Henry with an impish grin and hit the intercom.

"Driver, does this car just look like this or is it actually fast?"

"Ma'am, this car may be stretched, but by safety standards and pedigree, it's all Ferrari."

"Could you show me please?"

"My pleasure, please buckle up."

They put on their harnesses, way too much hardware to be called a seat belt. The driver's dashboard report acknowledging their compliance as he maneuvered into the left lane. This was a carpool limo lane reserved for multiple occupant vehicles. When the red light turned green, the only thing the closest cars to them saw was the rapidly shrinking license plate that said 'Drink mor Coke.'

The Ferrari was gone, stretch or not. Within five seconds they were topping 80 mph. After two lights, the driver decelerated smoothly, bleeding off the g-force that had pressed them back into their seats as if they were in a fighter plane. She noticed that they were at their destination. As she prepared to emerge from the Ferrari, she was thankful for the lap throw. The acceleration had pushed her dress up to her waist. Not only that, the speed had sent a thrill through her body that had an effect on her.

Unlike some young white pop stars, a swollen red punanni

was not what she wanted to have on page six in the paper. She used the throw to cover the exercise of pulling her dress down to a respectable length. Unwittingly mooning poor Henry, who wasn't exactly complaining. She was able to make her way into the hotel unnoticed. The concierge saw her attempting to fit into the back of a crowd and pulled her and Henry into an employee corridor. They took the room service elevator to her floor and Henry walked her to the room.

"Well D, more of the same, but different tomorrow. Do you want to go, or no? It's not customary for the client to be at the negotiation, but it's open for you if you want."

"I'll see Henry, I don't know how you do it; it's so much pressure. And this was an easy one, huh?"

"Yeah, he told you the truth there. It's gonna get harder from here, once the others see what Coke gave you. I'll call Pauline later and make sure she's gotten the contract and let her know to get in touch with me if and when anything looks strange. The contract was supposed to be couriered to her personally before we left the building. I'm gonna rest up and do some research on these guys I met this week. You relax and just think about playing tennis."

"Ok Henry,"

She opened the door and saw flowers and a box. She sniffed the box and opened it; it was the chocolate cherry cake she liked so much from the restaurant. There was an envelope stuffed in the side, it was from Carlos. Inside there was a short note and a stiff plastic card.

The note said 'Welcome, once again to the Coca Cola brands family. Enclosed, you will find your ID card to access your Wachovia Bank account. The starting balance is $6,626,775, representative of your win in the finals today. You now have a listing of all numbers needed to reach me directly or my assistant if I am not available. Get out there and win, Dutchess. I'm behind you all the way". When she turned around to tell Henry, he had already left.

Chapter 33

Upon coming back from the kitchen, the network news was airing a story about the Coast Guard boarding an out of control yacht, adrift in the Atlantic. The boat was non-responsive when hailed. Considering the terror Threat RED condition, the service pulled out three cutters and surrounded the seemingly abandoned vessel.

Lines were attached, and the boat was immobilized. The bridge turned out to be vacant; no power indicated at all. It was as if the $4 million vessel had been set out with the tide. Special Forces boarded the vessel to discover that the inhabitants of the luxury yacht were all in the main salon, in what the authorities would only report as 'compromising positions'. It appears an elaborate robbery had taken place, and the vessel had indeed been set adrift.

The rescuers had no knowledge of the amount of time they had been adrift; they were approximately 100 nautical miles off the southern coast of Miami. The trade winds were pushing them towards the Caribbean.

Experts suspect they could have run aground within another

day. The party was taken to Miami General Hospital, treated for minor dehydration and released. Coast Guard and Police have no suspects. The rescuees had no IDs and refused to reveal their identities. Dulcet got a good laugh at that, the famous poker players were actually everyday people. If you didn't know them specifically, they were not that recognizable.

Their recognition came mainly by their own admission. They were too embarrassed to admit what had happened. The fact was, they got fucked in all aspects of the word: out of their money, out of their bracelets, and out of their chips. And best of all, for the ballsy chick with all the mouth, up the ass by the big old prick of the dealer that she had no love for, priceless.

Dulcet was feeling the need for some excitement. Hmm, what would suit her fancy tonight? Undecided, she went back to the master bedroom into the walk-in safe. She completed the diamond removal from the balance of the bracelets. These, she stored inside a small black velvet drawstring bag. The diamonds were all flawless, considering the source. They should fetch a nice price, even considering the amount the fence would screw her out of. She could still clear low seven figures.

Dulcet wanted to go out, but the idea of crowds turned her off. She didn't have any type of people she wanted to be around. So, she would go people watch, maybe she would find a victim that begged to be taken. Pulling on a black calf length duster and a pair of knee high riding boots. She counted out $5,000 and grabbed the keys to the SL Mercedes.

Stopping by the weapons closet, she picked out a riding

crop, a Mardi gras mask of dark purple with peacock feathers, and a shoulder length platinum blonde wig. Her trusty Sig Saur was staring at her, but she chose the 9mm Walther Pk7, a sexy, midsized semi-automatic that she kept exclusively in Florida. Dulcet braided a tight crown with her hair and affixed the platinum wig with bobby pins.

She finger-combed the front thick bangs that covered her eyebrows. She locked up the closet vault and proceeded to the kitchen. The pantry swung away and she descended back to the concealed parking space. Still gloriously nude beneath the duster, she cranked up the powerful Mercedes and slowly motored out from beneath the house. She wasn't really worried about the National Guard checkpoints, since she didn't anticipate leaving the high rent district. Dulcet rode through the streets of the mansions in Miami. There was an undercover commercial district in the midst of the super residences in this area of Miami. The façade stated loudly 'old money'. But, behind that face, she pulled into the long driveway of the Tudor styled old mansion. She went straight back instead of taking the circle to the front door, and parked.

Dulcet nudged the small Mercedes into an outdoor covered alcove that was hard to see during the day. In this darkening night, it was invisible. She pulled on the Mardi Gras mask revealing her emerald eyes. The Velcro strapped the Walther securely into the inside pocket of her duster. She walked to the rear side entrance to the house and knocked a tune. The slide was pulled open, a pair of critical brown eyes sized her up, and then it was closed. The locks were thrown and the door opened.

This secret club was a secret among secrets; one could only be admitted while wearing a mask. There was no talking of any sort allowed, which was fine with Dulcet. There was also a color-coded hierarchy; colors denoted what you were into: straight sex, bondage, submission, water sports, gay, pain, toes, scat, and etc. There were no limits to what you could do or have done to you at the 'Mansion'.

Dulcet chose to wear black, which denoted she was a dominant. This gave her the upper hand in all situations in the house. That was the reason for the riding crop. She walked down the dark sloping decline to the Dungeon club. She saw 'X' braces on the wall, static and spinners. There were latex bags affixed to the wall, where slaves were zipped in and all the air was sucked out with their genitals and nipples still exposed.

Dulcet felt slow chills run all through her body. She walked by a man with a sky blue dog collar on, and three piercings in his nipple. She raised the riding crop and whacked him on the shoulder, leaving a wicked red welt. The man gave no response. She was just whipping him in passing, but his strong response caused her to take a small interest in him. The submissive man was smaller than her, standing with his back to her submissively.

She pulled her duster to the right exposing her knee high riding boots as well as her naked thighs all the way up to her flaming red-haired pussy. Its clit began to harden and grow. The slave knew better than to even look at her pussy; he went instantly to the boot. He knelt and licked the toes of the boot. He was rewarded by several lashes to his back and arms.

The slave was really getting into the boot licking, and made the mistake of touching the boot; he was only supposed to be licking and kissing. She viciously punished his knuckles.

For that, she was rewarded with a high-pitched yelping noise. That was what she wanted; the only sounds that were allowed in the Mansion were pain and pleasure. She used the crop under his chin to raise him up from his kneeling position to stand. His little dick was hard as ever, actually, vibrating and leaking pre-come, like clear oil.

She put her shiny clean boot back on the floor, covering her leg and turned to walk away. Almost as an afterthought, she whacked his dick with a quick up and down stroke with the flexible leather tip. This caused tears to squirt from his eyes and a thin soupy blast of come to shoot out of his dick.

She walked away in search of something that interested her. She walked down the various corridors, witnessing all types of sexual depravity. When it interested her, she would step in to participate, leaving raised bloody skin on white bodies in her wake. It's amazing what some people use to get off. Occasionally, Dulcet would stop to watch something particularly interesting. One room was similar to her machine room at home in Springfield. This one was much more equipped. Currently, there was a housewife; you could tell by where the fat was. She still had her kinky desires, but she had truly let herself go.

She was draped over a pommel horse-type support with her arms stretched around the girth. A machine with two appendages was working both her holes with large life-like black dildos. At the same time, an actual black man in an African war mask, was pulling her hair standing in front of the horse, steadily fucking a minimum of ten inches of live dick all the way down her throat. What seemed to be her husband, was tied to a chair placed directly next to her stuffed mouth, close enough for his face to be slick from flying spit from his wife's oral activities.

Dulcet chose this show to stick around and watch. She stepped up to a seat raised above the action that was designed to give ample access to her crotch. As she watched the action, she began to masturbate. Below her perch were women wearing orange dog tags. They were oral/annals; three of the five attractive women had butt plugs with ponytails, and stayed on all fours licking anything that came into the zone of their reach. The other two stood so that their tongues could lick the ass, balls or pussy of anyone in the chairs.

Dulcet stayed just out of reach of the greedy women's tongues, while she continued to play with herself. All the visual and sensory input took her over the edge, she came. She shot two fingers up inside to squeeze her g-spot, causing a stream of creamy liquid to shoot down into the faces of the two oral/annals, which elicited moans of delight.

The big black man had been watching her; he must have liked what he saw. He pulled his unreal dick from the woman's throat, stroked it like a shot gun loading a shell, and blasted the husband right between the eyes. Then, he turned his cannon back to the wife and covered her across her cheeks, brows and eyes. Once done, he slapped the trussed up white man across the face with his spent tool, turned and walked away, leaving the machine to handle its dual business. Dulcet climbed down on shaky legs. She made her way out of the Mansion, whipping a few people along the way. At the last door before the exit, she saw the black man. His penis in full glory pointing at her, threatening her. She reached out and wrapped a hand around the big shaft. With her fingers almost closed around it, she used her strength to move him aside like a door handle, and walked out into the night.

Dulcet sat in the Mercedes thinking about the Mansion. The amount of money in that undercover building tonight was astounding. The crème de la crème of Miami society is in there right now being degraded, beaten, and peed upon. It's amazing what the guilt of having money can do to a person that knows they don't deserve it. She started the Benz and put it in reverse. As she negotiated out of the alcove, her cell phone beeped, a text message. Slowly negotiating the driveway using only her parking lights, she checked her message. It was Recipe letting her know an 'orange marmalade' would be ready tomorrow.

Situations must have aligned themselves into a job that was sweet in Florida, the orange state. She would have to check the system at the house. She turned her lights on and motored towards home.

The SL didn't have tint on the windows like her car at home and she fought the urge to take off the duster. She really wasn't feeling clothes tonight, though the long thin coat left her thighs and lap bare. It didn't feel like enough, any truck that rolled next to her would need only to look to get an eyeful. But images from the Mansion kept running through her mind, especially the housewife and the black man. She had often considered giving herself to a man. But, she had vowed after the gang rape years ago she would not let a flesh and blood dick find its way inside of her. The pulsing heartbeat she felt as she gripped the huge mahogany spear the large black man possessed was tempting. She had something that size, if that was what she desired, but still.

She passed two National Guard patrols; neither bothered her since she was staying clear of the freeway. She had meandered into the seedier side of Miami very quickly. It's interesting how the worst parts of most major U.S. cities lie right over the line from the best parts. No degrees here, from million dollar homes straight to Orange Blossom Trail, porn shops, liquor stores, several different venues of ill repute. It's like the rich want their separation from the poor and immoral. But, when they choose to partake, they don't want to have to go too far.

She stopped at a twenty four hour lingerie shop, a euphemism for a porn/head shop. Anything you could want from Ben Wah balls: vibrators, cherry raspberry flavored rubbers, glass pipes and hookah bongs were available all day and night. She stepped in to look and see if anything tickled her fancy. Well, well, well, pervert central.

She walked up and down the aisles of pornographic magazines. The men were instantly ashamed of being caught looking at their particular fetish; but they were turned on all the same by being seen by such a tall stacked woman. She had decided that this was a wonderful opportunity to get an exhibitionistic set of orgasms.

She walked to the end of an aisle and turned the corner. Before she started down the next, she unbuttoned her duster. Free at last, her breasts were allowed to swing. The light brown nipples stiffened in the air conditioning, her compact-shaved red bush, framed her puffy excited lips. She reached down to separate them and stimulate her clit so that it was displayed prominently. She walked back to the aisle she had just left. The men stopped looking at the books; all eyes were on her. One man even went as far as to pull his dick out and stroke it as if that was sexy.

Dulcet put on a show for these desperate masturbators. She left the magazine section and browsed the DVD's. Her coat still open, not bothering to conceal anything, she picked through titles reading the backs. Looking from time to time at her fans, she was feeling so hot. Being nude where it was allowed was one thing, but where it was not, so much better. She picked a title, something about huge black dicks and went to the counter to buy it.

The cashier, a young pimply faced nerd trying to earn money to buy a life-sized sex doll on discount, stared. He couldn't even process the transaction. Dulcet placed a $100 bill on the counter and walked out of the shop, leaving the magnetic shoplifter alarm braying behind her. Done with the public, Dulcet rode back to the house, parked below and went to the computer room.

Logging onto Recipe, she saw the meal, Orange Marmalade. It was a rural check cashing establishment. Usually staffed by ten people, but because of the National Guards rollout, there would only be one person there from 7am to 2pm. There was a listing of National Guard weekend warriors that would not be coming in to work until late because of the alert status.

The store layout was incredibly simple: no bulletproof glass, only wooden and glass counters, shopping mall within two miles, plenty of small motels, and a convenient freeway exit. It looked like it could be a profitable little diversion after all, something to keep her blades sharp; she would need to get a car. Tonight looked as if it would be too busy for, no, never too busy for herself. She went into the toy cabinet and removed a suction cup dildo, quite close to the baby tree trunk she had held earlier, and adjourned to the large round garden tub. She ran herself a bath, stuck the towering phallus on the bottom and added bubble bath, as the steamy water began to fill the tub she climbed in and on. Fully refreshed. Dulcet went in search of her new temporary car.

She had a face she was going to use in the morning; it was good. She would keep the platinum wig and don a Marilyn Monroe dress and use a surgery mask to draw her disguise. It would be marvelous, she had a plan for Ms. Margie Summers.

She parked the Mercedes in the all night garage and strolled around the corner, still in the black duster. It would be gone tomorrow in a real burn bag. A shame, but she could always get another one. The Ford Escort she had identified was sitting sedately, just a piece of the neighborhood. She used an old car thief trick. She took a pocket knife and pulled the top edge of the window away from the rubber stripping and pulled back steadily. The safety glass bent outward until she could fit her arm inside and unlock the door. The one she chose was old enough that an alarm system would have been worth more than the car. She would be doing the owners a favor by stealing it.

Driving the beater was a snap; it was a five speed manual. The ignition was so worn out, she didn't even need the key to turn it over, amazing. She drove the five miles to the money exchange to recon the ins and outs: Stop signs in each direction, no lights to worry about, and now she would go into prep-hiding. As fortune would have it, while she was turning around to recheck the exact mileage to the garage when she happened to see the grandest sight in her profession. She saw a Brinks truck pulling up, armed guards piling out and bringing in money. "If Recipe was a man, he could get every bit of this pussy."

She drove back to the motel she intended to park behind. Maybe tomorrow would be a good day to leave Miami.

Chapter 34

Atlanta

They got back to the car after discussing their plans for the evening, she wanted to dance someplace that wasn't a fashion show, a local spot. Ron got back on the street, driving towards the freeway, noticing the National Guard patrols sitting in the darkened parking lots of closed businesses. Apparently, these were the looter lookouts they had been talking about on the radio. It was still early, so they were not really worried about curfew. As long as you were somewhere spending some money, they didn't really care all that much.

Ron went to the check point; they checked his ID and driver's license. Working for TCSS gave him privileges he sometimes didn't realize. Outside of the private sector, TCSS was also a large defense contractor, so the checkpoint stop was a breeze. They rode and listened to a jazz CD, mainly sax jazz with some soulful piano jazz mixed in. They approached the exit to Chits, it was apparent that the club was jumping.

Ron exited and showed his work ID. They breezed through the final checkpoint. They pulled into the parking lot. There was a spot opening up right by the door; they slid into it and got out. Sylvania was feeling a little self-conscious, not having a bra on, and having her feel-so-free park clothes on at a club.

To be on the safe side, she tied extra stout ties on her skirt and blouse. She was anxious that her breasts and nipples would show if the lights hit her blouse. Ron asked if she wanted to go back home. She said,

"No. I'll stay in your arms and nobody will see anything but my back."

"I didn't want you to be any place else."

She held his hand and they went into the club. Ron paid the $10 cover for each of them and they stood for a second, determining whether to go to the band side or the dance floor. The dance floor won out. The DJ was playing the first of the slow jam set. They made their way to the floor and got into a nice cozy corner. He wrapped her up in his arms. They slow grooved; the chemistry between them was so pure they didn't even notice anyone else was in the room. After the Ojay's 'Let me make love to you', the pair felt as if they had just finished making love; he was stiff, and she was hot. But, they weren't ready to go yet; they made their way towards the restrooms.

Ron was poking her in the back as they shuffled off the dance floor. He was as self-conscious about his erection as Sylvania was about her nipples. The slacks he wore held no potential for hiding, so, he reached down into his pants to try to re-adjust himself up against his stomach using her as a shield. At that moment, when she felt Ron's hard-on doing acrobatics, she looked over her left shoulder to see what all the commotion was down there above her butt. Ron was looking down, adjusting his Johnson. He looked into her eyes as they walked by Sylvia and $eduction on their right at the bar.

Sylvania went into the ladies room and Ron hung around looking at the crowd and waiting. $ensation had discovered the gold tooth guys each had a pocket full of money. She automatically saw a much needed couple of invitees to the party. While Sylvia was on the dance floor practicing her table dances for free, $ensation was, true to her name, getting paid at the bar. She stood between the two men so that each one always had a view; either tits or ass. She tested their pockets.

"You, my man, can see my titty right now, but it's gonna cost you $40, and you Mr."

She pressed her separated ass cheeks around his hard dick.

"Mr. hard dick, for $50 I'll let you get one good. handful of my ass. Y'all come to the party tonight over on Cascade and I might consider that a down payment on somethin', somethin'."

The money slid across the bar in front of her almost before she could close her mouth; she knew she had a pair of marks. She scooped it up as quickly as a magician. As she was putting the three bills under her left breast, she palmed her right breast and pulled it out for goldie in front.

At the same time, she used her bar side right hand to tug the hem of her dress up in the back. She felt the strip club experienced palm and fingers get a wide hand grip on her ass cheek, while the trailing pinky slid its way on a mission deeper.   Yea, these dudes need to lose some weight in paper she thought.   She saw Sylvia coming back and handed her, her drink.

"I gotta pee girl. I'll be right back."

$ensation tipped away after giving Sylvia the palm scratch, the universal signal that they had a mark on the line. She made her way to the bathroom. She didn't really have to pee; she wanted to transfer her money from her titty to her purse. The titty was good when nobody knew it was there, but she knew some expert pick pockets.

She deposited the two twenties and the fifty into her clutch, then pulled up her skirt to her waist and pulled her thong strip out of her crotch. The goldie in back had pinkeyed her panties all up inside of her. Then he stepped his hard dick print all into the crack of her butt causing further wardrobe complications that she couldn't pluck out at the bar. She had been bold, as far as she knew. Still unseen, she recruited a couple of money bags for the party, not bad. Now they would get the real test, when their $300 asses found out this ass cost two grand and ooo weee. If they tried to get Sylvia's panties, shit they better own a house.

She chuckled, walking out of the stall and bumped into a woman turning from the mirror on her way out the door. She was waving to the attendant. She saw that hair, those heavy swinging tits, that ass! She had the same body as her girl; how could that be? If she didn't know anything else, she knew female bodies.   She was straight, but for the right amount of money, she would participate in the girl, girl shows.

They were designed not to make either girl look like a butch, which threw the fantasy off for the guy. Each girl would lick and in turn each girl would wear the strap-on; the girls always knew who was who though. But, she knew that was Sylvia's body in some other clothes. She didn't get to see her face but she could imagine. She was about to run out after her, when the attendant squirted her hand down with cucumber hand soap forcing her to abandon the pursuit and wash her hands.

Ron was still waiting for Sylvania when he saw Fuscia's shoulders and black tits. The tits were swaying hypnotically above a slim waist. Flowing into a pair of perfectly grippable hips and the familiar swell of ass. She was book-ended between a low budget pair of ying yang twins at the bar. She paid them absolutely no attention.

Ron's dick was once again confirming a sighting, he was still chilling in his readjusted angle straight up his stomach and getting stiffer. A ghetto-beautiful woman came side winding out from the rest room. Ron turned to the side to let her by and his johnson notched in between her butt cheeks. She stopped without looking back. She dipped down and wiggled a bit, not too much, sizing him up. He realized she had to be a stripper. She tossed a quick glance over her shoulder and noticed his size. Just as he was looking for Sylvania, she missed his eyes. $ensation rejoined Sylvia and the goldie boys. Sylvia handed her a $50 dollar bill from her bra,

"They wanted to talk to me, and for me to actually talk back I told 'em it'd cost 'em a yard; that's your split."

"Girl you trippin; you trap it, you stack it."

She gave her the fifty back by sliding her hand into her shirt and under her breast while the men stared. 'Leave 'em hard and hangin' was one of $ensation's mottos; she claimed a thousand of them. So the decision was made to give these two an invitation with directions to the party tonight, and then make a hasty exit.

They gulped down the last of their drinks and turned to leave. $ensation was physically getting excited, mentally getting ready for the party. The liquor was flowing in their veins, off the chain wasn't far away. They were walking out with Sylvia on the left, they walked by Ron who was caught off guard, still looking for Sylvania.

$ensation used her passing palm to stroke bottom up on Ron's zipper while leaving, in that instant he realized the woman that looked like Sylvania was leaving with her. Ron walked back to the bathrooms to see what had happened to Sylvania, she was on the pay phone checking her messages. As soon as she hung up, the look on Ron's face told her something wasn't right.

"Baby, what is it?"

"I saw her again Sylvania, she was here."

Then without thinking he grabbed her hand and ran to the door. They looked through the door and saw a BMW Roadster and a big bodied Mercedes roar out of the parking lot and turn right.

"That's the car you mentioned earlier, right?"

"Yeah, I don't know who that was in the BMW, I think she was a stripper."

"How do you know that?"

"She had the stripper vibe. It's hard to explain, but after you've been to a few strip clubs, you recognize it, the way they walk, their mannerisms."

"And the one you said looks like me, did she remind you of a stripper hooker too?"

He knew he was on thin ice now. If he said yes, she could say he was insinuating that she had a stripper walk too. Though it was sexy, it wasn't as slutty as a stripper's. If he said no, then how come he's paying so much attention to her? If that was what he wanted, then he could go chase her then. He could already hear it. He tried to base the decision on past events but that was never good strategy.

"Not really, more high class I guess you could say,"

"Like a call girl huh, the call girl stripper hooker looks like me? That's what you're saying?"

He could tell by her controlled delivery that she was trying not to become upset.

"More, high class madam than worker, you know what I mean?"

She looked at him steadily for a while then broke the gaze,

"I wanted to know because the attendant said something strange to me in the restroom. She asked me if I had run home to get into something more comfy; then, she complimented me on how the shoes matched my fuschia skirt and could I recommend a designer." They looked at each other wordlessly. Then, they both looked out the window where the Mercedes had roared off from seconds ago. Ron looked at the bar and saw the gold mouth twins still talking excitedly. They approached the bar as if for drinks, but really to listen with Ron between them and Sylvania.

"Shiiit I'm a hit da ATM god damn and I'm a hit dat shit; I don't give a damn what it cost me."

"Sheeit dawg, we can go in on the double plan, but the pink one gonna cost a grip."

So, from what Ron overheard, the women were prostitutes, but that didn't seem right. Then he looked on the bar and saw the invitation. It said '$ensation and the Pusse Posse Presents: Album release after party fo'. The rest was covered up by the closest gold mouths arm.

"Yo dog, can I peep that invite? Is that where them broads is gonna be?"

"Yeah playa, but don't come shawt dog; this pussy party, you gotta pay to play."

He obviously hadn't turned to see Ron was with a lady or he wouldn't have said what he did, Ron hoped. But then, he thought that may not have been the case. Either way he was determined to keep himself between the goldies and Sylvania. The invite mentioned some low level Rapper and a $100.00 cover charge, twenty five strippers and special shows. He memorized the address off Cascade. He was familiar with the neighborhood. He just may have to find out the depth of this mystery. He turned to share the information with Sylvania and goldie #2 caught sight of her ass protruding out behind Ron. For some reason, he thought his mack was called for.

"Hey lil momma, ain't I just get done holla'in atchu?"

Sylvania looked appalled; Ron was calm. She looked up at him and watched him look at the gold toothed man. He towered over him in height and width. Ron looked down, and with baritone turning to bass he said,

"What did you say to my woman?"

The voice was totally different from the voice he used with goldie #1; so, he didn't even turn around; then, goldie #2 made a sneering gesture as if he was going to do something. He turned and looked down at him and goldie deflated totally. Ron looked at Sylvania, the strained expression still on his face.

"Baby, you wanna go?"

"No, not yet Ron, I want to dance with you some more, are you ok?"

"No, I don't think I am, but I'll work it out. You want a drink?"

"Ok, bartender, Hennessey Alexander. Have you had one of those before Ron?"

"It sounds familiar, but I'm not sure."

"It's a creamy brandy drink usually on the rocks, but its good, warm too, when it's chilly outside."

"I'll keep that in mind, make that two."

They sat on the stage side of the club on the back wall in one of the single-sided booths. They were facing the band, with Sylvania sitting on Ron's lap. They ordered one more round of Hennessey Alexander, and they added an extra shot of Hennessy this time. The drinks were delivered and the waitress tipped. Sylvania, not noticing the occasional stares from people that had seen Sylvia wildin out earlier, leaned her head back into the hollow of Ron's throat.

"I heard you call me your woman earlier,"

"When did I... oh yea, I was defending your honor, that's all."

"I have never had my honor defended before. I really liked it; if some woman comes up jockin you, can I step in front of you and claim you as my man and protect you?"

"Only if you really want me to be your man."

She stopped to think about this and took the hand that had been leisurely laying on the table by his drink and brought it up to mold it around her breast. Using it to weigh the heavy flesh, she scissored his fingers on her nipple making herself moan. Since losing his erection earlier, he had slipped back into his natural position down his pant leg. Holding her breast in his assisted hand caused his mind to go back to the sight of her in the park. The image of the little shimmery panties she had on beneath the wrap-a-round skirt had overwhelmed his concentration.

He took control of his hand and massaged her breast; he weighed the heavy orb and pinched the stiff nipple. He moved his other hand down to explore inside the folds of the wrap skirt. The skin of her inner thigh was the creamiest, smoothest, and felt most incredible. He lightly traced circles while the bands female lead sang 'the softest place on earth' by the '90s group Xscape.

They lounged in the booth. He was drawing his circles closer and closer to her sex; she was lightly scratching him from head to shaft, back and forth, using her fingernails over the fabric of his pants. By the time the band had taken its break, they had moved farther back into the booth and she had spun around with the table at her back. Her skirt pooled around them both and her arms draped around his neck.

She was slow grinding him, fully dressed but very effectively. His stiffness provided a perfect speed bump for her not to slip off.

The waitress stepped to them, then away, seeing that they were busy, regretfully wishing that she still loved her man like that again. Now, Ron understood why she called them emergency panties; they were the only things keeping them from getting arrested, even though...

"Babe?"

"Yea babe."

"The band stopped playing. You wanna go dance?"

"I thought we were dancing."

"You know what I mean. If we keep this up I'm gonna have to dip you."

"You mean dip into me?"

"I mean scoop you like ice cream and fill you like a waffle cone."

"Do it."

"No."

"What do you mean no? Are you in the habit of telling your woman no when she wants you?"

"To tell you the truth, I'm not in the habit of having a woman of my very own. But, I must admit, you do seem to be very habit forming, addictive even."

"Well Ron, like the woman said, if there's a cure for this, I don't want it. I got a love hangover and the hair of the dog that bit me is you."

Ron was once again thrown off by this incredible school teacher. She had chosen him; it felt like the nexus point between a dreaming fantasy and the reality that you're not asleep. How often does that happen in a lifetime? This was a first for him; he suspected that it was for her too. Hennessey Alexanders were surely going on his hit parade of alcoholic drinks. He looked deeply into her brown eyes, staring for seconds, then, he gripped her around the waist.

He looked back at the nearly deserted band side of the club and spun her around to the left, laying her down on the bench seat in the booth. Her skirt cooperatively remained out of the way, the wet spot on her panties clearly visible. Once again Ron felt that he could do anything with this woman; his woman, and she would lovingly participate. He gently nudged her legs until there was enough room for him. He touched his zipper.

He looked a question at her, leaving the final decision up to her, she underhandly stroked his hardness. She bit her lower lip, a subconscious show of her frustration. She sat up, pulled her skirt back around herself and pecked him on the lips.

"Ok, ok. I won't turn you out on our first trip to the club. Hell, what would you be expecting at the movies?"

That broke up some of the thick sexual tension with a laugh. Ron held out his hand to help her up out of the booth, now that she was rearranged and decent. One of the managers appeared with the young server from earlier.

"Excuse me ma'am, my staff has informed me that you and

your girlfriend have been using my club as your own little enterprise this evening. Is this true? Were you lap dancing on the dance floor, exposing yourselves at the bar, and, to top it off, turning tricks in my booths?? Madame may I."

"No you may not little man! I don't know what the hell is going on here, but I intend to find out, my woman hasn't done anything of the sort. She has been with me the entire time we've been in this shitty little club, with the exception of a trip to the bathroom where your attendant mistook her for someone else as well. It seems there's a look-a-like running around besmirching my woman's good name. I demand an apology from you and your little traitorous waitress. I tipped her $10 and my woman was sitting on my lap while we were listening to the band. Does this turn into a hooker turning tricks? Who owns this dump anyway?"

"Mr. Marshall is not on the premises right now Sir, but, if you'll come with me."

The manager turned and proceeded to the bar with Ron and Sylvania in tow. The waitress had been relegated to washing dishes until they got to the bottom of this situation.

"ReJohn,"

The manager called,

"Come here please."

The familiar bartender approached wiping his hands on a bar towel with the Hennessey logo stitched in the middle.

"Rejohn, is this the woman we got the complaints about?"

"It's uncanny sir, but no, this lady was drinking Hennessey Alexander's paid for by this gentleman, $10 tip, very nice gentleman. The other woman was drinking Remy Martin XO, paid for by the Dude with the Gold Teeth; $1 tip. Those were also the ones paying the women to expose themselves. The first one we have on tape exposing her breasts, we don't know what the other one did, but we saw her accept money." The manager got very nervous, he took two steps back from Ron, and he looked as if he wanted to run away. Then he looked up and everyone at the bar and the employees at the door were all looking at him. His response would be the turning point in his relationship with his employees, stalling for time he cleared his throat.

"Uh hmm, a grave error has been made. A pair of our valued customers have been mistakenly identified as a problem. I would like to apologize to them before everyone within the sound of my voice. Sir, Madam, I am sorry for the mix-up, on behalf of the staff and the establishment."

Ron and Sylvania looked at each other, and grudgingly accepted his apology. Ron shook his hand perfunctorily, but the look they exchanged let the manager know he was still on very thin ice with him. Looking down, Ron saw two more of the drinks that they had been drinking sitting a top two gold cards with embossed 'VIP' in black. The bartender, Rejohn, had slipped both onto the bar while the manager was going through his theatrics. He urged the cards at them. Rejohn leaned into the couple whispering.

"He knows he overstepped his bounds. This is my family's club; that's why he deferred to me. I signed these. They are good for as long as I work here, unlike the high falootin clubs downtown. VIP here is all inclusive: cover, bar, and seating. All you need to do is tip. That's why we don't give them out like coupons. I apologize for that idiot and for the comments of my new dish washer."

Ron had to think about that for a second. Then, he laughed when he realized the waitress' demotion was permanent. This guy, unlike the manager, Ron could deal with. His hand he shook firmly with eye contact.

"You ok baby?"

"Yeah Ron. I'm cool, but I don't understand. Where did this woman come from? How could she possibly look that much like me?"

"I don't know baby, but I intend to find out. Come on, let's get you to the dance floor. Thanks again Rejohn."

"My pleasure, try to enjoy the rest of your night."

They walked back through the club to the dance floor. The DJ was in a mellow mood; so the slow jam set was flowing between slow and mid tempo hand dance tunes. The two of them stayed hugged up together through six tunes. Ron held and rubbed her body as she held on tight and thought about what had transpired. The look-a-like that Ron had been so stressed out about had proven to be real. She had almost seen her. She had to have been standing in the same space just before or after her.

This was the strangest feeling that she'd ever had, some prostitute was using her face. She tried to keep her mind from returning to it, but how could she not? She grabbed Ron harder as they steadily moved to the calming old school tunes. He felt the additional squeeze transferring her stress. He continued to rub her, taking away the same thing he had been feeling all day.

"You ready to go babe?"

"Yeah. We can go."

"Your earrings look incredible Sylvania," He nuzzled her ear and kissed her neck

"Mmm that's nice. Take me home Ron."

"Ok, let's go."

They left with a final wave to Rejohn. They noticed the manager, without his suit jacket, unseen since the confrontation, was now sitting in the booth taking cover charges and stamping hands.

Chapter 35

En route to St. Louis

James Butler and Belinda Hughes approached the helipad at Bethesda Naval medical center. The call had come so quickly and from so far above their pay grade that they both still wore lab scrubs and looks of confusion. Despite the stressed out look on the scientist's faces, they were professionals; in the medical realm they would be considered the military equivalent to Delta force. They stayed on twenty four hour call to go anywhere in the world to handle Hazardous biological material issues as the language qualified them; these 'Issues' included anything from a massive Radon exposure to an Ebola outbreak, and anything in between.

Since the Threat Level Code RED had been declared, they had been expecting something. Considering their cross training in forensic pathology, they had expected to possibly be called in for some sort of morgue duties in St. Louis, stemming from the system overload of qualified technicians. But, this call was totally unexpected.

That meant that an unknown pathogen or other bio-threat had been identified and they were on their way to neutralize it. This terrorized climate was something neither scientist, like the rest of their fellow Americans, had ever imagined would affect the soil of America; neither the freedoms nor the safety of their home turf. Their hard packs were at their sides. The collapsible medical biological lab could identify and neutralize 97% of the known natural and military weapons grade biological toxins. The Huey H60 was waiting; the co-pilot assisted the two scientists into the chopper with their equipment. The jump to the flight line was almost instant, almost like jumping off of a tall building. Once they saw their transportation, they knew from their experience this couldn't get much worse.

Before them, ladders at the ready, were two F18 Screaming Eagle Joint Forces Tactical Fighter, Trainer Editions. These supersonic fighter bombers were at work training fighter pilots in many theaters of engagement around the globe. The fact that those fast movers were needed to get them to their destination spoke volumes.

The hard packs were hoisted into the rear cockpits behind the ejector seats. Then, the scientists were assisted into flight suits over their scrubs. They were led up their respective ladders and plugged into the proper ports. The on-board computer monitored heart rate, oxygen levels, and more bio physical data than an intensive care unit. The system adjusted O2 and nitrogen levels to compensate for the excessive G-forces the plane required during supersonic flight.

The seats were designed to compensate for the numerous multiples of gravity one was subjected to as you were tossed horizontally through the atmosphere at speeds upwards of

1500 miles per hour. They pushed with a counter force cocoon and an increased pressure flow of pure oxygen with necessary mixtures of nitrogen to keep the level in the blood sufficient to maintain consciousness and clarity.

Connected, seated, strapped and helmeted, Belinda gave the universal thumbs up gesture indicating that she was ready to go. Similar gestures were being exchanged in JFTF #2. All-in-all, 240 seconds from the time they stepped into the Huey, the two passengers in their respective rides were beaming at 45,000 feet doing 2.5 mach. They were headed to a private airport along the banks of the Mississippi river in St. Louis, Missouri.

***

C.B. Peters had been in his lab as well discussing the probability of micro particularized toxins in the air, or around ground zero. He also discussed how they, along with the increasing number of burned wet bodies decomposing and rotting, could affect second tier survivors, when he got the call. As with the other scientific professionals at this level, he kept his mobile lab equipment updated, packed and nearby. He was expecting to be called to the helipad on top of the building; instead, he was bundled into a golf cart. A security driver sped through hallways until they got to the end of one leading to an overflow parking lot.

As they were exiting the building, the cart stopped. Massive hurricane winds assailed them; their combined weight was the only thing that saved the cart from tipping. Once the cloud of dust had abated, C.B. looked up and recognized a

Harrier. He had only seen the Harrier hop jet once at an air show. But to see the Vertical Take Off and Landing aircraft here in the CDC parking lot was amazing. He noticed the jet had two distinct cockpits covered by one long glass cowling; the message calling him up gave no time for wonderment.

He was tossed down an open flapped flight suit; the cart driver zipped him up at his right ankle and pulled the zipper up until he was snugly fit. The med-lab went up followed by C.B. himself. This plane only had one umbilical cord that had to be plugged into track his O2 levels, etc. Once in, the pilot gave the thumbs up. He returned the gesture and the massive engines on either side started blowing them up and forward. The motors eventually faced backwards as they vectored to 40,000 feet. The gauge on the cockpit heads up display indicated mach 2., 1522 miles per hour and rising. They had ten minutes to reach their destination; it took eight. The Harrier circled their target destination in preparation for landing. Not having had the crew available to clear the parking lot of debris, the pilot chose a grassy field and approached. He set to hover, de-elevated on its cushion of air to a perfect landing. The Task Force airmen rushed to help C.B. from the cockpit with his mobile lab.

As he was touching down, two Hueys came roaring overhead. The first held the two scientists and their gear; the second came along for the mission ahead. Chad at HQ in Maryland had control of the mission on the ground in St. Louis. He had assigned one of the original home Task Force members to be the tactical leader for the casino team code named 'blow".

The blow sub force consisted of three teams: each team had a Hazmat lead, a bomb squad lead, and a physical plant expert. TAC leader, Carmen 'dog' Roselli, was briefing each team with the combined Intel that they had accumulated that brought them to their current point. They received information from the Crypto team, the site security, the inferences of the experts, and the methodologies for the strike. The land casino had been evacuated; the stragglers were still coming out as the second Huey landed.

The scientists were changing out of their flight suits into self-contained Bio-bubble suits. They were specially outfitted space suits with life support filtration and environmental options even NASA didn't have. In addition, they had integrated harnesses so that the wearer could be dropped into a hot zone from a crane or winch.

The bomb squad's portable mobile sniffer was a combination of surveillance and high tech bomb detection tools. It was equipped with a flexible paddle that could slide under obstructions. The paddle included a special camera that could detect and view heat, chemical, and six other frequencies as well as a puffer. The puffer device was basically an electronic nose that puffed a high pressure shot of air, which was then sucked back in and analyzed by spectrometer, to indicate if any explosive components are present. This unit weighed ten pounds and can fit into a backpack.

Support personnel were assigned to each team for crowd control and subsequent duties necessary for the experts to accomplish their mission. The teams, thoroughly briefed and with throat mike communications in place, were set. The Hueys, throttled up and loaded, contained a team of eight, crunched into the small space. Two were sitting with legs out on each side; two inside with a scientist and a bomb tech. Belinda Hughes was in Blow 1, C.B. Peters in Blow 2, and James Butler was walking into the deserted land based casino.

The Riverboats were designated Torch 1 and 2. Each blow went into a Torch; as the first blow hovered above Torch 1 Belinda was lowered from her harness. Within five minutes, all the team was onboard. The Task Force members donned bio hazard masks and gloves and approached the maintenance closet. They secured a perimeter and sent one of their numbers to the bridge to discuss the operation with the Captain.

The fact that this mission was sent out on a threat versus an actual sighting made things much testier with the casino boats. They could not be ordered back to port until an actual threat was observed. The Captain was informed to turn the ship back to Port as soon as the threat was discovered. If no threat was found, the ship would be allowed to continue operations undisturbed. After all, this was municipal money that paid the National Guard that was protecting the state right now.

The bomb tech pulled out the puffer 'bot' and sent him on his mission. In two other locations, the same procedure was taking place simultaneously. Each team was in constant communication with Dog back at base2. The parking lot and dock for the land-based casino, and Dog's communications were real-timed to Chad back at HQ.

Chad was overseeing the master board in his and Kristi's office; a massive wall screen tracked all missions in play and could be configured to watch anything on the planet. He was splitting his attention between the space suit cams on the CDC Scientists, and the thermal site cams on the Blackhawk contingent. They had landed on the roof, thirty five stories above street level. Two teams split up: one of the 'hawks went back up to maintain an overall view of the operation; Ten Task Force special operators stayed on the roof and started assembling a rappelling station. The other thirteen with Kristi, Phillip, and James added, went to the roof access door to charge down to room 2720.

The roof team, all armed with suppressed MP5 minis, also had two NL specialists. Non-Lethal methods went south of the training for most of the Task Force members. But this scenario, 'Rabbit', depended on the subject being alive when taken. The inside team had its NL pair as well. The lead special operator on the roof whispered into his throat mike to the team leader,

"Team leader, Snare 1, are on the move, current level 34 ETA 27 in 90 seconds."

"Copy that 90 seconds Snare 1; Snare 2 is at level 30; hold Snare 1 at level 28 until confirmed that Snare 2 is in place, copy?"

"Copy that Team Leader, 28 and hold, over."

They were constantly moving down the fire stairs while Kristi was talking to Snare 1 team. The second man behind her, Phillip, kept the rest of the team apprised of Snare 1's progress. As Snare 2 reached floor 27, the lead man popped the internally locked door and used the periscope. He checked to ensure the hall was clear, visually checking that everyone had their Kevlar face shields in place.

They filed out like a python, taking up positions on either side of the door. Kristi's demo tech placed the entry charges on the door at hinges and lock; a special spider web of material was affixed to the frame to ensure blast shrapnel went in, not back out at them. The thumbs up from the demolition tech was Kristi's signal, the communicator hummed,

"Snare 1in place level 28 above Rabbit."

"Proceed to target, standby for countdown."

"Copy that Team Leader... Snare 1 standing by."

** **

Thony slept, spooned behind Suzan, their hearts beating in unison. His sleep erection nestled against Suzan's fluttering sex, and all was peaceful. Their last bout of lovemaking leaving them spent, satisfied, and more lovers than friends.

"Two, one, go go, go!"

The sleep, the serenity, and the tenderness all ended in an instant. A huge roar rocked the room as the door was blown in off its hinges from behind them. The glass sliding door to the balcony was shattered into the room in front. All these things happened in the second before Thony and Suzan were shocked awake; the next second found them totally surrounded by black clad figures on all sides pointing weapons at them. The initial reaction to being awakened in this manner is shock, followed by fear, outrage, disbelief, and finally anger. In less than two seconds, Thony had rushed through them all with Suzan in close pursuit. From the Task Force special operator's points of view, they had just captured the worst personal mass murderer in the history of the country and his accomplice. So, their first words were too many. The two NL Specialists hit their side triggers.

**   **   **

The puff was loud enough to be heard outside the door. Within sixty seconds, the handheld monitor gave the all clear for explosives; this was relayed throughout the team.

"Come in Dog, blow1has a negative puffer for explosives on torch 1, permission to proceed."

"Copy blow 1, torch 1 is a go."

"Copy Dog, torch 1 is a go."

"Blow 2 to Dog."

"Go blow 2."

"Blow 2 negative puffer for explosives on torch 2."

"Copy Blow 2 torch 2 is a go."

"Copy Dog, torch 2 is a go."

Dog still hadn't heard from blow 3,

"Dog for blow 3."

"Go for blow 3."

"Status?"

"Still working the data lock on facilities' maintenance door to get the puffer in, stand by."

"Where the hell is house maintenance?"

"Bugged out with EVAC, stand by Dog."

"Blow 3 for Dog."

"Go 3."

"Blow 3 is through; puffer is activated; negative, repeat negative for explosives torch 3."

"Copy that Blow 3, you are a go."

"Copy Dog Blow 3 is a go."

None of the three teams had an explosive threat yet. This was good on one hand, but distressingly frustrating on the other. If there were no explosives, then what was there or was there anything? Dog checked the time, it was 5:29pm, Torch 2, boarded the second Riverboat casino. It was actually the first boat to go out, and had gotten a late start because of the number of handicapped gamblers aboard.

So, the second ship was actually twenty three minutes into its oblong gambling cruise. C.B., Peters, and blow team 2 were approaching the central portion of the ventilation system, the main hub that fed the ducts all over the boat. All at once the spacesuit mike picked up a beeping hissing noise that made C.B.'s skin crawl inside his suit.

"Quick, lights up."

The shoulder mounted halogen lights on his suit flashed on illuminating the filter access door. He rushed to the door, and the bomb tech pulled him back. He lifted the puffer and slid the paddle under the access door. The puff went off and the negative light popped on for explosives while the amber light lit up and blinked red for the presence of bio toxins.

"Blow 2 to Dog."

"Go for Dog."

"Blow 2 has a positive for bio toxins, repeat, positive for bio toxins."

"Copy that blow 2, what's the 20 of the positive?"

"HVAC central, it's coming from the filtration bay, puffer scans negative for explosives, but still proceeding with caution."

"Copy Blow 2, stand by, this is Dog to all Blow teams, "Operation Blow" is now "Operation Blowback". Repeat, "Blow is now Blowback", Torch 2 is positive for bio toxins, 10-20 is filtration unit on HVAC central, 1 and 3 come back."

"Blowback1 copy, proceeding to HVAC central, Bridge you copy?"

"Copy, Coast Guard en route to Torch 2."

"Blowback 3 copy, en route to HVAC central."

"Copy Dog, Coast Guard approaching Torch 2, Bridge 2 out."

C.B. Peters on Torch 2 was devastated; the device was small, about the size of a standard pack of cigarettes. The empty tube affixed to the front center of the device was the problem. In addition, to the powerful motor was still running, the counter window read -10:02.06, and was steadily running and humming. The bomb tech approached the device with a long robotic arm. The hand on the arm encompassed the entire device. He used a razor-sharp circumference tool to cut out the filter and screen surrounding it.

"Blowback 2 to Dog."

"Go for Dog."

"Dog, this is C.B. Peters, CDC. We have the device; video feed should be recording on your screen right now."

"Copy Peters, feed is captured; sending to 1 and 3 over."

"Copy that, Dog. When we accessed the device, the timer indicated that it had deployed ten minutes ago with an empty vial attached. I'm afraid it's too late for the occupants of Torch 2."

"Copy ... attention all Blowback teams, Torch 2 is now Quarantine1; come back."

"Blowback 1, copy Dog."

"Blowback 3, copy."

C.B. cracked open the hardcase lab. The vial was placed into a sterile compartment and released. The device was clamped by the floor of the compartment. C.B. used the remote controlled appendages to manipulate it. Sweat was pouring off his brow as he tried hard not to think of the number of people poisoned onboard this vessel. But, it was his job to learn if the rest were going to live or die.

The robotic fingers gripped the tube and twisted left and the tube didn't budge; spinning right loosened the tube and stopped the countdown clock. The vial was then placed atop another puffer/sniffer device; similar one to the bomb squads.

It puffed a very gentle puff of air. He then vacuumed the

resulting particles to determine the chemical compound.

"Two, 3 stat override, all teams."

"Override authorized 2, go."

"Substance confirmed; military weapons grade Anthrax; repeat, Anthrax. Device fan blows a high pressure diffuse stream into HVAC central. Unscrewing vials stops countdown clock. Vials are reverse threaded; twist right, repeat, twist right to remove, copy?"

"Blowback 1copy."

"Blowback 3 copy."

"Dog to Quarantine 1, good work team, let's see if we can save some people."

***

Fifteen thousand volts of electricity shot through each of them causing their bodies to jerk and their fluids to release. It was totally unnecessary, but the task force members were taking no chances. Kristi called them off. They unhooked the barbs from Suzan and Thony. They picked them up and slid their on underwear. They tied their arms behind them with zip ties and sat them on the sofa on the far side of the room.

Eventually, the pair regained consciousness. They were still twitching as a result of their nervous systems rebooting. The task force operators trained their high powered L.E.D. lights on them and the interrogation was underway.

"Miss, what is your name? And you, what is your motivation for killing Mitchell Johansen? Where are you from? Who do you represent?"

Thony groggily said,

"I want my lawyer."

"Sorry, no lawyer for enemy combatants."

"Enemy comb...who the fuck are you people and how do you just come bursting into my room assaulting us? I don't give a fuck what color your fucking board is, I'm an American citizen, and this is still America. You can't do this!!"

Suzan sat next to him, seething with rage, also naked. Her hands were tied behind her back with a sheet tossed over her torso. Her silence was borne out of realization; realization that all the things Thony was screaming about: all the rights that were being trampled on.

She knew that there was nothing they could do. For God's sake, they were on the 27th floor of a downtown hotel and men in black had come through the window! Something was going on here that was way bigger than them. She was afraid, more afraid than she had ever been in her entire life. She started to cry silent tears.

The questions kept coming: who, what, where, what time, and how many? Their IDs and personal effects were laid out on the coffee table; their whole lives laid bare, and their dossiers were brought to Kristi. She perused both sets of information. She looked up at them occasionally, but not saying anything, not one word, no expression, nothing.

Phillip came over to her and showed her a still image that had been lifted from the video uploaded to the Blowback teams showing the device C.B. Peters had found aboard Quarantine 1, which was fast becoming Morgue1. The report from the boat caused Kristi to explode.

"Tell me what this fucking device is, now!"

Thony was drained. The infusion of adrenaline from the explosion followed, by the unconsciousness from the Taser was the fuel for his first outburst. But now, he had crashed. He couldn't even muster enough energy to voice his 'I don't knows'. She threw a sheaf of papers on the coffee table and walked away. Thony was shaking his head, he couldn't manage much else. Through her tears, Suzanne looked at the papers on the table. She blinked the tears out of her eyes and leaned forward; her movement caused a ripple effect throughout the black clad figures. She tested her voice, finding it she bellowed,

"Hey bitch! What the fuck is this?"

She was looking at the pictures on the table; her official headshot that she had given to Wilbert at the auditorium for this current role, and two shots that both looked like her lover, but only one was, she knew.

"Yeah you, little boss bitch, come here!"

Kristi turned at the obvious disrespect, knowing that she was the only one that the woman could have been talking to. She approached her, mind still fully on the dying people aboard the gambling boat.

"Are you speaking to me, you little murdering whore?"

"Talk your shit now you megalomaniacal bitch, because this little action is gonna bite you right in the ass."

Kristi caught a small shiver from that comment; what could she have meant by that? The comment had too much maternal venom to it. There was some undercurrent that disturbed her on another level that she couldn't put her finger on. She walked back to the sofa, the sight of Suzan sitting there, trussed with the sheet hastily tossed over her, barely keeping her dignity intact. The fact that armed men had moved her mostly naked unconscious body across the room was a disrespect for this woman that she would have to carry inside of herself.

"How can I help you?"

Back to the interrogators neutral tone.

"You can tell me why you have me and my boyfriend sitting here trussed like hogs when we've done nothing to deserve this whatsoever."

"Nothing whatsoever, huh? You call 1,474 bodies and counting nothing? Your boyfriend here, with or without you, is the reason the whole damned country is fucked up right now."

Kristi's patience was wearing thin with this innocent, 'who me?' routine. She knew they were actors, this switch tactic wasn't going to work. At first she's mute and he's ranting, now the switch; he's just sitting there shaking his head like a two-dimensional bobble head. And, she's ranting with pure outrage, but still, there was that undercurrent ...

"Ok, look lady, it's obvious that we're not going to get anywhere screaming, with me tied up naked, and you surrounded by flood lights and gun-toting thugs. Could you tell me why you charged into our midair rental house? Tell me like I'm a five year old. I'm sure that whatever Special

Forces reasons you have for violating my civil, legal, and human rights is so damn complex, that I'll need it broken down into chewable chunks."

"Ok smartass, I'll give you chewable chunks. Your boyfriend, the spawn of which you most likely carry, since we found no evidence of contraception, is responsible for the most heinous loss of life in St. Louis history, and the worst terrorist action to take place on U.S. soil since 9/11/2001.

You ma'am, have been laying up in a hotel across state lines with the most wanted terrorist in the United States of America."

"You have got to be fucking kidding me."

Suzan said with a marked lack of emotion.

"And I guess your information is based on what, his head shot from the theater? What kind of crock of shit is that?"

She was beginning to get heated again, despite the olive branch offered scant moments ago.

"No, the headshot was verification; this shot is the one that put us onto your boyfriend."

Kristi pushed the papers around on the table until the picture of Abdullah was clearly visible. She looked at Suzan as though the photo was the final nail in the coffin. Unfortunately, that look was not reflected in Suzan's eyes; the nagging feeling came again that something.

"That's not Thony."

"What do you mean that's not him? Look at the photo, what kind of denial are you in woman? Has he dicked you down so good that you're blind?"

"No, woman, I'm not blind, but maybe if someone was dicking you down, as you put it, you would be able to see details through your rose colored glasses."

Taken aback by her statement, she looked at the pictures again, still, she saw the same thing, the actor playing his part. But that nagging feeling was growing to a point that it could not be ignored.

"Ok, show me."

"Could you take these damned shits off my wrists?"

"Not until you convince me that I should."

Kristi looked at Thony. Then, Suzan looked at him. An objective outsider would have seen the look of love in Suzan's eyes, compared to the look of fear and confusion on Kristi's face. But this group contained no objective outsiders, they were all very subjectively biased towards Kristi's point of view. The woman to woman interactions made some of the task force members uncomfortable, they turned away to check the perimeter.

They were not used to seeing the woman coming out of their team leader. That made her just a little too human. But, then she was back.

"Ok, convince me."

"Alright, I don't know how far you have to go back to remember the last time you loved a man, if ever; try to remember. Well, I've loved this man for years, from far away, and from right next to him, but now we're lovers. I love everything about this man, that's why I can tell you that that picture is not my man. Besides the obvious lack of a scar, or beard stubble, his eyes are wrong. If you weren't such a fake hard-ass, you would notice that too. Put those things together and you can see, my man has love in his eyes. Those other eyes are dead. I'll admit that they do look scarily alike. But that's not him."

Kristi put the photos side by side once again. She shined a light on the scar, and then his face; lastly, looking into the eyes. What she felt, came rushing towards her like a freight train. She jumped up and walked back to the window. She saw the Blackhawk hovering, and knew that they were recording every move. She turned her back to the chopper. This woman had touched parts of her that the job had kept covered up for so long. She had forgotten how much it hurt for them to be exposed, her womanhood. Had she been so tactical to the extent that her womanhood was at risk? Her female intuition should have alerted her much sooner that something was wrong. Because of this woman, the numbers were now cranking up the gut feelings. She believed the woman. This man could have never pled his case like his woman just did.

Either she was the best liar that Kristi had ever seen, or, she was telling the truth. And if she was telling the truth, lord have mercy. If everything she said was true, they had damaged property, invaded their privacy, tazed them unconscious, and handled their naked bodies. They had basically kidnapped them by force, under the name of National Security.

"Cut her loose."

"Copy that team leader."

"Let her get dressed."

"What about him?"

"Cut his hands free; keep his feet tied for a minute. I've got to get to the bottom of this."

***

Robert handled the Heckler and Koch mp5 handily. The weight distribution with the attached suppressor was that of a perfectly machined throwing knife. Standing by in the large open space was unnerving. The constantly shifting dark shapes were looking, seeking, and investigating. He was near a group surrounding an access door to what looked to be a maintenance closet. Robert stepped around to look into the depths of the dark as his speaker crackled in his ear

"Blowback 3 to Dog."

"Go 3."

"Dog, we got two devices set to T-37:00.00 and rolling down, but we also got a note."

"Copy that 3, retrieve 'em decon and back to base."

"Roger that Decon and back."

So, there were two devices here and a note. Maybe this would be a link to the whereabouts of the face. Robert was going to find that face. The Task Force member, Crocker, his vest read, was the unwilling donor of the uniform and weapons; his body should be settling in nicely, at the bottom of the Mississippi. Unless, of course, the current takes him down river. It was kind of amazing how easy it was to take him while hanging by the pilings of the Boardwalk.

Robert had pulled his head back and drained his deeply sliced throat directly into the river. Once he bled out, he undressed him and became him. The Kevlar face guard was perfect. It gave him the menacing look of vigilance and provided enough disguise to stay close enough to find out what they knew about the face. Now, it was a matter of principal. He wanted to kill him for stepping on his kill. As unprofessional as it was, this was personal.

The astronaut suited figure came out dragging the hard case behind him. The black armored guy behind him had what looked like two packs of smokes attached to a thick window screen, holding them out in front of him and bringing up the rear.

He handed the two objects to a Task Force tech with a large zip loc bag with a single piece of paper inside. Robert needed to know what was on that paper.

"Blowback 3 to crypto."

"Go for crypto."

"You on site?"

"Affirmative."

"Coming in third, got you in site, one and two are gonna need some working room."

"Copy that 3, making room for one; two, three come straight to the truck."

"Copy."

As the penetration team exited the building, the balance of the force fell in behind and created a perimeter around the mobile lab and the crypto van. The message first went to the mobile lab, the sniffer cleared the paper, declaring it clean. Then, the two devices were put into the sterile compartment. This time, James used both robotic arms to invert the devices and remove the vials without spilling the contents. They were filled to the top with the off-white powdered death. He hoped that Belinda was in time on Torch 1.

Several pieces of non-secured equipment had fallen behind the door to the HVAC unit on Torch 1. Having viewed the video, she knew where to look and what to look for. The obstructions put an extra three minutes into getting inside to the device.

"Lights full."

The blinding shoulder lights illuminated the area; the filter access door was directly ahead.

"Bombs, pull that door; nobody else had explosives, but I don't trust this timer shit."

"Copy that,

He ran ahead and used a pry tool to snatch the access door off. The device was there just like in the video, but the timer read 00:01:50 and was rapidly drawing down.

"Shit, Shit, Shit, come in Bridge!"

She was striding towards the device.

"Bridge, go."

"Percent evac, stat?"

"48% got more Coast Guard en route."

"Copy over."

She knew there was nothing they would be able to do from there if she was late.

"Bombs, you got a bag?"

"What kinda bag?"

"Any fuckin bag bombs."

He pulled out a plastic sandwich bag; the clock was down to :37 seconds. Belinda stepped up onto a shelf, inverted the bag, and wrapped it around the cylinder. She twisted hard to the right; it felt so wrong, but there was a slight movement. It subconsciously felt like it was tightening. Her mind kept saying rightee-tightee-leftee-loosee. But, the instructions said it was oppositely threaded. :21, :20, :19. She twisted again to the right, more movement. But the clock was still ticking.

"What the hell, damn it.? Stop!!"

One more twist and it gave. With a full turn, she watched the numbers go from :04, :03 to fade off, as the screen went blank. She kept the bag securely attached to the tube and the device, while the bomb squad tech cut away the filter retaining screen from behind the device. The whole thing came loose and Belinda slowly stepped down and made her way out of the maintenance closet. The Task Force officers cleared the doorway. The bomb squad tech opened the mobile lab according to her instructions, and removed the secure lid on the sterile container. She carefully placed the bag and the exposed device into the box and closed the door before checking in.

"Blowback 1 to Dog."

"Go one."

"Threat is contained, repeat, threat contained; please advise."

"Copy one, threat contained; good job. Stand by. Torch 1 is en route back to shore with .5 capacity copy."

"Copy, over."

Belinda allowed herself to exhale. Still clad in her spacesuit, as she would be until she got back to the base camp, she prepared to leave. She looked into the container and shivered, then said a prayer for the victims on Torch 2, and to give C.B. Strength.

Quarantine 1 was receiving airdrops of hazbags, which were quadruple-ply quarantine body bags for hazardous material corpses. The anthrax exposure, for at least ten minutes, was enough to infect the lungs of every person breathing inside the Riverboat, which comprised 95% occupancy. The 5% not breathing inside had the worst luck, which had saved their lives. This group had squandered all their money gambling, and had either gotten drinks or food, had adjourned outside to the above decks, to enjoy the only pleasures left to the busted gambler: fresh air, and the scenic views up and down the mighty Mississippi River. Quarantine 1, the former Torch 2, registered as the Mississippi Comet started the day as a partial charter.

The Rolling Wheels convention had charted the Riverboat for the selection of their number. They wanted to try their luck while attending their convention in St. Louis, this fateful weekend. They were 22,000 in number officially; 650 were registered for the casino boat ride. Twenty-five of their number had been left at the pier due to a traffic jam at a National Guard check point. They had, subsequently, been evacuated from Torch 3.

The Rolling Wheels Organization held an annual convention composed of wheelchair bound individuals. They were disabled from birth, due to an accident, or other circumstances. This was a terrible blow to the conventioneers. In addition to the 'Wheels, another 650 non-charter casino patrons were aboard, including an unlucky extra twenty five, that took the place of the scheduled Rolling Wheels conventioneers, that didn't make it.

All in all, the Mississippi Comet had a crew and passenger contingent of 1,340. Roughly, seventy of those survived being outside, plus two bartenders, two waitresses, and a bar back. The Task Force had contaminant suits airdropped that were to be donned on the topside level that had been declared 'SAFE'. Although safe didn't mean 'STERILE', it was a far sight better than 'BIO HAZARD'.

The Task Force still wore their TAC gear with the respirator masks, so they were relatively safe. C.B. ordered anti-anthrax injections as a precaution before they were allowed to dress in the decontamination suits to begin bagging and identifying the dead. The two ounces of weapons grade anthrax was enough to kill as many people as could have been aboard the ship.

The absolute maximum capacity was 2,500 with a crew of ninety five. The charter rules of the company dictated that the number of charters could be matched to the number of non-charters up to a predetermined number. This would make the charters feel special, while still keeping enough people aboard to satisfy the casino minimum numbers for daily operations. Nightly operations tended to flow closer to the maximum numbers.

History will reflect that the young crypto logical technician and C.B. Peters were the heroes of the day. C.B. had major problems comparing 1,265 dead to being a savior. But, looking at the big picture, the 1,970 people on Torch 1, and the 3,000 people in the land-based hotel and casino complex, considered C.B. Peters their savior, none the less. As Torch 1 and Blowback team#1 were pulling up to the pier, the sky darkened with the foursome of Blackhawk's screaming, while coming into the base camp.

"Team leader to Dog."

"Go for Dog team leader."

"Status?"

"Torch 3 and 1 contained, devices captured and secured, 3. Vials of confirmed weapons grade Anthrax secured 3, :2 from Torch 3, 1 from Torch 1. No suspects. Torch 2 is officially Quarantine 1, with 1,265 casualties, seventy survivors."

"Copy that Dog, any rundown on the origin of the Anthrax?"

"That's a negative Team Leader. CDC types are handling the specs on origin; Torch 3 had a note, more crazy talk. Current location crypto."

"Copy crypto, Team Leader coming in plus 2, copy?"

"Copy that, team leader +2, standing by."

"Team Leader out."

The quartet of Blackhawks landed in a staggered formation. They disgorged their cargo. Then, one by one, elevated to altitude and met up with the KC3 tankers to refuel, one by one. Kristi's personal bird was last. Phillip and James flanked Thony and Suzan, dressed now in bright orange jumpsuits purposely, looking totally out of place amongst the sea of black clad figures.

They were not under arrest, but not free to go either. They were officially classified as 'visitors of the team leader' under protection, and two seconds from a fresh pair of flexi-cuffs. They complied with the situation but at the same time trying to get to the bottom of this mistaken identity situation themselves.

Chapter 36

Florida

Dutchess lay back on her bed still partially in shock over the negotiation. Could she even say it? She figured the intent letter was signed; the bank card was right there; the account was good. She had called the toll free number; had spoken to a customer service supervisor; had chosen her six-digit secret PIN code; and, had recorded her voiceprint for the online backup verification. After all those steps, she called in to check the balance. There it was:

"Your account balance is six million, six hundred twenty seven thousand, six hundred seventy five dollars".

She hung up the phone. Her body was flushed hot. She pulled her dress over her head and laid it carefully over the back of her office chair. She was still hot; she unhooked her bra now, she felt a little cooler. She sat on the edge of her bed and whispered,

"Six million, six hundred twenty seven thousand, six hundred seventy five dollars!"

She got another rush just from saying it. Her body had a rosy glow as if all her blood was coming to the surface. She looked to her left and saw the cake box, sweet! She retrieved a set of cutlery that had been wrapped and set in the front corner of the box; it was taped in place like a Buckingham palace guard. She slid the knife carefully out from the napkin and sliced a piece of cake so thin you could almost see through it. She used considerable skill to balance the slice out of the box. It mostly fell apart on its way to her mouth, but she scooped it up and ate it with relish. Then she thought,

"I can buy at least six million of these cakes, why am I trippin?"

She cut a nice sized chunk of cake; this piece held together wonderfully balanced on the knife. She pulled a tissue from the box on the nightstand and carefully floated the slice over to it. Not one crumb fell from the rich, incredibly moist cake. She lay it down with a small mouthwatering bounce.

She chopped off one bottom corner and popped it into her mouth, chewing with her eyes closed swinging her feet in front of herself like she was practicing her kick stroke. That's when the knock on the door sounded. In her mind she could hear the theme song from the "six million dollar man", a TV series she had seen on the old school drama series channel. It was appropriate.

She silently bounded off the bed, quietly pantomimed running to the door to look out of the peephole to see who was knocking. The view through the fisheye lens showed various torso parts because there was too much person to fit in the lens, Franz. Her toes started to unconsciously wiggle. She took the security bar off the door and stood behind as she opened it to the empty room. He stepped in, silently invited,

"Dutchess?"

As he cleared the door, it closed behind him, he turned around and stared with his mouth wide open. Dutchess stood bare footed, and naked, except for the translucent silky French thong. Her hair was down; it draped and caressed her shoulders like a lion's mane, and those green eyes sparkled with amorous energy.

"Hey Franz, I got a sponsor."

"Congratulations."

Came squeaking out of his excited dry throat,

"Uhhmm congratulations Dutchess, who is it?"

"Coke brands, it's my first one. I went to the negotiations with Henry. I'd like to leave all that to him; but I know I'm going to need to stay on top of my business. That's enough about business; give me a kiss."

Franz bent down to wrap his arms around her and she jumped into his embrace. The feel of her warm breasts against his shirt and her calves wrapped around the backs of his thighs were indescribable. He felt as if twenty years had dropped away; he was eighteen again and she was the older woman. The time travel element of this live action fantasy was apropos as well. The heat and pressure of her molten red haired fire box was making him harder than he could remember being since he had been eighteen.

Those mythical uncontrollable late teenaged erections, scientifically proven to burst through zippers, known to break bricks, was how he felt right now. Dutchess was running her fingers through his hair and rocking up and down his marble hard shaft. They had the same thought: too many clothes. She leaped down and began unbuttoning his shirt very fast, with quick nimble finger work that would have made the bionic man's Doctors proud.

He was slowly undoing his pants at the same time. They finished in a tie. His pants dropped. She pushed down his boxers. He pulled her thong down. There they were, no more words necessary. She led him to the bed. He sat and she crawled over him pushing him down as she went, until she was sitting above his stomach, with her knees on either side of him. His throbbing bone was poking up her back. She looked down at him, he was looking straight ahead, directly into her deep red bush. She could feel him looking at her hard clit. It was pulsing out of its fleshy hood, the hairs on his chest was tickling it to excited stiffness. Franz was mesmerized by the tan colored lips hiding behind the sparse red hair. Ever since he had enjoyed her ministrations earlier, he had that sight, the smell, and the taste on his mind.

He reached down and grasped her womanly ass cheeks and pulled them forward towards his face, watching, as the treasure grew closer and closer. She helped by wiggling, pressing her lips to his chest to leave a trail of wetness. Then, it was there, his breath on her made her gasp. She pinched her own nipples, tossed her hair over her shoulders. Her head fell back and her mouth uttered a moan. He licked her from her opening up through her creamy lips to her clit.

Franz held her clit between his lips like a whistle. He began to suck and lick causing Dutchess to lose control. She cramped, her muscles contracting while he feasted on her. Her orgasms caused her to schooch farther up on to his face and her ass cheeks now cradled in the crook of his elbows. She was bent forward, holding on to his head riding and shaking. There were tears in her eyes from the intense pleasure of release. He rolled her over to his right, scooting back. She was still shaking; some pressure was abated from the sides of his head as he spread her open and licked her inner butt cheeks.

The cream had pooled there and he spread it around her totally open real estate; he flattened his tongue and licked up one side of her clit and down the other. Her entire body was flexing with her orgasms. He reached below and inserted one finger at a time until he had three wet fingers inside of her. He spread her tight muscles and dipped lower and tongued her anus. He spiraled his fingers deeply into her, preparing her for his wide dick. As he worked on Dutchess, he pulled her closer to the edge of the bed. With his foot, he retrieved his pants, reached down to pull out a three-pack condoms, while his hand was busily fingering Duchess.

He could feel Dutchess' orgasms cresting. He pulled his tongue away from its duty and ripped open the foil pack. He rolled the rubber onto himself, and, once again moved Dutchess back to the center of the bed. Drunk with the orgasms his mouth and fingers had brought her, Duchess' strong, flexible, body moved automatically into the perfect position. He knelt in front of her throbbing inviting wet hole. He held an ankle in each hand raised in the air.

He moved in and notched the head inside of her; her eyes flew open when she remembered what he was packing. There was no need to worry. He slid into her slowly; as the width began to expand, he gently pushed her legs open and down until in the end, her legs were touching the bed. He opened her legs wider than her shoulders and quickly he was all the way in. She had to reach down to feel her lips because they were stretched so wide, she couldn't believe it. But after three strokes to her clit, she started to strangle him inside of her and he began to thrust.

The love making was like none she could remember. For him, it was the first time a woman could take all of him and make him feel like he was normal. They made love twice on the bed, then, they went to the shower. This time when Franz slipped and slid in and out of the crack of her ass, she let him do more.

She relaxed and guided him, let just the head slide into her ass while looking back over her shoulder. He couldn't go in very far, but that impossibly tight two-inch in and out was too much for him. He held on tight to her waist while her arms were up against the shower wall and she felt him pump jets of hot come into her ass. This was a first for Dutchess and it triggered an orgasm she didn't expect, with the flexing and contracting of her sphincter causing more of Franz to slip into her. She gripped his still hard dick and eased it out of her anus; his come falling to the shower floor; she felt so stretched and open. She washed him off again and pulled the last condom off the shower caddy. They made love one more time in the shower with him holding her up leaning against the wall, and finally, with her riding him on the floor of the shower.

Afterwards, they sat in each other's arms. Franz turned off the water with his long legged talented foot. He kissed her all over from her forehead to her belly, back up to her plump lips, sucking her tongue. He leaned back and saw the love and satisfaction in her eyes. Words could never be enough; so, he stayed silent. They rose and dried off. Franz carried Dutchess to the bed and lay her down on the sheets, bypassing the wet spots on the blanket. He kissed her, congratulated her, and stroked her hair until she slept. He then dressed and left.

Chapter 37

Dulcet drove the Ford around to the block behind the "All Nite" garage and walked to pick up the Benz. She made the trip back to her house. She emerged in the kitchen, using her infrared goggles, so that she didn't have to turn on any lights. Afterwards, she made her way to the master bathroom. The plastic surgery mask was waiting where she had left it; the steaming drip from the water closet shelf had softened it up, until it had the consistency of smooth skin. She went into her tool chest of makeup. It was the same rolling cart you would see in an upscale auto repair shop or mechanical enterprise. It was fully five feet tall by three feet wide, with all its drawers, cabinets, and compartments. She selected a base that matched her light skin; she blended the makeup on the mask to fit seamlessly around her face.

Next, she drew on some features using blushes and glosses. She highlighted and visibly sculpted the face to look like a Japanese aneme character, a pretty power puff girl with the biggest eyes ever. Her work bag was packed with the tools she would need including a small Asian memento she would miss dearly and an inflatable ballgag. But, it would serve to keep her personal signature intact. Ms. Summers would enjoy this; she had no choice. Ready to go, she closed up the house and set out in the baby Benz, still under cover of darkness, although not for long.

She drove back to the "All Nite" parking facility up to another level. She parked. She adjusted the veil that was integrated in her vintage 1963, Jackie Kennedy pillbox mourning hat, and shuffled to the Ford around the corner. The black duster was tossed into the back seat, soon to be discarded. She made her way to the money exchange. She rolled around to the same place she had observed from hours earlier when she had seen the delivery truck. But this time, she turned around and parked in the lot. The money exchange was empty, the time was 7:19 a.m. Dulcet strolled in with her double stuffed bra. Her pillow bottoms pushed what she had damn near to her chin with cleavage. She used almost a full roll of toilet tissue underneath to create truly massive, but realistic tits. The Marilyn Monroe dress that she wore so well on her tall frame, as she walked into the exchange, that the exotic face at first didn't seem that far from real, even with the big bambi eyes. She approached and called Margie by name.

"Hey Margie, where you at, honey?"

"I'm out back; I'll be there in a second."

Poor thing she had no idea. Dulcet looked around at what she had to work with; perfect, a wheel chair with wooden arm rests, didn't get much better than that. The access to the business area was simply a wooden raised top like one would see at a bar; Dulcet raised it and walked through the counter while Margie came from the bathroom wiping her hands on a paper towel.

As soon as she saw Dulcet, a hundred different emotions flashed across her face. Seeing this beautiful platinum Marilyn Monroe, the aneme face, the semi-automatic pistol, and, the fact that she obviously knew her name, was more than her mind could process. So, after her face finished its juke box run through emotions and expressions, she simply asked if she could help her. The innocence in her voice tickled Dulcet.

"Yes you may sweetie, take all your clothes off for me."

"Huh?"

As Dulcet approached her, she didn't move, and her mouth was still open. Dulcet placed the barrel of the gun inside her mouth.

"Now listen well, I'm not going to repeat myself again. Take off all of your clothes right now."

With gun in mouth, Margie began ripping the buttons off her money exchange button down. She tore her bra trying to get it off, but she finally did. She unsnapped her pants and let them fall while kicking off her shoes. Finally, she stood in her panties, loud, busy pastel panties at that. Dulcet Bent down with her to allow her to remove and step out of the ugly panties.

Dulcet led her to the mail cart and pulled the gun out of her mouth long enough to let her clear out all the non-alarmed or dye-packed cash. Once the cart was full and the folded duffel bag from her large purse was filled, she pulled out her duct tape and placed the Asian contraption on the roller chair. Dulcet led Margie to the chair and put the pistol back into her mouth. She had to move quickly; she was approaching five minutes, and she had allotted herself six to eight.

After taping the Asian toy to the seat cushion, she spun Margie around and bent her in half forcing a ballgag into her mouth. With latex gloves on, she stuck two fingers into her pussy and lubricated her ass. She pulled her back up and aimed the two headed toy up into both her holes. They both started to vibrate, thrust and spin as soon as she hit the power. Dulcet taped her arms to the chairs arms.

She figure-eight taped her thighs to the chair seat. Ensuring no separation anxiety or attempts, she taped her feet to the wheel boards and rolled her into the back room. She saw a convenient VCR running under the cash register; she took the tape, flipped the door sign to 'be back at 12:00' and hopped into the Ford. Serenely pulling out, she made her left turn to head back to the "All Nite" parking deck. She replaced the Benz with the Ford, took off all the clothes, tissue, the black Duster and put them into a specialized titanium case. The case was designed to destroy sensitive information in the case that it was inevitably going to fall into enemy hands. The bag contained chemical phosphorous guaranteed to destroy anything inside it within thirty seconds, Dulcet flipped the switch. The outside of the case heated up measurably as the chemical reaction took place; then, a minute later, it began to cool. The bag sat on the back bench next to the duffel. Dulcet was ready to go. One more stop by the house and she was ready to hit Atlanta to get prepped for the scheduled recipe meal-Soul Food

She stepped back through the pantry, lugging the duffle bag into the safe. Dulcet counted out $680,000; of that, $400,000 was $100 bills; $130,000 was $50 bills, and the last $150,000 was a mix of lower denominations. She put the $530,000 in large bills into the cash carousel and kept the

$150k in the duffel. She separated out $1 and $5 bills to give to the homeless.

She had a heart, and nothing keeps a good myth going like a healthy dose of Robin Hoodism. Dulcet planned to leave for Atlanta within the next five hours; she repacked the kitchen, put her TV back on the TV guide channel, dumped all the trash into a bag and staged it in the pantry to take with her. All the vaults were relocked; she had enough cash for anything that might come up. She gathered up her roller bag and the trash, then exited the Miami house through the pantry floor.

***

Dutchess woke and stretched. She was sore in ways only a woman would ever know, but yet she smiled. She hadn't expected Franz to stay the night, but she could still feel the ghost of his good night kiss. She felt an exhilaration she had never felt before. In one day, her world had changed so much. In many ways, it was totally unrecognizable, but, there were precious few things that remained. She rolled out of bed onto her feet. Everything she owned felt the presence of Franz. As soon as she stood, her thighs vibrated and sent reminders throughout her body. She stiffly walked to the bathroom and turned the water on as hot as she could stand it.

She sat in the tub, and the water started creeping up her calves and lower body. The water pressure was high, so she wasn't sitting there long before the water had crested over her hips and made its way to the bottom of her breasts. She added baby oil, bubble bath, lavender aromatherapy, and essential oils that immediately went to work soothing her ravished body.

She lay back and smiled, raised her hair on top of her head, thinking about last night. She could see how Franz could be rejected often, because of the size of his package. A lot of people talk about wanting men with huge dicks, but once confronted with the real thing, they run away. It's so unfair, especially to a nice guy, which Franz seemed to be, so far.

Dutchess knew how it could be to get your hopes up and then be left hanging. It was similar to the ways racism reached out and touched her; she knew she wasn't white, and her friends knew. Strangers for the most part, ignored her modest amount of pigment. Some, you could tell by their faces, were very disappointed when they discovered that they were wrong about   her race.

With Franz, having been on top of his game for so long, had to have had swarms of admirers. But, all it took was the wrong groupie to try to wrap herself around all that flesh nature had given him, for him to run away scared; that could affect anyone's self-esteem. Having a penis that big, but, nobody to practice on, was a wonder that he could ever learn how to use that big thing on a woman, without killing her.

The way they had made love, the foreplay with his fingers, caused everything to work, literally, like a well-oiled machine. Once her body got used to his size, it felt good, and he was very enthusiastic. It was as if he felt that he was young again. But there was a price to pay; and she was soaking that price away now.

Franz was a good lover, but for her his loving was only for special occasions. Yeah, he was nothing for every day, but it was good to feel a man again. There's only so much a woman with a strap-on can do to replace that feeling. Women were best at being femmes, women; soft and leave the men to being who they were. Her mind slid sideways, and she drifted off to sleep. She awoke to discover that the water was almost cold; she turned the hot water back on and flipped the drain lever with her toe, sucking out some cold replacing it with hot.

With the tub back to steamy, she started to explore her body. She rubbed her thighs, and they felt much better. Pulling her knees to her chest, she felt no stiffness in her hamstrings like she did as she rolled out of the bed. The stretching, bunching, and releasing of her legs re-awakened her sex. Opening her knees to the limit of the tubs width, she tentatively explored the recent love war zone. She gingerly fingered her labia, probing for tenderness. She felt relatively little.

This was the site of the previous majority of her discomfort. But the probing and remembering boosted her blood pressure, and gave her a nice flush that had nothing to do with the heat of the water. She probed an experimental finger inside; it was welcomed by the powerful bite of her muscles and she smiled knowing she wasn't stretched for life.

She knew that she would have Franz again; but, it surely wouldn't be this week! She stood to exit the bubble bath, and heard the phone ring. Casually, she stepped onto the fluffy, shag, bath rug. She reached out and pushed talk on the hands-free phone console, which was built into the bathroom wall.

"Hello, Dutchess,"

It was Henry

"Hey Henry, what's up? It's awfully early don't cha think?"

"Yes, I know; I've been up all night. Word spreads fast with CNN being worldwide 24hours, and located in your hometown. I've been getting e-mails, texts, and voice messages from everywhere: Australia, Europe, Asia, damn near every continent but Greenland. Even Antarctica had called with some interest in you. Before I allow myself to sleep, I wanted to discuss some things with you."

"Okay Henry, I've got you on speaker; so, go ahead."

The phone system was 'aware' similar to the bathroom lights; if there was movement inside the bathroom, the lights would come on. Movement at least once in five minutes caused the lights to stay on, or else they would turn off. Similarly, when the phone was on speaker, if the local talker were to move out of range of the mike or motion detector, it would switch the function to the next phone that sensed your motion. So, as Dutchess walked out of the bathroom into the bedroom, the sound of Henry was coming from in front of her by the bed.

"Well, firstly, I've been thinking about shopping for an agent for you that will be exclusively tasked with your sporting side. I'll get you all the money you could ever imagine and take care of everything regarding you and your brand. But I'd like to let the sports agent handle everything that deals with tennis: matches, ranking, and tournaments. This week has shown me how brilliant I am with marketing, but yet, how far out of my league I am with the actual sport part. How does that sound to you?"

"That sounds like my amazing, robotic, cross-marketologist got a human programming upgrade. I know you can't do everything, Henry, I never expected you to. I appreciate all that you do; you do so much, that I would never ask you to stretch yourself any further. So yes, I think that's a good idea. Do you have anybody in mind?"

"Not yet, I'm gonna check some sources for applicants when we get home."

"Yeah, home, whenever that'll be."

"Uh, Dutchess?"

"Yeah?"

"Did you mention anything to Carlos about wanting to go home?"

"I'm not sure; so much happened yesterday. I'm sure I probably did."

She looked at her trophy in its place of honor across the room, reflecting the first orange rays of sunlight rising from the Atlantic.

"Why do you ask?"

"You're on the same side of the building I am Dutchess, look out your window."

Slipping on a robe, in case any paparazzi was staked out there with a camera focused on her window. There'd not be any voluntary tabloid pictures if she could help it, she looked out the window. At first she didn't see anything. Then, the red, white, and black mosaic tiles artistically morphed into 'Drink More Coke, Go Dutchess Go.'.

"Henry! What is that?"

"It just pulled up D, I thought it was some performer until I read the top."

"But what do you think it can be? Is it a city bus promotion you hooked up and forgot about?"

"No, I think I'd remember something like this D. I mean, it's a bus."

"Yeah, I noticed that too."

The silence was impossible to keep, simultaneously they both said,

"I'm gonna get dressed."

"Meet you at the elevator."

They laughed like school kids from the verbal collision.

"Ok, I'll meet you in about five minutes or less."

Dutchess went into her wheel bag and pulled out a plain grey sweat suit and a pink baseball cap. She gathered her hair and pulled it through the back of the cap, slipped on some pink anklets, and a fresh pair of bright white Nikes with the swoosh removed. She took her trophy and put it in the bed on the pillow and pulled the cover halfway over it. She put out the "Do not disturb" sign and made sure that she had the card key. She actually skipped to the elevator where Henry was waiting,

"Henry what the hell is going on?"

"Dutchess, I don't have a clue. If I hadn't looked out the window when I did, we might have been told, but I couldn't not tell you I saw that."

"So we see when we see huh?"

The elevator seemed to take forever this morning. They finally reached the Mezzanine level, and took the escalator down undercover. She almost made it past the concierge desk when the photo pack awoke to her presence. The nonstop flashes began for the day. She walked through them casually, hoping that she didn't look like a zombie. As she came close to the door, she could swear that she saw her eye, giant sized. She slowed her approach and grabbed Henrys arm, as they stood behind the floor to ceiling glass doors.

"Unbelievable!"

Neither could think of anything else to say. They walked outside and noticed that security had blocked off the entire carport in front of the hotel. Peripherally, from the right, she noticed a figure closing in with a hand outstretched. She turned and saw Carlos; his entire face was taken up by the smile that filled it. She noticed how much pleasure he derived from their shock and surprise,

"Dutchess, all the cars in my fleet would not be enough to continue to send to pick you up. So, we, in our infinite wisdom decided that you should have some transportation. You can call it your official company car.

Carlos theatrically opened his right arm to present to Dutchess a fifty three foot tour bus with pictures of her all along the sides. The two large rectangular cuts in the wrapping indicated that this was no ordinary bus. It was the Prevost Superliner Royale Dual Slider with expandable sides at the front and middle; this was the top of the line.

"And for the times when you want to be a little less conspicuous."

They walked around to the back of the bus. Carlos handed the remote key fob to Dutchess and indicated for her to push the trunk release button. The back end of the bus began to rise, revealing a backed in Mini Cooper convertible wagon nestled perfectly inside the space. Dutchess' eyes began leaking once more. She hugged Carlos, squeezed Henry until he was almost breathless, then, turned, still stunned and speechless. She looked her 'new ride' over.

Carlos was overcome with joy.

"Come on, let's do the tour."

Dutchess and Henry both blindly followed behind Carlos, who was strutting like a proud papa. As they approached the door, it hydraulically whispered open. The man in the driver's seat was waving at Dutchess,

"Meet Max. Max this is Dutchess Singletary and her manager, Henry, the core members of... How did you put it Henry? Oh yeah, 'Team Dutchess'. Dutchess, Max is your driver, but not only that, he is a major multi-tasker. He provides security and mechanics; he's an electronics whiz. That'll make sense later, plus any and everything else you need to ensure your personal comfort and safety. Not to worry Henry, he doesn't do business; his purpose is specifically to ensure the privacy and security of your charge and entourage."

The word entourage didn't fit too well into Dutchess' vocabulary; she never was one to hang with many people. Although she knew that her crew would increase by a few, she wasn't looking forward to multitudes. She looked at

Henry, he saw her hesitation,

"Don't worry D, no roaring crowds, this is all about you, ok?"

She felt the building weight lift off her chest.

"Ok Henry"

She looked at Carlos.

"Ok, ok, let's go."

They went on with the tour. Once atop the stairs, it was extremely difficult to remember that they were on a bus. It was actually called a Coach, which fit much better, since the trappings made her feel like Cinderella.

The sofas on either side pulled back and became dual height sectionals; when the sides expanded it was the size of a nice living room. Two flat screen TVs were integrated into the front wall. There were cup holders and plate clamps on all the eating surfaces. Beneath each cushion was a storage space; the sofas were plush enough to be wonderful beds. They continued down the hall: on the left, were cut out bunks, two sections of three each. Each bunk had a privacy curtain, a small flat screen entertainment center, and a charging station. Everything had wireless headset audio, which allowed the occupants to enjoy themselves without bothering others.

To the right of this same hallway was the restroom; the toilet had an adjoining door to a full sized water closet and shower. Farther down was the kitchen, with a two-burner induction stove, mini grill, and a side table tray that flipped into a griddle surface. The refrigerator was integrated into the knee panels. Not an inch of space was wasted; moving past this section, the next expandable area was the living/meeting room.

The walls expanded out the same way as the front section. The extra captain-styled chairs unfolded and sat around a central space. The oblong design on the ceiling, at the flip of a switch, lowered on covered wire rope cables to hover and form a meeting table. The entire living room area doubled as a fully functional office meeting room. Dutchess had never seen anything like this before in her life, much less the thought that it could be on wheels. Henry had seen a host of tour busses through his work in the music industry. So he knew the quality of the conversion compared to the stock installs that go out on tours. This was impressive.

The final rearmost section had the only door other than the bathroom. This was Dutchess' master bedroom suite. The bed filled the majority of the space; all the amenities were full sized: a 42" flat screen, full multimedia entertainment system, a Macintosh computer, a titanium G6 was wirelessly connected to use the flat screen as a monitor. Spread out on the bed was a comforter with an intriguing mix of Coca Cola colors; the tiara D logo was prominently displayed in the center.

Dutchess sat on the firm, yet cushiony, bed and looked at the two men.

"So, this is my life now, huh? Well, where do I park this thing?"

Carlos and Henry sat in the bedroom's companion chairs, and Carlos started.

"Dutchess, I know this is a major change and it's all come at once. But, it's what you have worked hard for, and now it's here. Right now you have a chance to make decisions most people will never have in their lifetime. You can change as much or as little as you want. It's at your disposal, don't feel as if you have to do anything. This coach is a symbol of my appreciation. It will be on call whenever you want it, and we have facilities for the bus and driver anywhere in the country. Are you ok?"

"Yeah, ok, but you're right. I'm very overwhelmed. Is there a handbook for this sort of thing?"

Carlos chuckled and said,

"Oh yeah, there's a handbook; you'll get it as soon as the contracts are signed. It is a job, don't forget. But, your job, your primary job, is what?"

"To play tennis well."

There were nods all around at that statement.

"And this bus, the signing bonus, the pastries,

are simply things to help you relax". He smiled that smile that made her relax in increments. "If they don't do their job, let me know; we will get rid of them. Your security and well-being are of the utmost importance to us. When you get home, you decide what you want to do about your lodgings. If you want to move, we have staff that can help you relocate, although, we would prefer that you stay in the Atlanta area. The choice is yours."

"Thank you Carlos. I have a lot to think about, but that gives me a good place to start."

"I'm glad to hear that."

Carlos stood up to leave.

"The bus has been wrapped with integrated O.L.E.D layers; therefore, every so often you will have a different exterior. As long as this interior is to your liking, it will stay the same, ok?"

"Ok."

"I'll be in touch. Take care, Henry."

"Thanks for everything, Carlos, really."

Carlos left Henry and Dutchess. She looked at Henry.

"Henry, I wanna go home."

"Ok, I have three or four more meetings today to get you settled into an apparel company so that we know what gear you will be wearing to your next tournament. There will be no more blank outfits Dutchess. I'm working to ensure that whatever company we go with, your diamond tiara will be part of the design."

Dutchess was laying back on the bed. Her thoughts were swirling like a tornado. After all of the years that she had been playing tennis, it still felt like fame came too soon.

"Ok Henry, you let me know what the outcomes are; keep me up on any decisions you need me to approve. I'm gonna go pack. There shouldn't be any problem going back to Atlanta on the roads, should there?"

"Nothing I can think of. I'll check with Max. For some reason, it seems that 'I don't know' isn't in his vocabulary."

They walked back through to the front of her new home on wheels. Dutchess was touching every surface, making sure it was real. At the door, Max gave her a diamond encrusted dog tag with his contact information on the front and one ruby on the back.

"That ruby is a call button; if you need me, push that ruby. Wherever you are, I'll be there. There are only four of those in the world, and you have number two."

Dutchess thanked Max, and exited the bus. The door closed, completing a picture of herself. Still floating on a cloud of disbelief, she walked into the hotel. She entered the elevator and went to her room to pack.

***

Dulcet piloted the Mercedes through Miami avoiding the National Guard as much as possible. At the first check point, she was stopped; she showed a fake passport and green card that identified her as Rebekah O'Brien, a legal alien pub master. She still had a year left on her work visa, so she was legit. The riding outfit she chose to wear was nothing that would stick out.

She'd chosen a zipped up grey hoodie with huge channel sun shades, and an emerald green Hermes scarf casually fitted on her head that was barely keeping her hair controlled. The roof was down and the matching leather grey, knee-length skirt with bobby sox and cute low top tennis shoes, made her look like the perfect Miami socialite out for a drive.

Of course, nothing was as it seemed with Dulcet. Her bare legs were a hint to the lack of anything else that she wore. So, when the guardsman wanted to look deeper than the requisite inspection of the identification, she called and told him that she may have found another piece of ID, using her best Irish brogue.

When the Guardsman walked back to the car with her ID's in hand, he looked into the car. The first things he saw were both Dulcets breasts framed by the pulled down zipper of her top. Next, he saw two fingers of her left hand thrust deeply inside a flaming red, Irish pussy. Dulcet had her right leg cocked open, languidly fingering herself, looking at the guard.

The Guardsman, totally not expecting this penthouse letters moment, first, looked around. Dulcet was the only car at this particular on-ramp to I-95 north. The weekend warrior had just recently joined the Guard at Miami Junior College, through ROTC to pay for school. Besides, since his once yearly month at Ft. Benning, GA, the Threat Level RED was the most official military that he had felt during his three years in. A bad luck collarbone break that had never healed correctly, kept him from the wars. But because he was hurt on duty, they couldn't let him go. Check point duty would be his lot in the military; the uniform was the only way he felt that he got respect from women. At home, he had an overly extensive collection of magazines and DVDs. Even with a special computer for his cyber porn, which was similar to Dulcet, he was addicted to masturbation; but not on purpose, he was just unlucky.

So, for Staff Sgt., Robert Bennett, this was a 'Don't ask, Don't tell'. 'No shame in my game moment'. He whipped out his little weapon, and proceeded to jack off right there at the check point while looking at Dulcet. This was unexpected; she raised her leg up higher, showing him more and allowing him to hear how wet she was.

She watched this guy's dick. It seemed like the finger indentations from his frequent handling were visible. He was so casually stroking it that he looked like he did this a lot. She was approaching her orgasm; she could see his skinny winkie turning all purple in the head. It seemed like the guardsman thought he was going to come all over her tits, but he was mistaken. She turned on her tantric practice, and used her vaginal muscles to swallow the orgasmic energy back into her body. He was past any possible point of return; he was stroking and holding his breath. When he let the breath out, she knew that he was going to blow his load.

She reached up, this time with two fingers it was nothing like the long, dong, log from the hugely hung black man. She directed his surprisingly hard, spurting, skinny, little dick so that he wound up splattering his semen on the ground, next to her car.

With his face flushed red, and his shrinking dick still soggy in his hand, and a stupid ass 'don't tell' grin on his face, he tossed her passport into the passenger seat with the green card sticking out of the top. He pressed the button to let her onto the Interstate. Ninety five north loomed in the windshield. The chill-speed wind felt good on her wet crotch; the post- masturbatory energy she had redirected back into her body made her feel extra awake. It was as if she had taken a double shot of Adrenaline. The breeze didn't last.

Long before she even got out of the Miami city limits, the traffic kicked in; it was not rush hour traffic nor night club traffic. It was anybody's misfortune, or, fortune, depending on which side of the debate you were on, to travel thru Central GA., on I-85, I-75, I-20, or I-285, during Freaknick, 1994. Then, you know the traffic Dulcet was facing, a slow moving massive parking lot. In this world, the two wheelers ruled. Cars were pushed to the side of the road forming another lane: the out of gas lane. Motorcycles, three wheelers, scooters, even some mountain bikes, were the only things moving with any type of regular speed.

The entrepreneurs were on the case; because of the number of people, flight stranded anti-gouging laws were updated from previous iterations to the current new version. Not only would any gas station selling gas for over the national average be locked and taken over by the National Guard, but the new law took the national average of gas to $1.50. Gas prices hadn't been at this level for over seventeen years.

The record number of cars on the highways allowed the amendment to the National Fuel Bill to pass within twelve hours of the threat level RED. This was done under the auspices of the PATRIOT ACTs tools. The two-wheeled entrepreneurs used whatever they had at their disposal to sell gas: soda bottles, gas cans, anything that wouldn't melt from holding fuel. Some unknowledgeable ones learned the hard way not to sell gas on the side of the road. Like parasites creeping, they were plying their trade. No matter the price they charged, they got their money. The life blood for their vehicles was worth anything they had. Dulcet wasn't worried, she had quite a while to go with the forty-two gallon tank. Not including the emergency overflow, she had hours or miles before the side of the road became a problem.

At one of the periodic stops, she got on her knees and bent over the drivers' seat, totally exposing everything she had to the cars in front. She pulled the spring loaded cowl hood to access the soft top roof. The exposed, vaginal, wiggle exercise lasted a little over a minute. This was enough time to: start a final separation for a couple whose marriage was already on the rocks; to start a heated sex education discussion between a preteen virgin brother and sister; and to start a cigarette fire, as an amorous cocaine sniffer stared with his mouth open and dropped his cigarette, setting his synthetic fiber jogging outfit on fire.

By the time she had the convertible's rear nub set and was ready to key lock the front two nubs into the top of the windshield, the damage was done. Scooting up in traffic, she motored past the tinted out foreign car with the smoke streaming from the windows. The Lincoln Continental with the arguing couple was moving steadily to the right for the rest area. And the ogling eyes of the two young kids in back of the station wagon looked as if they were pulling at each other's clothes.

The High Occupancy Vehicle lane was flowing as if it were an opened tap river. It was fenced off from the five lanes of stuck in syrup traffic of which she was a member.

There were only certain places where you could jump on and off the free flowing lanes of travel and they were restricted to three passengers or more. After what seemed like hours, because it was, Dulcet had watched a movie and listened to a portion of an audio book, a small break in the traffic occurred. She saw a sign; she had finally reached a bypass that would get her to I-75 north quite a bit faster. She shot a gap and got onto the bypass. The Mercedes hummed along at thirty miles per hour. This was faster than she had driven since she had been on the freeway.

Then, she noticed that her gas level was falling. She saw one of the biker/tankers and flagged him down. He approached her open window. She had her skirt slightly below her sparse pubic hair. Her expansive thighs were exposed. She asked for a fill up. The biker made a move to adjust his crotch. She thought that she would have to wait through another jerk-off before getting served.

Apparently, he had some control. He told her that she could get as much as she wanted for $200.00. She told him again to fill it up. Once her gauge touched full (1/1 in a Mercedes), she took out ten $20 bills and clamped them in the window. When he came for the money she asked for her gas cap, for he still had it in his hand. The money in the window wouldn't budge.

He grinned a dumb ass 'oops you caught me' grin and replaced it as she watched. He had no idea that the Walther ppk 9mm sat between the seats. She caught him fair and square; her cap was on, no harm, no foul. As she loosened the window, the money slid out and she took off. The bypass seemed like a good idea so far. Her speed actually passed fifty mph for about five minutes.

After another two hours, she saw the sign Jct I-75. However much time it took from here, at least she was on the direct route to Atlanta. While she was waiting in the lane to merge on to I-75 north, she saw something she would swear on everything she would never see in her entire life. Barreling up the HOV lane from behind her doing at least eighty mph was a huge tour bus! She had seen plenty of them stuck, trying to get on the HOV from I-95. But this one was on I-75 North and it had a beautiful red and green motif, but the thing that was so incredible was that it had her face all over it!

L. Corbin Bey

Chapter 38

Atlanta

Ron opened the door for Sylvania and walked around to the driver's door, performing an age old test; he had unlocked the car door with the key instead of the key fob and let her in. While walking around to the driver's door he watched. When he saw her leaning over to unlock the driver's door so that he could get in, his smile grew so big it hurt his face. He got in looking at her still wearing the dumfounded face,

"What?"

He had no words. He grabbed her face and kissed her deeply. He was all but totally convinced that she was the one. He started the car to drive back to Sylvania's house. Neither one of them had much to say on the way. Ron looked at Sylvania and rubbed circles on the back of her hand lazily while he was watching the road. Traffic in Riverdale was thick, but moving. It took ten minutes from the exit checkpoint to get to her house; Ron parked next to her car. He turned off the engine but left the key in the ignition. Silently they sat. Sylvania broke the silence,

"Do you want to come in and take the tour, sir?"

"What's the cover madam?"

"Well, it's been rather slow today, the discount cover charge is two kisses."

"Two huh? That's kinda steep; do any amenities come with the tour?"

"Well, we'll have to see what the amenity of the day is. It's usually listed inside."

"You know, I think I'll take you up on that tour lady. When is the next one?"

"You're in luck; I can introduce you to the tour guide right now."

Sylvania stepped out of the car, and waited until Ron could walk to the door with her. As they got to the stoop, she walked up two steps and turned around to face him with her arms behind her back. She closed her eyes and pursed her lips for a kiss. Ron pursed his lips in similar fashion and kissed her like a kissing booth contestant. Then he walked up on to her step, wrapped his arms around her and kissed her for real, taking her breath away.

"Oh my, you just earned a coupon for the extended tour; come on let's get started."

She unlocked the door, stepped inside and said,

"Welcome to my humble abode."

And it was, she lived in a modest three bedroom with 2 ½ baths; the two smaller bedrooms were used as an office and a library, respectively. One area of the library seemed like an educational incubator. This was where she tried out new things, ideas to instill some of the more complex concepts into the kids. She used simple everyday things to explain scientific or technological breakthroughs. The living/dining room separated these previous two rooms, with the kitchen in the back. The stairs going up from the living room led to the master bedroom.

"As they say on TV, this is where the magic happens."

Sylvania had a beautiful teakwood sleigh bed with a flat screen TV hung on the wall. There was a nice sound system surrounding the space. She had a recliner and a day bed on the other side of the rectangular room. All in all, she had a nice cozy house.

"You are a wonderful tour guide madam."

"Thank you sir, I really love my job."

"I believe there was something about a tour extension?"

"Oh, the coupon, let me take you to the coupon reclamation center."

They walked through the walk-in closet. Ron saw the different sides of Sylvania Collins. The majority of the clothes would have to be considered school clothes; the colors and styles bespoke 'School Teacher'. But once draped over her body, the whole look changed.

One small corner of the closet looked like grownup, after-five outfits. Ron would have to try to expand on that. One other thing that he noticed, being the techie that he was, was that she had a lot of gadgets! Something usually attributed to guys, he also noticed that tags on quite a few things came from the Sharper Image. SI was one of the first mail order exclusive adult toy stores from back in the 80's. Their quality at finding things was so high, that they started to have things made and branded exclusively.

He noticed the air cleaner and the wall mount multi disk changer in the bathroom. The five-disk changer had three disks currently loaded and the screen displayed the mode 'shuffle'. Strangely reminiscent of his master suite, she had a Jacuzzi tub in her master bathroom too.

"I see great minds really do think alike."

He looked at the actual restroom area and saw two toilets; he looked at Sylvania with an eyebrow raised,

"His and hers?"

"No, I went on a trip to France as a teacher chaperone a few years back. It was my first time out of the country. The hotel we stayed at was set up very similarly to this. Their tub was much bigger though. But the two commodes, when I asked why, they laughed at me.

That one is called a bidet; it not only is a receptacle, it also has a powerful jet of water that cleanses you. So, I guess in a way, you could say his and hers. Of course, after the France trip, I vowed to install one in my house when I got one, the first thing I modified was the bathroom."

"I think they did a wonderful job Sylvania. Your house is a wonderful reflection of you."

"Well thank you kind sir, do you mind if I run a bath?"

"I don't think I could mind anything less."

She walked over to the tub and leaned over the side. She slid a waterproof panel to the side to access what looked to be a complex DVD remote. The first preset button caused water jets to explode into life. The heat in the room instantly rose a few degrees. The next combination changed the color slightly and released aromatic smells throughout the space.

Ron looked over her shoulder, conveniently pressing his body against hers to see. He noticed level indicators for oil, bubbles, alcohol and salts; the tub had a virtual dispensary of additives that were insinuated into the water through the jets. Indeed, her tub was nicer than his, and he was happy that he had found someone that matched him so well. Sylvania stood and backed up on Ron molding her entire backside against his front. She felt him begin to grow down her molded body, and she didn't think she would ever grow tired of that particular method of appreciative communication.

She pulled her connecting string slyly and then spun around, not breaking their body contact. The skirt stayed locked between their bodies; he didn't know. She reached up to kiss him, feeling the hot steam rising up the backs of her thighs, causing her panties to feel heavy. He looked down for the kiss, and felt the weight of the skirt pooling on top of his shoes.

Without breaking the kiss, he pulled the tie from the blouse and felt the slight support it had given to her heavy breasts give way as they swung free against him. He stepped back and took in the vision in front of him, from the muted non-color of the hemp sandals to the cocoa bean legs up to the somehow shimmering white bikini panties. Her stomach was flat, her full breasts were awesome, with her nipples looking slightly up at him. Her beautiful face was framed in blinding light from the diamonds. This was his woman.

Ron wasted no time, he kicked off his loafers and stripped down to his underwear in record time. She stopped him from going any further, walked up to him and stroked him through his boxers. She leaned back against the side of the tub and descended to the floor taking his boxers with her. She reached the floor with a pronounced change of view, with Ron's bobbing erection in her face. Sylvania had never been big on giving oral sex. She enjoyed receiving, except for the fact that her reciprocation was expected. That wasn't a problem with Ron. She wanted to share everything with him and in time she would. Right now she wanted to taste him.

She wrapped her hands around him and stroked him firmly, pulling him to her. He took a step and leaned in putting both hands on the side of the tub to balance himself. She started to lollypop lick the tip while she two-hand stroked the rest. She was thoroughly enjoying herself, she felt him start to slightly thrust into her mouth through her fingers. All of a sudden she was so taken by the scene taking place in her mind and body that she seemed to float outside of herself on the steamy haze and she could see herself in front of Ron. She stroked his big unit in her mouth, as she squatted against the tub.

She was rushed back into her body as her orgasm struck; it was so unexpected and intense that she was caught off guard. She had never come while giving head before. Her body was reveling in it. She had removed her hands from his shaft and had them around his ass, pulling more and more into her mouth, until it was full. His tip bounced against her throat.

But she couldn't take that, not yet. She came back around

and slowly slid him out and caught her breath. Ron straightened up and looked down. He looked past his rapidly bobbing dick to Sylvania, still squatted below him, nipples sticking out like erasers, breathing hard. He offered his hands to pull her up, she accepted. Then, he stepped into the tub.

The floor of hers was simple, with seat cut outs in each corner, unlike his; the dry tub looked like a skate board park. Not releasing her hands he helped her into the tub, still in her panties. She stood with the water barely grazing them. Ron sat in one of the corner nooks and urged Sylvania by the hips to walk towards him as the bubbling water jumped at her with every step.

He brought his hands around to cup her glorious ass cheeks. He pulled her panty crotch to his face. The water wetness had soaked her crotch a touch more than she had soaked herself. Despite the additive flavor of the water, he could taste her through her panties. He attached his mouth to the right spot and sucked panties, lips and clit. All parts were rushed into his mouth; he began to gnaw on the package, doing special tongue tricks. Automatically, he felt her ass begin to flex. She grabbed a hold of his head and unabashedly began to ride his face. Ron loosened his mouthful with a 'pop' and wiggled her wet panties off. Then, he tossed them into the sink.

She asked him if he had rubbers. He pointed to his pants pocket. She leaned over the edge of the tub as she had at his house earlier, her plumpness appearing from between her cheeks as she ripped open the pack. She put the rubber in one hand and pulled him up like a fat broom handle with the other, he went willingly. She rolled the condom down and let him relax back into the cut. Free of her panties, she stepped to him again, no shyness now and grabbed his head and deposited her clit on his tongue.

He licked in butterfly flutters until he felt her lips quivering and juice escaping. She slid down his wet chest gripping him from behind and rubbing her clit down his chest. By the time his stiff head had penetrated her clamping lips, she was coming very hard. They lay back making muscular love, mostly hugging and kissing and licking, not much thrusting. Ron marinated inside of her, loving the feel.

She had come countless times while riding Ron and he was as stiff as ever. She wanted him to come for her. So, she started to ride him like she had at the club. Remembering the club, made her think about the look-a-like. Would she do this lovingly to her man or just do whatever whores do? She didn't care; this was her man and she didn't give a damn about that bitch. She lifted up on Ron and let her body take over.

She felt him stiffen and raise her up all the way out of the water, then the heat came. Ron sighed into her mouth as he came. The orgasm he had been holding back ever since the park, felt massive. She felt it too and she was wiped out. They stepped out of the tub and dried off. Ron carried his clothes, tossed the two wraps into the hamper, and wrung the water out of the panties. She was dragging ass, but felt wonderful. They sat on the bed. Ron laid her back and kissed her, wanting desperately to complete this night the right way. He pulled back the covers to sleep with his baby, but there was something he had to do first.

"I've got to go handle something, baby girl."

"Will you be long?"

"No, I don't expect to be."

"Ok, are you going to come back to me?"

"Do boats float, do cars cruise, or do Muslims eat pork?"

"Two outta three ain't bad."

They smiled silly grins and kissed; Ron tucked her into bed. She reached into her nightstand drawer and handed him a key.

"Let me know it when you get here."

He held the key like Luke Skywalker held his father's Jedi light saber; this was now official, he had a key. He kissed her again and assured her that he would be back. He turned to dress and leave before he changed his mind. He had a mission. Sitting in his car he was more confused than ever, but he was determined to get some kind of answer. He reached beneath the floor mat, using a quarter to release the recessed lock. The door sprang open; he removed the .380 semi-automatic and closed the stash spot back, replaced the floor mat and slid the holster behind his pants. He pulled off.

***

The little rapper was cute, but the initial turnoff was that he looked like he was ten years old. He had not a hair on his face nor chest, but he did have some size on his frame underneath all those saggy-baggy clothes. $ensation had brought out all the local flavors that any young a hip hop appetite could desire: Lexus, Mercedes, Lotus flower, Coco,

Chocolate, Cherry, Destiny, Cristal, Cali. There were so many names for so many bodies that nobody cared anymore.

But the storms were raging; every other room seemed to have some action. Apparently knowing how the night would progress, the producer that owned the house had paid the neighbors and the police to leave his party in peace. In fact, they even had police in plain clothes for protection; they were private security tonight. Nobody knew who they were. So, they were as free to sample the delights as anybody else. $ensation was overseeing the party from her vantage point; the girl-girl shows were swinging, with Lexus and Mercedes deep into a 69 on the coffee table in the blue room.

She had gotten a text that Katt and Blackgirl needed fresh batteries out on the deck. They were working a twin light dual-headed dildo; it looked like they were fucking each other with a double headed fluorescent bulb. For now, the show was in the dark, but not for long. $ensation showed up. She unscrewed the dildo in the center, popped out the 4 AA batteries, and replaced them with fresh ones.

The huge twenty two inch appliance started to glow brightly from green to purple and vibrated softly. With Katt and Blackgirl being 'high yella' and 'coco black', respectively, the show was even more enticing. Out on the deck in the dark, you could see the deep dildo penetration into both slim women. It was like a pornographic health museum exhibit. This show was nothing new to $ensation, she designed the girl shows: two girls, three girls, four girls. She had done them all and had new pretzel-styled acrobatic shows planned. She had brought out the big boy package; she knew that the producer, by reputation, always threw money around, but never threw it away. He had a small video crew roving the party; certain girls agreed to have their faces shown for an extra fee.

$ensation charged $1,500 per girl off the top. She had one of the pusse posse busses parked out front. She showed up with twenty five girls, not counting herself. Sylvia, acting as Queen Untouchable, hadn't even taken off her club dress. But, she did roll up the waist until the swinging hem was grazing the tops of her stockings with every step.

She enticed everyone but only had eyes for the master of the mansion, the one man that she ignored. At first sight, he was struck. Her long, black, hair was divided and flowed down to her collarbone, to cover her stiffened nipples in the sheer black stretchy top. She grabbed his attention and would not let go. He tried to speak, but she kept walking away, until he wound up ignoring his party guests. He only had eyes for her. Her plan of seducing the master of the manor was progressing as planned.

She saw the gold tooth twins from the club tossing small stacks of money onto Lemon Drop, Sexation and Caramel. They were doing an intricate three-way that looked like something from a sexual circque de solei. They all had vibrating eggs of different styles: long, slim, fat, and two on one wire. They stood there steadily tossing money at them, gaining them the coveted spot right next to the action. You gotta pay to play; and they were paying. Sylvia was about to flip the script on Mr. Producer man when all of her attention was pulled away.

**

Ron rolled up to Cascade through the hills. He remembered when it was all woodsy up here; he had friends that lived in the rustic stone and brick houses as much as 100 yards back from the road. They used to shoot rabbits and squirrels and sell the meat and fur to dealers at the farmers market. For them, it might as well have been bear skin and meat.

Then the big sell out came; people sold their land rights for outrageous amounts of money. Some stayed and lived in the big house on the tiny piece of land that resulted from their sale. Some just moved all together. He still had three or four friends that lived in the old area in their new houses out beyond the golden gates. They had given him an access code to come through the gates anytime he came by. So, he didn't have to get them to punch the buttons up on the phone.

The big gates swung in and he rolled through on to the main road, knowing that whichever direction he took, this road would wind up back at the gate eventually. The main road went up and down the hilly terrain, disclosing the secret topography that was so well hidden from the road outside the golden gates.

He saw what he was looking for right away. Lights, a big tour bus with the same logo he had seen on the invitation: $ensation's Pusse Posse' with a group of what looked like black cowboys chasing stampeding cats. And, of course, the cars, of all types, were parked from the cul-de-sac up and down on both sides of the street leading to the house. The overview gave him the heads up that he needed. He two parking people; they moved like cops.

With money like this, he wouldn't be surprised that mercenaries were paid to do parking tonight. So Ron parked on the next street over, walked through the yard of another big house and came out right behind the bus. Ron casually walked into the garage, picked up a beer, and joined in with the festivities. Once inside, wherever he walked, there were dollars: tens, twenties, currency all over the floor. he bent down on the sly and picked up a large handful of money. He quickly straightening it and he held it in his hand like a fat bankroll. He reclaimed his beer and staggered a bit, looking drunker than he was.

It worked well, considering the condition of most of the guys here; nobody noticed him. He didn't know what it was. It probably was all the drinks at the club that he'd never gotten rid of. But the beer took him over the edge; his bladder felt as if it would explode. He went walking through the big house tipping strippers walking by, until he found a bathroom. It didn't look occupied, but, when he opened the door, he saw a cameraman and his assistant filming two people having sex. He had her from behind one leg up on the toilet with the camera shooting up from the floor.

He closed that door and went back to walking past the strange glowing goings on, onto the dark, back deck. He saw, what looked like, another bathroom with the door cracked and the light off. He slipped in and pulled out his pee hardened dick, and drained the lizard. There are very few pleasures that can rival the voiding of an overfilled bladder. He was midway through this process when the door cracked open quickly and the light went out.

He didn't have a clue what had happened, but he maintained his aim. He kept the same note going, knowing that he was still hitting the bullseye in the toilet water, even in the dark.

The next thing he heard was water running. Then, he felt a rough surface on the head of his dick. A faint orange glow almost showed him what was going on in the room.

He turned his head to speak and his head was grabbed by two hands, his mouth was pried open by a pair of soft lips. Then, he felt the heat, and smelled the smoke. Whoever this was, was blowing him a shotgun. He inhaled his breath and smoke at the same time; he choked and tried to regain his breath and was hit by another shotgun. The strong weed and cocaine hit him quickly, and his dick stayed very hard. The mouth left him and he stood there trying to get his bearings. He thought that he was still facing the toilet that he had been peeing into. He tried to feel his way in the dark as he would if he were at his house. He stumbled and found the lost pair of lips; they were attaching themselves to the head of his dick.

***

Sylvia saw the man from the mall, impossible! How could he be here? But his height and those unmistakable hazel eyes indicated that this was him all right. She wondered what she would do if she saw him again and there he was. She was feeling wild as hell after all the dry humping in the club, then, walking around with half her ass hanging out tonight. People, from all manners of hidden directions, were tickling her pussy, or slipping money into her panties when she wasn't looking or walking close by pinching her.

In one case, one short guy put her blouse covered nipple in his mouth and started to suck like he was nursing. She was horny as a Billy goat, and he was stiffly walking into the toilet over there, not ten feet away. This was perfect; she listened to him pee, It sounded deep and strong, like he had a nice tool to release his fluid. She smoked the primo joint one of the dancers had given her; it smelled like flowers. This damned hydroponic weed nowadays was so strong; they had genetically grown the smell out. That and the inclusion of the cocaine boosted the strength to the moon. Damn, she was high and she was going to do it. She snuck into the bathroom and turned out the lights.

She hesitated for a second, got a mouth full of smoke and made her move. She blew the smoke over his dicks' head and engulfed him, taking him all the way until her mouth was full on the first slide. She started doing the tongue and cheek tricks that had added the suffix 'fire fire' to Fantasia, during such exercises. She pulled him out until only the tip was still in her mouth, she then dropped to her knees and wrapped her hands around his ass cheeks. She held on to his pocket and pulled him all the way past her gag reflex and into her throat.

Whatever Ron had been about to think, flew out of his head when he felt that bottom lip and tongue pleasuring his ball sack. The mysterious mouth began to take the full length of him from tip to root, corkscrewing the slippery hand on the exposed parts. He was no match for this super dick sucker. His come blasted out of him before he even knew that he was coming. It was a pleasure overload of the highest magnitude.

She continued to suck him, slurping, and smacking his overly sensitive head. She pulled her mouth off him, but kept her grip. She moved over to the sink, put one knee up onto the marble top and pulled his still cocaine hard, sensitive dick into her. She was on the pill and right now she didn't care about much but getting fucked by the dick of this man she had conjured up.

Once his raw tip was engulfed in her super-heated insides, it was a wrap. He sunk into her oiled depths, and in his drug-fogged mind, he was right back inside Sylvania. Hitting it from the back felt better than ever. Sylvia was rubbing herself from side to side on the brink of a huge orgasm. Her pretty-eyed mystery dick was banging the bottom out of her, just like she had imagined. She clamped down, her orgasm hit hard and she cried out. The grip made his sensitive head skid against her walls and spit another load this time deep into the mouth of her womb. She dropped her leg and crushed him inside of her and she moved him back to the wall. She backed her ass up and down, milking everything out of him. Satiated for the moment and proud of her act of fantasy fulfillment, she needed to get back to her mission. She reached to where she remembered putting the washcloth earlier, and slid off his slimy stalk. She hung the rag over his penis, like a towel bar then slid her panties back up her legs, pulled her skirt down, and opened the door.

***

Ron's drug clouded mind was clear enough to know that he had just blasted a strong nut into the raw pussy belonging to the mouth that had attacked him, and it felt so good. Once again he thought it had felt like he was behind Sylvania, but everything in his faraway rational mind told him she was at home asleep. Now, he was being pushed back, 'Uuuh', against a wall and she was pulling that biting hot pussy off of him. "Woohoo, that's cold". He reached down and felt a washcloth wrapped around his dick. He grabbed it and a blinding light came in; fuschia and black slipped out the door.

He reached for the knob to see. When he pulled the door open the light washed over him. He had a washcloth in hand, and his cream-covered dick was sticking out from his zipper. After a quick look, she had disappeared. He closed the door to get his head straight, both of them. He flushed the toilet and went in search of some coffee or something. He staggered through the party, not faking this time. He finally ran into the kitchen where he found a coffee pot brewing.

He made himself 'at home', lounging against the counter by the coffee. He chose a mug, rinsed it out, and poured black coffee. He stayed right where he was and drank two cups of straight, black, coffee, figuring it would sober him up. But Ron, not having the pharmacological experience to realize that he wasn't drunk. The caffeinated effects that would reverse an alcoholic intoxication, which was a depressant, would only increase the effect of a stimulant. His foot started to tap, his leg was shaking, and his gaze would not stay still. What he actually needed was a strong shot of liquor to bring him to a state a little closer to normal.

But, before he could find a shot, he caught a glimpse of fuchsia. He spied the inky black hair walking with a guy a bit shorter than she. They were going towards a roped-off area of the house. He watched until he saw what room they disappeared into. He gave her some time. He figured she was negotiating a sex deal. He didn't know what had happened with him. Don't you have to pay for pussy up front? Doesn't head cost more??

While he was waiting for them to finish screwing, or whatever they were doing, he looked to the right and saw a snifter selection and a large strange-looking Crystal decanter with amber liquid. He poured himself three fingers of the $2,000 per bottle Remy Martin Louis XIV cognac. He tossed the ultra-smooth, almond-hinted liquor down his throat, its burning sensation raced through his system.

He instantly felt a little more in control of himself. He crept back to where he had last seen the woman and the man go; the door was cracked. He looked through the crack and saw the man laid back on the bed. He had a glass next to his hand and his dick was hanging out of his pants. It was shrinking and leaking sperm steadily, joining a puddle on his black slacks. But where was she? There she was!

There was another opening inside the closet. As he watched, she pulled her skirt up to her hips and pulled down her panties. Using her panties as a barrier, she reached in and extracted a piece of jewelry that looked like snow in sunshine. She picked up several pieces, not even bothering to turn around. But he didn't need to see much more; the ass was perfect, identical. He recalled feeling like he was inside Sylvania in the dark and that's why. She was a clone of Sylvania in every way, and, she was a thief. Now, with the strong liquor finally getting his thoughts working like normal, he noticed the skimpy thong panties that she was grasping those massive iced out pieces with. They probably had his come leaking on to them.

If she steals, his DNA would be left. Damn, what the hell is going on here? He couldn't stop watching her. It was like watching a car wreck happen in slow motion. She went through everything as if she were doing inventory. Then, she took something small and clipped it to her thong and turned to leave. First, she looked at Mr. Leaky Dick, walked out and fisted him to a fresh erection. Then, she went back and closed the closet door and left the room.

Ron stepped back down the hallway into an alcove and tried to hide all 6'7" of himself; apparently, it worked. She didn't look back. She just scooted up the hallway past the expensive cognac, back through the kitchen to the party. Finally, Ron was working the drug problems out of his biology. He went back to the kitchen. The cognac was making his head throb. He filled another mug with coffee; this time, he added sugar and cream. To drink it as a drink, not as a drug, it was much better. He put the mug in the sink and turned to leave when he was confronted by $ensation.

"Hey, I remember you, you were at the club earlier weren't you?"

"Guilty as charged."

"How did you find me, honey? I know I only dropped one invite. Was it the broke-ass ying yang twins?"

"You gotta know it; they left the invitation on the bar, then came back to get it. By then, the name Pusse Posse was kind of stuck in my mind; it's catchy."

"Yeah, catchy alright, until the Posse catches you."

She reached around and stroked Ron's shaft. Being the ignorant appendage that is was, responded, growing down his leg.

"Ooooo yeah, I knew I wasn't mistaken, and it looks like he likes me."

$ensation pulled his hand below her mini dress and rubbed it against her shaved lips. She was wet, very wet. Her muscles throbbed against his hand. Then, she grinded down on his appendage so that she could stimulate herself on his palm.

"Who was that you were at the club with?"

"Fantasia, don't worry about her, she has her eyes on another prize. Is there something wrong with me?"

She had separated two of his fingers and slid them up into herself,

"Mmmm, thick and long, that's my song."

Like everywhere else that he had been that day, she was tight. She was getting herself off, while her other hand was jacking him off through his pants. He had to put a stop to that. He pulled his hand out of her and stopped hers; ten more strokes and he would have been done for.

"I can't do that right now, I need to talk to your girl, for real."

"Well, damn," She pouted. "I ain't never been dissed for my girl before."

Ron figured he wasn't going to get anywhere with this woman unless he gave her some kind of sex or satisfaction. So, he reached into his knot of money, pulled out a $50 bill, and rolled it into a tube. He stuck it between her lips and it unraveled tickling her clit; it was an old trick he used to use back in his strip-clubbing days.

"Ooooo, hey, that was nice. Ok, I'm not mad no more. Fantasia's out there some place, and if I know her, she's either trickin or table dancing."

She was doing a dance. Her entire thigh was crammed with

bills. She had a drink in her hand. She the balls to have the big-ass diamond ring she had just stolen on her finger; she was bold. Once again, Ron had to wonder what the hell was he doing here? What was his undercover mission? He had found the dead ringer for his woman.

Now what, could he even tell her how he had found her? The more he looked at her, the less she looked like his Sylvania. She still physically looked like her, but her essence was harsh and slutty. The drugs and abuses showed; they wore on her like makeup. He didn't ever want to feel the corruption that he felt coming from her, coming from Sylvania. Fantasia was a rotten version of his girl, and, she was a thief. What happened to the guy she had been with?

He was missing in action. Fantasia had found her way to the rapper of the evening. She embraced him, then, turned her back to him, and started riding his lap in a hot table dance.

The camera crew came to catch his face as she jumped up and ran across the room; obviously, she wasn't one for videos. Two other girls rushed in to fill the void. The camera didn't care. Ron felt so pulled apart. He wanted to talk to her, yet, wanted nothing more than to be out of here and back with his version, Sylvania.

L. Corbin Bey

Chapter 39

The picture came across the desk of the concierge. The face looked vaguely familiar. He walked over to the registration desk to inquire. The North Town Sheraton employed individuals from all over the world; the reception desk was currently represented by three different continents. He showed the picture around. One of the current associates that had been working overtime, remembered the gentleman. He was a military officer, and said that he was expecting his family, his wife and two kids. He said that they should be in before midnight and to hold an extra key.

"Ok, and where did you put him?"

"Well, since we were almost at maximum capacity, I gave him one of our bigger suites. After all, he was a decorated military officer. In my country, it's always best to treat the military well, as it creates a circle of protection around you."

He always had to remember that when dealing with an international staff, also meant dealing with many different realms of experiences. This young Israeli, though she looked well Americanized, had been forced into military service at an early age. Although she seemed an innocent girl of twenty, she was actually a retired soldier.

"Ok, forward the specifics of his check-in to my desk, please."

"Yes sir, right away, sir."

He walked back to the desk to the 'ping' sound of an internal communication received. Military efficiency did have its place.

Apparently, this was a one-star general here from overseas, supervising a contingent of National Guard troops. He had a military diplomatic vehicle in the parking deck. Hmmm, he would keep an eye on this 'General'. No use reporting him he thought to himself. The mistake that the night concierge made was a common one, with people not used to dealing with bureaucracy. The fax that he received had been washed through three different machines. The innermost fax was stamped from FBIs Homeland Security Mobile Command unit, which was the originator. The outer two National Guard post stamps were the least important and most local; he saw the order of importance in reverse.

One fact of life about the chain hotel culture, word travels very quickly. But, it travels in parallel; not often does it cross lines. The Marriot hotels had an internal memo circulating that one of their people, name to be withheld until the story went public at one of their properties, was most likely going to be in line for a commendation from Homeland Security.

They had recognized an international terrorist hiding out at their property. They were told to keep their eyes open, and that there may be more alerts during this current terror Threat Level RED. The company needs you to do your part to protect the USA; be a patriot, don't just watch, act; Of course, this memo was internal, for Marriott employees only. Michael Robinson worked for the Sheraton. This was his second week, and was also the first of two mandatory shifts. Michael Robinson didn't like his job. He put the photo into his desk drawer.

***

Abdullah stretched out in the suite. He had just finished his evening prayers and was studying the maps that he had printed off the complimentary internet computer in the suites office nook. The over view maps with all of the key CDC facilities in the Atlanta area used large red 'X' markings; how appropriate. His research was thorough. The mapping program already had the hotel's address programmed in; and the maps with the driving directions were complete, with the green arrow with 'you are here' and the red destination 'X'.

He could go to them all tomorrow, and make his decision as to which one was the most likely to contain the P-4 labs. These labs were the most high security designated ones in the CDC arsenal. The location of the vault that contained the most dangerous viral pathogens known to man, are actually stored to use in research for cures. But, in order to find cures, a lot of infected animals have to be used.

Not only did his dreams include losing all the plagues of the vaults, but also the pissed-off, deranged animals. The animals can mate, infect, and continue to deliver the fatalistic toxins. The American infidels let their hubris think that they alone could trap and tame nature's killers. This could backfire on them and Allah. Let me be the trigger to lose the fusillade of their destruction. These were his last thoughts before dozing off to sleep.

He awoke a couple hours later and looked at the uniform. He wanted nothing more than to get the car and driver, and start doing his in-person research tour. But, there was only so far he was willing to go with the false document that he was using. The real General he was portraying was still alive and operating in Afghanistan. The cover of the mountainous theater of operations was the only way he could justify the beard on his face.

The ribbons on his breast jacket kept many questions down. But, the questions of an innkeeper, at a checkpoint, or from a roving band of curfew patrollers, was an entirely different situation. No, he would pray that Allah would grant him patience. He went over his inventory: the sarin gas, the two remaining vials of anthrax, and the remaining C4 with triggers. If Allah granted him time, he could still do some damage. He would also have to develop a clever clue.

This time, he would have it delivered, instead of being found in the death-trash aftermath. He turned on the twenty-four hour news franchise, looking for news from St. Louis, and saw nothing. There was nothing on the ticker, nor new lead story. What was this? He had to think; could something have gone wrong? No, not possible. They had to be covering up something. That's it. Ok, publicity will have to be bigger and unavoidable. He knew how to make these infidels pay for covering up his messages. Oh yes, and he would make them pay now.

***

Sylvia was in the zone; she knew where the score was to be made. She had already sucked off the man with the key, she had found her mystery man, and had him every which way. "Oooo, he was good." Now, the little rapper's music seemed to be pretty catchy; he should make a lot of money at this. She gave him a table dance. But here come the cameras,

"Sorry kid, no cameras."

The camera crew saw the most hard-to-get stripper at the party riding the lap of the client. They rushed in to capture footage. They got her back and ass as she was raising up and running across the room. She was replaced by two other girls. He didn't seem very upset when one unzipped his fly, and the other one settled on his crotch.

Sylvia rearranged her skirt and went out on the deck to get a breath of air. She had let the party atmosphere get to her. The years had rolled back to the life with the Pusse Posse. It was the fountain of youth, and she had drank from the fountain once. She had to clear her head and get back on track.

The fresh air was doing the trick and she was focusing much better. She was thinking about the jewels she had seen in the vault in the closet. Sylvia put an action plan into effect. First, she would need another guy, somebody jealous of the guy that owned the place. From her earlier investigations, she had compiled a short list of who's who. While she was trying to determine the owner, she ran across a prospect.

He seemed as if this could be his home: the way he spoke

about the neighborhood, and the cul-de-sac in general. But, it turned out to be a neighbor. She had directed enough attention his way, and then, had taken it back. Of that, she was sure. There was still some interest, especially, since she hadn't been seen with anybody.

She peered around the party goers until she saw him there. He was sitting on a day bed with his hands stroking the thigh of the only white girl here; he thought he'd found the prize. Sylvia quickly changed that thought. With a single moment of eye contact, and the come-hither finger crook, the white girl was left alone on the sofa, and the neighbor was by her side.

"Are you having fun yet?"

The gentle backhand stroke down his cheek made his eyelids flutter,

"I,I,I wwwas doing ok."

"Well, how would you like to be doing better?"

He found himself regaining some of his composure, now that he was actually standing next to Sylvia and she was talking to him.

"And how much better are you suggesting?"

She smiled. This part took her back some years. It was always so simple separating marks from their money. She slithered her hand down the front of him until she cupped his balls.

"How much better can you afford to be doing?"

"Well, that's no object little lady; I came prepared."

"Mmm, I like that, have you got condoms?"

"Shit, I, uh damn. Nope."

"Don't worry. I know where some are. Come on."

She embraced his hand like a lover and led him to the roped off area. She was Constantly looking for the horny dude that, no doubt, didn't remember if he had screwed her or not. They made it back to the bedroom. Ron had just emerged from the bathroom again, returning all the coffee, and cognac, and other assorted chemicals from his body back into the toilet. As he finished washing up, he stepped out and saw a flash of Fuchsia and an older man.

They disappeared past the cognac service back to the bedroom hallway. "Damn", he thought, "This whore put in a lot of work in a night". Curiosity was too much; he stepped further down the hall so that he could see into the room. Sure enough, she had dragged the man into the same room that she had been in before. She shut the door. Ron was curious, but not enough to barge into the room. There were too many things that could go wrong. So he decided to grab a seat next to the cognac and pretend to be passed out, drunk until he heard the door open or somebody else came. Sylvia had gotten the man undressed first. She then pulled down her top exposing her breasts and flat stomach. The man had already given her $700 for the sex. She made sure that she didn't touch anything in the room. She directed him to the bar to mix himself a cocktail, then sent him to get a condom from the fish bowl. He gripped the fish bowl tightly with unsteady hands, to keep from knocking the expensive glass to the floor.

She slipped the knock-out drug into his drink, as he was

grabbing for the condom. Now, his nice sized package stood rampant while sipping his drink. He looked around with subtle contempt.

"So this is the great mans' lair, huh? This is where he lays his head. I've always suspected that he fucked my wife. Judging from conversations I overheard about some of the things I see in here, I think the bastard fucked my daughter too! Come on baby, I don't give a damn what it costs. I wanna come all over his pillow. So when he lays his stealing-ass head down, I get to come in his face."

He downed the drink and she approached him, rolling up her skirt and pulling her thong to the side,

"Come here baby, let Fantasia ease that anger. If you want, you can pretend I'm your daughter and fuck me like he did."

The man's dick started bouncing around like crazy; she had struck his fantasy zone,

"How did you..."

"Shhh, turn around you dirty old man. Put your hands against the closet door and spread your legs."

Sylvia knelt down and began to stroke him from the back, the other hand fondling his ball sack. The hand job he was receiving was world class. She started to pull him backwards from the door, and his hands slid down and gripped the door knob, perfect. She kept jerking him, working on getting his first quick orgasm out of the way. Her ministrations were increasing his heart rate, causing the drug to flow through him faster. He started to moan. That was her cue to blow soft, hot air right onto his asshole. His moans turned into a continuous sigh as he came. He filled the condom and passed out. He was still twitching and spurting more into the condom as he lay on the floor, unconscious.

Sylvia dragged him to the right and positioned him half on half off the bed. She wrapped his hand around his still-hard dick. She pulled a pair of latex gloves from her purse and gripped the neck of the door knob and opened the closet. The drugs had affected the producer like they had her earlier. He hadn't checked to make sure the vault was relocked, and Sylvia took everything.

Whatever she could fit into the large-sized Gucci bucket styled purse. And she did. There were going to be a lot of label mates upset from their lack of 'bling' for their videos. But there was a certain Israeli jeweler who would have no problem replacing the "one of a kind' pieces.

As the coup de gras, she selected a small, diamond-encrusted doghouse with Snoopy and Woodstock on top and slipped it into the unconscious neighbor's pants. Damn, she didn't even know his name. Oh well, he shouldn't be hard to miss on the news. She stood and viewed the scene; she wondered what would point more blame in his direction?

pair of emerald earrings, set in Lapis lazuli, caught her attention. Surely women's earrings, oh yeah, jealous husband suspects he sees his wife's earrings. Well, it's a start. So, she took one earring and folded the other one into his free hand. Now she was ready to go. Lugging the purse, she slid to the door and fixed her skirt and shirt. She pulled the door opened with her latex gloved hand and carefully closed it behind her. The great escape was underway.

***

"Click', that was the door. Ron opened one eye and saw the woman, Fantasia, slipping out of the room without the man she took in with her. She walked right past him with one of those giant Gucci bags; it looked heavy. The party on the other side was winding down. He followed her from a discreet distance. At one point, he pulled up right before crossing through a door arch and saw her talking to her hard to deny girlfriend/pimp, $ensation. She looked around warily and agreed to whatever Fantasia had said, and started rounding up the girls. After their conversation, Fantasia walked boldly out the front door, not looking back. Ron quickly stepped to the garage door.

From outside behind the bus, he noticed the parking security still on duty. One of them was walking her to the area where her Mercedes and $ensation's BMW Roadster were parked. He was casually rubbing her ass along the way; usual cop behavior if he had ever seen it.

With his attention distracted, Ron ran through the open space to get back to the next block and to his car. He still didn't know where this was headed; he was following his instincts. He did not know anything, except that this woman looked exactly like his woman. Considering the casual way she had basically raped him in the bathroom, then, proceeded to rob this man in his own house, he had no doubt that that was the reason she was leaving. He couldn't bank on anything else. All he really knew for sure was that she wasn't Sylvania. He pulled out as fast as he could, trying to beat Fantasia out of the cul-de-sac. He figured she would suspect someone following her from the back, so he would try to follow her from the front.

He got to Cascade road and took a right to take him back towards the highway and slowly pulled off. The golden gates were opening. He could see the maroon sedan peeking its nose out to detect traffic as he was passing. Now she had to take a right, or else his plan had failed. Holding, who knew how much, stolen stuff in her car, the last thing she would want would be a ticket. There went her blinker, and she turned right.

Chapter 40

St. Louis

Carmen 'Dog' Rosellis' office trailer in the casino parking lot, officially, became the TCU tactical control unit, or MCU2, as soon as Kristi stepped inside as Team Leader. Currently, she was over the shoulder of the young analyst that had broken the last code. Jon Eagle had informed her of what she had done. This break was of the highest caliber; not a simple feat at all. So, whoever did this, is someone to watch. The tech was poring over the note left at the Torch 3 site; apparently the note was intended to be found after the mechanisms had finished spewing their deadly payload and killing all the occupants.

Unlike before the level RED was declared, there was no news coverage of the casino deaths. The media was given ultimate scrutiny regarding what they were allowed to release. FCC security was present at every outlet of information. Only the censored and sanitized information was allowed to be disseminated. After the code RED was lifted, there would be another dam burst of sanitized news to assuage the data hungry populace; but the full stories would not be available for twenty to forty years, under the Federal Freedom of Information Secrecy Act.

The initial stories got out before the code RED. But now, this situation would be kept under wraps, the need-to-know ruled. If you didn't have access, it never happened. The evacuees from the casino and the boats were being held in quarantine. The majority had not been exposed, and the ones from Quarantine 1 were still anchored on the Mississippi. It was standard operating procedure. The newest note was just as cryptic as the other two if not more so:

3M4E3E3i4 D3D3i 4A3A3 i4L3D3i 4E3E3M4S3

Se habla a Martha por el ultimo tiempo

Vaya con dios anamales

The tools of your

Destruction

Bites

This was obviously distressing the young tech; he was sweating profusely. Kristi put her hand on his shoulder reassuringly. Not knowing whose hand it was, he looked around impatiently to see the beautiful woman in the tactical uniform. He had never met Kristi, but he recognized her from what he had heard.

"Take your time, do it right. You aren't alone, all of Crypto is behind you. Take a breath and tell me what you have so far."

Thony and Suzan looked on in disbelief. Was this the same woman that blew up their hotel room door, tased them, and subjected them to draconian interrogation? Looking at her now, calming the stress of the young technician was absolutely dumbfounding. It made them look at her differently, and Thony's hand-squeeze signaled that he saw the same thing. As actors, changing faces was something they were intimately familiar with.

"Well, so far, I took the message and fed it into the Crypto Sleuth program. It's chugging along; there were a couple of things that I saw that looked interesting. These doublets, like here, where the double 'D3', double 'A3' and double 'E3' are tickling something in the back of my mind, with the Spanish. I'm trying to figure out why the individual would use that language instead of an Arabic language? It seems that from his message before, everything has a significance. So I'm not trying to leave anything to chance."

"You're doing a great job. I don't want to hinder your progress by insisting on speed. But your quickness this last time was the major difference…"

"I understand SAC Johnson, I'll work harder!"

Again, Kristi discounted the additional dimension her beauty had on her subordinates. Once people met her, they felt the desire to work hard for her, if for no other reason than to catalog the pleasant expression on her face in their direction. Beauty had its bonuses, but she never counted on that. She rationalized; she already had the job. So if she got shot non-fatally in the face, would they fire her? Not if her skills were beyond reproach. The Spanish was the easy part of the translation:

[Talk to Martha for the last time, go with god animals]

then

[The tools of your destruction bites].

The Crypto sleuth was set to the same parameters, surrounding St. Louis, but while the first run came back with nothing, the next run came back with more data:

Dios=god, Mexico, deity, travel safely; Martha: Washington, vineyard, animals=animals, Spanish Mexican animals, American dogs; Tools = patriot, weapons, strategies, methods; destruction=annihilation, extinction, no more, genocidal; bite= sucks, not good, masticate, teeth, sting.

The output came from the words, the other part; the nonsense numbers, were still stuck in a loop. The human Crypto team was crunching down this piece to see if it would render any of the other data useful. The big screen had a picture-in-picture view of the remainder of the Crypto team at the MCU shredding through. A young Asian woman stood in the small view

"I've got something."

"Full screen Dog."

The views swapped and the multiple views shrunk to small views and the PIP took up the main screen. Her white screen showed this:

343 343 343 343 343 343 MEEi DDi AAi LDi EEMS

"Ok, what the hell is that?"

She stepped next to the white screen to explain herself.

"Separating out the numbers from the letters, we get 6 sets of the 343 string, then the letters give you a sequence of repeats, if you take out every other letter, you get:"

MEEiDDiAAiLDiEEMS

"That spells out 'media lies', leaving Ei Dai DEM, inverted that comes out to be 'media dies'. So now I see 343 x 6 and media lies media dies."

"Ok, so now, we have that, but what is it?"

"That's all I could come up with SAC Johnson. The rest was the Spanish translation that still has me at a loss."

The analyst in the TAC offered,

"The numbers have me worried. In the last one, he had four 'HA's and it turned out that he had four of those devices split between three casinos. So, what could the six mean here with the 343?"

They were all staring down at the current status board when an image on screen stepped into view.

"Eh, excuse me SAC?"

"Yeah, go for the SAC."

"SAC, my name is Francisco Collazo. I saw something that may be nothing, but I remembered your speech from earlier."

"Ok, go ahead Francisco."

"Well, in my language, we would not use the name 'Martha'; we would use 'Marta'. That's how it's spelled in Spanish. It struck me as odd that, that was included that way."

"Thank you Francisco, that insight may be...Oh shit!"

All eyes swung to the SAC from both facilities.

"Dog, switch screens, stat! One, click up a search for 'Public Transportation' countrywide."

The results came back quickly. They looked as if they had been spilled directly from a can of alphabet soup:

BART, CALTRANS, CCT, COTA, GCRTA, GRTA, IRT, LIRR, MARTA,

METRO Cincinnati, METRO D.C., METRO Indnap, PATH...

The list went on, but there was no need for more. The analysts in both locations came up with the same conclusion at the same time.

"Francisco Collazo, I'm going to remember your name."

Kristi vowed. Still, confusion ruled. Kristi was seeing something forming that she dreaded. She was thinking back to the Homeland Security Scenario Training sessions she had been forced to attend by the DD FBI. The Worst Case Scenario Terrorist Simulations always had their epicenter in one place. From this epicenter, the plagues of the world could be spread with biblical effectiveness throughout the country followed by the world. Now, the numbers made sense as well: Marta stood for Metro Atlanta Regional Transit Authority; 343 was a first graders alphabetic code:

ABCD 3=C 4=D, 343 = CDC…

***

Robert stayed in formation around the TCU, with gun at the ready uniformly mixed in the perimeter. He was unidentifiable from any of the others. To keep their visual perspective fresh, the task force perimeter scheme had the entire squad revolve. Every ten minutes the circle took one step to the right, thusly, insuring a fresh pair of eyes on every sector of the perimeter. It took one hour to navigate 360 degrees; any anomalies were to be reported to the perimeter leader.

Other than reporting in, this was also an exercise in silence. All communications would come through whisper throat mikes. As Robert, aka 'Crocker', revolved around to get the Blackhawks within his sights, he noticed the sounds he had heard from the rooftop perch. The Blackhawks were cycling up; something was going on in the TCU and a rollout was imminent. If the team leader was moving out, then, that had to mean that the face was on the other end of her mission.

Robert didn't know that Thony and Suzan were inside the TCU with Kristi. He had been coming in with Blowtorch 3 to secure the mobile lab and the CDC guy; he had missed their exit from the Blackhawks. But he knew when those black birds flew, he would have to be on board.

***

"So are you going to let us in on what the hell is going on, now that we're your 'guests'?"

Kristi looked sharp daggers at Suzan. They had reached a detente of sorts, as long as neither one spoke to the other, they would be civilized. Kristi's look softened a tad bit, as she realized no amount of anger towards this woman would solve one piece of this puzzle. In fact, what the hell, she may have an insight.

"Top level: your boyfriend here, that you know as Thony with an h, is suspected in the bombing assassination of Mitchell Johansen as well as this mass homicide here at the casino."

This was news to Thony and Suzan,

"WHAT?"

They said in unison. The looks on their faces were pure surprise and shock. Kristi had withheld this information so that she could purposely drop it on them to check their reactions. Knowing that they had been in her custody for the past five hours with all their conversations monitored and observed, they had shown no classic signs of collaborators. They had barely spoken. They held hands and comforted one another tenderly. These were none of the actions of terrorists. Kristi had been privy to undercover ops in Boston. Specialists from Interpol had flown in to take custody of IRA terrorists identified in several murders and a train assault in London. There were mainly males and two females.

The females, like in all other species, were the fiercest. But the relationships, when they put them together, were nothing like this. They were cold and distant when alone; when put together, they could not stop talking. Mainly it was the women berating the men for being such fools, and cowards for not killing themselves. But none of the characteristics of the terrorist dynamic was evident here. Could she be wrong?

Kristi had no problems admitting her mistakes. That was one of the reasons she was such a good leader, and why she received the respect she did from all levels. But how could this be a mistake? This man said he was an only child, adopted to a middle-aged couple who was now deceased. There was no other family that he knew of, outside of an elderly aunt in Phoenix.

Nothing came up on prints for him nor her. All she had was the picture; the picture was a match. Although the scar and facial hair does throw a wrench into the identicalness, there was too much of a match to disregard. And now, they both passed her reaction test.

"We are here because one of our shining stars in Crypto analysis deciphered a message that was sent to our attention, damn!"

All activity paused, Kristi spun.

"Dog, get me a report from the Atlanta office and any info regarding the initial message investigation. Who was the caller Wolf...uh,"

"-stein SAC, Wolfstein."

"Right, get me that ASAP."

Phillip was on it. She turned back to Suzan and Thony.

"Something just snapped into place; I had to act on it. Now where was I? Right, the message was a tip that there was going to be an incident here, and we got here with teams from across the country in world record time. But we were still too late.

Over 1,000 people were killed on one gambling boat. Gladly, we got here in time to diffuse the other three devices. It was a tragedy, but it could have been worse."

"When did this happen?"

"Right about the time we were blowing up your hotel room door."

For part of a second, Suzan saw her crack. Then, she realized, by the way that all eyes stayed on her whenever she spoke, that she was in charge. She was *really* in charge. Damn, what kind of responsibility was that to have? Every one of those lives were on her hands. Suzan couldn't recall ever reading about or playing any woman with a responsibility like that. Yet, this woman was living it, live, in front of her. She squeezed Thony's hand hard; he looked at her and almost saw the twin laser beams of her eyes locked on the woman in black. He fully focused, trying to pick up what Suz was getting.

"So now if, in fact, what you say is true, that you alibi this man for the times in question, then, there must be somebody else that is still on the loose killing innocent Americans without the courtesy of killing himself. And now, we are immersed in an unprecedented lockdown situation involving 300 million. This includes people that refuse to lockdown quietly. We have unprepared National Guard troops shooting people like nobody's business. I've got to find one man that's on a mission from Allah, to destroy us."

The weariness that came from holding the world's weight

was apparent in this agent's voice. The more it showed, the quieter she spoke, until she was almost whispering.

"So now you see why I want your man to be the one, because the needle in the haystack search is too much to bear. But that's my job, lady: making the impossible look easy, while being a Black Woman. You feel me?"

"I can't lie. Hell no, I don't feel you. I don't even know what senses it takes to feel that. But I'm praying for you and this situation. I'm sure you're not going to tell us what comes next. But are we ever going to be allowed to be free to go?"

"Ever... yeah, most likely, anytime soon. No, who determines what's soon? Me; do you have a need to know any of this, no; so if and when you get, if you get any knowledge or information, consider yourselves lucky."

With that, Special Agent in Charge, Kristi Johnson went back into team leader mode, and totally ignored her captives. The same way she had been doing since their casual incarceration, this exchange took place right before Francisco Callazo made his great breakthrough. With the scant information that Suzan had gotten, and judging by the tension in her voice, Suzan, originally a Butler, Georgia native, knew what Kristi dreaded.

This guy's next target was the Centers for Disease Control and Prevention in Atlanta. Suzan wasn't privy to the note, but she did know that the CDC was home to all the knowledge about all the most lethal viruses and poisons. They were housed and studied there. If terrorists were to, no, that was too terrible to think about. So, she stopped thinking and buried her head in Thony's chest.

Kristi called for the Blackhawks to get ready to ride.

"Get me Director of Operations Security and the CDC military attaché, three way video."

She turned to check the Atlanta office reports with Phillip. Nothing looked out of the ordinary. A text message had been sent via e-mail from a prepaid cell phone, virtually untraceable. Nothing in the server that could track down the origin. Cell phone internet uses a new internet protocol address every time, like dial up connections.

Unlike the current broadband and wireless connections. The address is permanent and is always on. The dial-ups couldn't be traced once they were disconnected-dead-end. The Commanding officer alerted Kristi that the link had been established. He sat in the chair before the camera and introduced her to anyone that didn't know her and explained the findings and guesses that they had, so far.

The last piece of the puzzle fell into place when the operations guy mentioned the lab animals. He then explained the level of toxicity that they carried.

"It seems by the 'bite' word being last, that he has some twisted idea that he can let loose the test animals on the population to inflict untold disaster. I've got to admit that this is a very ambitious plan, but the animals are in a secret location away from harm."

"May I remind you Mr. Director, that this is the same person that left a crater in the middle of St. Louis, then poisoned an entire Riverboat, while trying to get two, plus, a land side casino, all full of people? We're erring on the side of caution, one of our current scenarios is covered in the Doomsday Dance, remember? We had the CDC worst case scenarios in the Homeland Security training."

"Yes, as a matter of fact I do: pathogens, animals, mutations, and airborne threats, all at once."

"Well, we have reason to believe that something ambitious is coming your way with any or all of the above on his mind."

"What proof do you have besides the bombing in St. Louis?"

"Currently, we have a news blackout in effect. The three of you, my boss, and his boss are the only ones on the NTK list for this, acknowledge?"

All three men verbally acknowledged for the camera.

"We have over one thousand dead on a Riverboat Casino from military weapons grade Anthrax. Your scientists are working, as we speak, to trace it back to the place of origin; no luck so far."

Looking at the screen, the bureaucratic faces were gone. In their place was horror, outrage, and fear. Kristi waited, trying to see if any words of wisdom would come. Nothing did. Finally, the military man suggested a full and total lockdown of all CDC properties, triple internal security, especially labs and vaults. The operations director added

"We're gonna have some pissed off scientificos."

"Well sir, they will just have to be pissed off. This is a matter of National Security. If need be, you can remind them who will be liable if something gets out of a lab that they are working in after this recorded meeting. Liability will totally go to them."

"Copy that."

The military man said,

"I'll get on top of that right now."

"Good thing, keep in mind that we don't know who inside the CDC may be compromised. We are leaving nothing to chance here. Who would I need to confer with to have detailed maps of all the facilities sent to me? I have to have all the top and mid-level facility info. I need strengths, weaknesses and targets."

The security director came on,

"I'll have that to you within five minutes or less, SAC."

"Good man. As soon as I'm up, I'll be in touch with my ETA. Any questions, anything, don't hesitate to get in touch with my assistant, Phillip. He is never more than two steps away from me."

The conference signed off and she went over to Dog.

"What have we got coming from the checkpoints?"

"Whole lotta data, but no matches."

"Nobody knows about the POI Ops in Springfield, but the Marriott, right?"

"So far as I know, that's still solid, but you know how hard it is to keep a secret's lid on once more than two people know about it."

"Yeah, that was before we had a green light to shoot 'em..."

***

The Blow Torch 1 crew had rested once they docked; now it was their turn to relieve Blow Torch 3. Instead of going to the rest area, Robert went to the staging area that secured the Blackhawks. He approached one of the identically clad task force members and inclined his head toward the rest area. He quickly nodded and stepped out of his clockwise rotation. Familiar with the perimeter procedure, Robert stepped right into formation around the pre-flight Blackhawks. Now, he was in place to be aboard one of the four birds when they took off to wherever the face was. He was going to be there, nothing was going to stop him. For now, he watched, waited, and observed. He moved to the right.

Phillip was at the Command Center speaking to someone. James approached Kristi with four interlocking pages of maps with symbols indicating CDC facilities. The legend was color-coded to show the sensitivity of the facilities. The screaming red buildings were the ones with the vaults of hazards. The light blue facilities were strictly administrative. Of course, this scale was relative to what Kristi had requested, and no government entity could function without its paperwork.

The computer centers were spaced all over the metro area, which extended out from the center city proper to encompass approximately 29 counties. The main target sites were within the central five. The rest were considered low priority targets. The next sheaf of documents that James handed Kristi were route maps for the Metropolitan Atlanta Regional Transit Authority – MARTA; it was a mess.

The bus routes formed a tight, dense spider web of lines traversing six counties. The train system overlapped the bus lines and stretched out like an octopus from the center of the city of Atlanta. The system was made up of so many tunnels, bridges, and trestle ways, that it was a nightmare security scenario. One good thing that showed on the Marta report was that the Threat Level Red was adhered to stringently. Their new Breeze rapid automatic fare system tracked every passenger throughout the system, whether train, bus, or Para transit.

The Marta police force was the second largest police agency in the state of Georgia. During any alert level ORANGE or above, they rolled out their military SWAT teams. The teams were complete with explosive sniffing dogs, machine gun-toting officers, and several camera layers, which were computer controlled from the satellite recon centers. It seemed that the transit system, as far reaching as it was, was secure. She put that on the back burner.

"Dog, check the go status of the scientists 1, 2, and 3, and the techs too, I think I'll take them with me, this fucker seems to have a lot up his sleeve and I want to be prepared."

"Copy that team leader."

As far as the team cores, 1 and 3 were decontaminated and packed; 2 was still on Quarantine 1, disposing of bodies. With their mission's critical steps done, Belinda Hughes and James Butler would ride in the Blackhawks1 and 2 separately, with Kristi and her squad. C.B. Peters would stay and handle the rest of the bodies aboard Quarantine1.

Once they were tagged, bagged, and placed in HAZMAT transportation containers, and were safely on their way to a Hazardous Materials approved morgue, he could leave. The Harrier was left behind to get him back home.

"Phillip, are we good here?"

"Yeah boss, the maps and data are secured. The CDC has turned on beacons for the Blackhawks. Each facility will pulse a dark blue to aid in identification."

"Great, gather those two, whip up the birds, and we're outta here in five."

"Copy that, out in five."

"Two to Bird leader."

"Go for Bird leader."

"Bird leader ramp up full, we're flying south in 5."

"Copy that 2, ramp full, out 5, over."

All four Blackhawks got their engines up to full idle; the perimeter protection broke up to prepare to board. Robert was stepping up to board bird #3 when he saw the Team leader. After hearing the female voice on the Command, and now seeing the protective wedge that preceded her, there was no way to miss her.

But it was not her that caught his attention, but the other two people inside the wedge, the face and the woman from the apartment! What the hell was this? That was who they were looking for, wasn't it? His thoughts were cut short by the order to board. They boarded and sat scrunched together on benches down both walls. Once all four Birds were loaded, they leaped into the sky heading due south.

***

The little that they could see out of the blacked-out windows seemed to be going by extremely fast. The helicopters were inclined forward, and Suzan could barely make out the others. She knew that there were four, from what she had seen on the ground. She could just barely make out blinking lights next to, but slightly behind, the vehicle they were in. She already knew none of her questions would be answered. So, she did not even bother to ask. As far as conversation went, the memory of waking up next to Thony long enough to blink twice, and then to have her system short-circuited, wasn't something you forgot easily. And of course, subsequently, she awoke smelling of urine and worse; she found herself naked under a sheet with spotlights in her face. At least they were alive, but these things would not be forgotten.

She looked at Thony. His face was granite; he had no emotion, but had extreme concentration. She had seen that face before; that was a face of concern. It was the same face that she had seen on their first rehearsal without scripts. He was trying for a full run-through with no script and no mistakes. Once you accomplished that, you spent the rest of the show trying to repeat it.

But now, the look was much more intense. This was no play; in fact, that entire piece of life that made up so much of them seemed small and very far away. This set was real: the guns, the killers, and the speeding blur of scenery zipping by below. She didn't even have any idea where they were going. The only noise came from the rotors and the jets of the helicopter. The people in black had earphones with springy cords running down their necks like the secret service. Their communication was silent.

She and Thony were left out. Now, looking at Thony in deep

thought mode made her feel absolutely by herself. She looked at his hand; it was gripped tightly in his lap, and his concentration was very deep. She took his hand and gently tried to pry his fingers open; reflexively, it tightened then, began to let loosen, little by little. Suzan stared at his hand as if it were an oyster about to show its pearl, as each finger reluctantly opened to reveal his palm. Without looking away, she took one finger from her other hand and licked it, then spelled out 'I ♥ U'.

She looked deeply into the spit graffiti, then her masterpiece was clouded by another drop of liquid. She brought his hand up to kiss the palm and realized she was crying. Thony had been in a zone ever since he had looked at that table and saw the picture that had his face. He was stuck. How do you look at a picture of yourself that you never took, and tell someone that it's not you. That was the reason he'd been mute since they had left the hotel; he didn't trust himself, he didn't know what he would say, so he said nothing.

But now he looked at Suzan. He felt her kisses on his palm, and saw her warm tears rolling down his wrist. That brought him back. He held her face in both his hands, and looked critically into her eyes. He used his thumbs to wipe her tears. He brought her close and kissed her. He didn't care who was looking; he didn't care about much right now.

"I love you too, Suz."

That little crooked answering smile was all he needed. They held hands and tried to be each other's strength, while attempting to wrap their minds around the strange doppelganger mystery.

***

Kristi was overlooking the CDC maps and estimating the fly-in direction to determine which facility they would fly over first. She caught movement out of the corner of her eye.

The man and the woman were sharing a moment; she caught the kiss, the intense gaze, and she tried to force herself to look away, when she read the man's lips telling her that he loved her. She forcibly ripped her eyes away. She wished she hadn't seen that. That right there solidified in her mind that this was not the person she was looking for. But the odds were too fantastic that this could be anyone else. As the sun was peeling the lid off the night sky, she got the call,

"Team leader this is MCU, come in."

"Go MCU."

"Team leader we just got a priority patch through from Homeland Security out of Atlanta ,over?"

"Copy that patch thru, subject?"

"POI sighting in Atlanta."

The flesh on Kristi's scalp started to crawl; her skin goose-bumped. she looked at Thony. He and Suzan couldn't hear any of the earphone commands, but they were both looking at her intensely. She didn't trust chance, so she didn't trust them. This feeling was half guilt, half professional paranoia.

"Copy that."

She said slowly and thoughtfully.

"Run that patch thru."

"Copy team leader, running."

A beat went by and she heard a scratchy recording of a very southern voice. She was straining to understand the bad recording when she realized it wasn't the recording, it was the voice,

"Stop, rewind, play."

The order was complied with at once.

"... Victor Stephens at the North Towne Sheraton, we have a guest that fits the description on your flyer. My overnight concierge is a fuckin idiot and needs to be dealt with. I'm an old man. The young bastard won't listen to me. I found the picture in a drawer, and a young foreign girl mentioned it to me when I relieved her for lunch. Young punk came back and hit me for going through his things. I believe in my reservationists. She's been here for years. She says the guy with the beard is some kinda military official; he's gotta car and everything. I can't handle this youngun if he really wants to mix it up. Call me back and I'll be in facilities maintenance, Victor Stephens."

"Team leader to MCU."

"Go team leader."

"How old is this call?"

"Patch through says two minutes; Homeland tag is seven minutes ago."

Kristi conferred with Phillip for ATL ETA. He passed back

from the original mission data; they would be flying over the Northern most CDC facility in fifteen minutes. She inquired into time to CBD; Phillip checked back with the pilot.

"Central Business District is six minutes straight flight after flyby of CDC-A."

"Ok, do that, coordinates on the way."

"Team leader to MCU."

"Go Team leader."

"Send coordinates and all relevant data regarding North Towne Sheraton ASAP data channel."

"Copy that team leader, data coming now, over."

"Copy MCU stand by."

"Standing by."

The data channel took Phillips attention. The sheets flowed in.

"GPS is locked in for North Towne Sheraton; ETA twenty minutes max."

Suzan looked at Thony they had heard snips of the exchanges; the last one being 'ETA twenty minutes'. So, whatever was going to happen, they'd know in about nineteen minutes...

Chapter 41

<u>75 North</u>

Dutchess lay back in the master bedroom flipping through channels on the satellite TV. She watched programs filmed in America but with voice-over work done in Russian. It was so funny watching Col. Hogan talking and hearing it in Russian. Then she watched a few videos. International time zones made the satellite TV schedule crazy. BET's uncut videos were on and it was almost daybreak.

She had her blinds cracked a little and she could see the subtle differences in sky from the right side to the left. There was a guest Video Jock on the show. They were filming live from Atlanta, Lil Tooky's album release after party. It was a rerun. This feed was coming through a European satellite, and the live icon was blinking at the top of the screen, but 'recorded earlier' was at the bottom. Dutchess could not believe what basic cable could show and say after hours.

The after party was obviously an excuse for every full bodied

Georgia stripper in town to come out and get paid. Several times, you could barely see what was going on for the money flying in front of the camera.

This party was off the hook. She slid around on the big bed to lay on her belly. With her feet in the air, she saw the little boy rapper; he looked so young. The camera was rushing up on him. There was a pretty, thick woman riding his lap; her hair was so black, and her body looked really familiar. She turned her face, almost, then, she got up and ran away.

That was strange. But, no sooner had his lap been vacated, when he was attacked by two other pretty women. They, oh no they didn't on TV! One girl opened his pants, then, the other one sat on his, uhhh. Then, the first one pulled off her top. Dutchess turned the channel. She was appalled and turned on at the same time.

There was something about that first woman. She was pointing the remote at the TV when she saw the tall brother walk on to the screen. She wouldn't have looked twice, except that she had seen those eyes.

The man she saw on her big flat screen was tall and brown. His eyes were so beautiful; the hazel almost glowed in the lights that the cameraman was using. She got stuck staring at this guy, then, she blinked and he was gone. She wished she could have rewound the TV, but no luck on this one. But she already knew she'd remember that face.

She flipped through the rest of the channels. Nothing was really interesting on, so, she turned it off. She rolled over and looked up at the ceiling. She thought fleetingly about the guy on the TV. Is this a result of Franz being in her life? She couldn't remember herself looking at a guy like that before the tournament. As a matter of fact, the last person she had felt that same tingle for was Ms. Collins.

Yeah, that shiny black hair reminded her of Ms. Collins. That's who that woman reminded her of, but that couldn't have been her. No, not the precisely, beautiful, 4th grade teacher, although you never knew who was stripping in Atlanta.

Then, there was the camera run away. If Ms. Collins was stripping, she wouldn't want her face on TV. But hell, everybody at the party saw everything she had. She really wish she could rewind the show just for that split second piece of face. Now that she was looking for her, she knew that she could tell if it was her. But in her heart, she knew it couldn't have been her. Ms. Collins was beyond reproach as far as Dutchess was concerned. She scooted to the front of the bed and walked forward to the coach.

Henry was sprawled across one of the sofas in the living room area. He had his phone plugged in with papers, catalogs, and legal looking documents all over the place. Wheeling and dealing was this side of Henry. Dutchess never saw the frantic looking face. The heat energy coming from him was a shock to her system. After all the different feelings that she had gone through back in the room, then, to come out and feel all this wild energy radiating from Henry, was a real turn-on.

Then she heard his voice, the same calm placid 'Henry voice' that she was always used to hearing. But it was so strange to see that this was how he was on the other side of the phone. He was a little power station; he could probably power his phone without the plug. She felt enough energy to light up a nice-sized town. She mouthed

"What's up Henry?"

He answered in sign language: index finger, thumb up; two fingers, flat hand with the so-so motion, three fingers, another thumbs up and finally four fingers. Then, he pointed to a big smile. Dutchess was confused, but happy. No thumbs downs and no frowns meant things must be doing ok. She walked further forward to speak to Max. His concentration was on the road, but he instantly knew Dutchess was behind him. Without turning, he said,

"Hello Dutchess, is everything ok?"

"How did you do that Max?"

"Ancient drivers secret, I can't tell you everything now, can I?"

"Ok, I'll let you slide this time."

"I thank you Dutchess. Now, are you enjoying your new home away from home?"

"I love it. I need to go shopping. Can we stop to get something to eat?"

"Stop? Did you look in the galley?"

"The what?"

"The Galley; it's only a kitchen when we're not moving."

"Ohhh."

"Don't worry, the next time we ride, I'll have a list of terms and instructions about everything on the coach. I will include a map to all the storage areas so that you won't lose anything, ok?"

"Thanks Max, you're pretty cool."

"You should see me dance"

"I can't wait; you want anything?"

"No, I'm good. You know you have communications with me from almost anyplace back there. Look for the letter (M) on a button, press that and you'll get me."

"Ok, thanks Max."

She went back rear, taking her time to sit on every cushion on each sofa. When she arrived at the galley, she started opening cupboards. To her surprise, they had spices, and dry goods, noodles, and beans. She stooped so that she could open the lower cupboards; there were cans and heavier items. The fridge contained some of her favorite foods: Cajun turkey sliced thin, four different cheeses sliced in the dairy compartment, eggs and real butter.

The crisper was full of colorful fresh veggies, and the separate fruit container was full. She plucked a small bunch of grapes and checked the little freezer. It was filled with flat packs of butter pecan ice cream, French vanilla ice cream bars, Dove chocolate, and gourmet ice cream sandwiches. She didn't know when he had time, but Max had stocked the coach before they had left with everything she liked. She didn't even know that Henry knew all of these things.

The pressurized bread box held big fluffy croissants, potato, wheat, and French breads. She grabbed a croissant, turkey, and some cheeses, and put it in the microwave for a few seconds. It was enough to melt the cheeses and she was ready. She found a large variety of liquids: everything from square bottles of Fuji water to Heineken beer and a couple bottles of wine.

Somewhere in her mind, she knew that she could get used to this. She selected a bottle of orange-banana-tomato juice. She had never heard of such a thing, much less tasted it, it was great. So, feeling marvelous, she made her way back to sit across from Henry and the paper storm on the other side of the coach.

"So what's good Henry?"

He had turned off the phone after the last call, and had his head tossed back against the sofa back.

"Everything D, you have been invited to a tournament in Vegas in three weeks; we have to accept or not within forty eight hours. I'm waiting for a fax from a designer in South Korea. You will be wearing Reebok from head to toe."

She sat up,

"Reebok? How'd you make that happen? I thought it was the no names from France?"

"Well, they heard about the contract you got from Coke and backed out on their own. They felt that they couldn't compete."

"So, what did Reebok come with?"

She was afraid to ask, but she had to know.

"They came with an exclusive shoe and wardrobe design line, both sport and sportswear, and with three contracted after-five looks, for a three year contract of $22 million!"

"Are you serious Henry? Are you for real?"

"Yep, you're the flavor Dutchess, you gotta strike'em while the irons hot, and our friend, Carlos, did us the biggest favor ever."

With him starting her out with a $60 million deal, nobody could ever call her a bum. The rest of the suitors knew if they wouldn't come with the big dollars, they wouldn't be using voices or images of Dutchess Singletary.

"Dutchess, I'll need your approval. Once the shots come off the line, I'll need you to sign off on what you like; don't sign what you don't like."

"Are there anymore earth-shaking things I should know about? Come on, tell me. I'm not sure how many of these I can take back to back."

"Ok, let me see. If everything goes as I negotiated, which it never does, you'll be worth $132 million. But, of course, that's if nothing falls through. I'm only speaking of endorsements. That doesn't include purses. As long as you keep winning, you will be a very, very wealthy young woman."

Dutchess stared at Henry. Her eyes were huge and unblinking. She stood up, walked to the bathroom, soaked a washcloth in cold water, and splashed it against her face and neck. She dried off, and walked back to her seat across from Henry.

"One hundred thirty two million dollars, Henry?"

"D, you told me to go ahead and make you rich. One tiny $4 million part of that is a voice over for an animated character in a big budget movie. That may be three to five days' work, depending on your schedule.   To be totally realistic, if nothing else comes in, your total right now is $90 million. Oh, that's right, I forgot. Reebok has a $2.2 million signing bonus for you. The account is set up at the bank of the United States. We can pick up your access card at any major branch."

She leaped across the space separating them and knocked Henry down on the sofa. It was pure joy and emotion. But Henry, having been up all day and night, was caught off guard. Dutchess sometimes forgot she wasn't a kid anymore, and Henry was a man. He couldn't help his reactions.

When she had stood up from the Ferrari and mooned him with the strip of thong being the only blockage, it stuck in his mind. Instantly, this site created a horny, little devil to stand on his shoulder. Now, with Dutchess laying atop him, obviously bra-less, hugging him, he tried in vain to tell his ignorant dick that this was innocent exuberance. But, his opportunistic appendage wanted what that little devil wanted.

He wrapped his arms around her, feeling her braless back that made this harder and harder to be objective about. She was thanking him and thanking him, wiggling and gyrating. The cotton shorts doing nothing to separate their sexes. He understood her excitement at now being a single rich woman. His rational mind knew that this was innocent appreciation.

But, his irrational mind could feel his rock-hard member burrowing its tip through the thin layer of slacks, shorts, and panties, molding itself between the boiling hot lips. His mind saw him unfolding and sinking deeply into his client. He could actually feel the slick hot wetness of her as he reached down and pulled those perfect ass cheeks apart, and thrust deep inside her with all of his might. He could see himself rolling her over on top of the laptop and paperwork, humping her, while getting as well as he gave. He Came deeply inside of her, experiencing satisfaction like he never knew. Then he could see her pregnant trying to move around the court. He could see multiple little Henrys with their ties half loosened; he could see his child support checks growing taller than himself. That did it.

It was better than a bucket of ice cubes poured down the front of his pants seeing the image of him being poor because of one good bout of sex with his franchise. This thought scared his dick way back behind his balls; he felt like he had just gotten out of the pool. He did roll Dutchess over, away from the computer, not on top of.

He kissed her chastely on her forehead and congratulated her. She regained her senses and thought about what she had done, and grew embarrassed; she had attacked her manager. Henry was flushed and out of breath. Dutchess had never had a reaction like that; she had literally thrown herself on Henry. She had felt his raging hardness poking her directly on her clit, the stiffness of him spreading her lips. Damn, what the hell was coming over her? If Henry had pulled out his dick, she would have let him put it in her.

She was losing her mind. Was she turning into a nympho? She couldn't figure it out, but it seemed that her assertiveness with Franz was manifesting itself in other ways. She was so glad that Henry was all about business; that one move could have ruined everything. Then, she felt his big old stiffy start to shrink right before he lifted her off of him.

He stood and looked away. Dutchess couldn't meet his eyes;

for an awkward moment, they said nothing.

"Thanks again Henry."

"Oh, no problem, Dutchess. Uhh, let's not do that again, ok?"

"I understand, I'll try to control myself."

"Not that it wasn't nice."

"Oh yeah, it was very pleasant."

"But…"

"Yeah, I know."

She hugged him, her breasts squashed against his chest and she felt him rise up to meet her again. Having a dick must be frustrating, she thought, especially when you have to keep it in your pants. Sitting back on her side of the coach, Henry told her that last call he had made was to the Coke Real Estate Holdings office. They were assigned to poke around and see what was available. They were due to call back any minute.

"What do you want as far as living space, Dutchess? How many bedrooms, baths, kitchens etc.?"

"I don't know Henry. I know that I don't want too much, but, I do want the Coke people to understand that I appreciate the money."

There was a beeping styled ping sound from the pillar next to the window; looking at it for the first time, they both noticed the indentation. Henry reached in and a small latch was released. A compartment was steadily filling with pages from the fax machine/printer function, of an integrated all-in-one business center. Henry pulled out the stack of papers and took them to the sofa for Dutchess to look over; they were pictures of houses, floor plans, maps and a letter.

'Dear Ms. Singletary, congratulations, and welcome to Coke Brands. We are very excited that you decided to join our happy family. As the chief liaison for contractor relations, I am available around the clock for any company or contract-related issues you may encounter. Regarding the housing information, please peruse the selection of Atlanta area properties for your approval. Any property listed can be arranged for your private tour within two hours by a member of my staff'.

Henry stopped and pushed the small (M) button on the wall next to the conference table control panel.

"How can I help you, Henry?"

"How do you do that, Max?"

"Ancient drivers secret; I can't tell you everything, now can I?"

"Ok, ok, Max. What's our ETA to Atlanta?"

"We'll be in the city limits in five hours."

"Ok, thanks."

"Anything else?"

"No. That'll do for now."

The faint recessed light behind the (M) went out.

"Well, you got three hours to look-see if there's anything you like, and we can take a look when we get into the ATL. How's that sound?"

"Sounds good; was that all in the letter?"

"Nope, let's see. Once solid, your selection will be leased in your name. All basic needs arrangements are already taken care of by the company. All other expenses will be outlined within the terms and conditions of your contract. Once again, welcome and congratulations.' It's signed Midge Scott."

"Midge huh? Ok, Miss Midge, I'll take a look."

***

Traffic on I-75N was still bad, but it broke up in spots and Dulcet got some speed. When she could get it, she took all that she could get; one stretch found her tipping 120mph. It only lasted about thirty minutes, but it felt good; she needed that. The image of her face on the side of that bus had disconcerted her as nothing ever had in her life. She was hoping and praying that its destination was Atlanta. If it was in the city, she would find it. But then what? Who in the hell was this impersonator? Her entire life had been a solitary pursuit.

She thought back to her childhood: The vague memories of the orphanage, the taunts about all the kids with the dead parents, the everyday haters. Children are the worst, the most evil creatures on earth to each other. She thought of the presentation days when the prospective parents would come to look over the kids as though to buy a pet from the store. They would line up in their uniforms and look desirable in hopes to steal someone's heart and be taken home.

The kids knew that she was a light-skinned black girl. The real white kids would whisper 'bleach nigger', 'oree-ho', and all manners of hurtful things to make her cry. So, she could never have the pretty happy face the elders told them it took to get adopted. Often, she would step out of line and run away, crying.

Then came the fraud. At the age of four years old, she was becoming too old to be desirable to a young couple. But, a middle-aged white couple with red hair like hers, had found her adorable. They took her home that same day.

Everything was wonderful as long as she stayed quiet, minded her manners, and maintained her temper; she could pass for a young white girl. But, after a few months in her new home, small things started to creep into the routine of getting along in the house. Little Dulcet didn't like watching the same things on TV. She didn't like 'Little house on the prairie'; she liked 'Good times' and the 'Jefferson's. She didn't like the country western or mournfully soulful Irish melodies; she liked black music, jazz, soul, and hip hop.

Her foster parents knew she was not of the same Anglo race, and they knew there that were going to be genetic differences, but this was a bit much. Eventually they sent Dulcet to stay with relatives in the country, to see if the city was the reason for her preoccupation with all black things.

The country was fabulous; this branch of the family was not cursed as the foster parents had been with not being able to reproduce. They had a clan: five redheaded boys and three girls. Dulcet should fit right in for the summer, so they thought.

As far as the grownups were concerned, the summer went great. The kids played all day, and stayed out of their hair. Even their young city cousin, Dulcet was learning to get along. What she actually learned was how to fight. That first summer set the rules for the rest. The siblings all fought amongst themselves during any other time of the year. When Dulcet came for the summer, it was all of them against her.

Summertime for Dulcet was survival camp; the simplest things for anyone else turned into life or death situations for her. A day at the lake turned into an exercise in staying alive: it was between the boys dunking and almost drowning her, to the bigger girls stripping off her bikini and tossing it out into the lake. Then they left leaving her naked, young, undeveloped body to the elements.

They would leave her, after taunting her all day, to walk home alone; she often got lost. They ate her food if she wasn't at the table to get it; they pulled her hair because it grew longer and prettier than theirs.

Her young life was basically a nightmare. She learned to appreciate the home in the city. She imitated some of the actions of the country kids and that backfired. Her parents thought the country getaways were doing her good. So, they continued.

Her early teen years were the worst. By this time, the country summer cousins had changed tactics from physical to psychological torture. The only thing that kept her sane was Emma, the black cook/maid. She would look out for her after the red headed gang would eat up her food.

She would care for her scrapes, and ice pack needs when

the fights were over. Once, she even sat her down, combed, and brushed her hair. It was during one of these instances, that she dropped the bomb on Dulcet. This was something that she'd always known, but had never heard.

"Dulcet, you are different from these kids and I know that you know that it's more than the fact that you come from the city. You can stay outside in the sun longer than they can; your skin turns olive, while theirs stays pasty white or burns red. They see the way your curves are filling in, while the other girls are older than you, but still are straight up and down. Baby, they don't have no kinda know-how. But I know what I see: a little high-yella, black girl, sittin in the middle of a basket of white kids."

Dulcet was stunned; she had felt so confused for so long. Emma's hair-brushing revelation had brought everything into instant focus.

"So, is that why all these kids, my cousins, hate me, and want to hurt me, and be mean?"

"I'd say so, baby. They have been as confused as you, that you look just like them. But, you don't have freckles, and, you tan, instead of burning. Its human nature to despise the things you don't understand. Now let this be our little secret Dulcet; if you ever need to talk, you can always come to Emma."

Dulcet hadn't realized that tears had started to flow, tears of relief for finally knowing what the mystery of her difference was; tears of joy for having Emma as a confidante. She could talk to Emma like she couldn't even talk to her own parents.

That day, as she walked out of the kitchen with her silky hair brushed to perfection, gave her an entirely new outlook on life. She was happy, but not for long.

The girls were in the tree house with the three oldest boys; this was their getaway when the sun was too hot. The boys had bullied the girls into all sorts of things over the years and they had relented. They would sit up in the tree house and jack their brothers off, while letting them look at their less than womanly, naked bodies. This had progressed to giving them blowjobs. The line they wouldn't cross was letting them actually screw them. To get some sort of satisfaction they allowed their brothers to lick them, but that was it.

Now, they had decided that this summer things would be different. The girls formulated a plan; they would get out from being their brothers' oral sex slaves, at least for a little while. Their campaign during the summer of Dulcets 14th year was to make friends; to use the honey instead of the constant vinegar approach.

They invited her up to the tree house to look at fashion magazines. Suspicious, at first, Dulcet followed them through the small heavy trapdoor entrance to the tree house for the first time. When she saw the pillows and the stack of magazines, she felt a little more comfortable.

It was very hot in the enclosed space, so the sisters began to take off some of their clothes. It took some time in the hot box to convince Dulcet out of her clothes. They sat in the sauna-like heat naked, comparing their bodies: their pink little nipples vs. her tan ones, their flat chests vs. her nice, plum-sized breasts.

The next thing she knew, the trapdoor opened and the boys came rushing up the ladder, already naked and hard. She

asked about her whereabouts, they all claimed ignorance. One of the girls volunteered that she had been seen by the lake with one of the local bad boys. With looks of disdain, their parents set out to the lake to find her.

While they were at the lake, Dulcet was by the well using cold water to wash the dried cum and pussy juice off of her body, face, and hair. Her clothes were caked with dirt and everything else. She hobbled her pain-wracked body to Emma's apartment off the kitchen. There she laid on her floor. When the little search party returned empty handed, the kids started to worry; maybe they had gone too far and killed her.

Then, they heard the scream.

Emma had gone to her room to hang up her coat. She found Dulcet lying on the floor, a cold, shivering, bruised mess. She was in the hospital for a week before she was released to go home. Her cousins had come to visit her to let her know that there would be hell to pay if she told anybody. Dulcet stayed mute. She did not speak to anyone at all until she got back to the city. Even then, saying nothing about the assault; her decision was already made.

She began to work out. Her body was blossoming and her muscles were firming up. She spent the winter and spring running, swimming, and weight-training. The Boys and Girls club in the neighborhood offered archery and target pistol courses. She took advantage of everything. She had also taken her other hobby to another level: stealing. Her thievery advanced from petty trips into the purses and wallet of her foster parents, to the homes of the non-attentive people in the neighborhood.

She was well set for cash; when she saw it, she took it. Her collection was well into the thousands by now, and she had nothing to spend it on. With That fateful summer approaching, Dulcet placed all of her cash into the lining of her suitcase. Then, she packed all the things that she thought she would need and left it packed; every night, she would look at her packed bag and think about the coming summer.

She caught a taxi for the bus station; it was a day before she was due in the country. Nobody was expecting her.

Just as she suspected, the siblings were in their tree house. She pulled out the large zip lock bag that she had been holding in her purse the entire trip. The plastic Smith and Wesson .45 caliber squirt gun was filled with gasoline. She stood on the ladder, that was nailed to the tree, and squirted the sides of the tree house, the roof, front and back, until the gun was empty.

The spark from the wheel and flint zippo lighter sent the slowly leaking dribbles of gas flowing down the tree trunk, whooshing back up, as she climbed down. Retrieving her suitcase, she walked away. She didn't hear the screams until she was midway to the road. She stuck out her thumb after unbuttoning her blouse, revealing an impressive swell of mature 36c breast. It was no time before she got a ride back to the bus station. From there, she took a taxi to the airport, and a flight into her new life.

These thoughts ran through Dulcet's memory as she rolled up the featureless highway to Atlanta. That long-ago flight to this very same city was the start of all things Dulcet: her solo-sexual decision, and her first bank robbery. Most of her adult firsts happened there, so it held a special place in her heart. She hadn't been back in three years. 'Soul food', from Recipe, was directing her. But now that she'd seen that bus, there was nothing that could turn her away. She had to know.

***

In Springfield, Illinois, a young man, by the name of Mikey Siljan, was enjoying his first day off in a long while. He was a cashier at the 'Surf and Turf' in the commercial district. The owners had paid a special tax so that they could remain open, even after curfew hours. So, they had given him all sorts of overtime. Now, Mikey sat in his little studio apartment watching his tiny color TV, soaking his tired, achy feet in a bucket of hot water. He sat there on his easy chair, in his boxers, drinking a beer. He lived alone.

By the time he was reaching for his fifth beer of the first six pack, the news was on. The top stories were about the wonderful job the National Guard was doing country wide. There was a lot of nothing about the search for the terrorists. There was a serial thief going around robbing people, and institutions alike, leaving all the victims in compromising positions. The FBI had named her the CPR.

In sports, somebody named Dutchess Singletary was quick-rich from playing tennis. She had won some tournament in Florida and was the tennis' new golden girl. They showed a short video of her championship win. Mikey dropped his beer; he spilled the cold contents all over his crotch. In no way decreasing the hardness of his instant erection. The woman he saw on the TV was instantly naked, fingering her fire red pussy while playing with her breasts. The vision from the drive-through window was unforgettable. That was her!

The news had gone on to the weather, but he had to have more. He turned to the all-sports channels. The tab ticker at the bottom told him that they were about to go to tennis. He grabbed himself. As soon as tennis popped up, they showed Dutchess in her winner's circle contract dress coming through the hotel; all of her curves were showing. In Mikey's mind, he could see a naked Dulcet walking down the stairs, kissing her own nipples, and fingering herself. He shot off into the Epsom salt bucket that his right foot was soaking in.

He slumped back in the chair and continued to channel-surf and watch whatever he could find about Dutchess Singletary. After all the Dutchess stories had faded out, they went to other topics. He thought back to that day; she had masturbated right there, naked in his window. Then, he remembered trying to talk to her. She had punched the gas and roared away, laughing. Was she laughing at him? Did she know that he had come on himself? All of a sudden his dick went soft. He started to think, he had a magazine somewhere, was it, ah, there it was.

Chapter 42

Forty five minutes before sun up, Abdullah and his 'Driver' pulled the military limousine out of the ramp from the Sheratons parking garage. The twin flags in the front with the Generals stars flapping gave the first hint. The diplomatic plates in back sealed the deal. They took the streets into downtown Atlanta. Once in the area, they did a tour of the checkpoints. He rolled up to the National Guard troop to inspect the salutes. Abdullah rolled the window down and demanded a status report. The report was given crisply by the nervous guardsmen, who rarely ever saw an officer above a Captain.

The limo continued to the center of the city. Gaining access to the central hub of the MARTA system below was a difficult task. Beneath the arena, behind the facades and beyond the loading dock roads, the MARTA SWAT Team patrolled along with the National Guard troops. This was good because he would be able to disrupt their routine by pulling chain of command rank.

Abdullah checked the package he would deliver to the transit Authority. The device resembled a claw surrounding an aerosol can; the claw had a small programmable timer window built into its outward facing side. Between the claw and the can was a small rolled cylinder of C4. The pin from the timer was embedded in this strip. Just a bit thicker than a standard pencil, it was the conduit of the volt of energy that will set off the C4, which would destroy the aerosol can that would fill the central train station.

His stated mission at this access point was to tour and inspect for recording purposes to ensure that the protocols of Threat Level RED were being adhered to. This was a major smoke screen. Abdullah was praying to Allah that no fan would come along and blow away the screen before the time he had chosen for their demise. Gaining access was much simpler than finding it. As soon as the car pulled up to the 'Restricted Authorized Personnel Only' gate, everyone came to attention.

The 'General' stepped from the vehicle with all the slowness and deliberateness of the uniform. Abdullah said very few words. He approached the access gate observing, then turned on his heels,

"Status."

He almost whispered to the National Guard First Sergeant.

"Status, All clear General, Sir. Three accesses, all employees, all verified, sir."

"Out-fucking-standing, Sergeant. Good job; give me two guards, one train man. I want to see this tunnel through to the middle."

"Sir, yes sir."

The young inexperienced guardsman ordered two of his eight men and one MARTA SWAT member to accompany him and the General into the tunnel. He left behind the three MARTA SWAT members, and the K9 bomb sniffer. The walk through the tunnel was surprisingly brief. This access point was close to the center. As the bright orange innards of the station tiles came into view, their eyes adjusted and the north-south bound signs now visible indicated that they were on the bottom level of the structure.

The General said that he wanted to see above the tracks to inspect the platforms. The guardsmen formed a ladder and climbed over each other to retrieve an actual ladder from maintenance. This distraction was all the time needed to place the can and claw device underneath the lip of the platform. The time was 6:54am the timer was set for 8:15. The emergency schedule he had consulted online indicated that trains should be arriving from the north, south, as well as the east and west on the level above at that exact time.

The flat faces of the Italian-made train cars pushed the air in front of them in huge clothes ruffling gales. This optimal timing would serve to move the deadly serine gas throughout every corner of the massive train center point. This would include all three floors as if there was a whirlwind inside a box canyon. His first mission deployed, Abdullah called for the car.

They exited the station from the front on the third level. The General bundled the small inspection team into the limo and dropped them back at their start point. He praised their vigilance and expressed confidence in the security of the tunnel system as inspected. He even mentioned the unseen men patrolling in the dark tunnels along the way. Duly impressed with the General's observation, the small team was in a self-congratulatory mood, as they were dropped off.

With salutes all around, the General rode off to inspect the check points adjacent to the Georgia dome. The SWAT man wondered why they had only inspected one tunnel. Abdullah praised Allah for another mission set against the foolish infidels. The nerve of them to try to keep his victories from the media; the proper publicity was essential for the spread of true terror. He knew that they would try to keep his victories from the media, but he had something for that. The next stop was the first RED X, the CDC facility #1.

Using his diplomatic status, Abdullah's driver jumped on to the freeway and sped to the fourth exit. Two turns later, he saw the large three lettered sign. He had heard these letters repeated like a holy mantra for years. To be sitting in front of the potential ground zero for the end of America, sent chills throughout his body. The obvious ease with which the limo rode up to the building, spoke to the low probability that this was a high security target.

So, Abdullah informed his driver to proceed to X#2. This facility was located four miles away from #1, using surface streets. The time was 7:05, and security here was visible which indicated, at the least, that there was something to protect. Deciding against the perimeter approach, Abdullah took the direct approach, and drove straight to the loading dock. The driver checked the area and sighted a likely target location. He went to the HVAC system once again, this time, for a diversionary charge.

The driver parked the limo perpendicular to the obvious surveillance cameras. He released Abdullah's door, who proceeded to the dock office. He interviewed the security chief about any anomalies in the schedule, and to retrieve a status report to be run up the chain.

While this was taking place, two quarter-pound, pear-shaped C4 charges with thirty minute timers were dropped. One was placed through a snipped hole in an intake vent to the HVAC system. The next, was dropped down into a dry drainage shaft below the truck dock. Within ten minutes, Abdullah had completed his security review, checked off the bogus information on a clipboard, and had offered a bored salute and stepped back into the car.

"To #3."

The driver left to get back on the freeway. The explosive placement should do away with the security supervisor he had spoken to, as well as two nice sized chunks of the physical plant. The huge towering liquid oxygen tank close by the blast zone, should add a nice touch to the remainder of the damage. As they headed northbound on the freeway en route to #3, a dark diamond sped overhead. Looking out the back window, Abdullah recognized the military hi-lo diamond formation of the speeding Blackhawks, and the faint outline of a tanker high above.

***

Sylvania rolled over reaching for Ron, and felt nothing but cool sheets; rolling backwards she felt nothing as well. This physical realization brought her quickly awake. The first thing she did was look in the drawer next to the bed to make sure that the key was gone. So where was Ron? She sat up in the bed and looked around. Nothing was disturbed, and nothing of his was left. She grabbed her remote and turned the TV on, which was a force of habit, and the news was on. She could tell that here was a lot wrong with the country.

First, by the red edges surrounding every channel; then, there was the emphasis on the weather, sports and entertainment. There was no real news. As she channel-surfed she saw every channel was showing 'Classic episodes; even the game shows. It was like everybody was trying to take their viewers back to the good old days. She dialed Ron on his cell phone, it picked up on the first ring, and she left a voicemail.

"Ron, call me baby. You should have been here by now. I'm worried. It's me baby. I hope you're ok."

She disconnected and tuned to the entertainment channel. Feeling totally out of every loop was not a normal feeling for Sylvania. Now, throw these feelings that she had for Ron into the mix, and her heart skipped a quick beat, thinking that something may have happened to him. She slipped on a robe so that she could feel engulfed by something. She paced the floor of her room and looked out the west window at the still, dark sky wondering.

"Entertainment sports news, Dutchess Singletary is now the 'It' girl for tennis. Coca Cola Brands has picked her up in a big way. Around Miami, the Dutchess' bus has been seen touting 'drink mor Coke' on the back, with the Red and Green Coke and Sprite color schemes. Rumors have it that she has been picked up by a clothing sponsor. The name of the apparel maker has not been finalized as of yet. But, you can be assured when the news drops we'll be there."

Sylvania's attention was taken by that report. Dutchess was still on her mind, but that also made her think of Barry. So many things were swirling around in Sylvania's head. Seeing that Dutchess was doing so well, so quickly, was good. This was proof that anything could happen on any given day if you stuck to your guns and followed your dreams. The last shot on the news coverage was the side of the Dutchess' bus; she was so beautiful. They used the same photographic trick that the Uncle Sam posters did; her eyes followed you, even through the TV.

The next program was garbage. She turned the TV off, and sat on the edge of the bed staring towards the window. How many hours ago had she been waking up with Barry snuggling up behind her just to leave? His work taking him away from her. Then today, she woke up making love to Ron. Her whole life had changed. She had been to the park, the club, the world. Now, after having made love to Ron here inside her personal space, he had disappeared with the key to the kingdom.

She had been with Barry almost a year, six months before he even saw her body. He begged for a key. But Ron was elemental. Like a force of nature, he didn't ask for much, he didn't have to. He made her want to give him things, from herself to things that money couldn't buy.

Unconsciously, she reached up and spun the diamonds around in her ears. She vowed that she wouldn't take them out because they were a token of Ron's love; keeping them in would be a show of hers. Sylvania stepped into the bathroom. She turned on the tub and pulled back the skylight tile; the last of the evening stars were being overtaken by the dawning sky.

She hung her robe on a door peg, ran a hot soak with baby oil, and peppermint essential oil to calm her mind. Looking over her shoulder, she felt a slight twinge. Heat rolled through her body as she spied the shimmering white panties in the sink. Now, they were dry, and formed a shape strangely similar to a swan.

This reminded her of the really nice restaurants that put swans top the to-go boxes. She stepped backwards into the tub. The hot water bought more tingling thoughts of Ron. She sat and soaked. The peppermint essence took away her tension, little by little. She soaked until she was in a meditative state...

***

Not willing to risk the possibility that she may go another direction, Ron pulled into a closed gas station, and pretended to check his tire. Fantasia drove past him not sparing a glance. She proceeded to enter I-285 North. Ron had put his money on south; it's a good thing he'd thought quickly. He pulled back out in time to get to the northbound check point one car behind Fantasia.

Getting on was no problem, though he did notice the guardsman looked tired. He was not so sharp; that wasn't good. This code RED was really a drain on everybody; he wondered how much longer it would last. Once he finally got on the highway, he had to squint to make out the Mercedes.

Ron had to downshift and punch his sports Maxima to catch up; the smooth multi-port v8 was equal to the test. They were both humming along at 90mph.

Ron passed the Atlanta freeway junction to get back to Sylvania's house the long way. He thought about her for the first time in a while. It shocked him that he hadn't thought about her recently. He had been so stuck thinking about the anti-her, all the things he didn't like, that the love he was feeling for his girl was pushed aside. Then he realized that there may be some things he's going to be forced to do that he didn't want associated with his version. He mentally tried to make distance.

He opened his armrest storage compartment and disconnected his phone from the charger. He punched it on and there was one message. He played Sylvania's message back-to-back three times; she sounded so sweet. This was his woman, he had to get used to that. He put the phone back into the armrest. She would only worry more if he called. He had no idea when he was going to be there, especially, if he admitted that he had no idea what he was doing here.

Ron was going through some morality issues; he didn't want to bring a web of lies into his new relationship with Sylvania. He figured that he'd tell her as much about this look-a-like, as he could find out. But could he tell her he fucked her? Could he say it felt like he was inside of her? How do you tell your woman, your **new** woman, that there's somebody else, and all the rest?

No, he realized he would have to keep this his one secret from Sylvania. As hard as it was to decide, he felt it would be for the best. Now he had to figure out the solution to the mystery before him. The mystery poured on more speed; he tried not to keep up with her click for click but he kept her in view.

After about fifteen minutes, she signaled a right and kept moving over. She was finally making her exit. Ron had to look around to see where he was. In all the years that he had been in Atlanta, he had never used this exit. He eased through the checkpoint, watched her turn directly into the parking lot for the X hotel.

He had heard of the X; a super luxury hotel chain that had four locations in this country, and another eight in the rest of the world. There were more single letter hotels under the umbrella. The closer they got to Z, the more exclusive the room; there was one Z. It was in the United Arab Emirates, the only ten star hotel in the world. The X rated six stars and the prices were only rumored.

Fantasia pulled to valet parking and stepped out. Ron's body reacted violently to the sight of her. He got so hard so fast that he caught a cramp because of the position he was in. Watching the hem of her skirt hang for a second, high up on her thigh, before sliding its way past the tops of her stockings, and on down her legs, had him stuck for a moment. The naked sway of her breasts in the fitted black shirt made him ache to touch her again. Then, he saw the overstuffed purse full of stolen jewelry and that signaled the difference. That wasn't his lover; that was her evil twin, the whore that raped him.

As long as he kept thinking like that, he should be able to keep the two of them separated. Before she could get inside the building, the valet began to pull off. Ron approached the driver's side window with a $100 bill preceding him. The tip motivated valet stopped, he already knew that he was going to give this person whatever he wanted. But it would be another bill for a blowjob.

"What's her name?"

"Diamond Jade, she's in suite 3030; she paid in advance, that's all I know."

Ron noticed the Mercedes was in valet mode; no key was needed. Once it went into park, the engine would turn off.

"Ok kid, I got another bill, don't leave yet ok?"

"Sure."

Maybe it was the blowjob after all, huh? The valet thought. Ron went to his trunk and pulled out a device about the size of a paperclip. He inserted it into a magnetized unit that resembled a match box and pointed the box toward the horizon. Within ten seconds, there was a double beep and a faint blue glow from the lower corner of the box pointing at Fantasia's car.

Ron slid the box open and removed the device, he looked for the perfect place and found it, inside the window track. The rudimentary tracking device shouldn't be noticeable this close to the power window motor and speakers, but the box had a strong satellite bounce back.

He knew he could track this car as long as it had this door on it. TCSS allowed him as much time as he wanted in the research and development labs. Because he had imagination and made money, anything he invented he shared in the patent credit; it was in his contract, and, so far, the arrangement was working out fine.

He passed the two crispy new $100 bills to the valet. He did not know that he was now ready to turn tricks or cartwheels for him, whichever he chose. Ron walked away, he popped on his hazards and stepped into the lobby; this was an experience that he was not prepared for.

The atrium looked like a scene out of a science fiction movie; there were things up there he could have sworn were alive. The uppermost levels were beyond his vision; there were clouds encircling them that had to be projected, holograms he thought, but they looked so real.

At the right angle, it seemed as if you were on the bottom of the ocean looking up through the layers of water to see the clouds and sky, complete with ripples. There was an aquarium, worth of creatures. As disrespectful as it was to the designer, Ron ripped his eyes away from the miracle. He knew that he looked like a tourist in New York City for the first time: Walking in a crowd of people, only the new guy was looking up; everybody else was used to the view, looking straight ahead.

Looking back through the lobby, he did see more people gazing up, less paying him any attention. There, waiting to be seated at the restaurant, he saw Fantasia. She was the definition of a smooth criminal: the purse tossed over her shoulder, a big diamond ring on her finger, waiting patiently. Ron suddenly felt exposed, standing there staring at Fantasia while trying not to be seen. That wouldn't last long.

So, he moved back towards the door, stopped, and pocketed a business card from the Concierge desk. He walked through the self-propelled revolving door, back to his car. Killing the hazards, he moved his car into the parking lot adjacent to the carport, and once again, tried to figure out what he was doing. Why was he following this woman? He picked up his phone and punched redial. The phone was answered on the first ring.

"Ron?"

He instantly knew the difference between the two; she was warm and genuine. Her concern sent a soothing feeling through him.

"I'm ok babe, you sounded so stressed on your message. I wanted to let you know that I was ok and I'm on my way back to you."

"Oh baby, I'm so glad to hear that."

Ron started driving towards the exit,

"Where have you been all this time?"

"I'll tell you when I get home babe. I don't really know what I'm doing out here; maybe you can help me understand."

"Whatever it is, babe, we can work it out, ok?"

"Have I told you lately that I love you?"

"No."

She sounded like she had the pout on her face.

"Well, I do."

"Well, I'm madly in love with the way you make me feel, Mr. Man. Hurry up, I'm in the hot tub."

"I'm kinda far, don't turn into a raisin on me. I'm looking for a nice plump grape."

"I got a grape for you, pervert."

As Ron was turning on to the freeway approaching the check point, he had to look twice.

"Hey babe, your girls' gone big time, have you heard?"

"My girl, who?"

"The one from TV, the tennis girl with the red hair."

"Dutchess? Yeah they said on the entertainment news that Coke gave her a big contract after she won down in Miami. But what made you say that?"

"I just saw a huge bus with her face all over it."

"Ooooh, for real? I'm so proud of her. I thought she was still in Miami though, that's what they said on TV."

"Well now, we know for sure that we can't trust what we see on TV."

Ron had meant that as a joke, but for some reason it felt more like truth. After he'd said it, he got quiet.

"Ron, you still there?"

"Yeah babe, I was thinking about what I just said, you been watching TV?"

"A little bit, it's all repeats and bad programming."

"Nothing about the terror attacks? No on-site reporters, nothing?"

"Nope. Not one thing on any of the channels I watched. I was flipping through trying to find something, but I didn't know what. I guess that did stick out because of its absence."

"Hmmm, let's get off these phones babe, I'll be there in about thirty minutes."

"Ok, Ron…Hurry, ok?"

"Ok baby."

She hung up the phone. It was 6:55

Chapter 43

"Oooo look Henry, this is the one, it's perfect and it's furnished. They have one of those serve machines on the roof top court, just like in Miami. I like it. The houses are nice, but it's only me. I think the condo would be better to start. what do you think?"

Dutchess looked like a kid looking through the Sears Christmas catalog.

"D, if you like it, I love it, what area is it in?"

"Dunwoody, I've never been there."

Northeast Atlanta wasn't where she usually went, but it's always good to expand ones horizons, right?

"So now what Henry?"

"Hold on a sec D. Hello Midge? Yeah, it's Henry. Yeah, we got everything. Ok, yeah, she loved a few of the properties....Right, she does want to take a look at one temporarily; maybe a change later, number G57NE. The X. oh yeah. That's nice. Hold on one sec Midge."

Henry pushed the (M) button.

"How can I help you, Henry?"

"What kind of time can you get me for the X hotel, Max?"

"The X, let's see, topside northeast, the computer says right around 7am on the nose."

"Ok, thanks Max."

"My pleasure Henry."

"Hey Midge?   Yeah. Max said that we can be there at 7am on the dot. ok, yeah?

Well D, we got the big girl treatment. Midge Scott herself will be giving us the walking tour."

"Well, I'm impressed. I thought that she was going to get one of her people to meet us."

"She probably reconsidered how to handle the new 'it' girl."

Dutchess threw a pillow at Henry.

"It that, Henry."

"Get used to it D, you're here. With luck, we're gonna keep you here."

Dutchess went back into the bedroom and laid out on the bed to get some rest before they got to the X. She curled up on the bed lowering the lights and put her hands between her thighs as if she were cold. The temperature was ok, but she wanted to be warm inside. The incident with Henry earlier had gotten her horny. As soon as she touched herself, the fire flashed hot. She rolled over and slid her hand down into her shorts; the other hand pulled off her top.

She sensuously stroked her breasts while she fingered herself slowly. As she got closer to her orgasm, both her hands got frantic. She rolled on to her back, spread her legs, pinched her nipples, and dipped two fingers deep into herself. Her hips started to buck, as she came. She had no idea how loud she was. Her mind was on Franz. She moaned sensuously,

"Yes, fuck meee, fuck meee."

Spread out on the bed all alone with her need. She was so hot by now, she had pulled her shorts and panties down. They were around one ankle. Her hand was still dripping with two fingers snugly inside of herself gravity rolled her over to her side; She fell asleep like that.

Henry had dozed off on the side sofa, when he heard a sound. All he could hear was 'eeee'; he thought it was Dutchess calling.

"Henry".

So, he groggily got up and padded to her door and heard the 'eeee' sound again. He cracked the door to see what she wanted, and was rooted to the spot. That little devil was back on his shoulder kicking him in the side of the head. Dutchess was naked, on her back, fingering herself and squeezing her nipple in the throes of a major orgasm. He watched for a few seconds as her orgasm passed. Her breathing evened out; she rolled onto her side fast asleep.

He closed the door and tried to lay down, but he was so hard from that voyeuristic moment, he couldn't sleep. He lay there with a tent pole sticking straight up and tried not to think about Dutchess, his client, the franchise, everybody's future. The last four days had been major for Henry as well as for Dutchess. Henry had to get a girlfriend, soon.

"Coming up on the X hotel, fifteen minutes to the X hotel."

The intercom woke Henry with a start; it was Max informing Henry and Dutchess of their wake-up call. Henry dragged himself to the bathroom to pee and found a little sticky business. He must have been dreaming pretty good. Then, the sight of Dutchess flashed in his mind and peeing became a lot more difficult. He managed to finish and re-tuck before things got out of hand, so to speak, and walked forward to talk to Max.

"Hey Henry, how'd you sleep?"

"Max...never mind, how're we looking?"

"The next exit is ours and the hotel is right around the corner from the exit. It's about ten til; we should make it for 7:00."

"Great, did you give Dutchess a wakeup too?"

"Yeah, I'll hit her again if I don't hear from her in a second."

"Ok."

Henry walked back rearward and thought, 'well, he didn't hear from me, but he knew I was up'...ancient drivers secret, can't beat it.

The wakeup call in Dutchess' space started softer than the one Henry had gotten and it amplified with repetition. As she awoke, the first thing she noticed was a sweet feeling between her legs. Then, she realized it was her fingers, and she wiggled them on their way out of herself. She stretched like a cat. Then realized where she was, butt naked on the bed on the bus!

How long had she been sleep? What time is it? The clock on the bottom of the TV said 6:53am. That must have been Max telling her that they were almost there. She slipped on a robe and walked forward to wash up. Fresh, she walked back by Henry

"Where were you?"

"I went up to talk to Max. We're almost there you know?"

"Yeah, I'll throw something on, be right out."

She chose a simple fitted sweat outfit that hugged her everywhere. She put on a natural motion front clasp sports bra and a matching pair of string bikini panties. She modeled for herself in the full length mirror on the side wall. She dressed, knowing that in a few days, she would be getting the Reebok wardrobe. All she had to do was pick it out and try it on. She liked what she saw in the mirror. She was going to need to find a gym to keep this body. She walked out and forward. Henry was already up front drinking an energy drink.

They were turning off the exit; the hotel was in front of them now. It was indescribable; she could say tall, futuristic. But the overriding thing that came to mind was 'Beautiful'. They pulled in and parked inside the carport to the left. Dutchess was ready to jump out of the bus and stretch. She wasn't stiff or anything, she surely didn't feel like she had just traveled 720 miles. But Henry advised her to wait until Midge came to get her.

Sure enough, within a minute, a medium height black

woman came striding from the front door of the hotel to the door of the coach. Her approach was seen by all on the driver's surveillance cam that was repeated on the flat screen.

"Dutchess?"

"Let her in, Max."

The doors whispered open and Midge Scott came aboard. Dutchess and Henry were sitting on the same side of the coach, allowing Midge to sit and speak to them both. Pleasantries were exchanged, then, Midge escorted them into the hotel. She had tried to explain the inexplicable atrium before they walked in. No matter what they may have expected, their mouths still dropped, and they stared up until their necks ached. Max, of course, kept his eyes on Dutchess.

Midge had seen it all before. As a yearly bonus, she had actually traveled to the Z in Dubai, which made the X feel to her like a nice Ritz Carlton. When their initial wonder was in check, they looked to Midge. She was smiling the polite tour guide smile that came from doing this job for so long. Her smile reached her eyes and beyond, letting them know that it was truly genuine.

"Are you hungry? The restaurant here is open at all times for room service or eating in. Whatever you desire is their pleasure here. The live-in executive suites have a menu of all the amenities and services. The names and pictures of the staff are available, etc. Come on, let's go take a look."

They walked by the restaurant on their way to the elevators when Dutchess stopped.

"Is something wrong, Dutchess?"

"No, no; I think I see someone I know, could you excuse me for just a second?"

"Of course."

Dutchess walked to the waiting area and approached the woman in the fuscia skirt. She was walking as if in a dream. All at once, she realized that she hadn't been dreaming about Franz, she had been dreaming about her, Ms. Collins.

"Ms. Collins, hey you!"

The lady didn't respond. But that had to be her. She had every detail of her memorized. She could see the tennis outfit on her, surrounded by the kids. She looked tired though, and she didn't recall her wearing makeup. She stepped closer, she was less than ten feet away. She knew that it was her, but still, something didn't feel right.

"Ms. Collins?"

The woman looked up at Dutchess with absolutely no recollection at all in her eyes, she didn't know her.

"Can I help you?"

"Uuuuh, well, I guess not, I thought you were someone I knew, you guys look alike. I mean, just."

"I'm sorry, I do hear that there are a couple of ladies out there that look like me. All I can do is thank them for keeping this old look going."

They both chuckled at that,

"Are you staying here? Yes, I am. Had a long night at the

club, I was gonna get something to eat and go up to my room, you?"

"I'm looking into a place here, I'll know in a few."

"Well good luck, maybe we'll run into each other again."

"That'd be nice."

Dutchess went back to join Henry and Midge,

"So how is your friend?" Midge asked.

"That wasn't her."

"Really, you were so close to her, you couldn't tell?"

"Oh, they look remarkably alike, maybe it's just that I haven't seen her in so long, too many faces in between."

"Yeah, that can do it D, believe me, I know."

"I know you do Henry. Ok Midge, if you're ready, I'm ready."

They continued their way to the bank of elevators. The car came and Midge poked a plastic key card into a slot then pushed the 67th floor.

"These floors are only accessible with the security key card. It protects your privacy from unexpected or unwanted guests."

The doors dinged open on floor 67, and Henry and Dutchess stared transfixed. The view was breathtaking, the floor-to-ceiling view of the Atlanta skyline was so clear, that you would have expected a breeze. The short hallway contained two doors, one ahead on the left and one behind on the right; Midge took them to the door on the left. The view through the open door was a panoramic vista. Dutchess went directly to the nearest window to look out; the balcony wound all the way around this side of the building.

The windows and French doors were made with dual paned glass with vertical blinds built in between the panes. They could be operated separately or as one. There were several sitting areas with different floor treatments from deep pile Berber carpet, to Persian rugs, to original hard wood floors, polished to a mirror shine. Casual, functional antiques were tastefully placed all around, with a roll top desk here, and an antique clock there.

"The artwork can be changed at any time, along with the amenities. If you choose this property, you will find an electronic catalog that includes an art inventory that features all of the pieces that you see here. If you see something you would rather have or would like to add, choose it and we will have a professional installer take care of it for you. It is entirely by your preference whether or not you want to keep your current residence. Of course, we have movers that can bring your personal effects at any time you are ready."

Dutchess was as attentive as a school girl; Max and Henry were listening too, in case she missed something. Dutchess wanted to be clear on her responsibilities. She wondered how Pauline was coming with the contract. She knew that once she signed the papers, she would make this all real. She would know this wasn't a dream, she could wake from her dream.

Once the tour was done, she thought, they were led to a door in the middle of the floor next to the kitchen. Beyond the door was a spiral staircase; as she touched the railing, the steps lit up and the group walked down. At the bottom of the staircase, the room lit up with the first step on the floor. It revealed a cedar sauna booth with two bench levels, a ten-person Jacuzzi hot tub, a full complement solo tech resistant gym, and a complete set of free-weights. The gym was impressive and fit perfectly with the wish she had had earlier.

A door on the right wall led to a hallway. The first door on the left opened to a tastefully appointed home movie theater, with twenty luxury reclining seats with its own stocked concession stand, self-service, of course. Everything in this room operated through a Radio Frequency touch screen remote. The screen took up the whole back wall, and there were even sconces and a curtain. The last door on the left of the hallway was the pool, the most beautiful, sparkling, cerulean blue Dutchess had ever seen. The small window strip was the perfect accent from the side the view was a slice of Atlanta from the pool to the blue, blue sky. Dutchess' heart was beating very fast.

"Midge, could I speak with Henry in private for a moment?"

"Absolutely, take your time. I'll be in the gym."

Once she had left, Dutchess turned to Henry.

"Henry, is this too much? I mean, do I need all this?"

"According to you, all you need is a one bedroom apartment and some tennis tools and you can be famous, right?"

This blossomed a huge smile through her fear and anxiety. Those were the words she had spoken when she was luring him from the music industry.

"You don't forget a thing, do you Henry?"

"Not when it comes to you D. Look, here's what I can tell

you: if you like it, it's yours, you can sleep here tonight. If you don't like it, we can look at something else. As a matter of fact, we can look at them all, if you want. The bottom line is, you don't have to worry about anything. If you want to live on the bus, I'm sure something can be arranged."

"I can live on the bus if I want?"

"I'll bet you're not going to find many people that are going to tell you no, Dutchess. These folks have seen this before. The new contractors are not used to this level of money; at least you're not coming right out of high school, ya know? They are going to give you what you want to make you comfortable. If you're not, believe me, Carlos will know and somebody will pay for your unhappiness. This is the big game. These things, choosing, programming and setting your personal preferences, this is the most you'll have to do.

Once you're set, your only worry will be about playing tennis, then, coming home to the place you want to be, wearing what you want to wear, contractually, of course. You getting me?"

"Yeah, I got you. So, how do you like my new place?"

"I'd like to get a look at that catalog."

"Yeah, me too, to personalize my preferences, right?"

They went to the gym and collected Midge. Upstairs in the kitchen, she made her decision. They signed the paperwork, with Dutchess, with Henry as her representative. Afterwards, Dutchess was led through the process of recording her finger print and eye scans, so that the locks and password-protected options in the house and the hotel would know her.

By the time Midge left, Dutchess lived at the X hotel on a private floor at the top of the world. She went out on the balcony and smelled the fresh air; up here it smelled clean as the mountains. She thought about that woman at the restaurant, who looked too much like Ms. Collins. Then, she thought about the BET uncut party. That dress looked a lot like the runaway strippers outfit. She went back in, grabbed her key card, and with Max in tow, stepped to the elevator. Her plan was to catch the woman and find out if she knew Ms. Collins or something about her.

She kept her destination and reasons to herself. Max was ok with it. Strange thoughts were going through Dutchess' mind; could Ms. Collins have a split personality? Was she avoiding her for some reason? Or, was it really someone else? Now her memory was in doubt. This was crazy, but there was only one way to find out.

The elevator doors opened and they stepped into the atrium, going towards the restaurant, doing their best not to look up. The greeter asked if they would like a table for two. They declined, stating that they were looking for a friend. They walked in and looked around through all of the areas, even the restroom. There was no woman that looked like Ms. Collins, not even a black woman in the restaurant. Well, she knew it was a long shot when she had run to the elevator. The woman did say that she was staying here; she would see her in time.

They went out to the coach and retrieved some of Dutchess' items from the coach bedroom, and took them upstairs to her new home. After she had stowed the bags in her master bedroom, she stepped out on to the balcony. The light see-through mesh safety screen helped; she wasn't afraid of heights, but safety meant security. She walked around and saw Henry sitting on a sofa talking on the phone. She waved and turned to look at Atlanta on the horizon. It was 7:27.

Chapter 44

The Blackhawk's blue beacon was showing the location of the building designated A-CDC on her map. She had the bird leader hover the formation. She took her bird down to check in at the 'Orange' coded facility. This facility did have sensitive data and research, but not the vaults with the major virulent strains of diseases and weapons grade microbes. Kristi, Phillip and James made their way to the head of security. Kristi interviewed him while Phillip and James looked through the logs.

The security man said that the day had been basically standard. There was no inside access, other than registered contractors and employees that check in at the same entrance every day. He added that they had expected the military attaché to the National Guard to come through at any time to do an inspection as well. The epidemiological site had called and given him a heads up. They had passed with flying colors for security. As a matter of fact, he had thought that Kristi may have been him, but his counterpart had told him they were traveling by limo. Phillip and James emerged with an all clear for the log books, but saw a storm rising on their boss' face.

"What's the problem SAC?"

"We got a possible problem Phil. Get National Guard HQ, ASAP. Have them double all personnel at CDC facilities now!"

Kristi pulled her map copy out of her TAC vest pocket.

"Which facility did you get the call from?"

He pointed to the facility marked B-CDC.

"James, get me the name of the person he spoke to and a direct number. How far is this from here?"

The security man did a quick calculation. "Southwest, fifteen miles as the crow flies."

Kristi pulled out her cell phone and dialed the number to the B-facility and gave the phone to the supervisor; he then instructed that supervisor to speak freely to Kristi, and handed back the phone. The trio then turned and went back to the Blackhawk. Kristi made a take-off-now gesture with her other hand.

"Tell me about this security check this morning."

"Yes ma'am. A two-star General said that he was over the National Guard deployment. He had stars with flags in the front of the car with diplomatic plates. He said that we had passed inspection with flying colors."

"Ok. And what did this 'General' look like?"

"About six feet tall, dark hair, short beard, really dark eyes. I figured he'd seen a lot of action. Oh, and he had a scar on his cheek right above the beard. He was wearing his dress uniform with all the colors on his boards."

"Lock up your shop, right now! National Guard is on its way to bolster your security and check for explosives. Have your HAZMAT team standby; you may have been set up for an action, sir. I'll be there in three minutes! Phil, do a Broadcast, lockdown on all CDC facilities STAT, and put a fire under the National Guard!"

Kristi was pointing out the facility on the map, sending the bird on its mission. They reintegrated with the hovering formation and shot southwest. Kristi made a decision to split the team; touching her throat mike, with no emotion, she gave orders.

"Birds 3 and 4, this is Team Leader. Proceed to original destination, advise upon arrival, 1 and 2 are breaking to possible action at B-CDC, copy?"

"Copy 3, Team leader, original DES and advise over."

"Copy 4, Team leader original DES and advise, over,"

"Copy out 1 and 2, Bird 3 you have the lead, Team leader, out."

The two Blackhawks peeled off to the left to maintain their original course, while the others continued to speed to B-CDC location, ETA 3 minutes. The time was 7:29am, and they were closing in on B-CDC facility. The soft blue glow of the beacon caused the building in the complex to stand out through the wind-shields Heads-Up Display.

Compared to the rest of the view, at one mile and closing fast, the soft blue turned bright orange. The Blackhawks' windshield automatically darkened to absorb the unexpected spike in luminosity.

"Wooeh! Sheeeiitt! Bird 2, this is 1 ABORT, ABORT! Break left, repeat break left!"

Bird 1 dipped and flew to the right as bird 2 did the same move to the left, putting the blast behind them as they continued around the radius of their turns. They stacked above each other in a hi-lo formation, all eyes were on the front window.

"Bird 1 maintain, I'm coming over."

"Copy 2, Bird 1 maintaining."

The second Blackhawk moved over and elevated to the same observation level as Bird 1. Kristi redialed the security supervisor at the B site; no answer. The voice mail picked up. She knew that there was no message to leave. The phone was dust.

"Bird 2, this is Team leader, how's your tank?"

"Tanks at .5 Team leader."

"Top off and stand by, copy?"

"Copy that, topping off and standing by, 2 over."

The second Blackhawk elevated straight up to rendezvous with the tanker. Kristi checked in with the National Guard, Team leader.

"Ops, what's the status of the CDC presence increase?"

"Just got word that one team, twenty men, rode into the bomb blast; the other five teams are en route, and are already on site."

"Copy that Ops, condolences for your team. Ops, I've got Intel on the POI. Currently, there is an impersonator of a two-star General checking your troops; you got ears?"

"That's a negative team leader, nothing on my squawk about a General, spot checking or otherwise."

"Check all of your positions, Ops; get back ASAP over."

"Copy team leader checking PoPs, over."

Kristi directed the Blackhawk to fly over the facility, now that secondary explosives didn't seem likely. They could see the mangled Humvees tossed around the area that used to be the loading dock. The entire structure was ripped from the asphalt. Small bits of camo cloth was mixed in with the crumbled brick, glittering with a thick layer of ice.

The fire and ice vision was terrible; thick, burning, black clouds were coming from the damage inside the facility. It was juxtaposed against the flash frozen destruction of the loading dock. The formerly towering liquid oxygen containment unit made for a surreal scene.

"Team leader to MCU."

"Go for MCU."

"Contact CDC, inform HAZMAT cleanup that they have a high volume O2 situation at rear of B-CDC site on their map, copy?"

"Copy that team leader, the calls going out as we speak, team leader. I've got Red beaming for fire as well, over."

"Copy that MCU, way to be on it, team leader out."

The action that they were seeing through the windows of the

Blackhawk and the tension from the Task Force guys, caused Suzan to grab and hold on to Thony with rib cracking fierceness. The explosion was so sudden, with the evasive maneuvers, caused her to be tossed all over the space they were relegated to. All throughout, Suzan watched and gained strength from, and respect for this Johnson woman. Not once did she break down. Suzan knew that she would be a crying mess by now. But then again, she wasn't; maybe she was stronger than she thought...

She was looking out the side window at the damage to the hospital-looking building below them, when she saw the other helicopter come back into view. The pilot of the one they were in, shot straight up, so fast it made her whole body dizzy.

Thony had been her rock during this ordeal. She didn't know if it was the silent treatment or simply his being there, but it made her feel safe in the middle of this madness. He was bigger than quite a few of these guys. Although he didn't have all the guns and crap, she still felt protected. The bomb blast shocked Thony out of his daydreaming, paranoid, pity party.

He'd never had any problems with his mind; he knew that he wasn't crazy, so he also knew this wasn't his doing. But knowing the rational while experiencing the irrational was a horse of two different colors. Whoever this look-a-like person was, had done this. If he wasn't sure before, the accusatory look from that woman in charge as soon as she looked away from the explosion, was enough to tell him that she still thought this type of thing was something of which he was capable, totally off base. But how was he to clear himself?

***

Ron was almost to Sylvania's exit when the sky flashed in front of him and a large black smoke cloud presented itself in the rear and side view mirrors. The extra brightness on such a brightening day was totally unexpected. He called Sylvania.

"Hello?"

"Babe?"

"Hey lover..."

"Turn on the TV."

"Huh?"

"Turn on the TV babe. Click around until you see some late breaking stories. Go on, I'll wait."

She had been laying naked on her bed, air drying, waiting for Ron to get back so that she could present the plump grapes he had requested. So the urgent tone in his voice sliced through her mood and caused her to react. She clicked through all the channels twice with no news briefs or updates.

"Nope, nothing Ron. Why, what's up?"

"I'm almost to you babe and something behind me over my shoulder just blew up; it's on fire now and I don't see."

The two Blackhawks flying frighteningly low came zooming overhead,

"Shit…"

"What Ron?"

"Oh shit, two black military looking helicopters just flew low over me, cutting across the freeway."

"Are they coming towards me?"

"No baby, they went the other direction from you."

"Good, come home before anything else happens, ok?"

She was pleading; it hurt his heart.

"Here I come babe."

It was the truth. It was 7:40, and he wasn't far from the exit, not far at all.

***

Birds 3 and 4 were en route to the Sheraton when they got the word of the bomb at B-CDC.

"Bird 3 for team Leader come in."

"Go for Team leader."

"Please advise in light of CDC action."

"Stand by Bird 3."

Kristi had to decide how to best use her assets.

"Team leader to MCU."

"Go for MCU."

"Dragon, what type resources are on the ground in Atlanta?"

"Fed Task Force advisors integrated into National Guard check points. We have two HRT teams on alert at the federal building, downtown Atlanta."

"Copy that Dragon, pull HRT 1 and put together a TAC Team with all flavors. Drop them in center city at Underground Atlanta. Bring ten K9 units, infiltrate MARTA SWAT, spread throughout the line…"

Coms rang twice, Phillip and James caught the calls.

"SAC, National Guard Ops, stat!"

She nodded to Phillip. James pointed to his phone and showed two fingers and tapped his forehead.

"Damn."

Kristi knew that signal: #2 head, the DDI FBI was on the line; he would have to wait. The National Guard operations center came first.

"Team leader, we do have a report of a two-star General officer with features matching your POI profile.

The Guard Sergeant says they were inspected at an underground gate point behind the arena. A two-star General officer took a walking tour beneath the train station, tunnels, and platforms on two levels."

"Good God, what have you got at the train Central?"

"Hold on. Ok, I've got four curfew teams rolling in; ETA two to five minutes, respectively."

"Copy that, contact MARTA SWAT, inform them full cooperation comes from the top, copy? Presidential, if they need paperwork. I can send it to your field fax."

"That shouldn't be necessary team leader, but I'll keep that close if I need it."

"Copy that, I got balls in the air, update status six minutes, over."

"Copy six minutes, out."

She went back to Dragon at MCU,

"Team leader to MCU."

"Go for MCU."

"Drag, patch up the Freeway See way."

"Copy team leader Free See coming up."

"Good, stand by."

"Team leader for Bird 3."

"Go for Bird 3."

"Pull up vids; stand by."

"Copy, vids up, standing by."

"MCU, patch to Birds 3 and 4."

"Copy that, patching to Birds 3 and 4."

"Bird 3, are you receiving?"

"Copy team leader, 4 screen Freeway See way real time incoming."

"Copy, Scan. Find limousine front, two-star General, staff flags, rear dip tag. Copy?"

"Copy that, advise on find?"

"On find contact Team leader, will advise, over."

"Copy that team leader, out."

The Freeway See way is a network of lights and cameras that create a seamless real time map of the freeway system in America. The cameras are located inside solar powered caps placed atop light poles that are situated in the median between directions on the Interstate highways. The poles are impossible to miss, as they are four to five times as tall as the standard street light pole. They are green in color and have a circle of ten construction quality klieg lights.

The cameras create real time rolling surveillance for every inch of the freeway territory. Of course, they are unmarked property of the U.S. military. The municipal surveillance camera networks that had caught on swiftly in the mid 1990's, all funneled into the state transportation department systems. These were under control of the National Guard in each state.

The views available to Birds 1 through 4 were TV quality video surveillance with picture-in-picture functionality. They were available for searching each of the four respective screens. With Birds 3 and 4 occupied, HRT-1 and the pick-up squad were on their way to MARTA Central. It was time to talk to the boss. Kristi took the phone from James.

"SAC Johnson."

"Kristi, this is Peter,"

That wasn't good, anytime your boss goes to first name basis all of a sudden, you had to be careful.

"Yes, Sir."

"What's the status? I've just come from the Hill, and, as you can expect, things are moving on a razors edge. This level RED is unprecedented, and the boss is keeping Frantic Panic at bay. The writers haven't got a clue as what to write to the public."

"Ok sir, for your ears only. James, is this comm secure?"

"Affirmative SAC, both ends."

"OK, pardon me Sir. Sir, the unprecedented nature of this operation is an understatement.

The level RED effectively suspended the first amendment and a good deal of the others, as you know. Because of the FCC action, the TV has stopped updating news. Three casinos in St. Louis, were attacked with timed Anthrax devices. All but one were disabled. The one resulted in the deaths of 90% of the Riverboats population. The POI that we identified in St. Louis, turned out to have an airtight alibi."

She looked at Suzan, still enclosed in Thony's arm. She actually saw him deflate slightly, as if he had been holding his breath all this time.

"The POI/perp left cryptic clues at the scenes. Crypto, human and tech, worked enough to get us to the scene to save thousands of people. We are now in Atlanta. There has been an attack on a CDC facility. We believe that one person is at the heart of all this. We have a lead on him and are acting on it as, we speak."

The pause was gigantic. Kristi heard a dramatic sigh; again, not a good sign,

"Kristi, I received a call not one minute ago from SAC Atlanta. He tells me you took most of his department. He thinks that you are running out of fuel, and that you should be reeled in. I'm telling you this because I promised I would handle you, no smoke up the ass, no soft indirection.

You know the faith I have in you. At this point, there are major parts of both of us on the line. Me, personally, I need all of those parts and I'd imagine you'd like to keep yours, as well. What I need from you, Kristi, is an answer; the most truthful, selfless, answer that you have ever given in your life."

"Ok, what's the question?"

"Are you up to this? Can you finish this thing that you have started?"

She took her time to evaluate everything in black and white. She considered the assets that she had in play: the men and women out there right now, willing to give their lives for a team leader most have not met, and will never meet in person. Dragon, Dog, Chad and the Task Force, were parts at their disposal on her command. Nothing short of success would be able to vindicate the expenditure. A negative response was out of the question.

"Yes sir, I have faith in my Task Force. My team is running like a lean, mean, machine. We will bring this perp to ground, one way or the other. I'll take full responsibility, sir." "You know I can't let you do that Kristi. The chain of command is still intact. Shit still runs downhill, but it must start at the top. So be it, SAC Johnson. God speed and good luck. I'll stall the boss as long as I can. By my next call, it will already be too late."

The time was 7:55.

Chapter 45

Dulcet finally rolled into the metro-Atlanta area. The entrance to the HOV lane was easier to fit into; she slid in between two overloaded mini vans traveling 75mph. Finally, she was putting some wind beneath her wings. The early morning traffic rush into the city was surprisingly light. Considering some of the backups that she had come through lately, the eight lanes of traffic probably had something to do with that.

She was in need of a place to stay, and a computer, as soon as she could get it. Just as these thoughts were fleeing through her mind, the freeway, the median, everything in the world started to glow like high noon on the face of the sun. Experienced instinct alone allowed her to keep control of the wheel. The minivan behind her didn't have such luck. The sudden brightness must have blinded the driver; He swerved right, then left, overcorrected, and spun out rolling, left into the median grass.

From what she could see, it rolled about three times before it came to rest. At least one person had been thrown out when the front windshield shattered and blew out, the body came right after. Dulcet kept her eyes on the van in front of her. It swerved dangerously, but kept control. She realized that the extra brightness came from the sky high lights in the middle of the freeway, the ones with the little hats. She had never seen those lights operational, since she could remember them being there. But now, they were all lit up like individual suns. The lights were having a blinding, reflecting effect. Dulcet was now in a rush to get off the freeway.

The next exit from the HOV lane was coming up. She had to slow down so that she could merge right into the main flow of slower traffic. There, now to get across the crap-shoot of lanes without being targeted by a blinded driver. She made it off the exit in one piece. The lodging sign pointed right. She cruised through the checkpoint and made the turn. The hotel was close, only yards from the exit. The sign read North Towne Sheraton. She drove to the car port; the valet opened her door, stealing a peek beneath her skirt and smiling, as he accepted his tip.

She grabbed her roller bag and walked inside to get a room. The registration agent, Michael Robinson, ex-concierge, still hated his job; more so now, because his salary had been cut in half. Now, he was looking for a way to get the old man back that had caused him to be demoted. Michael was doodling on a mouse pad. He was all alone at the front desk when, the redhead with the dick-stiffening body came strutting to his station. He hadn't realized that his mouth was open until she mimed picking up his chin and closing it.

"How can I help you ma'am?"

"I'd like a room for three days, possibly more, but three for sure. What do you have available?"

"I have a single with a double bed, but I'd rather have you in a suite with a King."

"Oh, excuse me. Did you say you'd rather have me?"

"Oh God, I'm sorry. I meant to say I'd rather put you in a suite. Geeze I'm such an asshole."

"Don't be so hard on yourself, Michael."

She stepped back and looked down.

"I don't blame you."

She looked up and smiled a seductive smile that reached all the way up to her sparkling emerald eyes, promising un-fillable dreams. He put her into a suite for the regular room rate on the 15th floor. She walked away, putting more pop than normal into her already sexy, ass-wiggling walk. Michael was distracted; he watched her until the elevator came and went, and was still watching after it was long gone. She made him feel like a horny, love sick, puppy dog.

Unseen by Michael, the registration desk micro camera had recorded every nuance and word of the exchange. This was one more nail in his professional coffin.

Dulcet made her way to door, number 1521, a corner suite with a nice view of the surrounding area. There was the mall, and a small park. In the distance, she could see a black plume of smoke; something's on fire, she thought.

"Hmmm."

Turning her back on the window, she powered up the computer. The hotel logo splash screen popped up, the icons blinked across the bottom of the screen; she clicked the internet icon and typed in yahoo.com. The home page came up quickly. Satisfied that she was connected, she unzipped her hoodie and slid off her skirt. She walked to the bathroom in nothing but her socks and drew herself a bath.

The steaming vapors coerced her into the tub. At first, she stood there allowing the tendrils of steam heat to crawl up her body; little by little she started to heat up. Imperceptibly at first, her skin began to pebble with light sweat; she felt the small drops start to connect, creating bigger drops that ran slowly down her salty body. The generous drops that ran across the sides of her breasts and down her stomach, mingled with the water vapor along the way to tickle trickle through her fiery pubic hair crossing her clit, to moisten her hot lips.

The sweat collecting on the tops of her breasts rolled down slope, collecting on her nipples, until a big dollop hung there fighting gravity. She watched her nipples grow hard from the tiny bit of stimulation. The act of the drop falling off felt like a kiss. Now that her entire body was warm, she squatted down, separated her legs and lips and submerged herself in the water. The hot liquid heat felt incredible as it engulfed her, and she slid neck-deep into the super-hot water. Her breasts floated; her nipples were like hard periscopes, quivering from the hot water-cold air dichotomy.

She soaked lazily, occasionally stroking her hands up and down her body, taking her time at every spot that she happened upon. The hot water was boiling; her fingers were so hot that when they penetrated her lips, they felt like molten iron. Sliding her fingers in and out, caused the most delightful orgasms to wrack her melted body.

Once all the tension from the drive had left her, she went all out for herself. She maneuvered herself onto her knees, and used two fingers to thoroughly fuck herself while using her palm on her clit. The other hand was tweaking and pinching her nipples from one to the other. As her orgasm was hitting her, the body quakes came hard. She flipped the tub/shower lever up to shower, and spun the water temperature to cold.

The icy water felt artic. Her nipples got instantly brittle, as though they would break off. The orgasms' intensity tripled under the hard rain of the cold shower while sitting in the still steamy water. She turned the water off and opened the drain. As the water gurgled down, Dulcet stood on rubbery legs, still after-quaking. Every move causing additional mini-orgasms to flow through her. She held onto the door, frame, and the wall, until she got to the bed. She flopped down on her face and dug the pillow out from the blanket. She pushed the pillow down her body between her legs, she rhythmically humped it until she fell asleep.

***

The Freeway See way was phenomenal. Robert had been watching the progress of those giant helmeted light poles for as long as anybody else that drove on the freeways in the U.S. But to actually see them in action, functioning as they were designed, was indescribable. Because of his location in the seating arrangement, he was tasked to assist the Bird 3 tech leader in working the search.

Four pair of eyes were assigned to each screen to scan vehicles. The tech rattled on the keyboard putting in search criteria. The views automatically showed all of the major

Interstate highways in the Atlanta area, 75, 85, 20 and 285. The search criteria put a digital search on the real time video feeds. The feeds looked for what the tech typed in: 'two star staff flags, diplomatic tag, and black limousine'.

Robert watched in awe as the images in the bottom corner of each screen started a stuttering fast forward. It slowed on possible hits and zoomed through misses, while the large picture hopped camera pole to camera pole in smooth video transition.

Some of the other guys murmured sounds of surprise, but none sounded like Robert felt. The pictures were so crisp and clear. Robert couldn't understand how the shadows were mostly gone, and everything had its own luminescence, until he looked away from the screen. One glance out of the window showed huge lighted corridors; the freeways were soaked by high intensity light from the green towers. They were so bright and dense that it looked like a physical thing. How could these people stay in their lanes with all that light?

Shifting his gaze back to the monitor, he heard a warbling sound; the tech stepped to the screen that Robert was tasked to watch, I-75 Southbound. There was a match. The screen showed the flags flapping, slowing the view down, until the human eye could see as fast as the computer brain did. Freezing it showed the flags. It was child's play to see and freeze the ID tag; both of these images were encoded and blasted to the team leader, any second now.

"Team leader to Bird 3."

"Go for Bird 3 team leader."

"What's this I just got?"

"Free See has this vehicle currently heading southbound into the city on I-75, please advise."

"Engage and capture, interrogate with prejudice, crypto keeps handing me sheets. Profile says that he probably has something going with the number six. I was told to expect it but numbers aren't adding up yet. Birds 1 and 2 are en route to MARTA's main hub; do me proud, over."

"Copy that team leader; will engage and capture, out."

"Bird three to Bird four."

"Go for 4."

"You got the synch on the perp?"

"Copy that 3; what's the plan."

"We go in on a flank. Stay above my blades and use the following path swoops before the bridges block our way. Bird 3 is taking the lead."

"Copy that Bird 3 is taking the point."

The two Blackhawks nosed down and flew at high speed to intercept the limousine. They made it to the stretch of freeway where the car had been spotted. The Freeway See way interpretation program ghosted a target image of the vehicle onto the actual vehicle, as seen in the heads up display on the windshield. The Birds were high enough not to be seen by the occupant of the vehicle; they split and took flanks on both sides of the car.

"Bird leader to Birds 3 and 4, we have been tasked with engage and capture, activity number 17 in the rules of engagement handbook. My suggestion is to disable the vehicle around the perpetrator, circle, track, and listen. Then, capture once the body scan indicates no weapons, mechanical, nor biological; any better plan?"

TAC Ops was an entirely different animal from any other branch of service. A subordinate could comment without having to fear chain of command reprisal. If there was a better strategy, it would be used. No one spoke up.

"So be it; we roll in 60 seconds, remember, we want this guy alive."

The copies came in groups, they were ready. It was 8:00am.

Chapter 46

Sylvania hung up the phone and stared at the TV. She wondered why nothing was being said about the explosion that Ron had mentioned. Usually, the news had a late breaking story alert for anything from missing children's Amber alerts to cats stuck in trees. But not today. There was nothing but that infuriating red box around the TV screen, making it look too hot to touch. She sat up on the bed and stretched. Tension was beginning to build inside of her about this situation. The lack of information from the media, and Ron being gone mysteriously, was all starting to take its toll. She picked up the phone book and looked up the number to one of the local TV stations. She called the news desk.

"Channel 16 agent Fleures speaking, how can I help you?"

Instinctively she hung up the phone. Sylvania sat and looked at the number she had dialed and felt a cold shiver run down her naked back. She blocked her number from coming up on a call back device and dialed another number

"WJKL twenty four this is Agent Woods, how can I..."

She hung up again. If asked, she could not explain why she kept hanging up on these agents. But somewhere in her mind, she knew the news desk phone number was supposed to be answered 'news desk', or at least something close. So, hearing both of those people answering the phones, sounding like she had called the local FBI office made her suspicious to say the least.

She tried one last number, CNN downtown Atlanta. If it was answered by an agent as well, she would be absolutely sure something was terribly wrong. First she turned the TV to CNN. The anchors were not the usual ones; the weekend anchors were on. They showed a companionable rapport, but on closer inspection, Sylvania could see squint lines around their eyes and between their brows. They were nervous and it didn't look like the on-air jitters, or anything that had to do with journalism; they looked scared. While paying close attention to the background, Sylvania made the call. As before the phone was answered

"CNN, agent Brocket."

This time she didn't hang up

"Uuuh, yes, I'd like to speak to the news desk please."

"This is the news desk, how can I help you?"

"Well I was hoping to speak to a producer, I may have a story."

The rear right corner of the screen looked as if it had gotten busier since her call, but she couldn't be sure.

"What kind of story is it lady? I can help to forward it to the producers, the on air guys are really busy. We have a threat level RED, you know, busy, busy, busy."

Sylvania was taken by the casualness of this 'Agent'. She decided to give him something.

"There was what sounded like an explosion about five minutes ago, I think there's a fire; I smell smoke."

"Well, hell, why'd you call here, why not call 911?"

He seemed to be kind of distant from the conversation. When Sylvania looked back at the TV, the activity in that rear right corner had increased dramatically. There were men in suits and blue windbreakers swarming around a bank of monitors. one man was sitting on top of a desk on a phone wearing a suit and tie; he looked very agent-ish. There was a young geeky looking guy with others crowded around him. She had been watching that corner so intensely, that nothing else on the screen was in focus. Then she heard the man trying to get her attention, she didn't answer, she just listened.

"I think we lost her, but I heard headline news in the background, can you get a lock?"

Sylvania was frantically scouring the bed for the remote. She hit the mute button as soon as she felt it; still listening in, she heard,

"Fuck it then, phone's dead; Try tracking the TV, if she ...".

He hung up the phone; but the most amazing thing was, the man on TV hung up the phone at the same time! Sylvania was befuddled. She was tempted to call back to see if the man on TV would answer, but she knew that was foolish. The people around the geeky guy paid more attention to what he was doing, and Sylvania's vision came away from the rear corner up to the middle distance. Here, there were the rows of televisions that always showed different video streams of things from different affiliates.

She supposed the one that caught her immediate attention was square in the middle; it was showing residential scenes. Each one flashing by looked like a home interior show, except none of these homes looked like models. They lacked the cleaned-up, polished look of reality show houses. They looked like regular people's homes; there flashed a kitchen, oh my God, a woman wiping herself on the toilet, a living room, another kitchen.

Hey, those look like her neighbors' kids down the street. That was when she saw the most frightening thing she had ever seen in her life. Her front door opening and Ron walking into the foyer. She screamed.

Still screaming like an insane woman, she dived naked to the floor scrabbling for cords pulling any and everything she could. When all were free, the power cords, RCA plugs, and clip-in HDMI. Next, she crawled over to expose the junction plate with the cable input and unscrewed it. She could hear Ron's heavy feet running up the stairs. That thought should have been comforting, but it was the worst; it made everything true. By the time he made it to her room, Sylvania was sitting on the floor crying her eyes out.

The small chest-of-drawers was turned on its side, all manner of wires were strewn about, and the flat screen had a blanket tossed over it. Ron surveyed the scene and went to his baby directly. He stooped and picked her up in his arms and carried her over to the now stripped down bed.

"Baby, what happened? Look at you, you're shivering." He took off his shirt and wrapped it around her shoulders. Her crying abated but her breath still came jerkily,

"Th, th, the...the TV, Ron..."

"What about it babe? The TV has you all in an uproar?"

"Damn it Ron, just hold me, the world is crashing down. I'm so scared ."

Ron did as she asked; he held her. She climbed around until she was sitting on his lap, His subtle stirring beneath her bringing her comfort. She wrapped her arms around him tighter. She gripped his head and kissed him deeply; their kiss lasted until her breath began to run out. Their heart beats synched up. Ron felt her body soften against him as the marble hard tension ran from her muscles.

"Ron, I'm not crazy ok?"

"Babe, who the hell called you crazy? Not me."

"I did. I thought I was until I saw you walk in the front door on TV."

"You watched what?"

"Just now, when you came in, I saw you."

"You saw me where baby? Now you got me thinking I'm crazy."

She smiled a little crooked smile,

"See it's contagious."

"Ok, deep breath."

She inhaled, her breasts causing the hastily wrapped shirt to pop open so they were naked chest to chest, her eyes were clearer now.

"Ok, I called the TV station to find out about the fire so that I could have some more information for you when you got here. Then, the screens started showing scenes from people's houses. I thought it was commercials at first, until I saw the woman wiping herself on the toilet. That's not supposed to be on TV. Then, I saw the neighbors' kids eating in their kitchen. But the final straw was when I saw my front door open and you walked in."

"So that means that these cable satellite systems are transmitting and receiving. The TV's are spying on us?"

"Have you ever thought about how difficult it is to buy a TV that's not digital nowadays? Even if it's not flat screen like most are, they're all digital."

"Right, and digital TV's plug into other digital media, shit. How many TV's do you have Sylvania?"

"Three, the one in the library and the one in the living room."

"Ok, sit tight I'll be right back."

"Noooo, don't you leave me again, Ron!"

Her tears were coming back. Ron tried to stand up and she tightened up every muscle, wrapping herself tightly, digging her heels into his butt and subconsciously grinding on his stiff member. Ron knew that grinding was giving her comfort. She had been through a lot since he had been gone; he was surprised that she hadn't broken down earlier. He reached around on the nightstand, grabbed a condom, and walked out to the hallway.

He walked down four of the carpeted stairs and turned

around. Sylvania had laid her head against his shoulder; now, she turned and looked into his eyes with a question.

He gently laid her back against the carpeted steps and groped for his zipper. He ripped open the condom pack and painfully released himself from his pants. He rolled the rubber on and fitted his head inside her hot lips. Ron leaned in and kissed her as he slid deep inside; she gasped into his mouth then moaned. He began to deep stroke her, with one hand on the banister, the one wrapped around the small of her back. He gently, but, firmly rocked her body, her loving murmurs were music to his ears. She whispered,

"Thank you Ron, I love you Ron". Over and over, her orgasm was building from the compressed position. Ron felt the clench inside of her as she started to come. He pushed himself deep, very deep into her; her orgasm triggering his. He pumped the condom full, and she felt the heat and his muscles flexing against her clit, prolonging the wonderful feelings only this lover could bring.

Ron lifted her, held her at arm's length in front of him and walked her back up the four steps to the landing. He laid her back and quickly stroked her to another orgasm and slowly pulled out. He crept back down the steps, one at a time while kissing her calves, thighs, and lastly, placing a kiss on her still quivering clit. He said,

"I'll be right back."

Satisfied, fear in check, she lay there, with her legs open just as Ron had left her, waiting for his return. Ron backed into the living room to the TV presenting his ass instead of his sheathed still-hard dick. He went around the side and unplugged the unit, disconnected the HDMI connection from the TV, and the cable cords. He disconnected everything, until not one electronic component was connected to power, nor to any other component.

He repeated the process in the library, flipping them both face down on the floor, and covering them with a sheet as the coup de gras. Climbing back up the stairs, he was face level with paradise. Without her seeing him, he approached with stealth, the first contact was his tongue licking from bottom to top. He continued up the stairs until he was poised at her entrance. The still full rubber probed itself between her lips, her muscles gripping him to pull him inside.

He leaned over her slipping in half way and her legs wrapped around him pulling him in the rest of the way. He picked her up and walked her back to the room. He sat on the side of the bed, embedded but not moving he asked her,

"You said that they answered with the title 'Agent', right?"

"Um hum, but when I saw the one that I was talking to hang up live on TV at the same time he hung up with me, that made me start thinking that there was something wrong."

"Well, when that explosion occurred and nobody reported it, that made me know something was wrong. I didn't hear one siren, only those military helicopters flying overhead in a formation. I got a really bad feeling about this babe, maybe we need to get out of here."

"I'll do whatever you say Ron, make me come one more time, please."

He let her lead the way. She put him on his back and unbuckled his belt and pants, then, pulled his pants open. She rolled again until he was on top. She pushed his clothes down his hips and grinded him deep inside. Naked now, she rolled him back over and rode him vigorously, sparking her orgasms while pinching his nipples.

Her muscles squeezed the condom until all the previous semen pooled around Ron's balls right in time for him to come again. She clenched her hovering pussy while holding his tip as he pulsed his come into the condom. She slowly slid her clenched muscular nether mouth down until she caught the last pulsing contraction, while she scrubbed her clit against his root.

Climbing off Ron, as promised, she was ready to go. She slid the full-again condom off Ron, playing her fingers on his sticky sensitive dick. She went for a warm cloth to wash him off and kissed the head. She went into her remaining drawers to find something to wear on the run.

Chapter 47

As she was aimlessly turning the balcony corner to come back inside from the sitting room door, Dutchess saw a flash out of the corner of her eye. She turned and looked in the distance, between her and the downtown buildings. Smoke was bellowing up from somewhere below the tree line. She also noticed the sleek, black, helicopters hovering and doing some kind of maneuver. There were two of them right by the smoke; did they drop a bomb or something?

"Henry."

She knocked on the window,

"Henry, get Max and come here!"

The two of them came quickly,

"What's wrong Dutchess???"

"Look, Max. Those two helicopters were over there somewhere before that big cloud of smoke got there. I saw a flash, then the smoke, then I saw them hovering there!"

"They look like special operations choppers; they are called Blackhawks, and they are mainly military use vehicles."

Max scanned the sky over his left shoulder and saw two more zooming towards that horizon. He walked a few yards away and pulled out a tiny cell phone with a thick antenna. He pushed a speed dial number and spoke very softly, while walking to the corner of the balcony, keeping an eye on both sets of helicopters. Max came back a few minutes later, he had a serious look on his face.

"That was a bomb at a CDC facility that you saw Dutchess. The Blackhawks out there are actually on our side. Apparently, the bombing in St. Louis, wasn't the only terrorist activity in the U.S. over the last few days. But there has been a blackout of the news. All the news copters and reporters have been grounded or put on house arrest. This has never happened before."

Dutchess and Henry listened to Max; both were at a loss for words.

"So Max, you're telling me the terrorists are here in Atlanta too?"

"It appears that way Dutchess."

"Who did you call Max? How did you know that stuff about the media?"

"Let's just say that part of my protection gig is information to keep from being certain places; it makes my job easier."

The perfect politician. Max was obviously a master of the 'No answer' answer.

"So what do we do?"

"We stay put Dutchess. If any information comes in regarding anything that has to do directly with you, we worry about it. Otherwise, we sit tight."

Henry felt the need to add something.

"If you want to look and see what happens from here, that's one thing; but if it gets any closer, I want you inside, you hear?"

"Yes Henry, I hear. It's just, damn, this is Atlanta, not Beirut!"

"But don't forget Dutchess, the whole country is at Threat Level RED. This could be an entirely different crew from the St. Louis, group. They usually include some suicide ritual in their attacks. To be on the safe side, I'm going to cloak the coach."

"Huh, what is that?"

"The artwork on the side of your coach isn't stick on graphics. The art work is very special. It's a technology called OLED, Organic Light Emitting Diodes. It's a film thin composite of sheets of organic molecules that emit light when you apply electricity. Imagine, it's like a micro fiber thin movie screen; instead of using the stick-on wraps, we had one of our research guys team up with one of the graphic guys and design the technology from what we had on the books, patent wise and viola.

The graphics can be changed according to several schemes that are loaded into the computer on the coach, or, I can download specials. The image goes to the screen and stays there until its updated and changed. To cloak it sort of makes the coach invisible. It's not truly invisible. The wheels and windshield, the uncovered things, would make it standout; but I can make it a regular black or white bus with nothing on it to identify you. The company frowns on these tricks because it cuts down on the real-time in the advertising depreciation column. But right now, I don't think I'll tell them."

Max pulled out his key fob, it had 12 more buttons than Dutchess'. He hit two buttons and it beeped a mini bus horn sound and a small digital 'B' showed up on his screen.

Now we wait. Why don't you go on and work out, maybe take in a swim? Let us worry about the worrying, you try to work on your adjustments, ok?"

"Ok guys I'll try, but it's not going to be easy; I don't want to get all crazy about something I can't change."

Dutchess went down to the gym and sat on the Universal machine. She grabbed the control bars and a voice came on. The inspirational guy was obnoxious at first. Then, he got kinda soothing as he started making the work-out time pass. She had a bad feeling about this day; she started to pray for her city, Atlanta, the people, and the city itself, that they all make it safely through.

***

For some strange reason, the car was rolling smoother than ever. Abdullah was almost lulled into a sense of serene comfort. He still had half a pound of C4 and the two vials of Anthrax. He knew the exact time when the first CDC bomb went off. All resources should be racing to that target, leaving the main target unguarded like a nest with Momma bird gone. Hopefully, there were some good things destroyed at the first CDC locale. But, the next one on the list should be the best. The day was looking wonderful, sunny and warm, a small cloud blotted out the sunlight on the left side of the limo, then it was gone. Abdullah settled in, it should be about another ten minutes.

***

"Bird 1 to Bird 2."

"Go for 2."

"Split on target area, 1 goes up, 2 down copy?"

"Copy that, 1, up 2, down."

"NG and internal waiting to comply copy, breaking in 5 ticks over."

"Copy 2, 5 ticks, out."

Kristi and her crew all donned breathing apparatus, full head cover over their blacked-out TAC gear.

***

As official guests, Thony and Suzan were issued bright orange secure zip jumpsuits to step into. Suzan rolled the hem of her dress up around her waist attempting modesty, even though these same people had accosted her butt naked in her hotel room.

The one-piece uniform fit like a deflated bubble suit. The black breathing device was fitted over their heads by a Task Force member; they were instructed in its operation: pull the tab at the left edge of the hood, and the filtered air would begin to flow. There would be a slight constriction when the seal tightened; it was normal, nothing to panic about.

The orange color of the jumpsuits marks you as non-combatants; stay that way, they won't stop any bullets. Fully briefed, they prepared to land. They watched Kristi morph: from interrogator to air traffic controller, to counselor; a bureaucrat, now, a tactical leader. They had no choice, they were about to go into battle behind her so they had to listen closely.

"Ok, here's the scenario. Since I can't leave you here, you will come with me. When you see my wedge go in, stay behind me and down. We go in through the upper level, bird 2 will go in through the bottom level. We don't know what to expect, so we will retrace his steps and meet in the middle. We don't know what he may have left, but we know it'll be a nasty surprise. You are here, I wish you weren't, but there's nothing to be done about it now."

":Twenty seconds to landing."

This was all being echoed through her throat mike for the benefit of both teams. When the bottom up team saw the bright orange and black, they would know that they had encountered the top down team. Directions given, a silent moment of prayer accomplished, Kristi gave the circle down gesture. They landed in the plaza behind the MARTA five points metro rail facility.

"Bird 3 to Bird 4."

"Go for 4."

"LLTA?"

"Copy 3, Locked and Loaded Target Acquired, waiting for countdown."

"Copy 4 stand by... going from ...5...4...3..."

***

Abdullah reached for a cigar, an illegal Cuban midsized. He lit the tip and pulled hard, and puffed out a cloud. He admired his glowing ash.

Four MP 5, submachine guns, set on full automatic, were aimed out the open door of the Blackhawk. Two guns were dedicated to the front quadrant and two to the back, with four shooters for each side. The limo was traveling at approximately 85mph. The first fusillade would go into locking up the engine directly followed by the rear teams, the spacing was calculated with a probability of survivability. Both Blackhawks were flanking the limo, and the pilots already primed to de-elevate on three to firing level at one. The rapid de-elevation caused Robert's stomach to lurch, but he didn't allow it to affect him. The face was in that car and he was going to get him, only the end of his life would stop him.

"Two, 1 engage."

Chapter 48

Max and Henry were still standing on the balcony looking at the still visible Blackhawks. They kicked around theories about what they could be doing in the city. Max revealed some small bits about his past; some Special Forces work in Grenada and Nicaragua, and a whole lot of off the radar stuff. But he had to admit, this was the first time he had seen a display like this in the U.S. He pointed out the silver reflection circling high above, as the KC3 tanker, for refueling. Then, their casual conversation stopped. Henry suspected, but Max knew, that some poor target was just turned to mush.

Forty floors below in room 2703, Sylvia was resting. The meal was heavy, rich, and fantastic; this was exactly what she needed to clear out her system from the blast from the past, which was one of $ensation's Pusse Posse parties. Damn, she was having flashbacks of the things that she had done in the club, showing out with $ensation, and then the party! Did she really suck and fuck that guy in the bathroom?

She slid her legs to the edge of the bed, her thigh-high

stockings whispering across the comforter. Her missing G-string was all the proof that she needed to know that something fly had happened below the waist last night. They'd turn up eventually. Her bucket was tossed on the night stand looking fully stuffed. She smiled as if nothing else happened however; she did accomplish her mission. She knew $ensation wouldn't want any jewels, so she would send her a chunk of the money.

She had to admit that being a total slut last night felt so good. Fantasia does, and will always, have a place in her life, That part of her needed to exercise from time to time.

She went into the huge bathroom after jumping down from the overstuffed mattress. Everything in the X was extra, for a total sum of X-tra plush. The bathtub was sunken two steps down. Sylvia brought the bucket into the bathroom and turned on the hot water. She stood in the middle of the sky blue tub; she waited until the water was at calf level.

She reached for the bucket, and dumped the contents into the water all around her feet. She found her G-string, wrung the panties out, and then hung them on the spigot. She squatted down, and she pushed the jewels out of the way, so that she could sit. One large piece got away and tried to force its rounded tip into her asshole. She caught herself before her weight could push it past her sphincter and chuckled. She sat in the steamy water looking at a true pirate's booty of loot.

There had to be at least fourteen different logos, nameplates, symbols, and initials. The diamond encrusted Turkish, link, necklaces were worth more than the gaudy plates hanging from them. But there were exceptions. There was a Homer Simpson with Marge made of yellow and blue diamonds. This took a lot of skill and craftsmanship; the only problem with these pieces was their originality.

The links and 48 and 59 inch diamond necklaces would not be too hard to get rid of. A couple of them could be cut in half, or thirds, even, and make two or three nice necklaces with bracelet's to match. But the signature pieces lost most, if not all, of their value by being so recognizable. These would have to be stripped and melted; the gems had to be weighed and categorized, before a sale could be considered.

One thing about 'Bling' versus jewelry is that 'Bling' only has to shine and reflect light. Often times, a hand full of junk diamonds surrounding a few major pieces would be enough for those rapper types. Most have never had any type of jewel related instruction, so they wouldn't know one compressed piece of carbon from another. But there were others, mainly the ones who bought their own jewels that knew the history.

They knew the terms, cut, clarity, carats, and density, which were all the things that you needed to know and knew to look for when purchasing Jewelry or actual investment property. Sylvia was bathing with a couple million dollars' worth of 'Bling', but there were some jewels mixed in. She knew how to separate the wheat from the chaff.

There was an interesting minority amongst the macho collection of trinkets. Along with the single earring, there was a string of black and white interspersed pearls. It was beautiful and inspired Sylvia's tub time. She twisted a loop in the long strand of perfect pearls, put her foot through the small loop, and put her other foot through the large loop. She shimmied the pearls up to her hips where the small loop rolled and adjusted itself, bisecting her body.

Once in place, she plucked the other baubles out of the water and set them along the edge of the tub to dry. Now, Sylvia gripped the pearls that circled her hip and started to spin them backwards. At first, they were non-responsive and stuck, then, they began to move slowly around her hip. As the pearls spun, the small loop moved from the bottom up. The pearls traced a path down the separation of her firm ass cheeks, and up through the oily, lubricated lips of her pussy, to uppercut the tip of her clit, on its way back around her hip again.

She lay back in the tub, lifting her hips and turning her body into a natural train track for the constant round stimulation train. She moved the strand faster and faster, until the orgasms would not stop coming. The extra muscular pressure of keeping her body lifted, added to the intensity. She was floating, not just with the buoyancy of the water, but every facet of her being was light.

She thought about her next move. The now dry hip-hop amulets would need to be separated and sorted. After separating the class from the trash, she stepped over the jewels to get a fluffy terry cloth robe. She liked the pearl G-string, and kept it on for a little while longer. She gathered up the pieces, took the 'bling', and piled it on one pillow with the jewelry on another.

She put the jewelry back into the bucket, and the bling into a provided laundry bag. Turning on the amenity screen, she ordered the apparel menu. She shopped through the choices, and saw a cute, French, vanilla colored coat dress. The length on the monitor was about two inches above the knees. It was a decent enough banking outfit, until she could put hands on something at the mall.

She ordered and charged it to her room. Within fifteen minutes, the outfit with matching shoes and gloves were delivered. She tipped the deliverer, the same Judas that gave up everything but her shoe size, to Ron earlier. This was unbeknownst to her. She dressed, retrieved her car and set out to the Wachovia branch at Lenox, where she kept her closest safe deposit box.

***

Within the next two seconds, a combined 480 rounds of 7.62 millimeter NATO steel shredder ammunition poured into the unsuspecting Limousine. Before Abdullah even recognized the noise of the projectiles attacking his carriage, the car had been dismantled, and was sliding perpendicularly down the freeway. From this angle, he could see his attackers: Blackhawk Special Forces attack helicopters; Allah, was this the last sight he would see?

Abdullah didn't want to leave anything to chance. These infidels would have no compassion for him as his most high God Allah would in the bosom of his mercy. Abdullah needed a way out of this world. As soon as he could get it, he looked around and saw his 9mm on the floor. As he reached for it, the husk of the limo decided to roll. The remaining midsection of the Lincoln rolled at least twenty times before skidding to a rest against the mile marker sign on the left side of the highway.

The Blackhawks were steadily tracking the disintegrating vehicle. After the engine compartment, wheels, and entire front end, and the rear disappeared, the remainder of the car slid down the freeway until it started to roll. The four shooters in each bird switched off with the four fresh shooters, while the original shooters reloaded. Once the carcass stopped moving, the Blackhawks became vultures circling, looking for signs of life.

There seemed to be none, until the driver's door started to move. The door was crumpled and wouldn't respond totally. But the small flapping informed the spotter that the driver, at least, was alive. Bird 3 swooped in to land, leaving Bird 4 up, keeping the perimeter on lock for 3.

The fresh crew from Bird 3 approached the hulking wreck. The driver got two guns, as did the passenger compartment. Simultaneous rifle butts cleared the glass; the driver was in bad shape, with his chest caved in. Two parts of the steering wheel were missing; presumed to be inside the limo. There was non-commissioned officer's cammo gear, but no general. The rear compartment was another matter altogether. Robert and another identical task force member, smashed in the passenger window and saw a General's uniform on a man that fit the description. He was moaning and moving jerkily, but definitely not out of the game yet, he had an array of objects scattered on the floor of the limo: two off-white vials, what looked like a glob of play dough, and a turkey timer.

Robert took no time to think, he didn't care what the instructions were. After all, those were for Coker. His orders came from inside himself: destroy the face. But for all the obsession he had harbored for the face in his crosshairs, he had an overwhelming desire to keep it intact. The man next to him started to bellow orders to the face about putting up his hands places, etc.

Everything faded into a background buzz, as Robert's already aimed weapon, raked an arc. His weapon made two-stitches, side-to-side perforations on Abdullahs body from shoulder to knee. The entire right side of his body was stitched with holes, effectively riveting him to the passenger side of the floor.

"Geeeezzzum crow dude, what the fuck'd you do that for? Orders were, 'alive'. Shit!"

Robert turned to the voice on his right and tucked the MP5 beneath the man's chin, and blew his head to bits. All of which were safely nestled inside his still connected helmet. The other two Ops at the front window missed the action, and presumed the shots were answers from inside the wreck of the limo. But Bird 4 quickly changed that misconception

"Bogey, Bogey, Bird 3 ground, rear window. Bogey, one, bingo, repeat, one bingo!"

Robert, not knowledgeable of the military lingo, but sharp enough to know they were talking about him and the outside guy he'd just killed, turned his gun on the other two.

The armor piercing bullets tore the two Task Force operatives to pieces point blank, followed by a full salvo from Bird 4 and the balance of the Bird 3 team. They emptied their clips into Robert, and ironically, his face was the only thing untouched.

"Bird 3 to Team leader."

"Team leader, go quick Bird 3, I'm going TAC."

"Copy. TAC mission over: 4 down, 1 bogey, two perps, bingo. Please advise."

Shit, that sounded like a long, fast, cluster fuck.

"Stand by. Will advise. Secure area, Team leader out."

"Shit, shit, shit, Team leader to 2."

"This CHAD, go Kri....Team leader."

"Have you been tracking everything?"

"Yes, it's been, stressful to say the least."

"Keep real time tracking. I'm going tactical, anything goes wrong, you already know."

"Copy that team leader. check your 6 and your 12. You hear me? I can't be you until you teach me to."

"I copy you 2, Team leader out."

The faith Chad had in his number one was enough to power her for a week. She needed that little snippet of encouragement to go into this one, knowing what was at stake.

"Bird team two status?"

"Bird Team 2 to Team leader, currently in the tunnel walking with sun, checking every nook and cranny. We've got bomb tech and CDC in tow, nothing yet, approximately 75 yards to station."

"Copy, team one is entering station top level. Stay open, report all."

"Copy team leader; Bird team two open."

Kristi entered the top level of the vast structure. She gave the signal for the team to pop their tabs and start the pure air. They stepped carefully through the station, parallel with the dogs. They checked for trip wires, and other booby traps. Nothing, so far, on the concourse floor. They took the solid stairs down to the second level. Kristi heard dogs barking in stereo, from her ears and from her ear phones.

"Dog's handler says it's the explosives' bark."

"What's your 20?"

"Ten yards inside the station, twenty yards to platform. The dog is forty yards up and stopped."

"Copy, proceed with caution. Put the bomb tech at point."

"Copy."

Shuffling noises were heard over the link. The bomb tech pulled out an ocular with night vision,

"Looks like a timer, but what the hell is that?"

He obviously didn't know his mike was on broadcast.

"Hey, get that CDC guy up here!"

"Butler, get up to the front with Bombs."

"What is it?"

"Look at that, what the hell is it?"

"It looks like an aerosol can."

"Ok, it's gonna take the both of us. I don't know what might be in that can, but I'll bet that strip is C4; come on."

They were on top of the bomb now. James Butler, in his nasa-esqe space suit, engaged the suction fans as well as the lights, in case the can contained a fast acting airborne neurotoxin. He could try to suction as much out of the air as possible, if the can was set to spray.

"Bird team 2 masks, masks stat, aerosol threat, any alternates without gear, clear now cl..."

As the bomb tech got a good clear look at the front of the down facing timer, his heart stopped. Kristi ordered the facility man to invert AC units to suck at max, everything from the station as soon as the area was acknowledged.

0:00:02 ...0:00:01, 0:00:00. Bye-bye... BOOM! The amount of C4 Abdullah had stuck to the side of the pressurized can was enough to do major damage to both sides of the platform, the tracks, and the team surrounding it. The NASA suit protected several parts of James Butler. Unfortunately, not the parts he needed to stay alive.

The suction fans, however, did perform as advertised. They sucked in the majority of the deadly gas and much of the smoke from the explosion. Kristi was thrown to the ground by the force of the blast, rocking the station.

"Bird Team 2, this is Team leader; status?"

"Bird Team 2 comeback."

Open air greeted the command. Kristi stood slowly, helped up by Phillip and James,

"Team leader to MCU."

"Go Team leader."

"Drag, give me vitals on Bird team 2."

"Copy team leader, I read two weak vitals. Damn, make that

one. Team leader Julio Vazquez still shows a weak heartbeat. Nobody else, team leader. Calling in Guard unit mop up from the tunnel. No numbers from outsiders, MCU over."

"Copy MCU, team leader out."

***

The explosion knocked Thony and Suzan off their feet. Thony kept enough sensibility to grab Suzan in his arms; they fell back together against a pillar, Thony was shaken, but Suzan was protected from the impact. The rest of the Team fared better; they were farther back. So, they rushed forward to help the others.

"Team leader, this is National Guard Center City post. HAZMAT is on site, my men are personally mopping up. With your permission, can we use your Blackhawk for Med runs."

"Affirmative, Center City. How's your count?"

"I've got six down from shrapnel, two walking wounded, lost eight out of ten dogs. It's a hell of a thing, but at least we caught it."

"Copy that, Center City; team leader out."

"Come in Bird 2."

"Go for Bird 2."

"Bird 2, did you copy? Assist all, NG medi-vac, over."

"Copy that; medi-vac all, out."

Kristi turned to walk out and noticed Thony and Suzan slowly getting to their feet. She rushed to their side. Now, for the first time she actually felt for these civilians, who were brought into this by some freaky coincidence and bad luck. Still trying to keep up the façade of Commander, she used her throat mike to make sure that they were ok. When the report came back 'Shaken, not stirred', she proceeded to the 'Hawk. She reassembled the team, Bird 1. They stood, joined hands, and said a prayer for the Bird team 2. It was the luck of the airspace; it could have easily been them. While they were still joined; they sent up a prayer for the men killed from Bird team 3, as well. Climbing aboard, they cycled up to go check on the origin of this whole damned thing,

"Bird 1, take me to bird 4."

"Copy that, team leader. ETA 4 minutes."

Chapter 49

Dulcet woke, still clutching the pillow between her legs, feeling better than she had in quite a while. The first thing she did was an acrobatic roll to the far side of the bed, where she pulled the comfortable office chair to her with her foot. Transferring to the chair, she wheeled to the computer. The screen saver was set to an aquarium, with tropical fish swimming back and forth. The bubbles, even the sounds of bubbles, were popping and splashing. She moved the mouse to disable the aquarium, then typed the address in to connect herself to Recipe. After the passwords and authentication steps were taken, she saw that Soul Food was a payroll distribution for the largest black grocery chain in the south. 'Way Far Foods', was headquartered in Atlanta and all of their employees got paid on off days of the week, so that they didn't have to wait long to cash their checks. The money traveled in cash to a central depository, to ensure the liquidity of the checks.

The depository was the meal, unlike a Federal Reserve depository. Soul food described the Way Far depository as strength through stealth. The fact that it wasn't public knowledge where they did their deal, was what kept their security tight. Apparently, their transaction was going to take place at a hotel, of all the original places. Couriers from five different areas of the state meet, the combined cash is counted, and taken to a large bank branch to be deposited into the high capacity overnight depository.

It sounded kind of weird to Dulcet, but Recipe had never steered her wrong before. This time, she was going to use current events. She started thinking back to the big tour bus with her face on it. The cute little hooker wanted to use her face. Well, she was going to do some borrowing of her own. Combined total among all of her houses, she had close to $280 million. That was not bad for a concentrated little career. But, if this one sent her over the top, she would be done with the U.S. of A.

Her latest rationale for retirement was one dollar from every man, woman, and child from America, and she would be done. She'd retire. The U.S. population was tipping past 300 million. So, she was really close. Yeah, soul food would be her swan song and she intended to make it a Duet.

***

Ron was watching Sylvania dress; she put on a royal blue thong, and matching barely there denim bra, a zip-up hoodie top, and a pair of fitted apple booty cotton sweat pants. She announced her readiness. Ron looked at her feet; he could not ever imagine not loving this woman. She wore matching tube socks with toes, five on each.

"I can see what you're thinking, they are not kiddy toe socks; they are adult foot gloves."

The serious look that she gave Ron made him consider the facts. Then, looking around at the abject destruction of everything electronic, he shrugged his shoulders. She burst out laughing, unable to hold it in any more. The sound was magical, exactly what was needed. She explained that her sneakers were downstairs in the closet. They held hands as they stepped past their last scene of love making. Sylvania looked back over her shoulder at the spot at the top of the stairs, as if she had never seen it before. Under the guise of school clothes, she had a full wardrobe of athletic shoes, from simple Addias low top plain white, to psychedelic lower calf wrestling shoes. She chose a royal blue leather pair that offset her outfit. But Ron knew that perfectly matched her underwear. They left in Ron's car, not really sure where they were going, but away from the CNN 'Agents', that they felt were sure on the way.

Ron looked at Sylvania, then thought about the differences between her and Fantasia. Fantasia was like a bruised peach in a basket. They were identical in so many ways, but you could tell the difference, once you brought it to your nose and smelled it.

"So, what was the deal with all the cloak and dagger stuff Ron? Ron???"

"I found her babe."

"You found who?"

"The look-alike; she calls herself Fantasia."

"Fantasia? Like Disney?"

"Probably more like American Idol. She's a stripper alright, and she's also a thief."

"A thief, strip…where did you go last night Ron?"

"I went to the party the two gold tooth dudes at the bar got the invitation to. It was like a live-action video for one of those kiddy looking rapper types at this mansion. I went there trying to find out who she was and wound up watching her slut around the party with her girlfriends. I saw her steal a bunch of jewelry from this guy's house and run off."

"What? So you say she played hooker to steal this guy's jewelry? And you followed her, and her girlfriend to make sure, right?"

Rolling up the freeway Ron felt small dots of perspiration on the back of his neck; this wasn't going at all as he had expected. He didn't know what the hell was going on then, so, he didn't know how he figured he would know now.

"Look, Sylvania, I can feel you baby. I feel heat coming from your side of the car and I don't know why. You have nothing to worry about babe; not even from a dead ringer. I can tell you the truth, from the first time I ever saw her, I've felt an over-riding need to get to the bottom of this mystery. It's got to have something to do with the feelings I have for you. Hell, since the beginning, I didn't want to share you, not even with somebody else that looked like you. Can you understand that?"

Sylvania looked at Ron trying to do just that.

"Baby, I was following her around that party looking for her to be you, and she never was. She was tainted; her actions, nothing about her, was genuine or sincere. The whole time I was there, all I could think was what the hell am I doing here?

If she walked right up to me, what the hell would I do? What would I say? Could I grab her face and try to pull her mask off? Then I thought, what you would want me to do with this obvious imposter. I still didn't know. I was about to leave when I saw her pull that guy into the room. Then, she reappeared with a heavy bag, running out of the house. That's when I followed her."

"You what? Ron, all this was going on while I was asleep? Then, I woke up worried about you..... Why didn't you answer your phone?"

"Ok, hold on Sylvania".

Ron braked and pulled over to the berm. Sylvania got nervous; she thought she may be about to get kicked out on the freeway. She had heard of that happening to women before. She'd wondered what would make a person put you out of their car.

"Look babe, I have to get this straight before it goes too far. Look me in my eyes Sylvania. I love you woman, ok? I'm not going to go out of my way and purposely make you cry, and I'll leave you alone before I beat you. But all this accusatory business, I don't go for that. I can't go for that.

I don't know the history of this part of your life, and I don't want to. Unless you feel the need to go there, just know, I'm down for you, Sylvania, ok baby? Work with me here, I've been out trying to understand my motivation for needing to know, and I still don't know. So can we squash the storm before it comes? We don't need to argue to make up; all you have to do is give me that look, and tell me what you want."

The suspicion and anxiety left her face. She threw herself into his arms, with the steering wheel blocking her, but she did her best.

"Ron, I don't mean to be so insecure, but I don't want to lose you to somebody, anybody else. If she looks like me or not. Until very, very recently, I thought nobody looked like me; now it's been proven otherwise. I've had people in my life leave me for someone else that they said was more exciting. A school teacher didn't fit their profile, they said, if they said anything.

Ron, I didn't want to give all of my heart to you, then to find out that you didn't really want me after all."

"Baby, that won't happen. I wanna be there for you, and I want you to be there for me too."

She looked sideways up at Ron not understanding. Then, she sat back in her seat and contemplated. Ron got back on the road and drove back in towards town. After more minutes of silence than she wanted, she asked,

"So, where did you follow her to, inch-high private eye?"

He took a moment to collect his thoughts first. His performance had worked. Now, the rape, the drugs, all the rest of the goings on from last night, could be locked away, and key destroyed.

"The X hotel, in Dunwoody."

"The X? That's the only one in the country, isn't it?"

"Not the only one, but there are only three others."

"Why there?"

"I don't know; maybe the jewel thieves union gets a discount there. But I bribed an employee to get some information, and followed her inside and got stuck again, wondering what the hell was I going to say if I walked up to her and called her name?"

"And what is her name Ron?"

She was getting a little toasty again, but he saw her catch herself.

"Diamond Jade was what my money bought; the valet was for sale. I knew the check in name was fake, I mean, what else would a jewel thief register as? I know Fantasia can't be right. So, that was another dead end, so I left. That's when I called after I saw the tennis girls' bus."

"Dutchess, not the tennis girl, she's a friend of mine, ok?"

"Ok, that's when I saw Duchess's bus; it was turning the same direction I was coming from. She may have been going to the X as well, but I didn't stick around to find out because I was trying to get back to you. That's when all hell broke loose."

All hell was right; Sylvania needed a cool drink, maybe some juice.

"Ron could you stop at a store so I can get something to drink?"

"Sure I can babe, but I want to get away from this traffic madness first, ok?"

"Fine, Mr. Navigator, I'm at your mercy".

"Yeah, and don't you forget it."

She smiled and punched him in his rock hard arm. Unconsciously, they both reached up onto the dashboard, where the beetle clips held two unisex pair of sunglasses. The brightness was automatically attributed to the bright sun. But, as they looked up, they saw that the lights on top of the big poles in the middle of the freeway had been activated.

They slowly inched through traffic. As they rode along, they saw the primary source of the backup: three sleek black helicopters were at the scene of an accident. Everybody there was dressed in all black, except two day-glow, bright orange, suits jumping out of the third helicopter. The speed of traffic picked up dramatically as they rushed past the accident scene. Two exits up, they got off at the Lenox road exit. They stopped at a convenience store and she slid out of the car. Those apple booty sweats did a job on his senses. In less than a minute, she came back and jumped into the car

"I'm penniless Ron. I totally forgot to grab any money."

"Shit babe, what do you need, a couple of dollars?"

Ron went to dig into his pocket.

"No, take me around the corner to the Wachovia."

"Ok, your highness."

"Wait, I will allow you to give me two dollars."

"Ok, here."

"I'll be right out."

She ran back into the store and came back out with a

tabloid; she guiltily tossed it into the back seat where it fell onto the floor.

"A little light reading, who knows, one day I might get a bird or something."

Ron laughed at her pseudo-embarrassment, and backed out on their way to the bank.

***

Sylvia's titanium briefcase was the perfect accessory with her three inch heels and Gucci shades. She walked through the side entrance to Wachovia and offered her index finger print to enter into her safe deposit box area. Once again, the finger print scanner atop the key slot for the older box holders was activated, as was the manager's scanner across the room. Her secure cubicle slid closed around her. She opened her lock box and tried to find some room.

She removed the jewelry. She draped the necklaces and large stone pendants around the stacks of cash, and pooled them in the corners. She kept the bling inside the laundry bag in the briefcase. When finished, she returned the box. She opened the cubicle door and walked through the bank, making her obligatory deposits into the savings and to the credit card accounts. She paid off her I-phone then walked down the stairs on her way to the parking lot.

***

Ron pulled in and did a U-turn, so that he could let Sylvania out on the sidewalk side to go to the ATM. He stood up to stretch, still trying to decide where to go to be out of the range of the CNN 'Agents'. He figured it would probably be best to lay low until the alert level dropped at least back to ORANGE. Ron walked around to stand by Sylvania to have her back. The dress threw him off. It wasn't fuscia, but it was her. She was coming up on his right side as Sylvania came around from his left.

"Hey sugar dick,"

She approached him. Sylvania stepped around Ron's left.

"What the fuck did you say to my man, Bitch?"

Sylvia stopped in her tracks looking Sylvania in the face for the first time. Sylvania, having already heard how much this woman looked like her, was slightly prepared, but still taken aback by the resemblance. She stood in front of Ron and stuck her chest out protecting him.

"And who the fuckin hell are **you** bitch, how come you look like..."

Sylvania punched Sylvia in the jaw with an impressive left hook, followed by a right jab to the nose that staggered her back. This caused Sylvia and her briefcase to fall. Customers were starting to pay attention to the scuffle. Cell phones came out and 911's were called.

Ron was stunned; he never knew that she had that in her. Damn, she was standing over her like she was going to stomp her out or something. Ron pulled her off of her, pushed her to the car, and got the hell out of there. Ron stared at Sylvania; she was breathing hard and cradling her left hand … and she was smiling a totally new smile.

"Damn baby."

She looked at Ron.

"I was defending your honor baby."

When he looked back, she had tears in her eyes.

"Why did she step to you like that Ron? And why'd she call you that?"

Ron was stuck.

"Well shit, I guess she remembered how I was hawking her in the mall, when I thought she was you. As for her comment, she probably says that to all her prospective tricks."

Her gaze was locked on Ron's eyes. He held steady, because he really did love her, he didn't want anything to come between them. Reboot and move on, keep it moving from there. He pulled her sore hand to his lips and kissed her knuckle, they had started to look slightly puffy.

"Damn, where did that punch come from?"

"I don't know babe, maybe from that first conversation. I wanted to do that, I don't want any woman to be me for you, but me. Wait a minute, what did you tell me before we got in the car?"

"I said I wanna be there for you, and I want you to be there for me too."

"Ok, now, I know I love you, and you love me too, right?"

"Damn Ms. Collins, I can't get nothing past you, huh?"

"Anything."

That brought a tension-relieving laugh, as the police, at full siren speed, zoomed by in the other direction going towards the bank. The curiosity was killing them. Ron spun around the block.

***

The Black Hawk designated Bird 1 circled the perimeter area and came down north of the wrecked used-to-be limousine. There were shrouded figures lined up on the ground in front of Bird 3; a total of six: the driver, the passenger, the bogey infiltrator, and three Task force members. They landed, causing the makeshift body bags to flap in the rotor wash from the Blackhawk. The team solemnly exited the chopper and approached their fallen comrades. The three bad guys were separated from the three good guys. Kristi went over and saluted the team members, showing respect for men who lost their lives carrying out orders from her in the protection of their country. Thony and Suzan stayed behind, while the ritual of respect was carried out by the team.

It was so amazing for them to witness the depth of these multifaceted individuals. Separate and together, you would never know. Any time they saw the term 'Special Forces Killers' from now on, the image of the stone cold killer would not be able to suffice.

They held each other for support thinking about the loss of life that had occurred over the last few days. Although these six were the only ones they had actually seen, these few brought the enormity of the many crashing home. Kristi was waving them over by the covered bodies farthest from the black helicopter, closer to the wreck of a car. They walked out still holding each other, despite the bulky orange suits.

"Thony, Suzan, I want to apologize to the both of you for all that you have been through. Know that it was all per my command; if there is any person you would like to file an action against, it would be me. Is that understood?"

"Yes Ma'am".

They said in unison.

"What I'm about to show you will not be made public for forty years, if I have anything to say about it. By then, hopefully, I'll be dead and resting in peace. This viewing makes you privy to National Security Directives that could and do fill an entire book, not to mention the PATRIOT ACT provisions that fall under Threat Level RED tools. Do you understand what I've told you?"

Once again in unison, and harmony they said,

"Yes ma'am!"

Pleasantries and politeness come relatively easily, when confronted by so many people that have the means at their disposal to kill you many times over. Kristi pulled the sheet back on Robert. There was no response, just another dead guy. He didn't look foreign; he looked like he was from Detroit or something. His still open eyes were a lifeless hazel color, which would have been mesmerizing had he not been stone dead. Next to him was a bearded man with rough skin and one remaining eye that was looking halfway back into the cave of his skull. Other than the body's destruction, there was nothing of much interest. That left the last covered body. Kristi, Thony and Suzan all stood, mouths open. The two women looking from live Thony to dead Abdullah, and back and forth.

It was simply unbelievable. The resemblance in death was the same as the pictures. The eyes, the dead terrorist's eyes, were the same as they were in the picture. Although he was dead, the eyes were flat pools of inky black. In contrast, Thony's eyes were deep soulful, lively, black eyes. Through all that they had been through, he was still the man Suzan had always loved. Kristi thought back to the screaming match they'd had in room 2720, when Suzan insisted that the picture was not her man. This one was an exact match to the satellite photos, no doubt.

"Team leader to MCU."

"Go Team leader."

"Vid cap my cam, wrap with POI file archive; Cc to base, TCU and the boss, copy."

"Copy that boss, base TCU, max scramble."

"Copy, what's the status at TCU?"

"MCU for TCU, Team leader patch thru."

"Go for TCU."

"Status, Dog?"

"Quarantine 1 is clear; all bodies on HAZMAT equipped barge heading to containment center, where the remains will be tagged again and arrangements made."

"Copy that Dog; and the rest?"

"The boat will have to be sealed until it can be dry docked, broken down, and stripped before it can go back into service. C.B. Peters is on an IV drip. Exhaustion got him, but he's stabilized now, and is almost ready for a slow boat home."

"Copy Dog, carry on with your mop-up. Will advise re: patron's status, keep'em fed and happy; you'll have refreshers to deal with them."

"Copy that Team leader, TCU over."

"Team leader, out."

"So, uh, team leader, SAC Johnson, whatever, what happens to us now?"

Suzan was trying to find out.

"Not sure, for now you stay tight to me. I'll try to get you home for tomorrow. Shit, that reminds me, Team leader to MCU."

"Go for MCU."

"Cancel the sparks on POI, and Cleaner to Bird 3, copy."

"Copy that Team leader wires on the way."

"Copy that, ensure slip in-out."

"Copy team leader. They'll never know that we were there, over."

"Copy, out."

"Now, to try to answer your question, you will be with me, as my guests as you have been. We will be going to FBI Atlanta

District Headquarters to debrief. You will be told what you can and cannot remember, recall, speak on, comment on, etc. It will probably last until tomorrow, at which time we will take you to where you desire to go."

"Well, my car is in Springfield."

Thony chimed in.

"No, it's at the Mobile Command Unit, right next to the park. It was airlifted for evidence investigation; it's in St Louis, now. Of course, it will have to be reassembled. But now that the POI is dead, you are no longer a suspect. So, that will be handled during your debriefing."

"Ok, hell, let's get this thing started so it can be done. We still at Level RED?"

"I'll have to look into that as well."

They moved as a group, surrounding the two orange figures, back to the Blackhawks. From there they elevated towards the Federal building.

Chapter 50

Dutchess had tried out everything on the bottom floor of her new digs: the machines, and the free weights. She took a long stretch in the sauna, cooking her sore muscles. Then she padded down the thickly carpeted hallway to the pool, and swam some laps. Now, she was chilling out in the pool, listening to the tropical rainforest sounds she had found available on the sound system. She admired the clear blue sky when, subconsciously, she was disturbed by the lack of planes. It was almost as if she couldn't remember the last time she had seen one. She knew that was silly of her, but she also knew it was not. She hadn't seen a plane since she'd gotten off one before the tournament. She recalled the fireworks at Carlos' place, and the clear skies. There hadn't been an airplane in the sky during her entire new life.

Dutchess got out of the pool, pulled on a long, fluffy robe and bent down to catch all of her hair in a towel, and wrapped it to dry. She stood up and saw Henry at the door of the pool.

"Hey Henry, what's wrong?"

Henry had his 'not a happy camper' face on, he stood

silently.

"Dutchess, come with me D, we gotta talk."

They went into the theater, Henry closed the door.

"Damn Henry, what's up? You look like somebody just…"

He held up his hand to shush her; that was a first. Now, she was getting upset from his strange behavior.

"Dutchess, when was the last time you were in Springfield, Illinois?"

"Springfield, Illinois, I don't think I've ever been there Henry. Why what's up in Springfield? Do I have a match there or something?"

"Apparently, there's a match alright."

"Well, out with it, who do I play?"

Something didn't seem right about this exchange to Duchess."

"It's not who you play, but how you played yourself!"

"What are you talking about Henry?"

She was genuinely confused; why was Henry looking at her so mean and accusing her of being in Illinois?

"D, look, I was thinking back to that little crazy outburst on the bus earlier, and how you have gotten a little carried away with yourself a couple of times lately, a little too casual about your sexuality, you could say. But, while I was upstairs, I got a phone call from Pauline. She told me that everything was good and in order with your contracts. That technically, the whole shebang, should be wrapped up by tomorrow, next day at the latest, except, for the 'Springfield thing'."

She couldn't take it anymore; she jumped up from the recliner.

"Henry, what the hell are you talking about in goddamned Springfield? I told you, I've never been there!"

Henry looked at her as if she were speaking Japanese.

"According to Pauline, the Country's Inquisitor, has an eyewitness in Springfield. Some geek that works at a drive-thru window at a restaurant, claims that Dutchess Singletary, came through his drive thru buck naked, and masturbated for him. She gave him the money for the food, then gave him the wrong number, and drove off. This caused him great emotional stress.

So he went to the tabloids; so far, it's an exclusive and because of the Threat Level RED, it's in limited distribution. This is a potential deal breaker Dutchess. You know that, don't you? What the hell were you thinking, D? Riding around Boogerville naked? When did this start? You could have told me, warned me, that you do this sort of thing, damn."

Henry was on a roll. Dutchess, whose anger had peaked for a second, was stunned to silence; she had no words. The more wound up Henry got, the deeper Dutchess sank into the recliner. She knew that she had never been to Springfield, Illinois. She knew damned well that she didn't ride around anywhere naked. Hell, her car didn't even have tinted windows. How could this be? After all of her hard work, finally realizing a dream, who wanted to do something like this to her? Why? Henry's rant was starting to lose some of its edge, but it still contained all the steam. He saw Dutchess' tears and stopped.

"I don't know how far those tears are going to carry you, Dutchess. What do you have to say for yourself?"

In the smallest voice she had ever used she said,

"It wasn't me, Henry."

"What? What did you say Dutchess, speak up!"

Henry was in full-daddy temper tantrum mode now, seeing this one stupid indiscretion taking them both down in flames.

"I said,"

In a voice more suited to the size of her mouth,

"It wasn't me, Henry."

"What do you mean it wasn't you? In case you didn't realize it, my dear, you have a very distinctive look. The man described you as if he had watched you in a porno movie. Oh my god. You haven't ever filmed yourself having sex, have you? Let me know now, spill it all, Dutchess. let's see if, somehow, we can save our careers!"

Now, Dutchess was pissed.

"Save our careers? Is that what you said Henry? What about my reputation?! Huh?! What about the fact that I just told you that the person you are talking about could not possibly be me? Huh? Huh?! Henry, what kind of a chance do I have to prove these scumbags wrong? When the one person on my side is on their side. Fuck you Henry! Get out!!"

She flung her arm in the classic get out gesture, pointing to the theater door. Her robe slipped open; considering the conversation, she quickly gripped the small opening closed, lest Henry get a peek. Even though she was wearing a bikini, she didn't need any more assumptions about her propriety or depravity. Henry started to say something else, but in the end, he just left. She rushed to the door and locked it. She stood there with her palms and forehead pressed against the soundproof door and sobbed. What was it about this day?

First, it was those helicopters, now this. Was there some kind of demon running around Atlanta that wanted to make sure Dutchess saw it? Who was trying to destroy her life? She had never had to deal with negative attention like this before. She had always been conscious of her image. She hated that her parents had to die; for years, she had suffered from the survivors syndrome.

When the car had gone off the embankment and rolled, she did what anybody would have done, she opened the door and got out. When she tried to open her parents' doors, they were locked because the car was still in gear. Little Dutchess tried and tried to get her parents out of the car, even crawling back in through the door she had come out of; but they wouldn't respond. They were laying on the roof of the overturned vehicle, still in seatbelts, crunched down to their waists.

Dutchess had run from the car to get assistance. People were scrambling down the embankment to help. When the rescue workers came, there was nobody to rescue.

The money she inherited as a twelve year old, helped to pay for her upbringing. The caseworker that showed up on the scene from Child Protective Services raised her, and bought her first Tennis Racquet. As a social worker, she had known solo sports to help break the cycle of survivor's guilt. By focusing on the game, putting everything into the ball, be it golf or tennis, Dutchess was exposed to both; but tennis called her name.

The publicity she received from the accident taught Dutchess early on that image meant a lot. So she cultivated hers carefully, and knew not to do things to tarnish herself. So, why now, would somebody want to destroy all that she had cultivated? She pulled the remote controller off the wall and dimmed the lights down to full darkness. The glowing remote was the only thing that she could see. Using it like a flashlight, she found her way to a center seat. She pulled up the menu of entertainment options and searched for a getaway.

She turned on cartoon network to lose herself in reflections of youth: the Power Puff Girls and Dexter's Laboratory. Flipping through the channels, she noticed that quite a few were playing cartoons, old ones: super friends, Yogi Bear and Friends. The return to classic TV was kind of refreshing, until she recognized that she didn't see anything current. She didn't want to see any sports or entertainment, because she feared possibly seeing herself in the worst light. But, she accidentally did stop on a sports channel. They were airing a story about her and the Coke contract. They were still showing footage of her bus riding around Miami. That footage had to be days old, but they were playing it as if it was new. What's that about? She continued to click through the channels, until she got to an input channel. This one overviewed the security cameras. She chose the one that showed the doorway camera; outside the door, she saw

Henry.

He was slumped on the floor in front of the door, with his head in his hands, looking down at the floor. She didn't know that the system did all this; she clicked another button and got a view of the front door, the living room and the balcony. She saw Max. Subconsciously, she touched the dog tag around her neck and fingered the ruby very lightly. The temptation was there to push it, if for no other reason, but to see him come running. But she didn't want to cry wolf. She went back to Henry; he was still slumped outside the door.

She clicked off the power on the projector, and plunged the room into total darkness again. She remained sitting there for a while, trying to collect her thoughts. She had some harsh words for Henry. If he was truly on her side, they would only hurt for a moment. But if not, it would be painful for a lifetime.

Chapter 51

They rode around the mall. Ron stopped at a fast food drive-thru and ordered a large drink full of ice with an extra cup. Before they left the drive-thru, he poured about an inch of ice into the wide mouthed plastic cup, then, gently placed Sylvania's hand inside. He poured the balance of the tea into the other cup.

"This is to keep the swelling down, champ."

"Thank you, baby."

"No, thank you! You're my hero."

Her blush and look-away was priceless. She turned back and said,

"Ok, I'll be that."

They were coming out of the drive way, more police cars were arriving at the bank. The parking lot was full, and they'd gotten out in the nick of time. Ron could see Fantasia; she was handcuffed behind her back and being seated in the back of a police car. The metal briefcase that she was carrying, went into the trunk. A black-clad figure was taking off a shielded face mask; he supposed it was somebody from the bomb squad making sure the briefcase was safe to ride in the trunk.

"Well babe, that's the end of her. I got you, you got to beat somebody up for free, my watch is still ticking, and the world still goes around."

"I don't know how free it was."

She said, flexing her fist with a grimace.

"But it does feel like the world is still turning. So what are we going to do now, Ron?"

"I've been thinking about that. Is there anything you have always wanted to do but could never find the time to do it? If so, I say there's no time like the present."

"The present is good, it's got possibilities. But everything I want to do is whatever I'm doing right here with you. You have no idea how badly I missed you last night. I don't want any more of that love'em and leave'em stuff. If I got to take a bite and hold on, I want you to love me and stay."

"There's a high probability that that can be arranged."

They pulled into a gas station next to the freeway, Ron jumped out to pump some gas. Sylvania reclined back and reached around to get her Countries Inquisitor. Using one hand, she shook the paper open and stared at the headline:

IS COKE'S NEW MULTIMILLION DOLLAR BABY A NYMPHO NUDIST? Inquisitive minds want to know. Illinois drive-thru worker says it's so. See page three. Ron got back in the car from filling up and saw clouds all across the horizon of Sylvania's face

"What's wrong, babe? Was I gone too long?"

"No Ron, look. They can't let a sister have anything."

She showed Ron the headline. Dutchess not being his friend, and him having never met her, he really didn't know what to say. He knew not to totally trust what any paper said to be totally true; it was usually unfounded, subjective bull. But there was a long stretch in the ratio of truth to fiction. Ron didn't really know what to say to her. It was obviously the first time that she had seen someone she knew in the tabloid she was so used to reading, so he said nothing.

"I can't believe this is Dutchess. She doesn't strike me as that kind of person at all."

"But how can you know how a person is behind closed doors? That's why I don't like the media. They can twist anything up. I mean that headline could say 'dirty talking elementary teacher runs afoul of CNN Agents'. What would people think of that? Or, what if some child's parent saw you doing the Ali shuffle in the bank parking lot? You see, none of it has to be true. But the more of a celebrity you are, the smaller the amount of trash it takes to make a story. I wouldn't put too much credence in the story, but it won't be easy for her. She has to deal with her sponsors; damn, that's a tough break."

They eased onto the freeway heading north, with no particular place to go. Ron was looking at the face of the guy that was supposed to be the eyewitness to the nudity and lewd behavior. He was a pimply faced, young, white guy, who looked about sixteen, but the article said he was twenty six. To Ron, from that glance alone, he looked like he could be paid to say anything. He turned his attention back to the road then glanced back, he saw an article on the World Series of Poker.

"Hey Sylvania, what's that WSOP article?"

"Uh, let's see it says there was a robbery, a bunch of ex-winners got together for a friendly game and got robbed of an undisclosed amount of money and all their bracelets. The paper says that they were victims of the CP Robber. No more details were available, but the sources say that the CP Robber leaves all of her victims naked, and tied in situations they would not want published. This made them less likely to cooperate with authorities. They also say she is suspected in at least three other robberies in two other states."

"Damn, how would you like to be stripped butt naked, robbed and left in public with a bunch of strangers? It truly wouldn't be my idea of something I'd want blasted all over the news. Whoever she is, she's sharp." She read several other stories to Ron: Alien Abduction, 'he probed me and made me see visions'; an 82 year old woman has a baby by a 40 year old father; the typical tabloid fare. There was another grilled cheese sandwich with the face of Jesus, that sold on eBay for $32,000, breaking the record for a sandwich at auction. But it always came back to Dutchess Singletary and the naked drive thru story.

"What could she have been thinking? Babe, the more I think about that situation, the more it bothers me. I know that you are a good judge of character. I mean, you chose me, right?"

She looked at him and stuck out her tongue.

"But really, if you don't believe this could be true then, I believe you. I know stranger things happen than you can imagine, but that guy got pretty detailed in his descriptions, you've got to admit."

"Yeah, and he could have a great imagination and an overactive fantasy life and want's to ruin Dutchess."

They both looked at the scrunched little face. He didn't look very smart or imaginative, but you could never tell. Sylvania's makeshift ice bath had turned to cold water. So Ron got off at the next exit. The convenient store sold sodas from a fountain, therefore, they had ice. For a dime, they allowed Ron to fill up the large cup. On his way out, he noticed the tabloid rack; the Countries Inquisitor had a different cover than the one Sylvania had. Instead of the story about Dutchess, there was a story about one of the Presidents' daughters and a leaked sex tape of a drunken, lesbian episode. He asked the cashier if they were up to date,

"As far as I know mister; you read that stuff?"

"No, no, my girl. Ah, forget it, thanks."

He walked out and told Sylvania maybe it's regional, maybe it doesn't come out the same all over the country."

"We can only hope for her sake."

There was a little inexpensive motel across the street. They went in and got a room. After ten minutes, they were on their way to Jacksmart to buy sheets, towels and a comforter. They also got some overnight supplies for a late night cookout, and a disposable Hibachi grill, before returning to their overnight house.

***

The black outfits instilled fear and uneasiness, but the Brooks brothers' suits and the wing-tip shoes were much worse. Thony and Suzan sat in the sterile office surrounded by grey men. They were black, white, and Asian. But they all were dressed exactly alike: hair, features, height, and weight; it's as if they had been cloned and painted.

Over and over, they grilled them about everything that had happened, from the time the window had blown in. This debriefing process had gone on for hours. There were no windows or clocks in the featureless room. The passage of time was relative to the switching of generic agents. It got to the point that they couldn't recognize the same agents when they came back into the room.

They were out of the orange suits, back in their street clothes.   Every so often, they were brought pages of paperwork to sign. This indicated that the things they had discussed were covered under a National Security Directive number such and such. They swore or affirmed not to speak of this or that under penalty of yadda yadda yadda.   They lost track of how many things they'd signed or why. All they knew was that they were not to speak of anything that had happened. They were to act as if they had been asleep for the entire time that they had been kidnapped under the auspices of Threat Level RED.

The absolutely real understanding that the constitutional rights that every American took for granted every day, actually meant nothing, once the declaration of a color on a chart was made. This horrified them in ways they never knew they could be afraid. Yet, they signed the papers in front of them as they came. They tried in vain to ask questions, but were informed that there would be a time for that. As long as the questions were not about issues that would adversely affect National Security, they would be answered.

They were also told that the forms that they had signed, in effect, negated any perjury charges. Even if sworn under oath, they could mention nothing about any of the events they had experienced, witnessed, seen, overheard or peripherally inferred. The Fifth Amendment pleading was not necessary, simply say no. This was a far cry from what they had expected. The debriefings that they had seen on TV had consisted of a dark room, with coffee, and cigarette sessions. There, the field man explained what he learned from the mission to the office analyst, which was followed by a few weeks of vacation time. This was not. After the 100th time of hearing how many feet beneath Ft. Leavenworth prison they would end up, if they mentioned anything about operations "Blow Torch", "Family Tree", and several other names they hadn't heard of, they were finally given a break.

The break consisted of two cans of Coca Cola and a deli tray with meat and veggies, bread and sauces. The agents left them in the room alone. The first thing they did was embrace, kiss and hold one another. They wondered aloud how long this process would possibly take; then, thought better of it. It could last forever, since they were switching shifts in and out. They made sandwiches and drank the Cokes.

The food and caffeine served to remind them that they hadn't eaten since the hotel in Springfield. At that point, they finished off the entire deli tray. Overstuffed, with physical exhaustion slowly taking over, they dozed off, and leaned against one another, in the uncomfortable hard-backed chairs.

***

In another world inside the same building, Kristi's debriefing was an entirely different ordeal. An ordeal it was, nonetheless. She sat in the Atlanta Regional SAC's office; the tech communication room was not up to par with her office in Baltimore. She had Chad conferenced in on one of the P-I-P screens. The other screens were split between the DDI-FBI and the Director of Homeland Security; in turn, they had local screens split with the remaining rungs of the ladder. Currently, what all screens in all locations had in common were the two pictures of Abdullah alive and Abdullah dead.

"So Agent Johnson, I'm to understand that this bearded, scarred, dead, son-of-a-bitch is responsible for the deaths of approximately 3000 citizens in two different states. This does not include at least 28 officers and scientists, both human and canine. One fucking man caused all this?"

Herve' Dominguez, Director of Homeland Security was livid. Right now, his outrage was directed at SAC Kristi Johnson. Kristi sat alone, still attired in her TAC outfit. She was well within herself, absorbing all the input, stoically. This would be expected from any male counterpart that would otherwise be sitting in this particular hot-seat. The difference was that at this moment in time, a first in history for a woman, especially a young black woman, to be in this seat, was unprecedented. The spiky, dangerous pause let her know that it was her turn to respond to the incensed Director.

"Yes sir, Mr. Director, those are the numbers we have, thanks to the work of my team: Tactical, Crypto, Transpo, Et Al. The number of lives lost was regrettable, but the number saved was many multiples greater.

We recovered five three-ounce vials of weapons grade anthrax. The CDC has determined that the sources were varied; they discovered signatures from at least four different countries, including the U.S. The pound of C4 plastic high explosive and state of the art detonation device are in the lab as we speak, the Chemical origin pending. The photos we have of the aerosol can are being analyzed to determine the origin of the gas, now identified as Sarin. This was the same deadly gas used in the subways of Japan, late in the 1990's.

Sir, my analytical team informs me that the worst case scenario would have been the bombing of the CDC Agrihormone Research Facility. The terrorist believed that this facility contained the Bio toxin vault. The fatality numbers would have jettsoned up to an inclusive hard number of 23,000.

Please understand that this is without the bio toxin, which was his prime target; we believe that this was his destination when he was eliminated."

Kristi's pause was purposeful; her statements were given with authority, her voice was unwavering, and her gaze was steady. The butterflies in her stomach made her uncomfortable. This was the first time that her voice has been simultaneously heard on so many levels.

After pulling so much rank nationwide, she had to face the

echo of the music that she chose to play. When the silence ended, it was broken by the off camera voice of the POTUS: the President of the United States. Both men looked away to their own vid screens.

"Special Agent Johnson, I need to speak frankly with you. The bombing in St. Louis, was communicated to all levels at the same time. Your quick action in getting to the scene and assessing the situation was admirable far beyond your pay grade, young lady. You showed much bigger balls than a lot of the people surrounding me, by invoking Threat Level RED, for the first time in history.

Having you on the sharp end of this operation is one of the best decisions you have ever made Pete. Dedicate a chapter in your memoirs, whenever you write them. And Herve', staying out of the way was the best thing you could have done. Special Agent Johnson, know that you have now felt some of the same pressures that I am faced with on a daily basis. Out there on your own, you lacked the advantage or the baggage, of a room full of advisors. Yet, you brought together disparate teams from all agencies, and accomplished your mission with loss of life at a relative minimum. Considering one life lost is too many, the stated alternative would have been much, too much, to bear.

I commend you, Special Agent Kristi Johnson, and, hereby, award you the National Defense Service Medal, the Distinguished Intelligence Cross, the Gold Citation of Homeland, and the Bronze Star. These awards will be presented to you in a private, Top Secret ceremony on a date to be determined. Special Agent, you have my thanks, along with the gratitude of all the American lives that you saved, that will never know that you exist."

"Thank you Sir. I was doing the job I love to do Sir, and I appreciate the opportunity to continue to do so."

The Director of the FBI came on the screen for Kristi.

"SAC Johnson, good work. Do you need some time off? It's well deserved?"

"Not yet, Sir, I still have some things actually in play. I need to check in with my number two, and see where we are with the other threads."

"As you wish, let me know when you feel you're ready. I don't need you burned out if you missed that part. You are now a National Treasure, even if the masses don't know. The powers that be are well aware."

Next was the Director of Homeland Security.

"So, Special Agent Johnson, congratulations are in order. You are the first person ever to be awarded the GCH. You are in the History books, classified and unclassified. I'm to understand that the threat to the country has ended with the death of this terrorist, correct?"

"That's right sir. The best Intel that we have, points to this single operator. Copycats and sympathetic cells should be few, if any, because of the information /media blackout. We have a pretty tight lid on information. A top rank time released disinformation leak campaign is set to start as soon as the level drops back to ORANGE."

"Based on your assessment of the situation, I feel comfortable dropping the threat level back to ORANGE, as of midnight tonight. Special Agent Johnson, with the exception of the final paperwork, this debriefing is complete, I thank you."

Kristi stood and saluted; it seemed like the thing to do, and she exited the Atlanta SAC's office. Phillip and James were waiting in the outer office with pensive looks on their faces. Like their boss, they had no idea what this mission was going to turn into or how it was going to end. When Kristi came out with a thumb's up, and a neutral expression, they knew that it was good news.

Kristi was never one to toot her own horn, so that was good for the guys.

"Nothing bad = job security". Kristi sat down at a secured workstation and connected to her remote access program. The notes Chad had been making regarding the rest of the list that she had been working on before the explosion had occurred, was updated. The sex robber had gained a name that slipped through the media gate, "The Compromising Position Robber-CPR". Leave it to these imbeciles to come up with something like that. She had been busy.

Similar to the rationale that she had given to her bosses, the lack of media was refreshingly helpful. There was no coverage linking loosely together, to confuse the facts. There were no worries about a copycat. Her trail dotted from Springfield, Illinois to Daytona, Florida, to Miami, Florida, all with the sexual spectacle at the end. Then, she disappeared.

Her media blackout will be destroyed at midnight. Their disinformation campaign will begin flooding the airwaves and internet for forty eight hours. Following that, the outlets would put the brakes on, and dribble conspiracy theories in all directions, but the truth, until they became ridiculous. This would then be bolstered by adding small dots of truth to send the real truth off into mystery land with the reborn Mayans.

Chad had been on the ball. In each of the instances, the sites had been visited by local agents. He'd kept each incident separated so that neither office knew that this was an interstate situation. The reports stated all different looks: the mousy brown hair and burned looking face, the black hair and flat mask, and the platinum blonde hair with the aneme features. But in that last one, the money exchange, the body was reportedly thicker than the other two, with huge breasts and matching butt.

It wasn't as hard to add distraction as it was to delete what you had. She printed the reports out, and laid them side by side. She wanted a profile of this 'too smart' woman thief. Banks, gamblers, money exchange: she wanted cash money. She goes where it is, and knows when to go. That's the amazing thing; she hits at the perfect times. Not one of her crimes would have worked outside of a 60 to 90 minute window; how does she do that? Nothing linked the crime scenes. None of the victims knew each other or were related. Somebody always wound up getting fucked, multiple ways.

In order for her to get anywhere right now, she would have to drive, since flight traffic was still grounded. From Miami, there was only north, west, and money, money. She wasn't fitting into the pattern that everybody else was trying to put her into. Ok, she'd table it.

"Phillip, what do we have on the hotel? What was the old guy's name?"

Phillip went through his note file as did James; James got it this time.

"Victor Stephens, concierge at the North Towne Sheraton."

"We got anybody there yet?"

"Not yet SAC, we relieved the bomb tech that we had. We're awaiting the alternate bomb tech; the guy was partnered with his buddy for fifteen years. He said that they'd been through seventy one detonations together. Then, today they got split up, and his partner bought it. He was gun shy, so we got a replacement for him."

"What's the ETA on the replacement?"

"One sec, Bird1 what's your ETA, ATLHQ's?"

"Ten minutes, SAC."

"Ok, pack to ride. We're going to the Sheraton. We need to check on the room that our John Doe stayed in last night."

"Copy SAC, will meet you at the heliport in 9."

"Copy, SAC out, I'm going to check on the other debriefing."

Kristi walked into the observation room for Thony and Suzan's debriefing. At first, she saw them leaning on each other, obviously, knocked out. It must have been difficult in this Spartan room. The door swung open, four agents came in, and she saw what was about to happen before it actually did, and screamed.

"STOP, DON'T YOU DO THAT!"

But the observation room was soundproof. The first agent crept into the room, the other three came in behind him and closed the door. The first one took the metal platter and slammed it on the metal table. The violent noise shocked Thony and Suzan awake, and knocked them out of their chairs. The other agents surrounded them with menacing looks, trying to intimidate them. She could see a thick book of papers in the hands of the Asian agent, she had seen enough.

They were receiving this treatment because they were listed as her guests, and these agents were subordinates of the SAC that she had de-balled here in Atlanta. If they thought that dealing with his petty attitude was bad, they had no idea; now they had her mad. She walked around the corner and stormed into the interrogation room with her MP5 drawn, and ordered the four agents to the floor. Their expressions were total disbelief; they were caught off guard and unprepared. Kristi wanted to let them know how it felt to have someone in a position to help, turn it into a position of hurt.

"Toss your weapons to me."

Four service 9MM Semi-automatics skittered across the floor. She kicked them to the wall.

"Give the woman those papers."

The Asian handed the papers to Suzan.

"Suzan, Thony, come to me."

Kristi took the papers and looked through them, shaking her head.

"Agents, stand up, line up on the wall, and face me."

They grudgingly stood up, two had pissed on themselves; all were pissed off.

"In case you don't know, my name is SAC Johnson. These people are my guests. I want to know whose idea it was to interrogate my guests instead of the common courtesy debriefing that I ordered? No takers, that's cool."

Kristi tapped her throat mike.

"SAC to 2."

"Go for 2, SAC."

"Chad, record these four names, 1, 2, 3, 4 speak name and agent number."

They recited the information.

"Capsulate and forward to DDI-FBI with comments to follow, Copy, over?"

"Copy, out."

"Agents, I'll call you that for now, I'm not sure how long that will apply. Apparently, you didn't know who I was. Now, I'm afraid it's too late. Abuse of official guests is not tolerated in this bureau. If you didn't get that in your training, now you know. Thony, Suzan destroy those pages. Rip off your signatures and dates, and bring them with you. You're coming with me."

Chapter 52

Dulcet slid into a flesh colored body stocking on top of her slingshot. She had a huge athletic bag with her duct tape, a small. 22 caliber pistol, and a .40 caliber Glock semi-automatic. She still had to get a car so that her personal wheels could stay clean. She slid a Sheraton hotel robe into the bag and put on a light weight raincoat. She cinched the belt and stepped into a pair of black, low top, suede, tennis shoes and was ready to go. She retrieved her car from the self-serve lot and traveled to the industrial area on the west side, using the surface streets. Several constants of industrial areas are: large parking lots, motels, drug activity and prostitution; not so noticeable are the hidden businesses.

With the downturn of the economy, many industrial firms have been forced out of business. The tenants of the big brick buildings were mainly invisible, when they were in operation, up and thriving. So, when they left, the only way to know was the 'for' signs: 'for sale', 'for lease', 'for immediate occupancy, will build to suit'. These huge Islands of plain sight invisibility were perfect for the underground sex industry. Like the undercover mansions of Miami, these areas of Atlanta held their own collection of perversions.

Dulcet, being on her own side of the 'takes one to know one' formula, recognized the scene. There was a large warehouse space, an eclectic collection of cars, leaning towards upscale, and, surprisingly, no semis. Dulcet rode through the parking lot as if it were a dealership; her instincts led her to a classic Datsun Maxima, the box. It was backed in off to the side in the low self-esteem section. Chances were, that the owner couldn't afford to be a regular, but came as often as he could, and stayed until he got put out.

She pulled the Benz three or four slots down from the Maxima. She grabbed her bag in case her intuition was right; it was. The door was unlocked; she looked at the interior it was about a 1982 model. She looked into the ignition and saw a glittering hint of gold (hot damn), a broken key. She pulled the knot loose from her belt and stuck the corner edge into the ignition, and stepped on the clutch. She gave a quick twist and the motor came to life. Dulcet put the stick in first gear and crept out of the lot.

Once she got to the street, she turned on the lights and worked through the gears. The old Maxima had a good engine, unlike the body. Air hissed through the door seams and window edges as she put the car through its paces. Recipe had said that the payroll process was usually complete and the deposit made by 3:30am. It was almost one when she got to the hotel. She parked in the rear parking lot, pulled off the coat, tossed it on the passenger seat, and pulled the bathrobe from the bag.

She stood and stretched, feeling so strange without a disguise on, but so free as the cool night breeze caressed her stocking clad body. She thought about the smiling face that looked like hers on the side of the bus, and the strange feelings went away. She draped the robe over her shoulders, pulled the bag out and walked to the door. She knew the number, as she approached, she pulled the .22 from the bag and crouched by the door, listening. She heard voices and the heavenly purr of a counting machine counting bills.

The first voice she heard was moving, coming towards the door. It sounded like a youngish black man. There were women's voices as well. They sounded farther away. The rules of the urban jungle dictated that the men would protect the money first, then the women. She readied her act; with bag in one hand, and gun in the other, she took several fast breaths and shouted.

"Help, somebody please help me, he's trying to kill me!"

She yelled into the hinge side crack in the door, so that it would be loud and clear in that room, but not in the rest of the rooms. She stayed clear of the peephole, but whimpered up against the door. True to his youth, the man she had heard, unlocked the security chain and opened the door. She dropped her weight against the door, forcing it open and knocking the young man off balance.

Her unseen .22 pressing hard against his heart kept him from sounding an alarm. She kicked the door closed losing the robe in the process, carrying through the charade, she said,

"Oh god, thank you he was going to ..."

Whirling the man around and sticking the gun into his ear she told everybody to

"Freeze! Put your hands in the air and walk over to that wall, NOW!"

They looked at the naked looking white, red haired woman, then, to their little brother, and the men walked towards the wall. Still holding the gun in the young guy's ear, she patted down their waists and underarms. She slid two guns and four cell phones across the room to the door. Altogether, there were three men and two women. She gave the order for them to strip, jamming the gun deeper into the youth's ear, pushing his head roughly. No one here was over thirty five; this youngest maybe twenty. Once they were all naked, she grabbed the tape and wrapped the youngster's arms and wrists behind his back and moved him up against the first woman. She roughly joined them at their waists and chests, locking down her arms at the same time, then she repeated.

The process was complete for three; she forced them down to their knees. The last two included the biggest man and the youngest woman. She reached around her and taped her arms to her side, with the gun at the back of the man's skull. She continued to run the tape catching his left arm against his ribcage. She pulled the tape around his right side, making her second mistake, since tossing the larger guns back into the corner of the room. She missed his arm. Running the tape again around their torsos, then taping their thighs and ankles. She went back for her bag and went to the table to fill it with the money.

Young Reynaldo was hating everything right now. He was blaming himself for this entire thing, because he opened the door. Why did he take off the chain? Now he was taped up behind his sister watching the beautiful naked woman tying and taping up Dexter to their little cousin, damn. It was her first payroll run and only his third. He was so mad that he was shaking. But despite that, his out of control hormones picked that inopportune time to kick in. He started to get hard. What the hell was wrong with him? This was his sister in front of him.

But all his body knew was that it was a hot body in range. She felt him, and he could feel her back stiffen. With her arms taped to her sides, there was nothing they could do. He tried to pull back to keep from making contact with her, but it was no use. His stressed out muscles tired eventually. He relaxed and his body fell forward and penetrated his sister deeply, to his additional shame.

***

Dexter played possum, while he watched the white bitch fill the bag with their money. When she was paying them no attention, he reached back and patted his little cousin to let her know he had a hand free. He looked at the others and mouthed a quick plan to get her, and turned back towards the money, but not before he noticed the look on Reynaldo's face. There was shame and disappointment, something else. His sister was biting her lip with her eyes closed. There was no time to think about that now. He had to try to stop this whore from bankrupting his family.

Gripping his cousins thigh they started a tiny baby step in unison, until she was only about eight feet away. They shuffled faster. Dexter got excited by what he wanted to do to this thief. As soon as they were upon her, she stretched up and over the table to pull the money out of the counter. Dexter ripped the tape from his left arm, at the same time gripping Dulcet by the back of the neck. Dulcet gripped the

.22 and tried to spin, but the big man's body had her pinned against the table. He had his hand on her neck, she tried to get a better grip on the little gun when a huge meaty paw gripped that hand and squeezed. He twisted the gun out of her hand and put it to the back of her head.

"Uh huh bitch, it ain't going down like that tonight. You got down getting this far, but it's the end of that shit now."

Dexter was punctuating his little speech by pushing down with pressure on Dulcet's neck against the table. Raising up on his toes, he used his elbow to slam down on the middle of her back. He knocked the wind from her, and jiggled her thighs against his. He used his knees to spread her thighs open; his ten inch missile was rock hard. He growled into her ear, while he was still smashing her with is elbow. She fully expected to be shot in the back of the head with her own gun.

The recipe run of luck was over once and for all. But what she didn't expect, was this huge black man to break through her sling shot and slam, what felt like an axe handle, up into her pussy.

"How you like that bitch? I'm gonna fuck you, then, I'm gonna kill you. Who the fuck do you think you are? Tryin to rob my family bitch. You wanna take us, you better kill us! Dumb-ass bitch with a double deuce!"

He was steadily fucking her hard and fast while he was talking. Her juices started leaking, despite her wishes. The big black dick she had gripped in Miami, flashed through her mind quickly. Her survival was at stake; she had to think fast. This man was raping her like a $2 hooker. Her face was being pushed across the table with every thrust. She reached her arms out in front of her, her right hand scrabbling into the bag. Under the money, she felt the butt of the Glock. Relief flooded over her, and she allowed herself to have a strong orgasm. She hoped that the squeezing of her tight pussy around his massive dick would make him come too.

"Oh, you like that huh, bitch, too bad. This is the last fuck you're gonna ever get."

She increased the squeezing of her muscles until she felt the pressure ease up off her skull, which was what she was waiting for. His pre-orgasmic distraction gave her time to put her thumb backwards through the trigger guard, pull the Glock out and shoot behind her head four times, deafening in this small room. She felt the big dick fall out of her and the two bodies crashed to the floor. Dulcet turned around to see the holes in her rapists face and chest. She kicked him anyway and blew his huge balls to pieces, catching the girl taped to him in the lower thigh. The threesome were crying and screaming.

"Just take the money leave us be!"

She turned and looked at them, and casually shot them all in the head. The young one underneath the rapist, was still moving. She shot her in the breast and went to the table to finish filling the bag with money. Recovering from flashback mode, she looked at herself in the mirror on the way out. She couldn't believe that man had been inside of her, and she actually had come. She attributed that more to the feeling of the Glock, than the cock. Dulcet noticed blood on her shoulder. She picked up the robe from the Sheraton and wiped it off, realizing that the blood belonged to the rapist.

She tossed the robe, and pulled the heavy bag after her out the door. Window curtains were pulled back; people saw her, and she laughed. She'd be on a boat to Brazil by nightfall, out of this country, and into a new life within 48 hours. She wanted an STD test.

***

Dulcets heavy foot matched up with the Datsun engine and sent her speeding the Maxima back to the Mercedes, she cut the return trip time in half. When she pulled in there was a bewildered looking man in his underwear holding a bundle of clothes in front of him standing by where the car had been parked? Damn, timing is crucial and this little bit wasn't covered by Recipe, she pulled up with the lights in his face, turned on the high beams and blinded him. She stopped, lugged the bag out and dropped it behind the Benz. She walked up to the obviously drunk man with the stains on his briefs, and smashed him in the temple with the Glock. He crumpled like a wet paper bag. She left the scene as it was; backed the Benz out, and squealed rubber getting out of there.

***

The 911 calls were coming fast and furious; every room on the back side of the motel had called, almost at once, followed by the cell calls from the parking lot of a commercial building on Fulton Industrial. The Atlanta police were in full force, passing Dulcet going back towards the motel. She stopped at a light and reached over to put on the raincoat. A trick in the car next to her supposed she must be a good quality hooker to be driving a Mercedes. He flashed a roll of money and pantomimed sucking his dick, then he looked twice and his mouth dropped open, the light changed and she pulled off. Four more police cars sped past her as she approached the city's center, about fifteen more minutes to the north side, a little nap and she'd be out...

Chapter 53

The Blackhawk landed atop the Sheraton. Victor Stephens met them at the roof access door. Like déjà vu, they made their way down the stairs to the suite level and she stopped Victor from using his master key. The bomb tech, in full regalia, brought the puffer and slid its paddle beneath the door. The green light for explosives let them know it was safe around the door. He used the broadcast quality micro camera and the pivoting lamp to detect trip wires attached to the door or in the room. Finding none, they used the pass key to enter the room. The first thing out of place they saw was the collection of hardened, diplomatic cases. There were the disguises laid neatly over the backs of chairs and the sofa: the Arab, the hip-hop hockey jersey, and a priest's cassock.

"This fuckin guy was prepared for a lot of shit, SAC!"

She looked to the bomb tech, grateful that he had come so quickly at the last minute.

"Well, luckily, he wasn't prepared for what we had for him. Phillip, do we have any 411 on the ID for the guy that shot the perp and our guys from Bird 3?"

"No ID yet SAC, but we did get word on how he infiltrated. He was ghosting one of ours, a Personal Protective Operative named Coker. Coker was found dead, bled-out, throat cut in St. Louis. He was on a foot patrol at the landside casino before the Birds landed. Somehow, the bogey wound up on Bird 3 and you know the rest."

"Damn, Phillip, was there anything that could have changed that?"

"We're instituting a full culpability investigation. We should know in a couple of days and changes will be made."

"Categorize this stuff, track the Dip signatures, see where it came in, and where it came from. We need to know if Mr. multitasker is an anomaly, or, if he is part of some non-suicidal sect that we're going to have to worry about."

Kristi punched a button on her wrist and spoke into her personal voice recorder.

"Note to self, create new additions to worst case scenario workup; include the non-suicidal sect theory."

A walkie talkie squawked. The noise was loud and distracting, since the Task Force used earpieces and throat mikes. The walkie was on a National Guard frequency, carried by the task force communications specialist. He was covered with any and every communication device that any first, second or third responder would be using, from walkie talkie cell phones to portable satellite uplinks.

"Come in, all points, multiple homicide, Fulton Industrial area. Checkpoints and curfew crews stay up 'til sunrise. Keep eyes out for white 82 Maxima, suspect armed dangerous. Four dead on scene, one stabilizing, waiting for life flight. Tentative description: white female, long red hair, jewel green eyes, naked, possible bruising from rape; for grid 67A Fox Bravo, contact Whiskey Echo division, over."

"Comms, where is that?"

"About a 30 minute drive, we could get there in about five minutes."

"No we're not going I … I'll wait on some more info on that; as you were, Team. Let's button up this scene and get started tracking these Dip bags. This priority comes from the lofty top of the ladder."

They looked at her and knew she wouldn't joke. The White House was interested in what they had, so they went to task.

"James, keep me posted on what you hear from NGHQ."

"Copy SAC."

James pulled out his Epad and took Comms to the side.

***

She stood and walked through the darkness to the door. Replacing the remote, brought a faint glow from the baseboards all around the theater. Dutchess put her hand on the doorknob, waited, turned the lock, hesitated, and opened the door. Henry fell over backwards. Under different circumstances, it would have been funny. But not now. He found himself looking underneath Dutchess' robe, at her long legs, and the dark junction of her bikini bottoms. He scrambled over on to his knees, then up to his feet. He automatically dropped his head,

"Dutchess, I'm sorry I went off on you without even thinking of discussing this with you first, I..."

"Stop it Henry, now."

She felt the weight of his apology. But she felt that she still had to do this the way she felt it, to ensure that doubt never occurred again,

"Look Henry, I know that they say that you have nobody to blame but yourself when you choose your own poison and get sick and die. But, I refuse to get this far in my life and have anybody attempt to berate or belittle me like a child. I'm a fully grown woman, Henry. I know what I do and I pride myself on not having to lie. I'm not ashamed of anything I've done in my life.

And if you think because of some money, I'm going to change, then I just want you out of here. I want you out of everywhere that constitutes my life, every piece. I don't need you, if you are on someone else's side. Before I hired you, I thought I had Lou. Now, I know I was on my own, and I did pretty damn well. So, if I have to, I'll do it again.

You make up your mind right now. This is your one chance. Either you are in, or you are getting the fuck out of my life all together, now! I don't need this shit, I've got a house; I'll go home, so what Henry: in or out!"

The air surrounding them seemed to turn to ice. Dutchess could almost swear she could see the condensation of her breath. Henry was frozen. The only movement was the steady tracking of tears down his face. Dutchess steely, unwavering glare ate its way through to his soul. He knew he had been wrong to jump to conclusions. But he had no idea how deeply it had hurt her. The words that had come from her mouth, now seemed written in the ice that the air had turned to. They echoed verbally and visually striking him repeatedly.

"I'm...ahem,"

He had to clear his throat in order to speak.

"I'm in Dutchess. For the life of me, if you'll forgive me, I will never betray you Dutchess. I don't know what came over me."

"You lost your god damned mind, Henry. I want you to draw up a nice little addendum to your contract, Henry. Call it a good-faith clause, that will make me rest easy. I'll know that you have to be on my side, and you'll feel better because you'll have faith that I'll tell you everything you need to know, deal?"

"Deal!"

They shook hands, then stood looking into each other's eyes. Dutchess was thinking of all the Hollywood types that had messed up, apologized and put their careers back on track. But since she was not guilty...

"Flash a press release, Henry. Let those people know that I'm suing them for libel and slander. Put the lawsuit together; file it first thing in the morning."

She continued to look Henry in the eye, then turned to walk back into the theater. She stopped, still with her back to Henry, holding the door knob, in a soft voice, with no venom whatsoever, she added,

"I know you want to make love to me, Henry. But that's not something I can let happen between us. If you don't think you can handle that, then, don't worry about the contract. Just keep walking when you get upstairs. I know it's difficult; it's something we both have to learn to handle. If you can, then carry on."

She closed the door silently, with barely a snick of the door mechanism to know that it had closed. Henry rubbed his hand over the ghost image of Dutchess standing there in the doorway, over her ghost breasts down to her ghost thighs. Then, with a long exhale, he went to blast the fax of every word that .Dutchess said to the lawyer. The information was disseminated to the media, wholesalers, and on down the food chain. After an hour between Henry and Pauline, a concise statement was ready and sent to the Associated Press and UPI, to be trickled to all the outlets. The statement established the corroborating evidence that Dutchess Singletary has never been in Springfield, Illinois. A lawsuit has been filed against the Countries Inquisitor for libel and slander for $20 Million dollars. Dutchess would not waste her time commenting for the media, no press conferences will be scheduled. The strategy is to kill the war before the first battle.

***

They lounged back in their foldable recliners, listening to the sizzle of the lamb kabobs on the Hibachi. The stars in the sky twinkled as though it were a show made for them. Ron cradled Sylvania's poor, swollen hand; he had gotten a flexi bandage to wrap it and she said it felt a lot better. He was the official outdoor chef tonight, with the addition of a bottle of wine in the chemical cooler, and a pint of liquor.

The Kabobs were the second course, coming after the barbequed Salmon with rosemary honey sauce. Sylvania was in heaven: at a tiny cheap motel, on lawn chairs, charcoal cooking with the man she loved, in the middle of freeway wilderness.

"Babe?"

"Yeah Ron."

"You're looking kinda content."

"No TV, got my man, thinking about all we've been through in this short time, to be away from everything right now. Yeah, I'm kind of content; you don't seem so bad off yourself, Mr. Master Chef."

"Aw shucks ma'am, it's just a little something I picked up."

They laughed at this attempt at a cowpoke. Looking down, the Kabobs were ready. Ron grabbed a skewer and handed it to Sylvania, the fresh veggies cut in big chunks, divided the lean lamb pieces, and with the barbeque glaze, they were simply wonderful.

Ron was actually impressed that they came out so well; he attributed it to present company. After the late, late night meal, they continued to recline next to each other. The Hibachi had long ago burned out. They were tipping the last of the bottle of Cognac into the plastic steri-cups from the room. They held hands and watched the stars.

Sylvania was content, more so than she had ever been in

her life. If anybody would have told her that this was possible, she would have walked off in another direction, shaking her head. But, this was proof, the way she felt had never led her astray before. With absolutely no words spoken, only light casual touches, they were having deep complex conversations. They discussed the cosmos and the blade of grass directly beneath her chair. Ron saw the fantasy woman he had half-glimpsed at 'Okey Dokeys. She was a fantasy no more; she was real life and really his.

He thought about the old wives tale that told of everybody having a twin on the planet somewhere. Who thought that they would ever meet? You'd think they'd be in Japan or something, not in the same club as you.

They decided to call the cookout a success. They cleaned up the grill, folded and stored the chairs. Then, as if trudging to the car after a perfect and amphitheater concert, they walked into the room. Sylvania had transformed the little cheesy motel room into a cabana-like getaway. The tropical island inspired comforter, the silk cotton blend sheets, the multi-colored scarves covered and colored the lamps, gave a deep burnt-orange and purple glow. Even the tub liner that she had bought, gave the bathroom ambiance, with the only lights coming from the array of candles on every flat surface, 4:00 in the morning. The night was just beginning.

***

"Thank you Major. Oh yes, your information was concise, and will be very helpful. Yes sir, in that event, I'll contact you back and connect you to SAC Johnson."

James had been on the line with National Guard Headquarters for over thirty minutes. He had a small book of data from the Headquarters' Major, regarding their joint investigation with the Atlanta police. The multiple homicide had gone from four dead, two in critical condition, to five dead, one in a coma. The twenty year old girl with the multiple gunshot wounds died within an hour of arriving in ICU at Grady Memorial Hospital. The man from the parking lot with the blunt force trauma was comatose, vital signs weak, but still alive in some other dimension.

The information they received from young Corrida Way far was incredible, added in with the evidence from the scene. One side of the room looked like a mob hit; the other, like a drug deal gone bad. The rapist was easily identified, the bull of a man with the giant remnants of dick and balls, pointed to the obvious perpetrator of the sex crime. The shot to his balls caused the initial injury to the young girl Corrida. A nicked femoral artery, and additional gunshot wounds, lead to her ultimate death. On her death bed, she claimed that Dutchess Singletary killed them.

Of the three executed, the male female pair in the rear, were connected sexually, with the males penis buried in the female when they were shot in the head. This bore the signature of the CP Robber that had been striking across the country. Of course, this was known to the FBI database analysts, but not to general law enforcement. The final piece of evidence, the piece that had James pulling rank to get next to Kristi, was the robe. A plain white terrycloth robe with no logo embroidery was left, ripped, bloodied, and discarded by the door. Inside the robe on the care and maintenance tag, was a small fabric tag that said, 'thou shalt not steal; property of North Pointe Sheraton'. Kristi received the information from James and tingles began to prickle all over her scalp, not only the obvious clue of the robe.

"James, bring in Comps."

Bradley "Comps" Haringden, was the computer expert; he was also a walking datacenter. What Comms was to voice, Comps was to everything else.

"Comps, I need a secure line to base."

"No problem."

He floated to the ground like a Buddhist monk and hit a switch on the inseam of his TAC jacket. Then, he pulled out a slim line notebook computer. The first switch created an NSA approved secure hotspot. He plugged in protocols to connect to #2 in Maryland. Within two minutes, Kristi had a two-way, multi-media, secure connection.

"Chad, bring up that file on the CPR. Now, query Dutchess Singletary. Ok, Tennis Open Atlanta, tournament Miami/CPR, Springfield, Daytona, Miami, Dutchess, Coke contract, new digs at X for Tennis star.

"Ok Chad, how old is the news?"

"According to these stamps, the X hotel and the Inquisitor, the first ones not out yet, the second is in limited print."

"Pull that up for me, you added all these to the file right?"

"Which file SAC?"

"CPR."

"Oh ok, adding now."

Sometimes Kristi had to remember Chad was really a glorified seat warmer for her, but he did learn fast.

"So, this reported sighting was in Springfield, the same place we picked up our guests, circles within circles."

"We also have eyewitness statements from tenants of the rooms surrounding the shots. They stated that the woman had long, red, hair, looked white, got into a white Maxima, and had a super, large, athletic bag', is how they described it. It had logo patches all over, with main colors black, blue, and red."

"And the woman that died said it was Dutchess Singletary. What does she have to say about that?"

"There was a 'ding' just got something new 'ding ding ding ding,' something is going on with this search SAC, let me toggle over. AP wire has a story, 'Dutchess tells Inqisitor to stuff it, it wasn't me, sues tabloid for $20 million'. Well, SAC, I guess that answered that question. I'm looking at 25 hits so far and building, this must have just gone out."

"Ok Chad, I think we got work to do, but something stinks, I'm out 2."

"I'm here 1."

"Comms, find me the X hotel, contact Duchess Singletary."

"Roger SAC."

"Phillip, get me the front desk."

"Front desk, this is Michael. What, I mean, how can I be of assistance?"

Kristi thought, this guy didn't value his job at all, maybe it's the third shift thing.

"Michael, this is Special Agent Johnson, from the FBI. I have a need to know if there is a Dutchess Singletary staying here in the hotel?"

"Dutchess, the tennis girl? Why would she be at this dump? Didn't she just get a bunch of money from Coke? Well, if it were me, I wouldn't , wait a minute, I'm looking at a two-door Mercedes, pulling into the self-serve lot right now. There is a white woman or a really light-skinned woman parking, getting out. Oh shit."

"Excuse me, sir?"

"Oh, I'm sorry. This lady is in a raincoat, its open, and she looks naked. Well, fuck mee."

"Sir, do you know you are on the telephone with a Federal…"

"Lady, shut up, it's Dutchess. How the hell did you know? This is crazy as hell."

"Does she have a bag with her?"

"Yeah, couple a handles, looks heavy."

"Stall her, I'll be down as soon as the elevator will get me there. Say nothing, Michael about my presence. I can lose you in a federal prison, sir, for the rest of your natural life."

She hung up. Michael looked at the phone like the woman could see him clearly. He hung up and thought about it. "Hell, it couldn't be a bad gig, chattin up a rich, freaky broad. Shit, I might get laid."

Dulcet was dragging the heavy bag. By the time she got to the carport door, she realized she didn't have a key. She patted all of her pockets, and all she had was the one Mercedes key and the Glock. The credit card type key probably flew out in one of the cars. She pushed the button marked after hours; a sleepy sounding man answered and pushed a buzzer. The door lock disengaged.

She tossed the bag inside the door and followed. Right by the door, she saw a tall, golden, luggage cart with, the Sheraton logo all over. She hoisted the bag onto the cart and rolled it, much better. Now, she needed the front desk to give her a duplicate key.

Chapter 54

The royal blue tennis shoes were jumbled on top of the apple booty pants. The thong and matching bra were spaced erratically on the way to the candle lit bathroom. Ron lay on his side with Sylvania wedged into the standard sized bathtub. They soaked in the still-hot water, splashing from wet areas to places that would never get wet without help. The candles and their constantly flickering lights and shadows made for such a romantic atmosphere. They kissed long and in all the places on each other that couldn't kiss back: eyes, chins, cheeks, foreheads, necks, and throats.

They kissed, licked, and loved in every way, but sex. They rolled next to, around, on top of, and beneath each other, through three full tubs of hot water. At one point, standing and covering each other from head to toe in baby oil. They rubbed into every nook and cranny, then, went back to the hot soaking water. They timed their exit with the sputtering, guttering out of the candles. This was the cue to leave the candles and go to the redesigned bedroom. Ron carried Sylvania, still dripping oily water along the towel strewn walkway, to the bed.

He laid her on the crisp new sheets. They basked in each other's arms until they had dried off between the sheets and the comforter. Their bodies were hungry for each other, but, the soaking waters and oil, the good food and liquor combined, made them sleepy. As the twilight feeling of sleep claimed them both, Ron rolled over above Sylvania, perfectly fitting between her thighs.

***

Four members of the team took the diplomatic bags up the stairs and loaded the shrink-wrapped containers into the Blackhawk. They tucked them into the cargo bins against the back wall, then climbed aboard and awaited orders for Bird1 to hop to the pavement, if need be. Kristi, the other four men, Thony and Suzan were on the elevator. As they arrived at lobby level, they dispersed throughout the shadows, behind sofas, and huge potted trees. Thony and Suzan were amazed that they had disappeared like magic. They knew that they were there, and still couldn't see them. They had been instructed to walk through the lobby, arm in arm, straight out the front door. The attention that they would draw would give the team the advantage of being able to take a picture, to get a positive ID on the perp.

They were nervous; they knew that they were not even supposed to be here. So, they made the best of the fact that they had no other way home. They trusted this woman, Kristi Johnson. She had gone against her own for them, when her team was wrong. She had done them wrong, but now, they understood why. The terrorist that looked like Thony was much, too much, too close for comfort. Now, it seemed to be happening again; the woman that she saw winning the tournament in Florida, could never have done what Kristi said.

Kristi disappeared. They were on their own, walking through the lobby. They heard a cart coming around the corner from that hallway. It was the woman with the red hair and the open raincoat. She looked as if she was naked, pulling the cart with one big bag on it. It was covered in logos and tri-colored, red, black, and blue. They kept walking, visually acknowledging the red haired lady. They stared at her, because she did look just like Dutchess Singletary. As instructed, they kept walking through the lobby to the front door.

The woman went to the front desk to speak to the light-skinned registration agent. He was, also, not aware that five tactical killers were in his lobby, with targeted sub-machine guns, aimed at various points of the perps body.

They used their throat mikes to do inventory:

"5, I got left thigh."

"4, I've got right."

"3, I've got right shoulder."

"2, I've got left shoulder."

"This is 1,"

Kristi said,

"I've got the head shot."

Michael was taking his time making her key to the point that he messed up the first two. Not being the typical registration agent, his customer service skills left much to be desired. As concierge, he was aloof and slightly condescending. Obsequious behavior was a class that he slept through. So, he felt stressed; he began to sweat. His hairline, nose and upper lip were all dead giveaway areas. She already felt the animal desire to flee, but acquiescing to the post-murder need to take a nap, Dulcet was on edge. Her hand slid unconsciously into her coat pocket. She lounged against the counter to shield her right arm while her left one reached up to caress her right nipple to hardness. Without a word, she looked at his name tag, it read Michael. She offered him a nipple.

The fool leaned forward to try to put the admittedly irresistible nipple into his sleep-deprived mouth. She moved lightning quick, wrapped his tie in her fist, and dragged him a quarter of the way across the desk. She put the Glock to his temple and slowly asked.

"Why are you so nervous? Is there something I need to know?"

Michael could have been a man about it, but with the advent of the gun to his head, all manly thoughts or actions went out the window.

"Yes, yes."

***

Ron felt his naked tip flirting with her wet, naked lips. The throbbing caused him to paint moisture up and down her more than ready sex. He lay at the gate to Sylvania's heaven, with her eyes closed and the sensuous look on her lips. She looked so sexy, so lovely, yet, thoughtful too. Then, all the deep-thought wrinkles left her face. She had made a decision; she felt Ron's head slip across her sweet spot, and before he could slide away again, she whispered.

"Yes, yes."

She thrust her hips up, sliding the first raw inches inside of her. Ron moaned and licked her mouth open into a kiss. He stuck his tongue into her mouth, and pushed himself deep into her to the root. This was very much like the first, and only, time that he had been inside Sylvania unprotected. She started to tremble from the first deep plunge. He pulled out before the sensation could take him over. Her first orgasm was intense, but not breathtaking. He stroked back into her deeply, fully covered in a layer of her creamy lubrication. He knew that he wouldn't be pulling out anymore. Their rhythm was slow, feeling everything for the first time all over again. Sylvania's orgasms were coming regularly, every few strokes. His angle on her clit was perfect. It was like she was following a map, taking progressively bigger and bigger streets on her way to the highway. She felt the big one was near. She wanted it with Ron. He felt so good on top of her, inside of her. She tested Ron's position; she started to roll to the right and he let her get on top.

***

Dutchess awoke with a start, she had no idea where she was; she analyzed her situation. She was fully reclined in a large plush chair with both her legs draped over the arms.

One hand was in her bikini bottoms, holding herself, with one breast hanging out of her top. Now, it came to her why it was so dark; she was in the theater of her house. She must have fallen asleep, but what the hell was she dreaming about. Or who?

Dutchess sat up in the recliner and spied the glowing remote. She hit the projector power. Thankfully, it had to warm up as her eyes had to adjust. The channel was still on the outside of the door. The area was empty. Dutchess now had the hang of it; the input channels were for monitoring the security system. She clicked through them, saw that Max was still awake and on the prowl. Henry was tucked in on a sofa,   knocked   out.

Chapter 55

Dutchess wanted a piece of fruit. She turned the projector off and replaced the remote into, what she now knew, its charger. She proceeded into the hallway and upstairs to the kitchen. She found the same type of fruits and veggies that were on the bus. She plucked a bunch of grapes and washed them in hot water to take the chill off, but left them nice and chilly in the center. She saw a few sheets of paper on the butcher block table with the knife rack built in; they were press releases. She read them and realized that Henry had done his job, all the way to the $20 Million lawsuit, which was inspired by Pauline. Things felt better again, but, there was still a nagging feeling, something.

***

The intake process at the Fulton County Detention facility has been known to take two days, or more, to get an individual identified, booked, fingerprinted, fed, medically checked, etc. At some point, midway through the process, you were informed of your bond amount. This amount can be posted in full or backed by property, to ensure that you would come back to court. Or, you could give a bail bondsman a non-refundable 10% for the pleasure of him hunting you down like an animal if you don't show for court. Sylvia finally got a bond amount, because she had a briefcase full of garbage diamonds, barely worth $100,000 altogether. She was charged with burglary and given a $50,000 bond.

She had been here all day and night. Now, the sun was running back around. The plastic bag of juice that they had given her wasn't cold anymore, therefore, it did her jaw no good. That bitch that hit her, she could have been her. She was with the guy from the mall. What the fuck was that all about? That was a question for another day though. Today, she had to get the hell out of here.   She was given her chance to use the phone; she called $ensation's house. The phone rang and rang, she let it continue. After the third ring, if nobody was home, it would start to ring numbers down a list, until it rang a number with a person.   After fourteen rings, someone answered.

"Hello, who the fuck is this?"

"This is Fantasia. Beeny, is that you?'

"Naw, hold on Yo, Bee, phone, dog; it's that American Idol baby-mamma broad."

"Hello, Taisa?"

"Beeny, baby, and damn, I'm glad to hear your voice."

"What's up ma, you straight?"

"No Been, I'm not. I'm in the Fulton County jail on some bullshit. I need $50 large to walk out. and I'm gonna probably need a car and a pack of Newports."

"Cool babe, I got all that. I'll get the 'ports in route to get you. Sit tight, I'm on my way."

Sylvia was glad that she had given Beeny some pussy now. There was nothing more dependable than a pussy-whipped man, especially one that wasn't easily whipped. She sat back and drank the little bag of juice. She was tired, but she would be damned if she was going to close her eyes in this place. Two hungry-looking women sat on the permanently mounted hard plastic chairs right in front of her. The female holding cells were not big enough to hold all of the women that they had arrested. So, there were about twenty three sitting out here. The outfit alone that Sylvia had on could have paid the bond for half of them. She felt so out of place here, being well dressed with class, sitting with the streetwalkers and the smelly crack-heads. The drunk white women had separated themselves into a section with the crystal meth whores; they all looked at her like she had called 911 on them.

One drunk white woman complained of the same thing Sylvia was thinking.

"Hey, hey you, with the badge, aint'cha gotta private room? These bitches stink, they're, uugh, they're makin me sick; I think I'm gonna hurl!"

She had to be about 45, matronly looking. Another time and place, she could have easily been a school bus driver, but not here and now. In response to her outburst and abrupt standing and lurching across the room, a red dot appeared above the nipple of her braless right breast. The next thing heard was the zap crackle of a Taser gun. The sound was followed by the thump of her body collapsing, and spazzing out on the floor, in a pool of vomit and urine. Sylvia kept her mouth shut.

***

With his assistance, under protest, trying as he could not to be strangled by his own tie, Michael was yanked over the registration desk.

He now stood eye to eye with Dulcet. Michael saw a deep hollow at the bottom of those incredible emerald eyes. He had no doubt that she would shoot him. He couldn't name it, but he could smell the recent use coming from the barrel that was pressed just below his nose.

"Ok, yes man. What is it that I need to know? Hmmm?"

"J, J, J, John, Johnson, Mmm Miss Johnson wants to see you".

It was the truest thing he knew to say, but it meant nothing to either one of them because Kristi hadn't told him anything for this very reason.

"This is SAC, go to target package 2, repeat target package two, acknowledge when on station over."

"5 on target, 4, on target, 3 on target, 2 on target, copy, SAC on target, stand by."

The target 'package' had been pulled in from extremities to

kill zones. Lowers were brought up to abdominals, uppers were brought down to heart and lungs. Kristi kept the head shot, but she adjusted down to a throat shot for facial evidence preservation.

"Who the fuck is Miss Johnson, Michael?"

She spat his name out as if it were something foul in her mouth,

"Where is she? And why does she want to see me so much?"

"I believe she's a fan."

The look Dulcet gave him was a blank stare. There was no recognition in it at all; then, she thought about the bus.

"Oh yeah, yeah, well, I'm not entertaining autographs right now. Where's my fucking key? Now, I've got to get my shit and flee, thanks to you mister fucking Michael."

"It, it's in the machine, right here."

He went to reach for the key and his face disappeared.

"Oh shit, dumb ass, why'd you move?"

She asked the slowly falling corpse.

"Freeze, drop the gun and live! Put your hands on top of your head!"

Dulcet tried to determine where the female's voice had come from, but the acoustics in the lobby made the echoes come from odd angles. She saw a shadow in the area she thought the voice had come from, she whirled and shot.

***

Sylvania grabbed Ron's face in both hands, continuing the kiss while the rest of her body was riding Ron smoothly. This feeling was unlike anything that she had felt before with any of her other lovers. She could feel his shaft begin to swell inside of her, she wrapped her arms around his neck as the massive orgasm she had been expecting hit, hard, jerking her body. Ron reached around behind her, gripping her shoulders in his hands and rolling back to the left onto their sides and slammed through Sylvania's tightly spasming orgasm, triggering his own. His whole body convulsed, pulling himself deeper than he had ever known inside Sylvania and he came thunderously. He caused her orgasm to peak over the top, with throb after throb into Sylvania's hungry womb. This drew out more and more of his essence.

***

Calmly, Kristi opened her connection and whispered one word

"Go,"

A fraction of a second later, fifteen .223 caliber rounds closed the distance to the registration desk, before Michael Robinson's body could hit the floor. The highly effective three round bursts from the five MP5's destroyed their targets, respectively and effectively. With the least amount of damage to the hotels infrastructure, the woman was destroyed. Thony and Suzan stood outside the front door and watched through the glass, as the red-headed woman shot the man behind the reservation desk.

Then, the licks of fire came from the dark end of the lobby. The last thing that they saw was the woman's coat flying open, her body was bouncing off the registration desk, as she landed on her face across the luggage cart, obviously dead. The five black, clad, Task Force members including, Kristi, walked towards the target. Their MP5's were aimed at her. There was no need, of course, but it was standard operating procedure. The bag was blood-splattered from the body draped over the top of it. Kristi radioed to the federal building for a CSU/CSI team. She then called the Blackhawk down from the roof, as Thony and Suzan stared back into the lobby.

Chapter 56

She just didn't feel right. She ate another grape, still looking at the papers on the chunky blonde wood table, when she felt pain, sharp pains all over her torso and her throat. Her body was rocked; she screamed out then collapsed over top of the low table. Max heard the scream and came on the run to the kitchen. Henry was slower to react, but still, he was right behind him.

They found Dutchess slumped over the butcher block table moaning, as if in pain. Max gingerly lifted Dutchess from the table, looking for any signs of blood or injury. There was nothing marking the pristine white robe. Max .stood her up, taking all of her weight; he lifted her and carried her to her bedroom. Henry turned on the lights as Max was laying her down, opening the robe. Max and Henry stared, open mouthed, in awe.

***

Beeny left the Cutt house, his boy's house of ill repute. There were stripper poles built into all the bedrooms. The central bar around every corner. It was way, way past a bachelor pad; it was a sleeper spot, really. The basement was a huge club that had been rented to the student union of one of the largest black colleges in the south. The women were phenomenal; having a club in the basement was like a dream come true, when you didn't even know you had been dreaming.

Upstairs was off limits to the club goers. But, of course, the owners could go wherever they chose. There was video coverage of every inch of the club, so they could see if there was any new 'talent' they may want to audition. One of his boys actually did own a legit strip club; another shot porn. Having a sister in the business the way that $ensation was, left no doubt that the different aspects of the life, the game, the entourage, the groupies, would always be there. He'd chosen his friends long ago, and had kept them.

He had heard somewhere along the way, that you can never make new, old friends, how true that was. Beeny was on his way out to meet with one of those old friends right now. He tried valiantly to leave the house. They had been watching the big screen, looking at the talent downstairs, and had seen some late teen wet dreams. A couple members of the official Cutthouse, The Cutt Club had the baby face syndrome, they were official scouts.

One of those scouts was exiting the elevator with four of those wet dreams. They were already half naked when they came to the club. He had convinced them to take off the little clothes that they had on in the elevator. The T-bar G-strings and tiny bras were all that the foursome was wearing. They looked drunk and were fondling the clothes that they were carrying, as if they had all taken X pills, the love drug. Watching the young girls walk, he knew that there was going to be a battle in here tonight. These thick, fit eighteen and nineteen year old women were no joke. He expected to see some broken furniture when he got back.

Beeny had to run by the house before he could go get Fantasia out of the Fulton County jail. First, he needed to get some cash. Once at the house, he went into the bus garage. The structure was built for housing, maintenance and repair. He walked down a set of shop stairs to the lower floor, then, to a manhole cover with a five step ladder. This led to one of the many tunnels underneath the property. The family vault was down this tunnel. He entered into the main room; each sibling had their own room in the vault, he went into his.

The system greeted him and asked for a sample. He spat into a small tube. His DNA was checked, and a door opened in the wall. He went in and collected ten bundles and retreated. He jumped back into is newly painted Acura NSX, and rolled out to his boy, Jesse's house. Beeny and Jess had been friends since elementary school. Jess would have the Newports. Beeny text paged his sister.

"Hey 'Sashe, you got a flick of Fantasia? She needs some squares and I'm on my way to JJ."

"Ok yeah, use this one."

"Thanks sis, you cool?"

"You know me, shaking this ass, making this cash."

"Yeah, you alright, I'll holla atcha later, ok?"

"Ok Beeny, go take care of our girl, with her old scandalous ass."

Jesse lived on family land in College park as well; he was on the other side of the semi-rural city. His people had been cowboys, and they still kept horses and participated in Rodeos to this day. He had always been the artsy one, like Beeny; Jess had been the techie, so he was a natural for the 'Newports'.

That was a code they used. It wasn't for the familiar green and white pack of cigarettes. It stood for a new identity package: driver's license, voter registration card, social security number/ card, passport, two major credit cards, universal insurance card and as many kids as you wanted, were optionally available. The package cost $15,000, which included a payment history on the credit cards and a personal line of credit. Beeny figured that he would skip the kids; it wasn't the extra five grand, he figured she wouldn't need the extra right now.

The distinctive sound of the Honda 'baby Ferrari' engine meant Beeny never had to ring a doorbell to announce himself. He pressed 'send' on his phone, as he pulled up, shooting the picture to Jesse's computer, along with a separate file with her description. He plucked two bundles from the floor and stepped into Jesse's spread. True to his ancestry, Jesse liked Ranch living. His personal place was single level, and went on forever. He had multiple kitchens, bathrooms were everywhere you looked. Each was designed differently; he said that was to remind you 'you are here'. Beeny had lost count of the number of bedrooms and studios. He was never surprised to see a new room or newly broken ground for another extension.

The only place not on the same level was the workshop. It was built below the master bedroom. Jesse had gotten Beeny to hook up his video surveillance and alarm systems, but his best defense was his crew of Neapolitan Mastiffs. He bred the giant, French, war dogs for protection, and to help herd the horses. They walked through the sprawling residence to the bedroom, stepped around the dogs guarding the closet, and went down to the workshop. Beeny had given him enough information to start a template. He pulled up the received file, inserted the picture, and description. On the short side of thirty minutes, they were on their way back to Beeny's car, with the Newport pack of suitably worn documents. The passport was stamped for ins- and outs from five different countries. He had made arrangements for a mid-level Lexus to be waiting in a parking lot downtown. Now, to collect Fantasia.

As Beeny was turning into the Fulton County Rice Street facility, he realized that he didn't know her real name.

***

The first rays of the new day were making their way across the sill of the eastward facing widow. The birds were performing their serenade, and for some reason inside this customized $32 a day motel room, the world felt right. Ron and Sylvania were wrapped up into each other like one brand new creature, one's part indistinguishable from the other.

"Ron, baby?"

"Um hum."

"You awake?"

663

He flexed deep inside of her to answer. She ran her hands slowly up and down his back and strong arms, feeling the boiled-in baby oil that caused the slippery friction between them.

"Ron you're not going to try to run away and leave me, are you?"

"Nope."

Seeing how he wanted to do the communication thing, she squeezed her inner muscles, and pulled back sliding him halfway from her. That caused his eyes to open, as he pushed back in to where he was,

"And what do you call yourself doing, Mister?"

"Marinating."

"Marinating? What, are you about to cook me? Stew me up like a fricassee?"

"No I'm not stewing in the pot; I'm thinking about baking in the oven."

"It's too hot for baking Ron... wait a minute, you trying to make buns on purpose.

Ron?"

She sounded incredulous, did he really think. Who said she wanted...

"Ron, did you think it was worth asking me first."

"We talked about it all night, remember? Out on the lounge chairs, in the tub, while I carried you to the bed. It's not a decision I made lightly nor was it one I made alone, was it?"

"No baby, it wasn't. But, can we make it plain; put our cards on the table, and tell it like it t-i-is."

Ron laughed, his muscles causing shock waves throughout Sylvania.

"That's old school there babe. Now you're talking like Betty Wright, Sylvania Collins. I want you to be the mother of my children, all of my children. Do you wanna? Are you willing?"

"Yes Ron, I'm willing, but only if you're staying, I don't want to do this on my own…"

"You just try it, no, on second thought, don't try it."

She reached through their tangled up bodies and kissed him passionately.

"So, are we going to live here or what?"

"Well, I do like what you've done with the place, but we may need a bit more room."

"Yeah, I guess you're right."

"You feel pregnant yet?"

"Uuummm, nope, not yet."

"You willing?"

"Yep, you able?"

"Yep."

"Nice to meet you, Mr. Able."

That sent Sylvania into a little giggle fit, that turned to moans, as Ron began to make love to her again…

Chapter 57

The loud abrasive noises sped through midtown Atlanta, on their way north. Every block that they passed was a universal wakeup call, made all the more significant by their recent absence. Police sirens, the military moving in don't need sirens; so the sounds of sirens must be significant. This was the first sign that the threat level was no longer RED. The next sign was the crowd of media surrounding the Sheraton North Towne.

The black clad figures, eight across, were blocking the front door access. The hotel was shut tight. All of the guests had received wakeup calls informing them not to leave their rooms until further notice, by order of the Atlanta police. Kristi didn't do media. She had noticed the growing mass congregating outside; she faded back to the murder scene.

She knew Thony and Suzan were still out front. But in their civilian clothes, they didn't stand out as anyone of particular interest. She would grab them up and get them out of here when the time was right.

For now, the techs were clearing the scene. Photos had

been taken; both bodies were bagged and on their way to the loading dock, where the unmarked federal morgue wagon waited. They would be transported to the Federal building for further processing. Comms had contacted the X hotel, but there was no way the Concierge, front desk, or even the manager, was going to get him through to Dutchess, so Comms went through other routes. Eventually, he got the contact number for her manager, Henry. By that time they were in mission mode. Once the perp was down, Comms continued on his last mission.

"Yes Sir, this is Bradley Harrington, Agent, Homeland Security Special Projects. You are the manager for one, Dutchess Singletary, tennis player, correct? And, do you currently know her whereabouts. Thank you sir, if need be, we will be in touch. Thank you."

Comms left his post at the front door, and the other seven filled in his spot. He found SAC Johnson at the kill scene.

"SAC, new Intel."

"Go Comms, what ya got?"

"I spoke to Dutchess Singletary's manager. He informed me that she is currently, and has been, in her home at the top of the X hotel. I told him that we would be in touch if we needed to speak to him or her further."

"Good work, Comms. Text my phone with the number. If what Chad told me was going National in the tabloids, she may need a call really bad."

"It's done SAC. The locals are here, they are working traffic and stacking up crowd control."

"Ok, get me two local agents, briefed and conversant with

media relations. Let them interface with the cops, as the cops come in, file our guys out and we can fly. The new SAC should be here to make his replacement announcement."

"Atlanta has a new SAC? When did that happen?"

"It's not out yet. I got a pre-heads up from the DDI. In about an hour, he'll get the news."

"Damn, copy that SAC."

He left to rejoin his post until the police replacements found their way in.

"Phillip, what's the status?"

"Cleaners are done with the first room; almost done with hers, two minutes, we were never here."

"Copy that Phillip, let's get our guests and get the hell outta here."

"Copy that SAC."

With almost balletic precision, the police officers replaced the larger black clad Task Force operators, creating the human media screen. The black line moved to the loading dock, and around the side of the building with a bulge in the line that contained National Treasure, Kristi Johnson. Thony and Suzan stood in front of the Sheraton's front door, doing their best looky-loo act, trying to see through the big, black, clad soldiers.

The media was stacking up behind them, jockeying for position to get the first coverage. When asked if they had seen anything, they pled ignorance of everything; it worked like a charm. When the police officers began replacing the Task Force, they started to automatically back away from the window. Photographers and reporters greedily filled in their vacated space.

They heard the Blackhawks rotor start to cycle up, and knew that it wouldn't be long. Then they saw the first of the Task Force come around the corner of the building. They quickly stepped towards the helicopter, as soon as they caught Kristi's hand gesture. Before one question could be asked, the Task Force, plus two civilians, took to the sky headed, for St. Louis.

Kristi pulled her scrambled SATAC phone and dialed the private number to her boss.

"FBI, how may I help you?"

It always amazed her how he answered the phone like a mailroom clerk; he said it was operational security.

"Hey boss, Johnson, I'm coming in."

"You in D.C.?"

"No, I'm just getting up over Atlanta. I had a nagging feeling that turned out to be true."

She told him the whole chain of events regarding the CPR, except, of course, how the after thoughts made her feel,

"So, ya wiped two more off of the illustrious list, huh?"

"Excuse me? Oh, yeah, I guess I did, huh? Just doing my job, boss."

"Are you sure you're not trying to get mine?"

"I can't do your job; the job I have is the job that I do well. I love my team, and I'm well compensated. I'm cool."

"Ok. But, whenever I leave this desk, I want to see you here, you got that?"

"Don't leave too soon, ok?"

"You got it."

"Is there anything else I should know?"

"Yeah, I left agents from the Atlanta office to do the mop up at the Sheraton. According to Bombs, the bag she had was device-free, and full of cash. Everything points to the Way Far grocery payroll robbery. I wanted to make sure something is done for that family. Rush the evidence process, start a memorial fund, something. After all, if it weren't for that youngest girl's death confession, we never would have caught her."

"But, had it not been for her relative raping the perp, they wouldn't be dead, according to her pattern."

"Touché boss, but the dead are all innocent, right? Can we sterilize those points from the media as well? Let's see, that's IA on ATL money, mem fnd for fam, got payroll, scrub media, is that it?"

"Outside of the charges against the four agents that tortured and intimidated my guests, and the SAC that put them up to it, my guests want to press charges, fully. But yes, I think that may be all."

Kristi hung up and looked to Thony and Suzan.

"I'm sure there is something that I'm going to have to do for you two. I've put you in harm's way repeatedly, because I didn't want to let you out of my sight. Then, you see what happened when you got away. As you heard, I told my boss that on your behalf, charges will be brought against the agents that treated you like criminals, as well as their boss.

Hopefully, your lives can get back to normal as soon as possible, though the base of your debrief is true. Nothing can be spoken of to anyone regarding me, the tactical team, our weapons, nothing. Officially, we don't exist. I do, but we don't. You understand?"

"Yes."

They said in unison. Kristi pulled out a note pad and jotted down a couple of sentences. She handed the pad to Thony, he read it.

"I have been fully debriefed by SAC Kristi Johnson. I understand the secrecy rules, and will not violate them, under penalty of life imprisonment."

There were two lines for signing and dating, Thony did, then Suzan did. They handed the pad back to Kristi. She signed and dated the page and handed the pad to Phillip, who scanned it and sent the encrypted file to Kristi's computer back in Maryland.

"We are going to drop you back off at the building known as your residence, Suzan. Do you have rooftop access?"

"Yes, I'm pretty sure. I've been up on the roof before."

"Good. I do want to make sure that I thank you for your assistance back there at the hotel. That one moment of distraction allowed our Photo analyst to get a positive ID from the scene, that she was the target."

Suzan hugged up next to Thony. She had an immense respect for Kristi Johnson. The concentrated time that she had been forced to spend in her company, allowed her to see parts of her that she knew she would not have ever believed existed on the first day they had met.

"Hey, I'm, uh sorry about the things I said, you know, back in Springfield."

"Don't be, I agree with you whole heartedly."

This comment drew surreptitious glances from the team members that had been on the Snare teams, as well as Phillip and James,

"I've got to find time to revisit who I am, the fact that I could have made such a huge mistake. Had your woman not loved you so much, Thony. That was a wakeup call for me. I'm going to try my damnest to take some time off, not think about the job for a while, and see what happens."

"I think that's a good idea. I haven't wanted to get between you two. I feared I might become psychically damaged, with all that energy flowing around you guys and all."

They looked at Thony, and then shared a look, reaching fists out towards each other. Susan's manicure was still fresh; Kristi's nails were cut down to the finger tips, and they bumped knuckles.

"It's all good and can only get better."

Thony watched the girl-power bonding in action. He had a feeling that no matter where they were in life, Kristi Johnson was going to be a part of them. They rocketed towards the Northwest, towards St. Louis, towards home.

Chapter 58

There were violent red marks on Dutchess' stomach, ribcage, and throat. They could see the red marks bleeding through from beneath her bikini top on the left. Her breathing was erratic, and she was still unconscious. Max was worried, he hadn't heard anything. Were the grapes poisoned, what could have happened so catastrophic on his watch?

"Henry, do you know of any allergies that could do this?"

"Shit, shit should I call 911 Max? What do you think?"

"I'm not thinking right now, Henry."

Henry watched Max take in what seemed like all the air in the room and hold it, then let it out slow. The exhale must have taken over a minute and a half; then he was calm.

"I was reacting and you're not helping Henry, control yourself, your panic is contagious. Take a deep breath."

Henry tried to control his breathing while Max looked closer at the bruises on Dutchess' stomach. He did not need to pull her bra top to the side, that bruise looked like the others. A large deep, red center with concentric rings of lighter red, rippling outward. Some had two or three center points with the same bruising effect. The bruising spread subcutaneously on her light skin, making her look like one big bag of bruise.

Henry saw this latest development and instead of getting the calming benefits of deep breathing, he did just the opposite: he began hyperventilating. Max spun Henry around and grabbed him in a Heimlich maneuver and pushed in on his solar plexus, squeezed all of the air out of him. This got the desired result; Henry took the deep cleansing breath, that clicked the switch in his brain, and calmed him down immediately. With Henry fixed, they both looked at Dutchess. The bruises that had been spreading red a moment ago, were turning yellow at the edges, and rebounding back in towards the middle. The bruises were retreating. Anyone who would have walked in on this scene would have seen two perverted men, ogling a young sleeping woman on her back, robe flung open, in her bra and panties.

What it actually was; was two caretakers in awe, once again staring at their charge as she went through a strange metamorphosis. Henry's phone rang, automatically he answered.

"Yes? Yes...yes right here with me, ok."

He hung up the phone still staring at Dutchess. The violent red marks were now pinpricks. As they watched, one by one they too disappeared. Dutchess began to moan, she was coming around. Henry pulled her robe around her, and sat on the bed next to her head. When she fully regained consciousness, and tried to sit up, Henry held her gently by the shoulders, and urged her to stay down.

"Henry, Max, what happened?"

"We don't know Dutchess. But it was something weird, what do you remember?"

"I was eating some grapes in the kitchen, and I felt the most incredible pain all over my body, all at the same time, uhahem,"

Clearing her throat,

"My throat still feels kind of sore."

Henry could see a slight redness remained there, as he lifted her chin to take a look...that last redness went away too.

"How did I get in here?"

"Max found you slumped over the butchers block. He picked you up and carried you in. Dutchess, you had huge red marks almost like hornet stings all over the center of your body."

Subconsciously, she looked inside her robe to make sure she still had her clothes on. It was a reflex, and she knew that she had to trust these two men with her life, so she might as well start now.

"Oh, no, no Dutchess, nothing like that, your abs, all over your body was covered in red angry bruises, right Max?"

"Yes sir, Henry, then they all disappeared. I've never seen anything like it in my life. How do you feel?"

"I'm ok Max, it's just, and I can't explain it. I have a headache, but it's unlike any I've had before."

Get some rest Dutchess, we'll get to the bottom of this, if there is a bottom to get to."

Max turned and walked back out to the porch and pulled out his tiny phone. Henry was holding Dutchess' hand, making sure she was really ok. He noticed how she caressed his hand, as she reassured him that her body was fine. Her comment from earlier came back to him, as she was walking back into the theater after dissing him.

She had spoken of how she knew that he wanted her. She had said that it was something they would both have to learn to handle. So, she had some uncontrollable feelings for Henry too. He pushed these thoughts away. Those little bratty Henry's were still in the background, begging to get fed.

Max came slowly into the room, knocking on the door while still slowly walking. After he crossed over the threshold, he stopped.

"Henry, let me see you real quick."

Henry saw the haunted look on Max's face and said no words. He patted Dutchess' hand, since she said that she felt ok. He suggested she get some blood moving, and she thought that was a good idea. Henry followed Max to the living room. Max showed Henry the picture on his camera phone.

For the third time in less than an hour, Henry was stuck, unable to move or even close his mouth. He stared at a picture of Dutchess, laid back in a see-thru stocking, that was barely holding the remains of a body together. The most horrifying part of the picture was next to the ruined body, Dutchess' head.

"Max! What the fuck kind of joke is this? Where did this come from? Is it that same geek in Illinois, that's trying to ruin Dutchess?"

"No Henry, this came from uptown Atlanta, less than half an hour ago."

"Where did you get this Max?"

Henry now had the same haunted look Max had had when he came to get him.

"I got it from a source I use, a security source. That's all I can tell you Henry. But it's real, too damned real. I think this is the explanation for Springfield. They say that this is the CPR; now, she's been post-humously designated as the CPR killer. And, she could be Dutchess' twin, that's what hit me the hardest.

Look here at the body; I know it's a mess, but look where the main areas of damage are: to the stomach, the breasts and the throat." Henry stared at what Max was pointing out, and his mouth flooded with water. He took flight, and made it to the kitchen just in time. He turned on the cold water and the disposal. He vomited powerfully enough to raise him up onto his toes.

He continued until it was only dry heaves. He cupped some water in his hands, and rinsed his mouth out a few times. When he turned off the water and the motor, Max was there.

"Henry, you're going to need a report from these people, to send to the lawyer for the lawsuit."

"Let her get it, I can't…"

"No Henry, man up. You have to do this quickly, before this gets swept under the rug. You know Threat Level RED has rules that you and I don't have any clue about. You get a report number, so that you can reference the Feds. Then, have the Lawyer use that reference to clear Dutchess' name. That's nothing I can do Henry, or else I would. I care about her *that* much in this short amount of time that I've known her; what about you?"

That snapped Henry out of his little boy-scared-safe space, back into the real world of responsibility. Dutchess came bouncing past, with her racquet bag from the tournament.

"Henry, I'm going up to the roof to work with the serve machine."

"Take Max with you, D."

"Come on Max, I'm gonna leave you."

Max left the image on the screen with Henry.

"I've got more phones; do what you have to do."

***

All of the prismatic colors of the rainbow were twinkling through the mid-morning window. But the sound that pulled the snuggling couple up from their satiated love sleep, was a droning constantly moving sound, it was so loud because of its alien absence. They both rolled to the edge of the bed. They looked at each other, then to the window. They stood and carefully stepped to the window and pulled back the curtain. Up there in the picture perfect sky, were two parallel vapor trails of what appeared to be commercial airliners.

"Those are what I think they are, aren't they Ron?"

"If you think they are non-military aircraft, I'd say you're correct."

The view from their little customized cabana included the gas station and the freeway entrance. There were no camo colored trucks, nor check point. They continued to look at each other, still not believing. They proceeded to spin the TV back around and plug it back in. The remote was retrieved from the bedside nightstand drawer, and the batteries replaced. They sat down on the foot of the bed. Sylvania draped her leg over Ron's and hit power.

It was a normal picture, no border, the news was on. She clicked through the channels, and every channel had news. She stopped on a local cable channel that they were discussing the recent eBay $32,000 grilled cheese sandwich with the face of Jesus. The pros and cons of healing sandwiches, and several other stations, were showing and discussing similar inanities.

The local Fox Station was giving reasons for the grounding of their air fleet. The first of the birds out of the repair shop was flying towards St. Louis, to get some live shots from the park blast that had caused the whole terror Threat Level RED escalation. When Sky Fox got there, the sky was full of helicopters from news stations countrywide. Whatever they were expecting to see, a huge condolence card, fabricated on a patchwork of tarps covering the entire blast area, was probably the last. The text read:

'In Honor Of The Lost Innocents We Grieve, We Pray, We Recommit Ourselves To The Cause Of Peace. Never Again... Sincerely, the United States of America'.

Ron looked at Sylvania and shook his head. It was a propaganda coup. Nobody knew what to expect, nobody knew what really happened, but they obviously mentioned worldwide. Who would be responsible for the cover up, figuratively and literally? They had enough already, when a teaser came on mentioning Dutchess. So Ron lounged back on the bed, and drew lazy lines up and down Sylvania's back.

He watched the shivers course through her body, seeing the incredible stiffening of her nipples as the shivers continued. She was only partially watching, she was lightly raking her nails up and down Ron's inner thigh. She learned quickly, giving her another toy to play with as well. Just as he defeated gravity and started waving around proudly, her attention went elsewhere.

'In entertainment news, Dutchess Singletary has filed a $20 million dollar slander and liable lawsuit against the Countries Inquisitor, for an article pressed into limited distribution. We tried to get a copy, but the print run was halted. In other news, the AP wire office was struck by a freak lighting strike.

The wire is back up and running again. Two technicians were injured, they are currently hospitalized and in guarded condition. As more information comes in, we will bring it to you live, here, on Fox 13. In other news, the flotilla traffic jam has cruise ships stacked up, attempting to get into the port of Miami. Waiting times are approaching two days; the parent companies have been offering coupons for free day's on subsequent cruises.'

Sylvania turned off the TV, she went to unplug it. As she bent over, she heard 'Meeting in the Ladies Room' by Klymax. She started to bounce to the old school beat, when she looked around Ron was searching through his pants. He pulled out his cell phone.

"Hello? What the hell? Wen, what's good, you on stage yet? Oh, that's new... hold up, I got news. I got me a woman now. Yeah, right. I hear you talking, huh? Ok. hold on."

Ron put the phone on speaker, and grabbed Sylvania to him, she came willingly, and sat across his lap with questions all over her face.

"Hello, Miss Lady, you don't know me yet, but you will, my name is Wensday. I work for Mr. Big Feet, at TCSS. I don't know what you did to snare the tall man, but, congratulations. Babysitting him was too much for me alone. I'm so glad to have some help, for-real-for-real. You got'chu a good dude, lady, and I want to meet you as soon as possible. Because, if he is imagining you, I want to find out right now, so that I can make him an appointment with the office shrink, you there?"

"Yes, I'm here."

"And what's your name?"

"It's Sylvania Wednesday."

"No, not the day of the week, Wensday, like it sounds."

"Oh, that's original."

"Damn, that's one more dime I missed. I tell ya, a dime every time, and I'd be rich."

Sylvania was laughing and looking at Ron being embarrassed.

"Ok Wen, that's enough."

"Oh no, not after all the hell you put me through because my game is better than yours. I will have the honor of cutting up your player card Mister. I might even throw you a party, on me."

"See, there you go. "

"Miss Lady, you don't know what you have done. Secret crushes all over the city have been squashed. I know, he didn't have a clue. What are ya'll doing in about three hours?"

They consulted each other, shrugged shoulders,

"Nothing I can think of."

"Ok, meet me for some food and drinks. I'll text you directions. I ran into some friends I used to party with out of the blue. We're hanging out, fly style."

"So, we need clothes, like that, Wen?"

"Just something casual, cool."

"Ok, three hours, we'll be there."

"We'll be in the lobby level restaurant; they'll be looking for your eyes. Can't wait to meet you, Miss Lady."

"Same here, Wensday."

After they hung up, Sylvania asked Ron about her.

"It seems like she really likes you, boss."

"Wens' cool; I like her. She works well, and she's good people. She's the first openly gay woman I've ever been around, and, if she is any indication, I'm not letting you spend five minutes alone with her."

"You don't have to worry Ron, I've always been strickly dickly, and I'm not about to change, especially since I've got the dick I've always dreamed of, and it's all mine."

They showered playfully and dressed. They made a quick trip to the mall, and they had upscale casual clothes to wear for drinks with Wensday. The speed that normalcy returned was surreal. It was as if nothing had happened, and all of a sudden life was back to normal. The radio stations were not yet playing commercials, just music and more music. Small things were still not ticking on time, but society, at large, had come away from the code RED, as if it were just another day, maybe a long weekend. They went back to their little cabana and changed to his and hers Notify jeans outfits; five pocket straight leg with a floral print button down the shirt for him. A mini skirt that matched with a solid purple short sleeved pullover for her.

It was very expensive nowadays to dress down. The two outfits set them back more than $850.00, when you added a pair of casual shoes for each, from the Ferrogomo Store that number went north $1,500. But, admittedly, they **did** look good. Ron helped Sylvania into the car and they were off.

***

Beeny was in the bond office to pay the money to get

Fantasia out of jail. He had her full document package, all the money for her bond, and some extra grease cash. When he asked for information pertaining to Mellysa Torando, their computers came up blank; he asked to speak to the watch supervisor. The Supervisor was a Lieutenant; Beeny offered a card that introduced him as Benjamin Whitmore Blankenship, Esq, Attorney At Law.

He explained that his client was currently being held in their intake process and he believed that she was being held as a Jane Doe. Benjamin requested from the Lieutenant the extraordinary exemption of being able to go to intake to see his client, so that he could get her released, most expeditiously.

The Lieutenant looked at Benjamin as if he had lost his mind, until he produced an envelope. The Lieutenant was no rookie, he knew what was going on to the point that he could feel the width of the envelope indicating approximately thirty bills thick, at $100 per. That would be $3000 for a trip back to intake.

"You know Mr. Blankenship, it's highly irregular to perform a tour at this time of night. But under certain circumstances, things can be arranged."

Benjamin made small talk as the lieutenant's clipboard came down atop the envelope. When the clipboard moved, the envelope was gone. On the way to intake through the employee access, Benjamin asked if anything could be done about the bail amount. He was there on orders from his client to pay the amount in full, but, if there were other arrangements that could possibly be more efficient, he was willing to listen.

Lieutenant Vonn was wondering how far he could push it with this lawyer. He had the three thousand dollars on his person now, so guilt was already established. How much farther was he willing to go?

They walked through the last door into the booking area. Walking in behind the counter, Beeny saw Fantasia. Benjamin nudged Vonn and indicated Fantasia. The Lieutenant pulled a Sergeant to bring Fantasia back to the booking area. She was escorted behind the counter, and into an office where she saw Beeny, in an expensive black suit and tie. His briefcase was in front of him on the desk he said,

"Good evening Mellysa, have you been treated alright?"

"Not necessarily."

She said, looking sideways at the Lieutenant.

"Can I get out of here? There's like, four people in there, paid their bond yesterday, and are still waiting to get out. I don't want to go through that."

She sat on the desk next to her lawyer, and showed more and more of her thighs. Sylvia scooted to the corner of the desk and exposed the crotch of her panties to the Lieutenant. She pulled the crotch to the side and asked,

"Is there anything we can do to get me out of here, Mr. Officer? Anything."

She already knew that her bald pussy was incredibly enticing with its thick lips and large pink clit. It was absolutely beautiful. The look on the lieutenant's face said it all. Benjamin dropped a $10,000 bundle on the desk and said,

"Ten thousand dollars, we walk out the way we walked in."

The Lieutenant was still looking between Sylvia's thighs; she was opening the lips now showing the inner pinkness. She was turning herself on, and small drops of creamy liquid began to run from her snapped-tight inner lips. When she saw Beeny put the $10,000 into the cops hand, and take the camera phone picture, she knew that she was out. She pulled the crotch back over to cover her pussy and hopped off the desk.

"Let's go B, which way?"

As soon as her pussy was recovered, Lieutenant Vonn snapped out of his daze. With a well-paid escort, Benjamin Blankenship and Mellysa Toranado, were casually walked out of the booking area, through the employee hallways to the employee parking lot. LT. Vonn stashed his $3,000 underneath the spare tire of his personal squad car, and drove Benny and Sylvia to the public parking lot.

Sylvia got directly into the NSX and grabbed a phone off the charger. Beeny stood with the light at his back, and Sylvia got a perfect picture of the Lieutenant's face, as he reached into the car to retrieve Beeny's $10,000 briefcase. She got the perfect picture with both their hands on the handle, impossible to tell who the giver or who the taker was. Beeny got in the car and drove to Grady Hospital's parking deck.

In space #678, sat Sylvia's still brand new Mercedes, with the key under the floor mat, waiting. Beeny got out of the car and asked her if she needed anything?

"Beeny, I really love how you worked that out; you really have grown up, huh? Come here man."

She grabbed Beeny by the neck and pulled him into a deep long soul-stirring kiss. As he was catching his breath, she jumped into the Benz.

"Keep my boxes paid, baby, I'll be in touch."

Beeny reached into the window and dropped three $10,000 bundles in her lap.

"Be careful Fantasia, I want to see you again."

"Don't worry, Beeny. Wild horses couldn't keep me away."

One more peck and she was out. Her first stop was to the World's Bank branch downtown. Preferred safe deposit box holders had twenty four hour access. Even though the bank wasn't open yet, she could still access her box, one of three she kept here. She withdrew as much cash as she could fit into the complimentary carry bag the vault services representative had handed her on the way in. She also pulled a small black drawstring bag. By feel, there were about ten, by the color of the bag she knew they were diamonds. These, she put into her coatdress pocket. Now she was ready for phase II.

***

As promised, the Blackhawk silently landed atop Suzan's roof, with rotors still turning, hovering, so that the full weight would not rest on the old factory's non-supported roof beams. Kristi hugged Suzan and Thony, actually feeling a bit of separation anxiety. She would have pulled their fingernails off, one by one, less than 72 hours ago, amazing. Phillip gave each of them Kristi's business card, and a copy of the note page that they both had signed.

They jumped from the chopper and ducked from the rotor wash. They ran to the pill box door sitting on the back edge of the roof; the Blackhawk was hovering two feet up. They tried the roof door, found it unlocked. They looked at each other; they had picked up something from being around Kristi, they had never really thought about security before.

Suzan was trying in vain to hold her wrap dress down with the gale force wind blowing. In the end, she gave up, and let it fly, exposing her teddy as she waved good bye. Her's and Thony's waves were returned by Kristi, Phillip and James. The Blackhawk angled to the right and took off in eerie silence, as if it had never been there.

Closing the roof door behind them, they made sure it was locked, and made their way down the fire stairs to Suzan's floor, her door was locked. They entered, feeling as if it had been months, since they had been here last. They walked up the middle stairs straight to the bedroom. Thony and Suzan looked into each other's eyes, and sat on the edge of the bed holding each other. Their minds drifted to the first/last time they had been on the octagon. It struck them both at the same time that this bed was trashed from their lovemaking, before Thony dressed her. They'd never made up the bed; they decided a tour was in order. They retraced their previous steps up to the bedroom, back down the spiral staircase.

The Towels were neatly hung, including the one Thony had used on her brow. The most blatantly obvious change was the playroom. The floor was spotless, the cardboard pieces that they had put in the widows were gone, and the glass was repaired. They had been here, considering the stealth with which they entered their hotel room. They must have been through here thoroughly, and reordered the place, once Kristi determined Thony wasn't a Terrorist.

"What do you think Thony?"

"I know I don't trust government types, first of all. Secondly, I'm not going to let you out of my sight. If not for you, who knows where I'd be right now. Suzy Q, I loooove you."

"Yeah, I agree. But, I do think that Kristi was a straight shooter, once we convinced her that something wasn't right."

"She shot straight alright. You saw what they did to that woman that looked like the tennis player. All of them shot straight."

"Thony, do you think there's something strange or weird about people looking like you or like Dutchess for that matter?"

"Well, off putting, a little uncomfortable, but I can't say weirded out. But it's surely a new feeling seeing a man that looks just like me. I can't imagine what it would be like if I would have been there when he was trying to kill those people. But then again, Suz, you've got to remember what times we're living in. Celebrity look-a-likes are an industry unto itself. You keep doing what you do, don't be surprised to see a Suzan look-a-like contests, like they do for Hemmingway, down in the Florida Keys. Not that I'll ever get used to it, but for now, we've got to move on. You want to call Wilbert?"

"You don't think we're fired?"

"They can't do that, we're stars, baby."

He picked her up by her waist and spun her around Cinderella style, and ended with her gripped in his arms. She placed her hands on his shoulders, looking down into his eyes.

"You wanna run some lines?"

"You gonna put on that purple thing?"

They laughed, he put her down, grabbed the script and exited stage left upstairs to bathe, rehearse one love scene, and perform another..

***

There were people on the roof top court, when Dutchess and Max arrived. One lady on one side and two on the other. The single lady was handling the other two with ease. She saw Dutchess getting off of the elevator and stuttered, allowing the black girl on the other side of the net to score.

She jumped for joy and did a little dance. It was clear that she hadn't scored a point in a while. The Amazon white woman with the platinum blonde hair and impressive body waved off the other girl's dance and welcomed Dutchess.

"Good morning. I was finishing off my light work; I think I have about twenty minutes left. If you're in a hurry I could cut this short."

"There's no need to do that for me."

"Oh, believe me, I'd have no problem doing it. I know who you are, Ms. Singletary. It's kind of difficult to earn a living with a racquet and not know you."

Dutchess was flattered.

"Well thank you Miss... I'm afraid that I'm at a disadvantage; you know me, but I don't know you."

"Oh, I'm sorry. That's my girl, Yukkio, across the net, and a friend of hers from here. I'm Jelina Aspelin, and I'm new on this side of the pond, from Sweden."

"Interesting, well, welcome to the states. Would you like to run one?"

"I'd be honored; hey you hoochies, clear the court so some real players can play."

Max chuckled at how quickly foreigners can come to the U.S., and learn every stereotype. He wouldn't be surprised if she had an IPod full of gangster / crunk / snap rap, but even that light distraction couldn't erase the picture in his head.

His brother-in-law was on the FBIs HRT, Special Task Force call up roster. He was a communications expert that was usually on the A or B teams, handling all the electronic signals work. He had informed Max, that there was a very bad scene involving a perp that was made up to look like his new assignment.

After the kill, they discovered it was not make up or contacts, the CPR killer was an exact copy of Dutchess Singletary. Max had no doubt, that in his other life as a Navy Seal, some of the psychological operations or Psy Ops, involved intensive, in depth training in ESP, code systems and languages.

These ops were developed by twins, triplets and more, for use only among themselves, Multiple Birth Syndrome Systems, they called it. The theories even bubbled over into partner Psychology, developing these attributes between you and your partner could save your life. The main lesson taught was that after forming in the womb, some parts of the developmental cycle became so intertwined that a telepathic bond is created; if one twin or triplet, etc., experienced pain, they all would.

Translate that into a situation, whereby, you're with your partner on a high priority stake out, and their twin gets clubbed in the head at some other location in the world; your partner passes out.

As soon as Max saw the picture that Comms had sent to his phone with the shots corresponding to the bruises on Dutchess, he knew. This was her twin, no look alike, an identical twin that she obviously never met. He hoped Henry got to the bottom of this. Could there have been three? Max couldn't worry about that right now. He was about to watch Dutchess Singletary play for the first time. This was going to be good.

The Swede had her outsized in all dimensions. The black girl and the Asian were friends and sometime lovers. Yukkio met Jelina on a tour a year before. They had been inseparable ever since. Jelina won a lot on the tour, and her career took off. So, Yukkio quit playing to support her woman. But, she loved clubbing in ATL, and the black girl was her connection to that world.

Deferring to her current status, Jelina surrendered the serve to Dutchess. Dutchess had not touched a racquet since the final day of the tournament in Florida. She felt strange holding her tool in her hand; it felt lighter, and slightly smaller. She realized once she tossed the ball up into the air for her first serve, it had been the workout yesterday, after being able to get so much rest.

She was stronger. She sliced through the green fuzzy ball with a ferociousness that was almost primal. The ace clock said the serve had been 119mph; not her fastest, but it didn't feel as if she had put anywhere near that much effort into the serve. She thought it may have been a fluke, but after she smashed four more aces at the same speed, or with one mph up or down, she was impressed with herself. But she wanted to play the Swede, to see what she had.

So, she took her game out of mercenary mode and went for play time. Starting out with a neutral volley, they sent each other scrambling back and forth across the back court and center court with a selection of drop shots, smashes spins, etc. The big Swedish girl's game was good; her power was impressive, but, true to Dutchess constant strategy. Her practice games used round-about renditions of her real game.

Despite her power, Dutchess beat her handily every time. She realized there was something familiar about her strategy and overall approach to the game. At the end of the last game, they approached the net, Jelina shook Dutchess' hand.

"You are the truth Dutchess Singletary."

She was breathing hard and looking at Dutchess as any type-A gay woman would look at an Alpha wolf that beat her at her own game. Dutchess asked her,

"Do you, by any chance, know Franz Gruber?"

Jelina reacted as if slapped. Her first glance went to Yukkio, satisfied that she had not overheard. Jelina confessed that,

"Yes, I knew Franz back in Sweden. When I first started as a youth, I took instruction with the Swedish National team. Franz was my coach. Why do you ask?"

"I met Franz in Florida; your national treasure is something else."

Dutchess could feel Jelina searching her eyes for, something. She couldn't tell what, but there was a pleading there for understanding. Then, all at once, she felt she knew.

"I recognized some of his techniques in your play."

"You played Franz?"

"Yes, we played by accident like we are now. Nothing planned, but I beat him that first time before I knew who he was. From there, we became friends."

Jelina still had the look; she was pleading to be understood on a level below the casual conversation. That's when she knew that they had been lovers when she was younger and he was less gentle. They stared into one another's eyes, psychically commiserating. Dutchess' foray into lesbian affairs was totally by choice. She was so grateful that she had not been forced into the arms of women, which seemed to have been the case with Jelina.

She reached out to hug the tall Swede; she felt a hot tear graze her neck, and she rubbed understanding circles on her back. Dutchess broke the embrace off cleanly, so that the woman knew that she also knew her current agenda.

"So Dutchess, do you play here very often?"

"This is my first time up here, I just moved in yesterday."

"Oh, you live here? Must be nice. I'll be here for a few days. Would you like to have a drink or something after you're done?"

"Sure, that'd be nice, you guys wanna meet downstairs?"

Jelina nodded, and the two girls on the sidelines chimed in with,

"That's hot!"

Dutchess laughed out loud at the homage to Paris Hilton. The three ladies left Dutchess to her practice and Max to watch.

***

Birds 1 thru 4 were back at base, post-flight Ops were underway; system use computers checked, engine rebuilds, the normal post action reports being were being filled out by the pilots. The Task Force members were reintegrated back into their regular jobs: Agents, Forensics techs, Communications Supervisors. All TAC Ops had support jobs as well as paramilitary training and duties. The FBI HRT trainers were the only truly full time warriors, though their position was that of warrior trainer.

Kristi was back in her office, with her specialty tactical gear stored back in its closet, her grip restocked, the electronics recharged, and waiting for the next deployment. She sat back looking into her drawer. She pulled out a calendar pad, and began to write in dates for increased training for Chad. She needed to know if he was totally up to par on both sides of her fence. He needed to be more than a number two; he needed to be a potential number one. She made a call to her boss regarding his generous time-off suggestion. She decided to take him up on it.

"Phillip…"

"Yes boss?"

"Are you going to be able to handle things around here with me on vacation?"

"Can't say, that's a first in my experience here. I'm sure things will be smooth; until they are not smooth, at that point, I have your private cell number on speed dial. That way, I'll look like the genius that nobody believes I am."

"You are too much Phillip, but I couldn't look as good as I do without you. Do you want some more money?"

"It couldn't hurt."

"Ok, you and James will get a retroactive raise, when I get back. Will that work?"

"That's affirmative. Thank you, SAC."

"Don't thank me yet, I only offered more money because I'm gonna work you guys asses off to deserve it."

She slapped her desk, and spun around in her chair laughing.

"That's all Phillip, unless you can find me someplace to go on this vacation."

"Well, if I were you, and wanted to get away from it all, I'd do a hopscotch La Caribe Island Tour. Do a couple days on a bunch of little Islands and beaches; get lost out there yacht style."

"That does sound top choice, can you put that together?"

"I'm pretty sure, if I can't make it happen, I believe James has a travel agent in the family somewhere."

"Ok, it's decided, make that happen. Hopscotch huh? You sure you didn't just make that up?"

"Scouts honor, SAC,"

He said that with a twinkle in his eye, that hinted that he had never been a boy scout. Kristi's debriefing was a more formal and civilized affair in the office of the Director of the FBI. She sat next to her boss, and broke down the past approximately 4 ½ days to **his** boss. She was commended for her outstanding leadership and she was awarded the medals promised to her during an unannounced, surprise walk in, from the President of the United States.

At the end of this momentous day, several things were brought to her attention. First, the Threat Level RED condition code carried with it time intensive escalations. The first came after 7 days, 21 days and 30 days. Each escalation takes the elected government more and more out of control, and cedes that power to the military, FEMA, and Homeland Security for overall management of the country.

Therefore, her expedience in getting the Level RED handled in less than seven days was commendable, because these provisions were not known until the level RED condition was invoked. Legislation was being considered to water down this escalation definition.

Second, she was receiving a $60,000 raise to her annual

salary. An office renovation was included in that package, if so desired, as well as a car, driver and additional staff. About thirty more minutes and the official and unofficial parts of the debriefing were complete.

Kristi adjourned to her boss's office, and had the post-action Cognac, a tradition they started after she brought in her first person from the top ten list. Those few years seemed like ages ago. They shot the shit about her upcoming vacation time, trying to keep the office off her mind. She told him that she hadn't made any for sure plans, though she knew he would know where she could be found if really really necessary.

Kristi rode the beltway to the Maryland exit, where she could get the final confirmation information that Phillip had placed on her desk per his text. As she was riding the elevator up from the parking garage, she got a transferred call from the office phone.

"Hello, Special Agent Johnson speaking, how may I help you?"

"Agent Johnson? My name is Henry Carlisle; I manage Dutchess Singletary, the tennis player? I was finally directed to you. It's been over an hour and I've been trying to get to the bottom of some information I have in my possession."

"And what would that be?"

Kristi was stepping off of the elevator, striding to her office so that she could take notes.

"It would be a picture."

"What type of picture Mr. Carlisle, I'm very busy sir."

"A picture of my client decapitated and shot all to hell."

Kristi stopped in mid-stride at the door to her office.

"Is this some type of joke, sir?"

"Joke! Are you fuckin for real? Ma'am, I'm to understand that you have some information tying this picture to the CPR killer. How the CPR killer looks exactly like my client, obviously has something to do with the Country's Inquisitor story from Illinois, that could quite possibly cost my client tens of millions of dollars. If you know something, I need to know what it is. I need some way to ensure my client's contractors that she was not involved.

Last, but by no means, least, I need to get to the bottom of what happened to my client for twenty five minutes around, five a.m. this morning."

"Sir, first I need you to calm down. Whatever information I can give you, I will, ok. Describe this picture you've got."

She made notes as Henry described in full detail, what he was looking at, on the picture phone screen.

"Ok, sir. This conversation never happened. Keep in mind that this portion with your agreement is being recorded. State your name."

"Henry Carlisle, President, the Carlisle Group Management."

"And you swear not to mention any details of the conversation of today with Agent Johnson, correct?"

"Correct, I agree."

"Ok, yes the picture is genuine. It is the CPR Killer and yes, it looks exactly like your client. Attempts were made to contact you previous to any action, but the person in question accelerated our time table, unavoidably. Efforts to contact and verify your client's location and living status bore fruit. One of my people spoke to you and determined that she was indeed alive and well and in your company."

"Wait, somebody said they talked to me?"

"Yes sir, they did."

"Shit, *that's* who that was?"

"Now, when you mentioned something happening to your client this morning, I'm afraid I don't know what you are referring to."

Henry explained, as best as he could, about seeing Dutchess sprawled over the butcher block table looking dead. Kristy recoiled, she thought about the CPR lying dead, sprawled over the luggage cart, with her shot to the throat, the decapitator.

"You say the violent red bruises were on her throat, chest, and abdomen?"

"Yeah, they looked dark enough to bleed. Then, out of nowhere, they just started to fade away. Within ten minutes, they were gone, and she was regaining consciousness."

"That I find to be unbelievable Mr. Carlisle, though the phenomenon has been recorded for sets of identical twins. In fact, Mr. Carlisle, the very places you say Ms. Singletary had her bruises were in fact the places the CPR was fatally wounded. Without DNA samples we can't be sure, but I'd say forgoing that, the case seems to be made for this theory.

The actual report is going to say the perpetrator had 'disguised herself to look like Ms. Singletary, and bore an uncanny resemblance'. I can arrange a copy to be forwarded to you to help in your lawsuit."

"I'd really appreciate that. So Dutchess had a sister, an identical twin, damn."

"That information is classified, Mr. Carlisle, even for your client. I'm afraid, as it is, it's better that she not know."

"You got a point, Agent Johnson. I appreciate your candor and your time."

"It's no problem, I have your statement on file. So, if you have any more questions regarding this non - conversation, contact me here."

Kristi hung up the phone with a mystery solved, and a paranormal occurrence documented. She picked up the tri-fold Phillip had prepared: tickets, itineraries, hotel captains, everything but the clothes; she'd get them when she got there. Kristi went on a long deserved vacation.

***

The Mercedes pulled up into the VIP lot at the private airport in Dekalb County, Georgia, right outside of Atlanta. Sylvia parked and adjourned to the pilots' lounge, where she sat at the bar, had a drink and listened. She heard pilots talking about flight conditions, and passenger loads. All very mundane topics to the uninitiated ear, but Sylvia was initiated into all things she participated in. She heard the snippet of conversation she was looking for on her second glass of White Zinfandel.

"Yeah, this Gulfstream, it's all kind of better than that Lear. I like the range and it's been fitted for the auto take off and land. Although I prefer to do both myself, it's pretty cool to know if something happens, it's just a two-button preset."

"Shit, now that the TTL is down from RED, I expect business is gonna spike like it did on 9/14."

A pilot of a jet, was exactly what she needed to successfully get away. Phase II sounded like a sophisticated plan, but it was nothing close. Sylvia's plan, phase II: find a pilot of a private plane, give him whatever he wants, head, pussy, ass, money or all of the above; get out of the country, simple as that. Now, she had completed step 1.

With the flight plan in place to the small landing strip on the Island of Tobago, Sylvia crouched above the naked pilot, riding him, and working professional pussy tricks, that would cost much more than the price of this plane ride. She went from riding him, to kneeling next to the pilot's captain chair and sucked him to a fantastic climax.

The pilot lay back smoking a cigarette, asking the youngish Island girl how she felt to be a member of the mile high club. She gushed about how it was the best, how big he was, how sore she felt, how it would really be great if he would eat her in the copilot's chair,

"Wow, we're going so fast!"

She said everything the pilot expected a college girl from the Islands to say, like she was used to traveling by fishing boat. He fell for it hook, line, and sinker, all the way down to insisting that she keep her $300, and thanks for the memories.

They landed on the Island of Tobago; Sylvia went to the local market and got some plain clothes to wear and a camping-sized back pack with connections for her IPhone, IPod controls, and a solar flap to keep all the electronics charged. She was thankful to the constant daily sun shining on the tiny Island. At the market, she found a poster board advertising places to live, roommates wanted, boarding available. She caught a taxi to an advertised home. They were the nicest family; Mellysa was welcomed at once.

***

Ron pulled off the highway at the familiar exit; he sat there for a minute looking at the directions that Wensday had given him. He sat long enough for Sylvania to ask him if everything was ok.

"Yeah, babe. I'm just tripping a little bit. Remember I told you that I followed that look-a-like chick to a hotel I had never been to before?"

"Yeah, why? What about it?"

"Well, this is the same exit, and that's the only hotel I remember seeing."

"Well, coincidence or not, we can't keep her waiting now, that we're here."

"Yeah, at least I'll get to go into the restaurant now, and I won't have to try to put the atrium into words.

A couple minutes later, they we're pulling in on the right lane of the carport, there was a plain black tour bus on the left. The place must have been popular with rock stars, Ron thought. He helped Sylvania out of the car. He didn't trust the valet not to sneak a peek at her brand new, sky blue, shimmery, La Pearla panties. He tossed the keys to the waiting valet, of course, it was the same one that he had already over paid. He grabbed the keys on the fly and, with a wink jumped in and drove off.

Ron walked Sylvania into the lobby's incredible atrium. The water motif that he had attempted to explain to her, was gone. Now, it looked like a view of the earth from the face of the moon. It was just as impressive, if not more so. There were comets and asteroids shooting by in the middle distance, slow motion giving detailed perspectives of the illusion.

Ron ripped his eyes away from the sight and looked toward the restaurant. He saw Wensday waiting by the greeters' dais. Wensday was a Gemini; she could change in a second, like her twin faced mutable birth description.

The last time Ron had seen her in the office, she had long hair, about mid back length and was dressed in a conservative business suit. Apparently, her tryst with the actress was completed, as she was sporting a totally different look. The China doll; inky black hair, straight, curved under just below her jaw line. She wore what looked to be a nicely filled out men's polo shirt, with nice medium sized breasts Ron never knew that she possessed. And a white tennis skirt that bounced around at mid-thigh; and oh what thighs they were.

Wensday had a killer body. Now, he saw what the women she attracted knew all along, she was a catch. She didn't help matters when she bounced her braless breasts while excitedly waving them over. Luckily, Sylvania was still looking up. They made it to the restaurant, and Ron made the introductions, as expected. Wensday took over from there.

"Boss man! Where in the hell did you find an oyster big enough to hide a black pearl like this? She is adorable, oooooo, I'm sorry, Sylvania, right? I didn't mean to talk about you as if you weren't here. I'm just shocked that the player of the year finally claimed somebody. Much less, look at him, I have never seen that look on his face; you gotta be the one, Miss lady. I tip my hat to ya."

She tipped an imaginary hat and gave Sylvania a high five. Then, mouthed for them to come on into the restaurant, just about everybody was here.

"So is this what community theater gets you nowadays Wen?"

"No boss, she was soooo last week. I'm into tennis now, sportsy Chix."

Sylvania's mind wandered for a moment, when it returned, she was shaking hands with Yukkio and Jelina. The waitress came for their orders. Wensday's party had already ordered food, the sampler platter of appetizers. It was basically a private buffet of all the appetizers the restaurant specialized in. Ron ordered two Hennessey Alexanders that brought a twinkle of recognition from Sylvania's eye that wasn't lost on Wensday. They all sat down and a lively discussion ensued; in the distance there was a ding ding across the lobby.

***

The workout on the roof had been rigorous, no one else had shown up. Dutchess had worked extra hard with the programmable machine. Max was amazed, as a bystander, first watching her whoop the Amazon Swede as if she were an amateur, then watching her return 130mph serves. He doubted that his hand-eye coordination was even up to par to return half of those. Although he could tiptoe through a firefight, and pilot a TAC helicopter through a radar net, in all types of weather.

Dutchess looked kind of beat up on her way back down to the residence. But, she was smiling, keeping her own council. It was almost impossible for Max to reconcile this athletically superior machine of a woman. This same woman that had the limp, was bruised, marked up, and a rag of a thing that he had carried from the kitchen this morning. But whatever the cause was, right now; it was, what it is.

He had a healthy, sweaty, superstar athlete under his care and his job would be done. Dutchess announced a spectacular work out to Henry and proceeded to shower and sauna directly. Henry ran down his conversation with Special Agent Johnson to Max, and the conclusions that they had arrived at.

Max agreed; they decided between them, to inform Dutchess of the least amount possible, unless they had to reveal more. But, they would not lie to her.

Dutchess lay back naked on the cedar bench inhaling the steam and cooking her body, thoroughly. She thought about Franz and she touched herself. She remembered his clumsy, new-found gentleness, and felt sorry for Jelina. Had her personal next day soreness have happened the first day, her memories of Mr. Gruber would have been much different, she thought. She stopped short of actual masturbation.

She wrapped up in a huge towel that was so luxurious, it could have been mink and she spiraled up to her bedroom. Dutchess chose a casual sweat outfit, something with a sexy fit that showed off her body and a nice camisole top with her tiara D necklace and earrings. She let her hair flow loosely down her back.

She announced to Max that she was going downstairs to the lobby restaurant. He was at the door as she was approaching. Max informed her on the elevator ride down that he would be in the lobby, if she needed him. Press the ruby and he would be there. The elevator dinged and Dutchess stepped out to the restaurant.

***

Jelina and Wensday had the lobby facing seats. So they saw Dutchess approach first. Ron was whispering something into Sylvania's ear and missed their wave. But they didn't miss Jelina standing and pulling another seat into the table grouping. Sylvania looked around and was struck by the beauty of the red headed Goddess. For about two beats the entire table was stock still.

Dutchess saw the face of Ms. Collins again, and felt that same sexual tingle run through her. But after somehow being wrong once in this same restaurant, she was more cautious this time, until the recognition she was expecting flashed in the woman's sexy brown eyes.

"Dutchess!"

"Ms. Collins!"

Sylvania bounced up from her chair into the waiting arms of Dutchess. They hugged as if they had been friends their entire lives. They pulled back and looked at each other as if they might kiss. The entire table watched this moment, with each viewer having different agendas based on their desired outcomes. They hugged again and laughed while catching up.

Sylvania's congratulations went to Dutchess. Introductions once again went all around, the drinks came and everyone made toasts. They ate and all had a good time. Dutchess asked Ms. Collins what they were doing afterward. They said nothing, so she invited them all up to tour her new home.

They started towards the elevator with Max in tow, the excitement could be felt growing; nobody knew exactly why. But this meeting could not have been an accident.

Wensday was out of her mind with joy to have been the instigator of this whole thing. She felt kind of like the fifth wheel. Yukkio was still stealing glances at her and sneaking small touches. Jelina couldn't take her eyes off of Dutchess. Dutchess was looking between Ron and Sylvania. Max oversaw the whole thing with his non-expression neutrality, knowing that the call he'd made to Henry a few minutes ago was going to make some pretty serious changes in Dutchess life.

They all got off on Dutchess private floor, she tried to be nonchalant about it, but it was still too new. Her excitement was adding to the pool of energy, the awe they felt with every step through the house. By the time they got to the pool, the visitors had to applaud. Jelina made a comment about having an appointment she needed to address.

Wensday knew better; she knew that she just wanted Yukkio to put the strap on to her big ass, and make her feel better about herself. She knew Jelina was a hater, that was the reason Wensday didn't mind fucking her girl. Yukkio was fair game because Jelina didn't care about her. She was incapable. She wanted her to stop her career and devote herself to Jelina, which made one less competitor to the crown.

Wensday wanted to stay and hang out with Ron and his new girlfriend, but she was the one that brought the hater, so she had to take her away.

"Dutchess, it was a joy meeting you and you too Sylvania. Take care of that man, ya here? I'll be seeing you."

Max walked that trio to the elevator, stuck in the card and pressed their floor. When he came back in, he caught a wink from Henry and asked Dutchess and her remaining guests into the kitchen. They learned small things about the water purifier and the wine cellar hidden behind the finished panel in the wall.

After the mini tour of the kitchen, they were led back to the window side seating area. Seeing the two wingback chairs facing the windows, Dutchess approached. She knew these chairs were facing into the room earlier. As she walked around back she saw Henry's legs crossed, foot bouncing and a hugely smiling Pauline.

"Congratulations Dutchess, welcome to Coke Brands!"

Both her hands flew to her face keeping the contents of her head from falling out. She saw the contract and pen on the table. She called Ms. Collins and Ron over to witness. Pauline gave Dutchess a small book.

"Those are the things you have to worry about, the rules. There is a 120 day period for adjustment; you to them and them to you. This flap won't bother your contract status, especially with the lawsuits filed the same day that the story was leaked. You dodged a bullet Dutchess. But nobody deserves it more."

Ron and Sylvania looked on as Dutchess signed her Coca Cola Brands contract. This made everything under her feet real. Reebok would come in a couple days and Henry promised an auto, liquor, makeup, gadget and restaurant sponsor by the end of the quarter.

Sylvania stood with her hands clasped in front of her breasts, tears of joy slowly tracking down her face. Ron was trying to get used to the flurry of emotion, knowing his woman's good friend was unimaginably rich. He liked Max though, and they had hit it off instantly.

They shared a lot of things, including an almost obsessive

desire and commitment to protect the ones under their care. They all took turns taking pictures. Max behind, the rest in front featuring Dutchess and the $60 million pen. The picture Dutchess prized the most, was her and Sylvania Collins cheek to cheek with Ron and Henry flanking. The evening was better than Dutchess could have ever expected and the most valuable thing she got... was a friend for life.

EPILOGUE

Over the next few months, Dutchess' star continued to rise. Eventually she would go on to win her first Grand Slam. Hers would go down as the most meteoric rise in one season in the history of women's' professional tennis in the open era.

***

The sold out production of 'Oh no you don't, Nanette'. was a smashing success, opening to critical acclaim. It went on to have an SRO run, with two weeks added by popular demand, a tour was in the works. Thony and Suzan sneaked off and got quietly married, unbeknownst to anyone else in the cast. Of course Wilbert knew; he was their witness, after all. Unknown to the happy couple, there was another surprise after the encore curtain call.

On the closing night, as they were tearfully making their way back stage for the last time. The twosome was approached by two dozen beautiful multicolored roses. They presumed that the huge arrangement was being handled by a stage Production Assistant.

But as they reached out to receive their appreciation gift, they saw an intensely beautiful woman with the most radiant face, a body like Ms. Universe, and a suit that looked to have been personally fitted by the designer, Coco Channel, then spray paint applied within the past hour.

It was Special Agent Kristi Johnson. She informed them that there were still privileges to being with the FBI. In addition to the flowers for a wonderful performance, she had a small box, a wedding present. She thanked Suzan for the suggestion that got her groove back, and let her know she thought of them often. They all enjoyed a closing night meal with the cast. 'Cousin Kris' was a big hit, they promised each other they would never be strangers...

***

Sylvania and Ron resumed their normal lives with the addition of 'we time' every day and night between the two residences. They fostered their relationship and stayed in close communication with Dutchess at home or on the road. Their photo book was growing, every major event in either of their lives, found them all together.

The photos documented Sylvania's external growth, within a two week window, Dutchess and Kristi both became godparents. First, Suzan had two identical baby boys, with her features and Thony's midnight black eyes. Sylvania had a boy and a girl with an even mix of both of her features and Ron's hazel eyes.

***

On the Island of Tobago, in a small house off the Ocean, Aisha Domingue, midwife, delivered the fraternal twins, a boy and girl with their father's electric hazel eyes, to her boarder, Mellysa Toranado.

FIN.

ABOUT THE AUTHOR

L. Corbin Bey is a master techno-erotic storyteller who enjoys educating, delighting, and borderline-scandalizing his audiences. Corbin Bey's unique gift of understanding basic human nature and creating believable, empathetically flawed characters place him in a class by himself.

Corbin Bey resides in Atlanta, Georgia, USA. He enjoys writing (of course!), film direction, and event management.

To learn more about L. Corbin Bey, visit www.LCBey.com.

Made in the USA
Columbia, SC
05 June 2020